Advance Praise for
SHOWBOAT *SOUBRETTE*

"Captivating characters? A fast-paced storyline? Cameos from historical figures? Brodie Curtis checks all the boxes in his novel set along the Mississippi River on the eve of the Civil War. Well done."

— Tim Wendel, author of
Castro's Curveball and *Rebel Falls*

"Readers of historical fiction will love *Showboat Soubrette*...a river adventure down the great Mississippi to New Orleans in the 1850s when racial tension is ripe in the Old South...an adventure worthy of Mark Twain's pen...Curtis is a master of description and atmosphere."

— Tyler R. Tichelaar, PhD and award-winning
author of *The Mysteries of Marquette*

Praise for Brodie Curtis' Previous Books

ANGELS *and* BANDITS

"This second novel anchors itself around the early days of World War II, specifically the epoch identified as 'The Battle of Britain' (July to October 1940).... The author carves out a creative niche that will enthrall readers."

— Historical Novels Review

"At times, I was reminded of the film *Top Gun*, and I think this book would make an absolutely wonderful film. I would love to watch it on the big screen. In the meantime, though, I suppose I will have to settle for reading this book over and over, for I missed reading it as soon as I finished."

— The Book Bandit

"*Angels and Bandits* is the kind of book that can appeal equally to fans of World War II accounts and women's romance/fiction. If you happen to like both, you're really in for a treat."

— Ruth F. Stevens, Author of The South Bay Series, Books 1 and 2 and *Stage Seven*

"For this reviewer, the characters' bonds and inter-action are one of the strongest and enjoyable parts of the book aside from the action…. We should give our thanks to Brodie Curtis for giving us such a fun and suspenseful story that helped us gain more interest towards aviation and World War II history."

— The Historical Fiction Company

"Curtis has proficiently mixed history, suspense, romance, and drama, and has given us a war story that's more than meets the eye…. *Angels and Bandits* is a heart-wrenching, suspenseful, well-written book that will keep you wanting more."

— Readers' Favorite

"I don't really have the words to describe this novel, and it's rare a book leaves me speechless. What could I say—this book is amazing, spectacular, brilliant. I felt like I was watching a movie as I was reading it. It is in all ways a complete success in every sense of the word."

— Whispering Bookworm

"This novel was absolutely impossible to put down, and I feel the author has completely succeeded in telling the story they set out to tell. This is the kind of book I would happily read again and again, and I miss it sorely now I have finished reading it."

— Lost in a Book

"With very special appeal to readers who are fans of World War II themed action/adventure stories, *Angels and Bandits* is a rewarding read from first page to last. Showcasing the narrative driven storytelling style author Brodie Curtis, *Angels and Bandits* is unreservedly recommended for community library WWII Historical Fiction collections."

— Midwest Book Review

THE FOUR BELLS

"An engaging, gritty novel of World War I and its decades-long effects on England."

— Kirkus Reviews

"[Brodie Curtis] aimed high and original in his debut novel…. As the worst memories of his past force their way to the surface, Weldy discovers that his future may lie right there in the town of his youth."

— Callahans Books

SHOWBOAT *SOUBRETTE*

Brodie Curtis

Westy Vistas Books

Contents

PART I

THE LADY J

"During the 1840's and 1850's dozens of small showboats swarmed over the river systems of the Middle West,
bringing entertainment to hundreds of river landings."

— Philip Graham, *Showboats:*
The History of an American Institution

Chapter 1

STELLA PARROT STOOD AT THE rail on the hurricane deck, high above the riverbank.

A tall gentleman approached and doffed his top hat. "Allow me to introduce myself. I am John Dee Franklin. I've seen your name on the playbill, but forgive me, Miss—."

"Stella Parrot. I am pleased to meet you, Mister Franklin."

His blue lapel sheened in the afternoon sunshine. "Tell you the truth, I recognized you standing at the rail here." He raised his newspaper. "Picked up the *Natchez Free Trader* in the barbershop and wanted to share it." He opened a page. "Let me read from the Society column: 'The Singing Soubrette of *The Lady J.* Her voice captivated the audience and they grinned at her comedies. The slight woman performer swept away the press of time into a memorable evening's entertainment arranged by Mr. Jenkins of New York City.'"

My lord, that's me! Stella blushed, concealing an uplifting warmth from the *Free Trader*'s review. An important newspaper giving accolades to a Cherokee riverboat singer! Its endorsement would surely boost ticket receipts from shows in lower Mississippi river towns. She burned to share the good news with castmates, but something about the man's kind smile wouldn't let her excuse herself just yet.

The first notes from The *Lady J*'s calliope pierced the sky like a sweet-ringing dinner bell. Far below, Friars Point locals scurried toward the landing like they did when the big side-wheeler arrived in river towns from New Orleans to St. Louis. The curtain would drop for the *Lady J*'s seven-thirty show in just a few hours. Judging by the gathering crowd, the auditorium would be full. Her heart beat quickly as she anticipated looking out at their faces from the stage.

Space at the handrail filled fast. Stella's understudy Mary had disappeared, leaving her standing next to Mr. Franklin and near other businessmen who wore jackets, vests, and ties, enduring the May Mississippi heat. Some were northern land hunters, others gold hunters. Cotton planters stood shoulder to shoulder with Quakers. Where had Mary gone?

Well-to-do women on the hurricane deck wore day dresses and headdresses a cut above her own bodice and bonnet. To aft, where the view wasn't as good, were Black folks: uniformed chambermaids in plain white wrappers and aprons, firemen and deckhands in dungarees and cotton shirts.

Mr. Franklin said something to the man next to him. She couldn't hear a word over the calliope's melodious peals.

Only Mr. Franklin stood next to Stella. The White folks kept their distance from the Black folks with her somewhere in the middle, same as always. She figured it was her skin color, which was too dark for the White folk and too light for the Black folk. Most people didn't recognize her out of costume, so to White folks she was just a brown-skinned woman with high cheekbones and long black hair. Dressed too well to be a squaw on her way north to reservation lands and pretty enough to be a whore, but a whore would be at the bar, well away from the good ladies on the top deck.

They could just go ahead and wonder who this mysterious woman was, for all she cared. A Creole-planter's wife. A Spanish traveler. Or maybe the *plaçée* quadroon mistress of a White gentleman. Standing next to Mr. Franklin, the latter assumption was surely reasonable, so she inched down the rail, away from him.

The *Lady J*'s deckhands threw down spring and bow lines to flapjack hat-wearing roustabouts who tied them to iron cleats. Then they snugged her hull to massive, hemp-wrapped fender posts.

Stella sensed someone approaching and looked up. A White lady twirling her parasol passed by, knocking into Stella's forehead with the wide brim of her hat. Stella jerked away, stunned. Everything was fuzzy. *What was that?* The brim had a metal clasp to hold colorful feathers. Had it jabbed her? She touched her skin and found a drop of blood on her fingertip. *Oh no!*

The White lady shrugged half-heartedly and said in a flat voice that was barely audible over the calliope, "Make way, please."

Blood pounded in Stella's ears, swelling up anger ready to explode.

"I believe an apology is in order," said Mr. Franklin, loud enough to be heard. Who was he talking to? Stella faced the back of his suit jacket, so he must be addressing the woman who had bumped her.

"Oh, I suppose," the White lady said, and walked away without another word.

Stella breathed deeply, gathering herself. She stepped nearer to Mr. Franklin in order to be heard. "Thank you."

He nodded. "Do you need assistance? Can I get you a doctor?"

She dabbed at her forehead. No more blood. "No need. I'm fine. Thank you for asking."

He turned his attention to the riverbank.

She retrieved a hand-held mirror from her handbag and examined the wound. Barely noticeable. The blow hadn't left a cut or, thank the heavens, marred her complexion to prevent her from going on-stage. Nothing an extra dab of makeup couldn't cover.

Glancing up, Mr. Franklin's classically handsome, clean-shaven profile quickened her pulse. Being taller than other men at the rail, he towered over her. He was probably close to her own age, perhaps a few years older. Upright posture, shoulders square. She hadn't noticed him on the boat, but she wanted to know more. It wasn't just his looks or chivalrous defense of her. Maybe it was an aura of confidence and success he projected. But now was not the time because his attention was on the riverbank crowd, like everyone else at the rail.

The calliope paused. The giant wheels stopped turning. A sudden, almost unnatural quiet settled over the top deck, disturbed only by water spilling over the paddles and cascading down to the river's surface. Stella repositioned her feet to adjust to the motionless deck.

She wrinkled her nose at a stench that rose from horse pens, slaughterhouses, and massive coal and cotton warehouses, saturating the air. Quite common in river towns. A rude displacement of the fresh scent of willows and pine from downriver, when the *Lady J* had steamed close to the bank.

A fast-walking man dragged a woman by the hand, her skirts billowing as she ran to keep up. Two in a procession of townsfolk coming from the warehouses, taverns, dry-goods store, and other buildings of commerce. Stinky air didn't prevent them from coming out.

Mr. Tobin, the calliopist, switched tunes, and "Cricket on the Hearth" floated over dozens of Friars Point's locals with toe-tapping intensity. Black children danced to the tune—one boy spun in circles, throwing his hands to the sky. Soon, field workers appeared out of the reeds and creepers north of the levee, leaving their plows in the furrows.

Stella rocked back and forth, feeling the same mystical magnetism that pulled lower river locals to the boat.

Friars Point's riverfront swelled with townsfolk mostly dressed in workmen's clothing. The calliope was doing its job, drawing them for a break from their labors to welcome the *Lady J* and to the barkers selling tickets to the show. Scanning the working people, a light-hearted sensation flowed through Stella. She was them. They were her. If she couldn't sing, she'd be a cook or a cleaner. A perpetually-tired house woman, married to a roustabout or a free Black man. Southern society would never grant her anything more.

The rousing calliope tune took Stella's thoughts to the evening's work. Dress in finery cut to display her charms. Take the stage. Sing to stir the emotions of the entertainment-starved lot below. Together with castmates, bring the joys of song and dance to their grimy river town.

At the edge of the crowd, four men sat high in the saddle, not moving. The man on the left had on a red vest and a bowler hat like a clerk or merchant's. The other three looked a far cry from men of business. Two wore flapjack hats over their long hair, and one's bushy brown beard hung down his chest. The fourth man was hatless with a massive, nearly bald skull and monstrous shoulders, sitting half a head higher than the others. Stella's grip on the rail tightened. River thugs in colored shirts, with rifle butts pointing up at their hips. Just the types she always had the good sense to avoid.

The calliope's tune changed to a heart-pounding circus rhythm. The crowd clapped along, and seeing happy expressions on so many faces made the riders fade away. Mr. Tobin worked the twenty steam-powered whistles with a fury. Stella looked his way, but the Texas Deck stood between them. A silver filagree climbed to the deck's roof, perfectly in line with the white puffs spreading from Mr. Tobin's steampipes into the cobalt sky.

Roustabouts lowered the gangplank. It banged loudly when it hit its resting block. Drays lined up to tender wooden barrels and boxes. Filled with coffee, salt, and whale oil, according to a chatty deckhand at yesterday's Vicksburg landing.

Cargo waited while the *Lady J*'s brass band in their silly white sailor suits and round hats disembarked. One by one, a trombonist and assorted horn players filed over the gangplank. The top-heavy tuba player wobbled close to the edge, nearly falling into the river. *Oh no!* A deckhand grabbed his shoulders until he regained his footing. Stella breathed easier. On land, the band members lined up for a Friars Point parade. Their conductor shouted, "March!" and deckhands followed, carrying placards that promoted tonight's performance.

Stella grinned knowingly at the choreographed chaos that didn't vary much from landing to landing.

"Quite a gathering," Mr. Franklin said.

"Oh!" Stella, idly pondering the scene, twitched a little at the sound of his voice. "Yes, indeed."

He moved closer. "Friars Point is the largest cotton shipping stop south of Memphis. Our landing has generated more enthusiasm here than in Arkansas City or even Greenville."

Stella hesitated, uncertain whether to reply further to his unsolicited attentions. "Perhaps steamboats of our size and adornment don't land here often."

"Well, boats bigger than the *Lady J* load cotton bales here. You're right; she is pretty." He chuckled. "First time I've seen gilt acorns atop the derricks. But still just a boat. One stump and this bonny craft is at the bottom of the river like any other."

"Oh! I hope that won't happen."

"I'm sure it won't, ma'am."

"Tell me, Mister Franklin. If the *Lady J* is rather ordinary for this landing, as you suggest, then why have the people turned out?"

"This afternoon, they're coming to the riverbank to hear the steam organ and see the band parade through their shabby little town's muddy streets. For a break from loading bales and counting stocks and whatever else they do." He winked. "But tonight, they'll come to the auditorium to see you."

Stella drew back. Had he just winked? And personalizing his views on the audience's adoration was a bit much. What was the objective of Mr. Franklin's attention? Being forward? An over-awed admirer of her performances? Some angle to further the business of the *Lady J*? She didn't care to find out and was about to make her excuses when a light-skinned Black man, nearly the height of her flatterer, approached. When Mr. Franklin nodded at the Black man, he joined them and handed Mr. Franklin a drink.

Her gaze fixed on the Black man's straight-backed and wide-shouldered, confident posture. His midsection was trimmer than Mr. Franklin's. A round bulge at his shoulder meant powerful muscles. How would his manly torso feel to her touch? *Stop! I will not think about him in the same way men leer over me!*

Mr. Franklin took a sip. "Rum punch with milk and nutmeg. Delicious."

"Would you like one?" the Black man asked Stella.

"No thank you," she replied, jarred from her musings.

"Miss Parrot, this is my partner, Toby Freeman."

The words "free man" and "my partner" registered, and Stella took a closer look at the Black man. His size and shape and even his white linen shirt and waistcoat resembled Mr. Franklin's, so much so that the two of them standing side by side created what almost seemed a light and shadow mirror image. Toby wasn't a man forced to serve his master a drink.

Reacting to her attentions, Toby said, "I'm a freeman, ma'am." He chuckled. "Named Freeman, but you can call me Toby."

"I see." A curious situation indeed, Stella mused. A White man and a Black man standing together in a public area, with obvious familiarity. And Toby's expression was warm and disarming.

The two men grinned. Their comfort with one another was apparent, but the lower Mississippi is a strictly segregated world. White people assumed that Mr. Franklin owned Toby. A fair mistake since most Black people on riverboats on the lower river were enslaved. Some were traveling with their masters and others were hired out by the plantations between planting and picking seasons and used by the captain as inexpensive human equipment for cleaning and firing the boilers and other labor-intensive tasks.

Toby's kind, knowing smile sparked a moment of kinship. A Black man and a Cherokee woman trying to make their ways in the White man's world. She mused that their bond was the shackles of Southern society's intolerance for the advancement of their respective kinds.

"Get yer ticket to the greatest show on the river!"

The *Lady J* herself drew better than the barker's shouts. When locals paid their fifty cents and strolled through the main cabin, the grandiose chandeliers, porcelain door-knobs, and oil paintings awaited them. Oh, she'd seen it before. They'd marvel at Wilton carpets that came all the way from England and massive floral arrangements that exploded in a rainbow of colors before settling into their padded seats in the boat's velvet-curtained auditorium. Two-hundred small-towners experiencing opulence as foreign to their dirty river town as the governor's mansion.

They'd happily pay to see Mr. Jenkins's variety theater. A New York showman, Jenkins took elements of Eastern vaudeville, singing and dancing and comedy skits, and fashioned a program that was proving a perfect draw for the river traveler as well as the denizens of the little river towns from New Orleans to St. Louis. The curtain came up and rarely a seat was open.

Mary returned and handed Stella the evening's playbill.

"I wondered where you've been," Stella said to her red-headed understudy.

"Sorry, mum," Mary said in a thick Irish brogue. "I should have told ya I was going off to fetch this."

"BEST RIVER SHOW OF 1858. *THE TIMES-PICA-YUNE*. NOTHING LIKE IT! THE SWEETEST SINGER, PRETTY GIRLS, ELEGANT COSTUMES, AND GORGEOUS NEW SCENERY!" Stella glanced down the list of acts and laughed. *Sorry, Professor Butler*, she thought, *when you lecture on phrenology, the men in the audience will get up to refill their drinks*. It wasn't the lecture they came to see — it was *her* — singing and performing comedy scenes.

Stardom. Yes, stardom was hers. Since the *Lady J* had left New Orleans, seats were full and applause exuberant. Audiences cheered loudest when she hit high notes and looked pretty. Just glue them to their seats with mournful ballads and pop them up with fanciful jigs. The *Lady J*'s tour had started well, but what about bigger stages? Could she draw in New York? Europe? She must take that up with Mr. Jenkins. She hummed softly to the tune of "The Sailor's Hornpipe," which was listed a third of the way down the page.

Mr. Franklin took notice and glanced her way. She acknowledged him with a slight nod. God Almighty, he was handsome. Who was this man? Her stomach fluttered a little as she waited for him to say something. But he simply smiled and turned back to the riverfront scene. If a little humming disturbed him, he was a sensitive fellow indeed.

The crowd surrounded the brass band's parade like bees around a hive. At the boat, workmen carried cargo across the gangplank. Stella scanned the riverfront and began to hum again, softly this time so as not to attract Mr. Franklin's attention.

A barker sold tickets to customers lined six deep. *Sell away!* Of course, sold tickets sustained the troupe.

The four horsemen walked their mounts toward the crowd and halted them behind the line of buyers. *Who are these men, and what are they doing here?* Taking stock of ticket collections? Whatever it was, she couldn't take her eyes off them. Motionless in the saddle. Menacing, humorless figures contrasting with bustling townsfolk who'd come to meet the boat. Uninterested in the band or buying a ticket. She shuddered. Mounted gunmen presiding over the scene.

A horse-drawn buggy obscured the horsemen for a moment, then zigzagged through the crowd and pulled up at the gangplank. A well-dressed man got out and waited. A golden watch chain dangling from his vest gleamed in the afternoon sun. The *Lady J*'s captain greeted the man at the gangplank. So, the man in the buggy was somebody important. Hopefully enough to hold sway over the people of Friars Point and encourage ticket sales.

In the middle of a swell of townspeople, the brass band and sign-stumping deckhands popped in and out of view. The band's colorful uniforms almost put a coat of paint on Friars Point's shoddy riverfront buildings.

The band broke into the opening notes of "Dixie." Mr. Franklin smiled at her. Had he just glanced at her chest? She was conscious of her tight bodice; why hadn't she chosen a more modest one with a higher neckline? She crossed her arms tight to her bosom and focused on the riverfront scene.

Mr. Franklin hadn't picked his spot randomly because well-dressed Whites kept their distance from her. She bristled at the thought that he had more on his mind than a newspaper article and backed away.

"I'm sorry if I've crowded you," Mr. Franklin said.

Stella took a deep breath. Maybe she had misread his intentions. After all, every one of his overtures had been exceedingly polite. "You say the two of you are partners?" She looked from Mr. Franklin to Toby.

"We're business partners in the river trade," Mr. Franklin said. "We've delivered our goods at the port of New Orleans."

"I see. What did you take to New Orleans?"

"Mostly northern hardwoods. And grain and quite a few barrels of bourbon."

"Now you're going home?"

"We're returning to St. Louis with two barges stocked with barrels of sugar and molasses."

"I see." Stella made a show of looking around. "Where exactly do you keep these barges?"

Mr. Franklin laughed. Toby flashed a toothy smile and replied, "We've hired a stern wheeler to push our sugar load upriver, probably two days ahead. Our agent will be waiting at the wharf with his stevedores to unload."

Mr. Franklin held his cocktail below his chin and looked away, studying the crowd on shore.

Stella followed his gaze to the four men on horseback. Their scowls contrasted with the excited, eager faces of Friars Point townspeople like musk thistle in a bowl of roses.

The horsemen sent a shiver down Stella's spine. Mr. Franklin and Toby's wary expressions matched her feeling that something wasn't right.

"Know 'em?" Toby asked Mr. Franklin.

"I think the one on the left was cast off the *Bayou Rose* at Plum Point Reach in fifty-six."

"Cast off?" Stella asked.

"The boys in the *Rose*'s men's cabin were playing a friendly game of Euchre," Mr. Franklin said. "Once they started wagering, they found a Jack of Spades up his sleeve. So, they chucked him and his valise onto the sandbar off Osceola. Lots of river rats and pirates up that way—good company for him." He rubbed his chin. "They called him Barton as I recall."

"Mister Barton?" Stella asked.

"Well, they don't say their r's south of Cairo, so I could be wrong 'bout that."

"I take it you are a gambling man, Mister Franklin." Stella's haughty air didn't conceal her disdain. Was card-playing the real reason he and Toby were returning to St. Louis on the *Lady J* rather than with their barges?

"Now, Miss Parrot, games of chance are not the depths of wickedness that your tone implies. Why, a card player on the Mississippi once pointed out to me that in biblical days it was determined by lot which of the goats should be offered by Aaron and how the land of Canaan was divided. Great thinkers like Cato and Descartes were seduced by wagering, and even the father of the Methodists, John Wesley, was known to be a card player. So, sitting in on a game or two is not just a diversion; it's for my betterment."

"Hardly convincing, Mr. Franklin." Stella crossed her arms. Hopefully for his sake, his specious argument had been in the spirit of a farcical jest. "Please tell me you don't leave a wake of destitutes in river towns when you disembark."

Mr. Franklin smiled. "All in fun, ma'am. There's a fair bit of idleness on a journey between the Missouri and New Orleans, Miss Parrot, as you're surely aware. I've been known to play to pass the time."

Stella shifted. "And you?"

"They don't allow my kind in the card rooms, ma'am," Toby replied.

She nodded, acknowledging the offense he took at segregation that burdened him but not his partner.

"Look at that sonofabitch," Toby said. "Sorry for my language, ma'am."

She accepted his apology with another slight nod and followed his gaze to the river scene.

The bald-headed horseman pulled sharply on the reins to bring his horse around, impervious to people standing next to him. The big bay's head snapped left, striking a man and pushing him into a group of others. Two of them tumbled onto their bellies in the muddy street. Baldy's three companions took up their reins and followed. One man sat up in the mud and shook his fist at the riders, but it was too far to hear if he shouted at them or not. None of the riders acknowledged the blow.

"The three on the right aren't your average river gintys, Miss Parrot."

Stella raised an eyebrow.

"Don't get off the boat often, do you?" Mr. Franklin chuckled. "That's what Toby and I call long-haired ne'er-do-wells who slink around river town landings. Looking for a drink or some unattended cargo to pinch. No, these men are different. They have the look of bandits who will come aboard tonight after an easy payday. The *Lady J* has quite a few well-armed security men. I suggest you stay near one while we're tied up at Friars Point."

Stella took note that the tone of Mr. Franklin's voice had lowered, a little ominously. "Thank you, sir. I'll keep that in mind."

But in truth, his words rang hollow. In her off-time, Stella often wandered the boat bow to stern, deck by deck, passing gents who acknowledged her with a tip of the hat and ladies who signaled their envy of her stardom with a slight smile. Since leaving New Orleans, the *Lady J* had been as safe as a fortress.

Mary turned her attention from the riverfront to the three of them and smiled sweetly at Mr. Franklin and

Toby. "Miss Parrot," she said, "you should take a rest. Later I'll help with your makeup."

"Thank you, Mary," Stella said, feeling a little empty that her chat with the handsome strangers must end. She curtseyed to the men. "Have a nice evening, gentlemen. I hope you enjoy the show."

Mr. Franklin bowed. "We look forward to the boat's first-rate entertainment, especially the singing soubrette." Toby nodded in agreement.

"Thank you," Stella said. "I hope the locals agree with you."

"I'm sure they will."

"Come on, Mary." Stella hesitated. "Mister Franklin, may I take your newspaper to share with my castmates?"

He handed it to her. "Why, of course."

At the stairs, Stella took a last look at them. Business partners in the Deep South. How unusual. Races didn't mix much. That alone made them intriguing. Each man had been easy to talk with and carried himself with a confidence that suggested he was worth knowing. Beyond that, they were two of the best-looking gentlemen on the *Lady J.* Another thing struck her; they were faintly familiar. Had she seen them before?

She put those questions aside. Leisure time was over. Get into character, pull back the curtain, and deliver the good people of Friars Point a *pièce de résistance.*

Chapter 2

STELLA CLUTCHED THE STAGE DRAPERY, her heart beating a pitter-patter. Same as always before she took the stage.

The full-capacity theater crowd fidgeted, clapped, and called out for the show to start, charging the backstage air with excitement. Cast members bantered happily, eager to go on. God, she loved performing for a packed house. Her voice soared, and the troupe's performance matched her own. Stella bounced on her toes. Showtime couldn't come soon enough.

Finally, the piano player, Teddy, pounded out a lively jig and four female dancers came on, Stella's understudy Mary among them. All young and shapely, wearing matching swallow-tail coats over red vests, knee breeches, and green stockings. Their black soft-soled shoes quick-stepped in a light-hearted folk dance in front of scenery boards portraying the green hills of Ireland.

The tops of the orchestra players' heads bobbed in time over the proscenium's edge. Fiddler Knobby's bald pate gleamed with reflected stage light. Customers filled twenty rows of seats and probably the boxes at the edge of the stage, too, although the curtains blocked Stella's view.

The dance ended to spirited applause and the girls filed past Stella. She squeezed Mary's shoulder, drawing a big, toothy smile from her understudy. Big exhale. Time to pull back the drape. The crowd spotted her and cheers rose. She took five steps forward into a sunburst from the oil footlights. To buy time for her eyes to adjust, she waved to all corners.

Stella flashed a wide smile while surveying the showboat's auditorium. Maybe the most democratic institution on the Southern frontier. A gray-haired man, wearing a paisley-patterned vest over a frilled white shirt, sat beside a younger one, who wore a work shirt with rolled-up sleeves. Could be a cotton planter next to a poor White Irish or German roustabout. In the same row, a woman with fancy brown ringlets of hair and a string of pearls or possibly diamonds across her bosom accompanied a well-dressed man holding a top hat in his lap. A frontiersman-type in his worn buckskin vest sat next to them. In front of them, a man with slick blond hair looked like an Eastern, cravat-wearing heiress hunter. Several rows of Black customers sat at the back, behind a divider rail. All of them had come to see her, a Cherokee. The star of the show.

Teddy smoothed his mutton-chop whiskers like he didn't have a care in the world. As the show's accompanist, they had worked through dozens of performances, so Stella was confident his attention would not stray for long. When he tilted his head to her, she nodded slightly. He played the opening notes of her first solo.

"By the blue Alsatian mountains dwelt a maiden young and fair..."

Her strong soprano voice was not classically pure, but it had a thrilling edge, which was what had brought her success in a St. Louis theater and on other boats before Mr. Jenkins had hired her to sing on the *Lady J*. It held the audience silent, which was the highest mark of their approval. Stella lengthened the final top note in a vibrating crescendo, skillfully controlling her breath to keep the sound at its sweetest right to the end. When she relaxed, listeners gave a collective sigh; when she smiled, they broke into cheers. She blew kisses and, with an upraised palm, brought Teddy to his feet to accept his share of the applause.

"The Sailor's Hornpipe" was the last number in the opening act, and Stella sang and danced with a whimsical flair that had the crowd clapping in time. She forged a rapport with them, as if they were carrying her along. After taking a bow, she slipped behind the curtain and flipped her sailor's hat prop to a stage hand. The last of the applause faded as she took a seat. Grateful for twenty minutes of respite during the "filler" acts, she stirred a spoonful of honey into a cup of tea to soothe her throat.

When the good professor finished his talk, Stella went back to the stage drapery and peered at the crowd. Too many were slumped back in their seats with passionless expression. The buckskinned fellow rustled restlessly. The show needed a spark! Fortunately, Rawley went next. When the juggler tossed his sticks into a flying pinwheel, Stella sucked in a quick breath of amazement. He somehow coaxed three gentlemen to lend him their top hats. He juggled them across the stage, then tossed each one into the lap of its owner to loud cheers.

The crowd came alive with laughter. *That's it, Rawley!* He was a true showman, drawing her and everyone else into a happy world, one that must have given many in the auditorium a welcome reprieve from their hard lives in Friars Point.

Rawley took his bows. Time to concentrate on putting herself into the right mindset to tackle her own act. Stella fussed with the neckline of her dress and then with her hair. She mentally ticked through her lines, anything to get through the hardest part: standing just off the stage, waiting. She burned to go back on and give her very soul to earn the audience's applause.

Knobby worked his bow like a whirling dervish, fiddling "Natchez Under the Hill" at a *presto* two-hundred beats per minute. Mary and the other three dancers came back on stage. The girls spun and jumped in a weaving pattern, moving faster and faster. The crowd came to its feet in a clapping frenzy. Stella clapped along, savoring perhaps the best audience since leaving New Orleans.

The stagehands changed the scenery flats quickly in preparation for a comedy act. She lightly bit into her lip to normalize her breathing. The audience-facing side now had a painted kitchen with white cupboards, a cast-iron stove, some hanging pots and pans, and a woodpile. Stagehands placed a kitchen table with a small vase of flowers in the center of the proscenium. One of them handed her a mixing bowl and a whisk.

The Master of Ceremonies announced, "Newly-Wed." Stella exhaled and walked on wearing a kitchen apron and carrying her props. With the crowd cheering the sight of her, she set the bowl and whisk on the table, then picked up small sacks of sugar and flour and poured some of each into the bowl.

"Honey!" she exclaimed in the direction of the door she'd passed through.

"Yes, dear?" Her skit partner, Terry Tucker, was backstage, unseen, but his strong baritone easily projected beyond the stage to the attentive audience.

"Get yourself cleaned up and come in for supper," Stella said.

"In a minute, dear."

She silently moved through dramatic elements: Pour the floury mix into a pot and pantomime putting it on the stove. Set the table and pour glasses of water from a prop pitcher. Study the door, holding the pose for several seconds. Then face the audience with a perplexed expression.

She circled her mouth with her hands and shouted at the door. "Honey, dinnertime!"

Terry still didn't appear. *Now, let's hook them.* Pour half of the pot's mix onto each of the plates. Peer again at the empty doorway, then put her hands on her hips and frown. She pivoted to face her audience and sang to the popular tune of "Fanny Gray":

"Well, well, sir, can you come at last, before I think you'll come no more:

I've waited with my apron on from the twelve till the four...."

Terry's baritone answered from behind the scenery flat:

"Now pray, my love, put off that frown, and don't begin to scold;

You really will persuade me you're growing cross and old...."

"Oh!" She placed her hands on her cheeks, then widened her eyes and made an exaggerated sniff, holding the pose for several dramatic seconds. After studying the empty doorway, she put a finger to her chin, and gave a mischievous smile. The crowd chuckled. She removed her apron to reveal a bespeckled bodice with a low neckline above her tight waist and full, hip-hugging skirt.

Wolf whistles filled the air.

Stella sang in a sultry voice:

"Put down your hat, put down your coat, now Charles do stay;

Come to see me, or do you long to run away?"

The doorway was still empty. After a short pause she said, "Oh, honey dear. Come hither! I have something very sweet for you." With a hand behind her head, she pointed a toe and threw out her chest in a voluptuous pose.

The whistles grew louder.

Stella let the crowd's excitement build. With wild, lust-filled eyes, men ogled her from the front rows. It took great resolve to keep her eyes from narrowing with disgust. But it was her job to bring the audience to a frenzy, even if using female charms to do it made her feel like a working girl in a tavern. Having achieved the desired effect, she straightened and peered at the doorway again for several seconds. She hurried to the left side of the scenery flat. No Terry. She shook her head and ran to the other side of the flat. Not there either.

Stella went to the center of the stage and put her hands on her cheeks in a panic. She turned in a circle, looking all around. The crowd murmured, beginning to wonder if Stella's play-husband had missed his cue.

Finally, Terry burst through the door. "Hello, dear!"

"Why didn't you come when I called!"

"Why, my dear, I was out back hauling in the damnedest, biggest catfish you ever did see!"

The theater erupted in laughter.

The crowd was hers. Stella and Terry embraced. The orchestra triumphantly struck up Mendelssohn's "Wedding March." They danced around the stage, high-stepping in unison and flashing wide smiles like happy newlyweds. They finished the dance and embraced once again before bowing. Stella curtseyed to Terry, and he exited to loud applause.

Knobby stood and bowed his fiddle. Teddy pounded the piano keys to the tune of "The Old Rose Tree" with such vigor that his alpaca coattails were bouncing below his bench. Stella joined Mary and the dancers in a lively number that once again had the room clapping along. Her steps felt lightning fast and weightless, propelled by the audience's applause.

When the dance was over, Stella acknowledged Mary and the girls and the musicians, and caught her breath. Then the orchestra accompanied her on a slow, soulful version of "Dixie." She wouldn't choose the song to end the show because too many lower river customers seemed almost unnaturally roused by it, but Mr. Jenkins had insisted that "Dixie" be the finale at every show south of Memphis.

~ ~ ~

Seated in the back row, Toby thought Stella shone with grace and beauty that overshadowed anyone else on the stage. Her voice was a songbird's, sweet and melodic, creating a sense of contentment when she sang ballads and exhilaration when she raised the volume on up-tempo numbers.

Hah! What a scene! White men in front of the rail that divided the White and the Colored folk were mesmerized by a woman with dark skin. Up close on the hurricane deck, she had been unmistakably Indian with her big, round dark eyes and her pitch-black hair. Cherokee maybe since they tended to have the lightest skin tone of the tribes. Damn she was beautiful! Many of these White men would spit at a squaw they came across on the street, but here, every one of them bowed to Stella as if she owned the auditorium.

From his vantage point sixty feet behind the divider, Stella's skin glowed light brown in the lights. Like a woman from New Orleans—a melting pot of a city with many types of dark-complected beauties. In her costumes, carrying herself like a starlet, she resembled the fancy-dressed Creole and Spanish ladies on *Rue Chartres* that he'd seen through the open doors of boutiques, holding court while the clerks displayed the latest fashions on their manikins.

Something else fascinated him, something beyond her looks and musical talent. She was faintly familiar.

He sensed a man standing close and glanced over his right shoulder. One of the long-haired horsemen stood in the aisle, stiff as an oak, his face darkened by several days' stubble. He held a drink. He glared at Toby with drunken glassy eyes and lips parted slightly. Despising hardness in his stare pierced Toby's soul. Toby seethed. *River rat bastard thinks he's my better, and it ain't so at all.* Long-Hair turned back to the stage, drawn to Stella like everyone else. But his sinister panting chilled Toby. A wolf frothing over the livestock.

Stella finished the final notes of "Dixie" and took her bow. Toby applauded enthusiastically along with the crowd until she disappeared behind the draperies.

When Toby turned to his right, Long-Hair was gone.

Chapter 3

STELLA ASCENDED THE *LADY J*'s stairwell in nearly to-
tal darkness. While the forecastle shone with the red
glow of torch-baskets, the darker aft section of the hurricane deck offered solitude. She stood at the stern rail,
enjoying a silver shimmer cast across the river's surface
by the crescent moon. Inhaling deeply, cool, sweet night
air energized her, even though it was late, past eleven
o'clock, and still. A deserted top deck and quiet riverbank. Serene moments hers alone.

Applause rang in Stella's ears. She pumped a fist into
the dark sky, reveling in her triumph. She'd never tire of
basking in the adoration of two hundred strangers. More
than anything, their attentions affirmed her talents, and
that stirred her. Every night since the *Lady J* left New Orleans, the audience had loved her work and craved more.
Sometimes, like now, she savored the joy of it alone,
greedily.

Recalling Mr. Jenkins's reaction lit her up. Not five
minutes ago, he offered, "It's a shame the *Lady J*'s auditorium isn't larger. I could fill twice the number of
seats." He mentioned "The Swedish Nightingale" had
packed the biggest river town halls for two years—clearing $150,000! With only a pianist and baritone backing
her. An Easterner named P. T. Barnum had arranged the

Swedish Nightingale's tour, and Mr. Jenkins had said he might be able to do something along the same lines for Stella. Her chest swelled. Could it be possible?

Off in the distance a loon wailed. Across the Mississippi River, the Arkansas shore had faded into a straight dark line. Green canopies of pines, hickories, and maples were black now, blending into the night.

Time to return to the theater and have a celebratory drink with the rest of the troupe. Stella bit her lip a little. The happy adulations they'd share! Someone would serve up rum punch from a pitcher set in the center of the room and the toasts would begin.

Wasn't it a rum drink that Toby had given Mr. Franklin earlier? A fancier libation than the troupe's punch, indeed. Sipping one would be heavenly, especially if the two of them joined her. Mr. Franklin had been at the performance, in the third row, but she hadn't been able to make out Toby among the Black customers in the back rows where the light was dimmer. Hopefully, both were there, cheering as enthusiastically as the rest of the audience.

Boots clomped on the wooden planks.

Stella turned toward the back wall of the Texas deck, fancifully hoping to see Mr. Franklin and Toby. Moonlight illuminated a tall, long-haired man next to the ship's bell.

The hair on the back of her neck rose.

He took two steps toward her. After setting a glass down, he struck a match and light flared over several days' worth of stubble that covered his face.

God, it's one of them! One of the four men on horseback.

He lit a cigar and clenched it between his teeth.

Another two steps. He rocked back and forth like a drunk.

A sinking feeling hit her.

Another step. And another. So close now. His shabby brown jacket stunk like whiskey and tobacco.

Stella stepped back. The wooden railing halted further retreat.

He puffed his cigar. Smoke blew in her face, gagging her.

A menacing growl came out the side of his mouth. "Well, well. As purty in person as up on that stage." He pulled up a Windsor deck chair and sat down directly in front of her. "I'm a gonna take a good look at you." He took a long drag on his cigar.

When Stella started to walk past him, he stuck his arm out to stop her. He growled a menacing sound from somewhere deep inside him. Her legs started to shake.

He pointed his cigar at her chin. She recoiled from the heat. *Oh Lord, the look on his face!* Lust, hate, anticipation, dominance—all rolled into one.

How could she escape? It was deathly quiet; she couldn't hear a soul. Her throat tightened so much she wasn't sure she could scream. Would anyone hear her? *Run! Just run!* "I m-must be leaving, sir. My castmates are looking for me."

He didn't move his arm to let her pass.

"Uh. Uh. I don't want any trouble, sir. I need to leave."

"There's no trouble here, squaw." He tossed his cigar over the rail, set down his glass, and rose. He grabbed her around the waist and pinned her against the rail.

Stella couldn't breathe.

"I'm the opposite of trouble." He ground his pelvis into hers. "Calm yerself, li'l Injun girl. I'm gonna give you sweetness."

Stella gagged at his whiskey breath. "No!" She struggled to squirm away, but he was bigger and stronger and squeezed her like a vise. He pinched her cheeks with his thumb and forefinger. It hurt like hell, and she couldn't make a sound.

"Easy, girlie. Don't you worry; I pay well. More than your wages from this here riverboat."

Stella jerked her head free for an instant and screamed.

He slapped his palm over her mouth and snapped her head like a wet towel.

Stella's legs wobbled. She went limp. His face leered over hers with a predator's vacant eyes. He ripped her neckline and buttons popped, exposing her cleavage.

Her temples blazed impossibly hot. She reached to cover herself, but he pulled her hands away.

"Get yer hands off her!"

Stella couldn't see the speaker, but his voice was familiar. She muttered, "Please, please help."

The man approached. "Stella?"

Toby!

"Jeez Christ; get the hell outta here," Stella's attacker said. "I'm busy. Go to Jericho!" He nuzzled his head into Stella's neck, licking at her.

"No!" Stella shouted. She pushed him back.

Toby grabbed her attacker's sleeve. "Let her go!"

The man flung her aside. He pushed Toby backward over the deck chair. He pulled his pistol and fired two shots. Stella held her breath until she spotted Toby's large form standing in the moonlight. He'd missed! Click. Click. The attacker tried to fire again, but the chamber was empty.

"Goddammit!" The man threw his pistol down and pulled a long knife from inside his jacket.

Stella stepped back, but he thrust the blade at Toby. Toby caught the attacker's arm and spun him around, using his momentum to drive him into the *Lady J*'s jack staff. Everything inside her screamed "Run!" But she froze, unable to take her eyes off mortal combat.

The long-haired man shook his arm loose and swung the blade. Toby blocked his forearm and drove the man's back firmly into the staff. With his own hands, he circled the long-hair's grip on the knife's handle. Toby and the man grunted and strained; both of their grips locked on the handle. They swung the blade wildly. Metal flashed as each man tried to gain the upper hand.

Finally, Toby gained control and turned the blade away from himself, toward his attacker. He plunged it into the man's heart.

The man gasped, his eyes opening wide. A demonic hiss came from his lips. When Toby released the knife, the man slid down and crumpled on the wooden deck.

Stella had to force herself to breathe. She and Toby stood side by side over the body. Dark. Quiet. The only sound came from the flags up the jack staff flapping in the breeze. Time stood still.

"Oh God. Oh God." Stella shook. "Is he—?"

"Dead? Yeah, he's dead," Toby said. "Got 'im right through the heart."

The knife stuck out of the bloody shirt. The dead man's blank stare was right at her. Stella stumbled backward a step, disbelieving her beastly attacker was now a corpse. But the long-haired bastard deserved what he got. If Toby hadn't fought him, the bastard would have violated and probably murdered her.

She took Toby's hand. "Thank you."

"You're welcome, ma'am. Ain't gonna let that kind of thing happen."

Dark shadows and silence and time stood still. The two of them and a dead man on the deserted deck. Someone would come soon, maybe a passenger out for a stroll, maybe the watch. Then it registered with Stella that the deceased was White and she and Toby were of color. No White person would believe a White man deserved to die at the hands of a Black man or Cherokee woman. *What do I do?*

Mr. Franklin appeared at the top of the stairs. "There you are," he said to Toby.

He joined Toby and Stella. His easy-going grin disappeared at the sight of the body. "Good God in heaven, Toby. This one of those river gintys we saw?"

Mr. Franklin looked around the deck. Empty. He lit a match and crouched down to study the body.

"What the hell happened? Tell me quick!"

Toby did so.

Mr. Franklin turned to Stella. "I'm sorry this happened to you, ma'am. Are you injured?"

"No—thanks to Toby."

Mr. Franklin walked to the railing and looked toward the forecastle. Stella couldn't see anyone that way. The only sound was the haunting call of a loon. Mr. Franklin returned to the body. He put his hands in the blood that had soaked through the dead man's shirt. He wiped some of it on his own shirt. He rolled the corpse over, face down.

"Listen—both of you," Mr. Franklin said. "I did the killing here."

Stella flinched, not understanding.

"Now hold on," Toby said. "I can't let you do that."

"Christ, Toby. Get your head on straight." Mr. Franklin pointed a bloody finger at him. "You're a Black man on the lower river—you know how it goes. This ginty's from round here. His brothers and their thugs will never listen to your side. It'll be a lynching court, and your neck will be stretched by morning."

Mr. Franklin turned to Stella. "You hear me?"

She nodded but didn't reply.

"Goddammit! Do you hear me?"

"Yes."

"Who killed this man?"

"You did," Stella said, her voice quivering slightly.

Mr. Franklin put his palms down. "Calm down, lady. Are you okay?"

Stella gathered her strength. "Yes."

He lit another match, sheening the side of his face bright yellow. "All right. Listen; you got to be convincing why I did it. Rip your neckline some more. You tell them he was ravaging you and don't hold back!"

"Okay." She tore the rip in her dress so she had to hold her collar to keep her breasts in.

"Damn good thing I stepped out of the salon and heard the shots," Mr. Franklin said. "What the hell were you doing up here anyway?"

Toby nodded at the dead man. "He was in the theater. Drunk. Licking his chops like she was a piece a meat. I knew he was fixing to come after her. After the show, I walked around to make sure he didn't do her no harm."

Stella nearly fell to her knees. Some unfathomable goodness in this man had made him look out for her. Like a guardian angel.

Two deck hands approached, apparently making their rounds. One of them held a lantern. He noticed the body and reared back. The other saw what had spooked his mate and grabbed the lantern. He bent down for a long look at the dead man. "Got a knife in 'im. Go get the captain," he said to his mate.

"You gonna tell me what happened?" The deck hand shone the light in Mr. Franklin's face.

"Let's wait for the captain."

Mr. Franklin took a cigar out of his coat and lit up.

They stood in silence. Mr. Franklin faced the dark river while he smoked. Stella wished she could read his mind. The prospect of him having second thoughts about taking the blame gave her an empty feeling in the pit of her stomach. If he changed his tune, Toby would be in grave peril, but where would it leave her? Would the authorities accuse her of being a wanton woman who had brought about the killing? Would Mr. Jenkins dismiss her? Even worse, would she face charges?

When the deck hand turned the other way, Mr. Franklin smiled slyly at Toby. Was he signaling that he'd bought himself a little time to think through his story?

Minutes later, the *Lady J*'s gray-haired captain appeared out of the gloom. The deck hand held up his lantern, illuminating the captain's fulsome girth and gray goatee.

"Captain Martin," Mr. Franklin said.

Captain Martin grunted his acknowledgment. "And you are?" He didn't say anything to Stella or Toby.

"John Dee Franklin."

The captain lifted the corpse's head. Stella heard him snort as he studied the dead man's face. She could hardly breathe. The captain turned to Mr. Franklin and said, "Ricky Burton. Gonna be a peck of trouble here that I most surely don't need."

Burton. Close enough to be the four horsemen's surname Mr. Franklin had mentioned earlier. The roils in Stella's stomach returned.

The captain pulled back his coat's swallow tail to reveal a pistol at his side, a move Stella assumed was meant to show he was in full control. She didn't know exactly what his legal authority was but, of course, he was well within his rights to investigate a death on his ship. She felt tiny as he appraised the three of them with the air of a judge sitting at his high bench in a court of law.

"What the hell happened here?" the captain asked Mr. Franklin.

Mr. Franklin pointed at Stella. "The long and the short of it is he was assaulting your singer. I told him to stop, and he took a couple of shots at me. Then he swung his blade at me, and I killed him."

"That right?" the captain asked Stella. "And what in hell's blazes were you doing up here so late?"

Stella drew back at the force of his question. *Breathe. Keep your cool.* "What he said is true. I came up for some air after my performance."

"To meet Ricky Burton?" the captain asked.

"Heavens no!" Stella scowled.

"All right," the captain said. "Then what the hell were you doing up here in the dark?"

"I was high as a kite after the show. I just had to be alone. The man—Mister Burton—backed me into the rail and wouldn't let go."

"And?"

"He ripped my dress!" Stella slightly parted her collar so he could see the long slash in her bodice. "Oh—my God—the things he said he was going to do to me! I thought he was going to kill me."

The captain took off his silk plug hat and sighed. He addressed Mr. Franklin. "So, you're saying he missed? Any bullet holes to back that up?"

Stella stepped forward. "I saw where he shot." It was a big risk. In the darkness, she hadn't seen exactly where Burton shot, but she knew where the gun had been pointed and the bullet holes had to be here somewhere. Her heart raced as she directed the deck hand to train his lantern over the plank flooring. "The bullet hit in this area." She ran her hand over the wood. Smooth. She widened her probe left, then right. Nothing. Where? Where is it? Her mouth was dry as sandpaper. Finally, her fingers ran over the splintered edge of a gouge. She guided the light to show the deck hand. Then she led him to the back wall of the Texas Deck. Her fingers felt splintered wood almost immediately. Thank God!

"That's where the second bullet hit," she said firmly, keeping to herself her lack of conviction that the damage was truly a bullet hole.

The deck hand said to the captain, "Looks like two bullet holes, sir."

"Hmm. Where's his gun?"

Stella pointed to the deck near the stern rail. "He threw it there when he ran out of bullets."

The captain had his deck hand light up the area. The pistol was on the deck toward the starboard corner of the stern rail. The captain picked it up. "Still warm." He went to the dead body and kicked the corpse's coat tail over its hip, exposing a holster. The captain inserted the pistol. "Well, it holsters okay. Summabitch weren't supposed to have one of these on my boat."

The lantern cast a faint glow over Toby and Mr. Franklin. Stella glanced over, wondering if they felt as helpless as she did. A red stain on Toby's shirt sleeve protruded below his jacket. She gasped and held her breath. *Please, please, Captain—don't see it.*

"Franklin, you said?" the captain asked. "You're a card player, ain't you? Away from your game, ain't you? Why are you up here?"

"Well, I was done for the night. I came up here with Toby for a smoke before retiring." He flicked off ashes.

The captain motioned to the deck hand to hold the lantern high, illuminating the group of them. He looked Toby over, but spoke to Mr. Franklin. "Who did the killing—you or him?"

Stella's heart beat quicker. Did the captain doubt their story?

"I told ya. Me," Mr. Franklin said.

The captain's narrowed-eyed stare at Mr. Franklin made Stella breathless. Finally, he nodded slightly.

The captain hadn't seen the bloodstain on Toby's sleeve. She thanked the heavens for that. What's more, Mr. Franklin had been correct: Due solely to the color of Toby's skin, his word meant nothing. The captain treated Toby like a piece of Mr. Franklin's property. He had no right to speak. Stella had been on the lower river too long to expect anything else. Nevertheless, the unjustness of the captain's bigoted thinking made her blood boil. Maybe this time it would work in their favor. If the captain had decided to question Toby, some little inconsistency could give them away.

"There's sumthing I don't understand here, Franklin. Why the hell did you kill Burton if he didn't have his gun no more?"

A quivery tremor shot through her. What was the captain insinuating? How in the hell would she get through this without screaming?

"The ginty pulled his Bowie knife and rushed me. I turned the tables on him."

The captain grabbed the lantern and shined light over Mr. Franklin, pausing to examine the blood on his hands and shirt. Then he trained it on Ricky Burton's body. He rolled the corpse over and examined the bloody shirt. When he fingered the tip of the knife handle, it wobbled several times.

With the captain's attention on the corpse, Stella discretely pulled Toby's jacket sleeve over his shirt sleeve. Toby looked down at his jacket sleeve. His questioning look turned into a knowing, tight smile.

"You telling me that ain't your knife?"

"I am. He pulled that knife from his jacket."

The captain pulled back the dead body's lapel, exposing a sheath. Then he stood up and faced Mr. Franklin. "How'd it get in his chest?"

"He ran out of bullets so he threw his gun down. He charged me with his knife. It was him or me. We rassled and I turned it on him."

"Ricky Burton here's a big man. Nasty, too." The captain paused and looked Mr. Franklin over. "I guess you got 'nuff size to you to give him what for. Franklin, you must be a tougher bastard than you look there in your fancy suit."

The captain fingered his thick gray moustache as he thought. "Jack," he said to the deck hand, "put Burton down below in cold storage for the night."

"There ain't much room in there with the ice blocks and the meat crates and all."

"Well, make room, goddammit! Throw some blocks in the river if you have to."

"Yes, sir."

"And swab Burton's blood off the deck. Do it quick, afore anyone comes round here." The captain grabbed Jack's sleeve. "Don't you say a word 'bout this."

Jack nodded.

The captain stood in front of Stella, Mr. Franklin, and Toby like an imperious lord. "You three. Come with me."

Chapter 4

John Dee Franklin followed Captain Martin into a small room inside the Texas Deck. Was his nervousness obvious? Not yet certain of the captain's predisposition on the legalities of the death, John Dee steadied his breathing.

A servant lit the last candle on the opposite wall, giving its curved glass sconce a yellowish hue. He nodded at the captain, and Stella and Toby stood aside at the threshold as he left the room. Then they entered.

A redwood table bordered with an ornate black resin pattern was surrounded by eight leather chairs. Gleaming brass handles, fittings, and a crystal serving set adorned the room. A decanter two-thirds full sat on a corner cupboard. Perfectly fitting, John Dee thought, for entertaining a rich plantation owner, a United States senator, or an English prince.

After motioning John Dee to sit, the captain took the chair at the end of the table. John Dee straightened his tie, waiting for the captain to point out seats to Toby and Stella. He didn't even look at them, so they stood silently behind John Dee, like a couple of servants.

"Nice, ain't it?"

John Dee nodded.

"Fanciest captain's dining room I ever had. Then again, the *Lady J*'s the fanciest boat I ever ran up the river."

"Yes, indeed. She's the prettiest steamer I've had the pleasure of traveling on," John Dee said.

"We'll finish our business here. Then we'll have a drink."

"I'd like that, sir." Did the captain's invitation affirm his agreement with John Dee's version of Ricky's death? John Dee breathed a little easier.

The captain addressed his underling at the door. "Go get Sam Clemens."

"Yes, suh." The young man left the room.

"Here's what's gonna happen, Franklin. 'Bout seven-thirty tah-marrah morning, my deck hands will load Ricky Burton's body into a wagon. I'll take 'im to the undertaker. That'll put me at the Magnolia Hotel 'bout eight o'clock. 'Spect Judge Thompson'll be there having breakfast."

"You know this local judge?" John Dee asked.

"Sure do. Fact, the judge met me when we landed. Pulled his buggy right up to the gangplank and gave me a ride to his chambers."

John Dee's heart jumped a beat as he remembered the buggy making its way through the crowd. His fate rode on the captain's relationship with the judge.

"See, me and the judge appreciate the subtleties of Tennessee whiskies. Had a drink with him and caught up on the goings-on here in the Mississippi Delta. Then I caught him up on river happenings."

While John Dee listened, he tried to work out how to influence the captain's opinion of the matter, which was undoubtedly the key to saving his neck, and Toby's. "The judge is a friend of yours?"

"Well, Franklin, we go way back, Judge Thompson and me. I've landed dozens of cotton boats at Friars Point. Hell, bringing on a load of five-hundred-pound bales might take a day. So, yeah, the judge and I became friendly. See, I'd take a drink and dinner with him to pass the time. When I stop in on my way downriver, I try to keep a cabin open in case he wants passage, which he does now and then."

The captain's openness about his relationship with the judge surprised John Dee. This kind of talk didn't go with a murder charge. He bit his lip to keep from smiling. But there could be a hornet's nest since quite a few judges turned up in steamboat card rooms, bars, and barbershops on the lower Mississippi. Most often, a jurist's arrogant estimation of his skills didn't match his card-playing abilities. After a game, away the jurist would go, red-faced and poorer. To John Dee's gain. "I know some judges down this way, but don't recall—"

The captain raised his hand like he was swatting the comment away. "He ain't one of your card players. He likes to go to New Orleans for a few days every now and then."

That was a relief; a sore-loser's grudge would have been most inconvenient. If he wasn't a card player, the judge took riverboats to New Orleans for its exotic vices. Traveling the western frontier alone to the Crescent City meant secret desires. Knowing more might prove useful. Perhaps their paths had crossed at a tavern or even a bawdy house.

"Oh?"

"I don't ask a man 'bout his pleasures, Franklin." He ended the line of questioning with an irritated snort.

John Dee instantly regretted prying into the judge's affairs.

"Once I find him, we'll go back to his chambers. He'll read my statement and hear the evidence. Then he'll decide what to do."

"Uhh…" John Dee lost his question. Was the captain on his side or not? Stella and Toby hadn't made a peep. They were surely locked onto the captain's every word just as he was. Okay, so the captain was friendly with the judge. Great. But their fates were in the hands of a stranger.

"Judge Thompson has the authority to dispose of the case?"

"'Course he does. *Lady J* is tied up at Friars Point, ain't she?" The captain shifted in his chair. "See, Franklin, a little river town is an unruly place. It needs a king. The judge is the biggest landowner in Coahoma County. He's chairman of the committee that runs the wharf. Decides which boats get to land here and how much they pay. The sheriff is his nephew. Judge is King in Friars Point. Understand?"

"I do."

"Now, Franklin, in my line of work, you need to be friendly with the man in charge every place your boat lands. Most trips, there's some damn kind of legal issue. A passenger goes overboard. Stealing. Surely you've seen a sucker accuse a gambler of cheating or even shoot 'im?"

John Dee nodded.

"And there's a crime of passion now and then. I'm the law on this boat to deal with anything that ain't worth no more than a few dollars or ruffled feathers. Serious crimes get settled on land. So I make it my business to be on friendly terms with the local judge—or whoever else is the big man. Makes my life easier."

"I suppose all that's true. I'll go with you in the morning," John Dee said.

The captain laughed. "No, you won't. Friars Point's a small town, and everybody here knows the Burtons. Once the undertaker has Ricky's body, it won't take ten minutes for his brothers to find out. They'd kill you sure as anything before you got back on the boat."

John Dee took out his kerchief and wiped perspiration at his brow. Who were these Burtons? This situation was spiraling and not in a good way. "So, you are going to write out a statement about Ricky's death?"

"My cub pilot Sam Clemens is gonna record my statement. Yours too. And the squaw singer's. He's damned good at writing things up."

The door opened and a young man with wavy red hair entered. "You called for me, Captain Martin?"

"I did, Sam. Sit down. There's been a death on board, and I need you to take some statements."

Sam took a seat and looked at John Dee, then at Stella and Toby, while fingering his bushy red mustache under an aquiline nose. Those features, together with his bow tie and bright red hair, made Sam one of the most memorable characters John Dee had ever encountered on the river. "Remember me?"

Sam set his papers on the table, dipped his pen in an ink pot, and took a second look at him. "Did we meet in Hannibal, sir?"

John Dee shook his head. "It was in Keokuk. Iowa, I believe."

"Iowa. That's right," Sam said.

"Came into the shop to get myself a flyer printed, and there you were: a young, over-worked printer's devil setting the keys on the presses."

"Ah. I wasn't just the printer's devil. I was the poor devil who ran the place."

"You told me I'd come just in time—before it got dark when the gas light flared on and a million bugs assembled on the board, led by President Beetle. And you proceeded to describe President Beetle's tuxedo and his scepter and other accoutrements of his regime. Isn't that what you told me?"

Sam raised one side of his red mustache in a wry grin. The captain restlessly adjusted his bulk in his chair.

"I remember the dusty volumes you kept in your shop." John Dee lifted a finger in a theatrical flourish. "Suetonius. Shakespeare. Pepys. Darwin. I'll concede that your study of the caesars qualifies you here."

The captain raised his hand, demanding attention. "We're wasting time here, boys. Let's get to business!"

Dammit! The idea had been to ingratiate himself with the captain by recalling his unforgettable carrot-topped scribe. All he'd done was irritate the old codger, who probably was antsy to make his statement and get to bed. Or maybe to sip good whiskey.

"Yes, of course," John Dee said.

Sam's pen oscillated over his paper. "Ready?"

"Yes. My name is John Dee Franklin. I'm a passenger on the *Lady J.*"

Sam recorded John Dee's version of the events, which emphasized the depravity of Ricky's assault on Stella and the mortal combat that ensued when Ricky charged him with the Bowie knife. When he described plunging the knife into Ricky, Sam was glancing at Toby, who was using his sleeve to wipe away perspiration. Sam's eyes narrowed, making John Dee wonder what the hell was he on to? The captain rocked back and forth in his chair. He didn't pick up on whatever had piqued Sam's interest and didn't ask any questions. Sam returned to his scribing until John Dee finished up. Having now told his tale three times, once in his head, once to the captain, and once to Sam—John Dee almost believed it.

Then Stella gave her account to Sam. She kept hers brief, exactly the correct tactic because Captain Martin clasped and unclasped his hands with annoying regularity, undoubtedly eager to get this over with. She finished and made a slight curtsey to the captain.

The captain started in, frequently using legal terms like "said" knife and "such" witness testimony. Sam recorded his observations regarding the dead body, the gun and bullet holes, the knife, the blood on John Dee, and Stella's torn garment. The captain concluded that "Ricky Burton was justly killed in self-defense of a mortal threat to Mister Franklin's life." John Dee couldn't stop a sly smile from forming. He glanced at Toby, who was muttering under his breath. Something about his prayers being answered, undoubtedly.

"Now," the captain said, "let's have that drink. Sam, pour Franklin and me a glass. And one for yourself." He ignored Toby and Stella.

Sam retrieved the decanter and three glasses and served up.

"I believe the judge will clear you, Franklin," the captain said. "But you ought to know whom you're dealing with."

"You're referring to the Burtons?" John Dee asked.

"They might be the meanest river bastards from Memphis to Natchez. You know 'em?"

"I've encountered one of them. A card player. He didn't strike me as overly mean. But he was a bastard—a cheating bastard."

"That would be Stevie Burton. He's the educated one. Two years at some college back east. His brother Cliff called 'im home when their daddy died. He's s'posed to be the smart one. Handles the money and such."

"And the other two?"

"They're the muscle of the family—what's left of it now that you killed Ricky. The big one with the bald head is Brick Burton."

John Dee chuckled. "Didn't get Stevie's brains?"

"I don't reckon he did. But that's not why they call him Brick." The captain took a gulp. "Brick's no joke, Franklin. They say his fist's twice the size of most men's. It hits a cheekbone like a brick. Wander round Friars Point, you'll come across Danny Jinks. When you see his smashed-in face, you'll know what I mean."

"Oh shit," John Dee mouthed quietly.

Stella gasped.

The captain's admonishing glance at her demanded quiet. He continued. "Cliff Burton's their leader. He's the oldest. Has a beard as long as ol' Moses. His eyes have a fire in 'em that makes 'im look half crazy. Sam, tell Franklin here what you told me 'bout Cliff and his brothers."

Sam nodded and leaned forward. His red mustache twitched a little.

"One trip downriver, I was a cub pilot under Horace Bixby," Sam said. "We'd followed a small cargo packet down from Lake Providence—that's where the hanging trees draped with Spanish moss start. Once you get past Vicksburg, you don't find any settlements to speak of until Natchez. Well, the packet was faster than we were, so we lost sight of her round a bend at Grand Gulf." He paused. "She never made it to Natchez. Skiffs looked for her, but no sign of the boat or its crew was ever found."

"Now listen careful," Captain Martin said to John Dee.

Sam continued. "When we landed, I saw Cliff, Brick, and Ricky Burton in the biggest saloon in Natchez-Under-The-Hill. Hell, they and their drunken mates had taken over half the place. Whiskey bottles were lined up on the tables, and whores circled those boys like fireflies. Cliff paid for everything from a stack of yellow boys."

Sam's gaze shifted to Stella and Toby. One of them must have given a questioning look.

"Those are gold dollars and sovereigns, ma'am. The missing cargo packet carried a chest of them for a bank in Baton Rouge."

"So, you think the Burtons are pirates? They killed the crew, took the gold, and sank the boat?" John Dee asked.

"Well, that stretch of river is perfect for an ambush. But a stack of gold alone wouldn't convince me. I saw Cliff pull out a pocket watch I'd know anywhere—it was silver, with a fancy embossed steamship on its back. It was my friend Joe Wilson's—Joe had been piloting the packet."

Sam let that sink in. "I told the sheriff the bastards had killed my friend. He didn't do anything. Maybe Cliff paid him off. Or maybe that old sheriff knew he was a dead man if he took on the Burton gang without an army of Pinkertons."

John Dee's heart raced almost uncontrollably. Hard, ruthless river men were everywhere on the lower Mississippi, but these Burton bastards might take the cake. It sunk in that they'd never, ever stop until they settled the score with their brother's killer.

"The Burtons ain't never bothered my boat," the captain said. "But word on the river is hell yes they're pirates, Franklin. You see, the judge told me that here in Friars Point, the locals leave 'em be 'cause they have women and kids and act respectable for the most part. They pay the parson, help poor folks out now and then; that sort of thing. None of that means diddly to you. Point is the Burtons are hard men, and y'all are in great danger."

John Dee took a drink and let the whiskey's burn calm him. He glanced at Stella and Toby. Her eyes were glassy, as if her emotions were tied in knots. Toby's expression hadn't changed much, but his insides had to be churning as well.

A junior boat officer entered the room and motioned for the captain. They went outside to confer.

"Miss Parrot," John Dee said, "we'll keep you safe."

"This—all this. Can it be real? My God, just minutes ago I was on stage."

The captain poked his head in the door. "Been a fight in the bar. Bloody one I'm told. I've got to go. Franklin, watch for me in the morning. We'll talk when I get back from seeing the judge." He paused. "In the meantime, none of the three of you leave the boat. And none of you say a word to anyone—I mean anyone—until after I'm back on board tomorrow. I'll have armed men at the gangplank so the Burtons can't get on. I'll get you to Helena, but from there, you'll have to find another passage. The Burtons will be looking for you, and I can't have that kind of trouble on the *Lady J.*"

John Dee felt like he was falling. He and Toby, cut loose on the lower river to fend for themselves. He didn't blame the captain; he had to protect his passengers. So, what should they do next? He took deep breaths to gather himself. "I understand, Captain. Thank you for all you've done."

The captain tipped his cap. "Stay and finish your drink. Take your time. Freshen it up a little if you want. But don't get corned. I reckon you're gonna need your wits about you come tomorrow."

John Dee waved goodbye, seeing the captain as far more than a fat old man past his prime. It took insight and intelligence to deal with Ricky Burton's death, and for that matter, the many types of wrongful conduct that must arise on weeks-long river runs packed with travelers from all walks of life. The captain had both, on top of the technical riverman skills he and the pilot surely possessed to keep the *Lady J* from becoming one of the thousands of shipwrecks at the bottom of the big muddy river. Maybe they were in good hands.

~ ~ ~

Stella's temples pounded as she tried to make sense of everything she'd heard. She settled back into the chair she had taken at Sam's invitation, after the captain departed. Toby was seated next to her.

My God, do I have to leave the boat? Mr. Franklin certainly had to; the captain had said so, but did she have to go? How would she manage? Alone in some lower river town. "If you have to leave the *Lady J* at Helena," Stella asked Mr. Franklin, "what are you going to do?"

"I most certainly must get off. Same for Toby and same for you. The dead bastard's brothers are killers, and they'll be coming for all three of us."

Leave her headlining role on the *Lady J*? Unthinkable! Stella gasped. "I can't!"

"Ma'am, I'm truly sorry," Mr. Franklin said.

"I didn't do anything wrong!" She paused. "I rose from a reservation in Oklahoma to the streets of St. Louis to singing on river showboats. Heights a Cherokee girl only dreams of. My castmates love me. Audiences love me. Walk away? Never!" With a clenched jaw, she said, "I'll be staying, Mister Franklin."

"Ma'am, you didn't do anything wrong. Ricky Burton attacked you. He was a ruthless bastard, and he got what he deserved." He paused. "But the three of us unfortunately must pay a price. His brothers will blame us and come for revenge. We need to get off the boat. To save ourselves, and you heard the captain—so innocent people don't get hurt by the Burtons."

"The captain was speaking to you, Mister Franklin. He didn't tell me to get off the boat. Besides, he has an armed security force. They'll protect me from these Burtons."

Mr. Franklin sighed. "I 'spect all this will sort itself out once the captain returns from meeting the judge. And let's drop the Mister Franklin and Miss Parrot, shall we?"

Sam nodded. "Y'all have gone beyond formalities tonight, haven't you?"

"Okay, John Dee," Stella said. "Tell me, what are you going to do?"

"The captain's right. The Burtons will look for us in Helena. Any ideas?" John Dee asked Sam.

Sam sipped his whiskey and looked from John Dee to Toby. "First of all, I'm not entirely certain the words on the paper match the facts of the event that resulted in Ricky Burton's death."

Stella's temples pounded. Had this red-headed young man seen through their deception? John Dee raised an eyebrow in surprise. Sam studied Toby. She followed his gaze to the bloodstain on Toby's white shirt sleeve that was noticeable below his jacket sleeve. Good lord! Was Sam going to tell the captain what he suspected?

"Be that as it may," Sam said, "I can't construct a version where Ricky Burton wasn't in the wrong. I have no doubts that he needed killing. All the Burtons need killing."

Stella let out a huge breath. "Nice to know we're on the same side here."

"I'll help you best I can," Sam said.

Thank God.

Sam took another sip. He sat back and murmured, "Hmm." He cocked his head to the ceiling. His focus bounced from there to Toby to the cupboard to her to the table to John Dee as if he was calculating all possible options. The red-headed young man's air of authority was beyond his years. She hung on his every word.

"Seems to me a little misdirection is in order," Sam said. "When we land at Helena, you'll need disguises. Let me think about how to get you off the boat; I'll come up with a plan and some costumes. Once you're off, get yourselves to the south end of the landing. Board a steamer for New Orleans. Hope the Burtons chase you north, and hope even harder that they're caught and thrown in jail or killed before you see them again."

Sam's gaze met Stella's without any hint of his usual playfulness. "Stella, I do believe the captain meant you'll have to leave the boat along with John Dee and Toby."

His words hung in the air. She heard Toby's measured breaths. Sam's creaking chair. Faint rumbles that must be the boilers. "You're telling me I have to run for my life?"

"That's exactly what I'm telling you. I wish it weren't so, ma'am. My advice is that you need to stick close to these two gentlemen." Sam stood. "Now, I must get back to the pilot house. I wish you all luck." He bowed to Stella. "Ma'am." He downed the last of his whiskey, shook hands with Toby and then John Dee, and said to him on his way out, "Come see me later."

Stella slumped in her chair, feeling the walls closing in, squeezing the life out of her. Her triumphant theater tour was over. Dreams of being the next Swedish Nightingale were dashed. Now she would play a role she was completely unprepared for: weak and defenseless prey running from cold-blooded killers.

Her heart pounded. Go on the run from the Burtons with only a few dollars hidden in her room? The troupe covered all her expenses, and her pay from the *Lady J* was in a bank account in St. Louis. How would she eat or let a room off the boat? Her gaze trained on John Dee and

Toby. Did they have enough money to run for it? John Dee's passage to St. Louis cost one hundred dollars for a bed and meals. His trading business must be somewhat successful. White men let cabins; Toby let a "deckers" place on the lower level among the barrels, crates, and livestock for five or ten dollars. So, they had some money between the two of them. But why would they support her?

Toby said, "We'll get through this, Stella." He offered his embrace.

His expression was kind. At least this large, powerful-looking man had a heart. Part of her wanted to bury her face into his chest and cry. *Pull yourself together!* This nightmare wasn't going away, and she had to be strong. She patted his shoulder but pushed him away.

"I won't lie to you, Stella," John Dee said. "It's a bad spot. But we're in it together. Sam's plan sounds like a good one. Toby and I will get you to New Orleans. You can find yourself a new show."

She gathered her strength and straightened her back. "Why would you do that Mister…err, John Dee? Neither of you even know me! You don't owe me a thing."

"It's the right thing to do, ma'am." Toby's large, clasped hands were as big as a cannonball. Her self-proclaimed protector would be able to handle himself.

"Thank you, Toby." It wasn't far-fetched to believe Toby would cast his lot with her. Two people of color equally wary of White men on the lower river. What about John Dee? Could this White man in fancy clothes be trusted? "You," she said to John Dee, "you stepped in and took the blame—you risked your life for a Black man and a Cherokee woman. No White man does that."

"Toby and I go back a long ways. We've stood in the fire together more than a few times. Truth is, we've been in worse pickles."

Toby chuckled.

"Stick with us, Stella," John Dee said. "You'll be fine."

She had no choice: *If the captain forces me to leave the* Lady J, *John Dee and Toby are my only chance to escape the Burtons.* She ticked through the tasks ahead. Pack her costumes—she'd need them for her new troupe in New Orleans. How many could she cram in two valises? Maybe if John Dee and Toby helped she could bring a third. Just as importantly, she must leave things in good order with the troupe.

"Well then, I'll find Mr. Jenkins and tell him I must leave the ship at Helena. And I'll wake my understudy Mary and—"

"No, you won't!"

The force of John Dee's interruption gave her pause.

"No one can know we leave the *Lady J* or where we're going," he added, in a softer, more sympathetic, tone. "We can't leave any clues for the Burtons."

The shock of her impending departure on her castmates made Stella's heart sink. Would they think she'd been kidnapped? Gone overboard? Run off with a lover they'd never met? The worries they would have, without any way to get answers, sickened her.

But knowing the truth might put them in danger.

"I suppose you're right."

Toby and John Dee each made tight smiles as if they had come to terms with the seriousness of their predicament. She drew strength from them and gained confidence in her guardians. But it was something more than the sense of security they projected.

Just for an instant, they were young boys again. *Good God in heaven! I remember these two!*

"We all go back a ways," she said.

Toby shot her a questioning look. "Ma'am?"

"When you were just boys and I was a little girl. On *nunahi-duna-dlo-hilu-i*. The Trail of Tears."

Chapter 5

North of the Tennessee River
October 1838

TOBY SPED THROUGH NIGHT CAMP, just a clearing in the wilderness six days north of the Tennessee River. He scampered around blue-gray wagons covered by canvas-ribbed tops with John Dee closing the gap behind him like a hound after a rabbit. Toby broke left.

Dang! Ain't nowhere to go.

Thick stands of black walnuts hemmed him in like a fence.

John Dee grabbed a shirt tail, but Toby jerked free. He jumped a water bucket and found himself in the center of camp. Toby weaved through women mixing scoops of cornmeal with water in cooking pots, catching a mouth-watering bacon scent wafting from crackling fires. He dodged stools and water jugs and heard empty coffeepots clanking together. *Oops!*

An old woman's cooking pot wobbled but didn't fall. "Get outta here, boys!"

Men were in the south end of the meadow, thank God, turning out the oxen and horses. Good thing 'cause they'd-a whupped his and John Dee's behinds for running through woman's work.

Toby rolled between a wagon's small, iron-rimmed front wheel and the brake shoe attached to the larger rear one. After clearing the far side, he sprang up for his getaway. Huffing and puffing now, he gritted his teeth and kept up his pace. John Dee flashed outta nowhere and snatched his pant leg. An arm circled his waist. They somersaulted head over boots, coming up laughing. Toby wriggled loose for an instant, but John Dee, two years older and considerably stronger, wrapped him in a bear hug.

"Goddammit, John Dee Franklin, get over here! Now!"

Toby cringed at the familiar rolling rumble that intensified into a guttural blast. John Dee released Toby and presented himself to the bearded, angry, middle-aged yeller.

"Yes, Mr. Tompkins?"

"Yer a goddamned nuisance!" He growled like a big dog. "Make yourself useful, boy. Get me some firewood! Take yer boy with ya. Go on now!"

"Yes, sir."

Toby followed John Dee through spicebushes into the forest. Twigs crunched under his feet. The musty scent of wet, fallen leaves filled the air. A thorny branch whipped off John Dee's shoulder. Toby ducked. Several minutes of walking in the brisk fall air cooled him off. After a few minutes more, being beneath the forest canopy was downright chilly—a blanket over his shoulders would feel great.

Branches and sticks suitable for firewood were everywhere, but John Dee pushed on through the bush, not speaking. Finally, he stopped at an elderberry bush, popped a berry into his mouth, and gave one to Toby.

"Ain't bad fer this late," John Dee said.

They each picked a handful and sat down. Toby popped berries into his mouth one at a time.

"Why does ol' man Tomkins yell at me all the time? One of these times, his eyes are gonna pop out of his head, ain't they?"

Toby nodded. "'Fraid we was gonna get a switch."

John Dee stared straight ahead. He threw his berries at a tree. "Damn ol' man! Can't wait till we get to Missour-a."

"Gonna be a long time yet, ain't it?"

"I reckon so. Come on. Let's get our wood an' get back to camp." John Dee led them toward a downed walnut tree.

They'd each gathered an armful of sticks when leaves rustled in front of Toby. He grabbed John Dee's arm and made the quiet sign with his finger. They stood still and listened. What was it? A bear? Wolves? Some bad men hiding in the forest?

A child's scream pierced the air.

Toby put down the wood, dropped to his knees, and crawled as close as he dared. John Dee lay beside him. Toby pulled back bushes and spied a skinny White man with long greasy hair hanging under a shabby brown hat. The greasy White man led an Indian girl by a rope tied around her wrists. She was maybe a head shorter and a little younger than himself.

The girl fell and stumbled back to her bare feet. Tears streamed down her little red cheeks, matting strands of her long black hair.

John Dee stood, then Toby, and the White man saw them.

"What in the hell!" The man pulled a pistol.

Toby drew back. The hammer clicked. He froze; sure a gun blast was coming.

"Get over here where I can see you, boy. You, too, nigg-ah."

Toby stood still as a stone beside John Dee. The man pointed his gun at John Dee's face. Then at his. The muzzle looked big as a hoop. His chest thumped.

"Anyone else with you? Any a-dults?" He circled his gun in front of John Dee's chest.

John Dee shook his head no. Toby's heart thudded faster. *Is he gonna shoot?*

"What the hell you doing here, boy?"

"I was gonna ask you the same thing."

Lordy, John Dee! Don't give him a reason to pull the trigger!

"Don't get smart with me, boy. Who you with?"

"The wagons in the meadow back that a ways." John Dee pointed through the trees.

"Where's the wagons headed?"

"Missour-a."

The man holstered his pistol. Toby exhaled.

"Get back to yer people."

"Where you taking her?" John Dee asked.

Toby wondered the same thing.

The man rubbed his scruffy chin. "My cabin. Found her o'er yonder so she's mine. What's it to you, boy?"

"Nuthin, I guess. What are you gonna do with her?"

The White man laughed. "Why, I'll play with her awhile, boy. Don't you worry—you ain't missing nothing. Hell, you ain't old 'nuff to get a hard pecker." His grin exposed three black teeth in a yellowed mouthful of them. "Then I'll toss her in the bayou."

Toby recoiled and stumbled back a step. This bad man was gonna toss the little black-haired girl in the swamp like a bucket of slop?

"Why would you do that?" John Dee asked.

"Yeah, mister," Toby said, "why would ya?"

The greasy man glared at Toby as if he didn't have a right to speak. "A little Injun squaw ain't good fer nothing. This one ain't old enough to do no cooking or cleaning. I wouldn't waste two beans feeding her." The man spit a stream of brown tobacco juice. "Fish gotta eat." He looked back at the girl. "Let's go!"

Her lip trembled. Her head tilted as if she didn't understand English. The man pulled on the rope, and the little girl's bound hands were out in front of her like a wagon tongue.

She didn't deserve this.

Toby's temples blazed red hot. This greasy White man had no right to hurt this girl. But deep in the Tennessee woods, far from a town, who was gonna stop him? Toby and John Dee had to return to the wagons and leave for Missour-a in the morning.

"Bye, boys." The White man grinned like a sneering demon, exposing his rotten teeth. He jerked the rope, and the little girl fell forward onto her knees. She rose and pumped her little legs to keep up as he pulled her into the woods. He would hurt her. Then kill her. She would leave the earth, and no one would know, not even her parents.

This was wrong.

Toby rushed the little girl's captor. He knocked the greasy man sideways, causing him to drop the rope. The man flung Toby down and cocked his fist to strike. John Dee grabbed the man's arm. The two of them wrestled to the ground. The man was thin, but older and stronger. He threw John Dee onto his back. He choked John Dee with a vice grip. John Dee tugged on the man's hands, but he couldn't get them off his neck. The man grunted. John Dee gurgled. Little bubbles came out the side of his mouth. His face turned red.

Toby grabbed a length of black walnut from his firewood. He whacked the greasy White man in the side of his head. The man fell off John Dee, onto his side, groaning. Toby hit him again and again, until he lay still. The man's face was a red, bloody pulp. Toby dropped the walnut stick like a hot coal.

John Dee sat up and moaned. He rubbed the red marks on his neck. "Holy Moses. He was gonna kill me."

"Then he would have kilt me," Toby said. "Then her—"

The little girl was gone. Was she scared of him and John Dee? They would never hurt her. "She run off?"

"Nah," John Dee said. He pointed to a rope end showing at the bottom of a thicket. He pulled back shrubbery to expose the little girl, who held a hand over her mouth. He held out his hand. "Come with us, girl. We won't hurt you."

The girl sobbed and didn't move.

Toby bent down and put his hand on her shoulder. She didn't back away. "You are safe now. We won't hurt you."

Dirt and tears smudged the girl's face. She looked him straight in the eye as if searching for something. Hope, he guessed.

Toby took the girl's still-bound hands into his and helped her out of the thicket. John Dee untied her.

"What should we do with her?" Toby asked John Dee.

"Well, she looks like an Indian. Maybe a Cherokee or a Creek. Or Choctaw. Bet she knows the woods," John Dee said. "Let's let her go home. We gotta get back, too."

"But she's awful young," Toby said. "Can't be more than seven or eight. Mebbe we should take her back to the other Indians."

John Dee took a close look at her. "I reckon yer right. Let's trace back the way she came with that bastard."

The little girl's attacker hadn't moved. Blood covered the stubble on the side of his face. Kind of reminded Toby of back in Carolina when John Dee had shot a deer through the head. Toby didn't feel bad for the man. He didn't feel anything. "Is he dead?"

"Hope so," John Dee said. "Maggots gotta eat."

Toby grinned.

At first, trampled underbrush was easy enough to fol-low, but in two hundred yards, a clearing ended the trail. Toby and John Dee hesitated, but the little girl looked in all directions and then led them west, past a tall blackjack oak. She touched little shards of red wool. Had she torn 'em off her dress to mark her trail? Toby'd underestimat-ed her.

They walked until the sun was low in the sky. The little girl led them to a wagon camp that resembled the one Toby and John Dee had left. Many more wagons were at this camp, most without canvas tops, and many more people. Dozens of Indians were gathered round a fire, watching a man wearing a wolf's skin circle the flames in a slow dance. White paint streaks lined his face. He chanted something Toby didn't understand.

Beyond the wagons, two soldiers in blue uniforms stood with rifles at their sides, smoking. Fires dotted rows and rows of army tents a quarter mile farther out. It was as if the soldiers didn't want to be near the Indians.

The man in the wolf skin stopped chanting and dancing. He and other Indians stared at Toby, John Dee, and the little girl. Five men approached. One spoke to the girl in their language. When she replied, she pointed to the marks on her wrists and on John Dee's neck, then to Toby, while pantomiming swinging a stick.

Indian women took the little girl away. The men shook Toby and John Dee's hands.

"You are brave boys," an old Indian man said in English. "You saved a life. We thank you. Stay and have rabbit stew with us after the shaman finishes."

The man wearing a wolf's head tossed more wood on the fire. Toby flinched at a loud crackle. The wolf's sharp teeth jutted out from his forehead as he stood over the fire, palms raised to the flames. Its furry hide hung over his shoulders. Bear claws hung from straps at the bottom of a leather bag tied to his hip. He chanted words Toby couldn't understand.

Toby pulled on the long, blue shirt of the Indian man who had spoken to him and John Dee. "The man wearing a wolf's head."

"Yes. The shaman."

"What is the shaman doing?"

"He is burning the blankets of the dead."

Toby made out blood-red wool in the flames. "How did they die?"

The Indian man sighed. "The Army took our lands. We must walk a thousand miles to new lands. Our people die every day—from the sickness or because they can't walk so far." He pointed to three freshly-dug grave mounds. "Shaman casts out evil spirits of the sickness that was in their guts, from their pain, their weariness."

"Where's he cast dem spirits?"

The man pointed to the river. "To the backs of the beaver. To go into the water and wash far away from us."

The pox sickness had killed several old people in the slave quarters back in North Carolina. Old Elijah gathered everyone to sing hymns and pray. Those hymns asked God to heal the sick. They prayed to God to take away the pox. Toby couldn't quite work out why the shaman asked the beaver to do what God was supposed to do. But Shaman's voice was strong and confident, so it must be okay.

Shaman finished his chanting and people returned to their wagons.

"Now. Come eat," the Indian man said to Toby and John Dee.

"Thank you," John Dee said. "But we have to get back 'fore dark." He turned to Toby. "They'll be hell to pay with Mister Tomkins."

Toby looked for the little girl and spotted her in the warm embrace of an Indian woman. She waved. Her face shone with happiness. He thrust his chest out and waved back. His insides felt warm all over. He nudged John Dee to be sure he saw the little girl.

~ ~ ~

John Dee sipped his whiskey. Stella, having finished her recollections, leaned her head back against her chair. Had the tale drained her, or saddened her? Maybe both. Toby's eyes were closed as if he were reliving the events in his own way.

"Well, I'll be," John Dee said to Stella. "You were the little girl in those woods. I haven't thought about that day in a while. What year was it—this Trail of Tears?"

"The summer of 1838. The army took thirteen thousand of my people from their homes and put them in stockades. White people don't know much about it. No one does."

"What happened?" Toby asked.

Stella sighed. "The Government passed a law that gave our native lands to White settlers. So, the Army marched my people to new lands in Oklahoma—right on through the dead of winter. Many of us didn't have shoes." Stella paused. "More than four thousand of my people died on the trail."

Four thousand dead! Had he heard her correctly? For Christ's sake, the Government had damn-near killed Stella's people off. What they hell had they done to deserve that?

"The land in Oklahoma was barren. It meant nothing. All spiritual connections with our ancestors were lost." She sighed. "Losing our native lands killed many of our people. Both my parents died after we got to Oklahoma. They never got over that walk."

"I'm sorry." John Dee noticed Toby was misty-eyed. Was it massive loss of life on the Trail of Tears that bothered him? Or his recollections of the day Stella had been terrorized? Maybe it saddened him that injustice had found her again, tonight, with Ricky Burton's violent assault and her banishment from the *Lady J*.

Or was it something more? Maybe the mistreatment Stella was describing made him reflect on the tyranny of enslaved labors that so many of his own people endured.

A lump formed in John Dee's throat. Toby and Stella and their peoples endured despicable mistreatment solely due to the color of their skin. Understanding their pain was impossible.

A ceramic eagle sat on the top shelf of the cupboard. America's symbol of freedom, of powerful elegance the nation aspired to, of the Western Frontier's wide-open spaces. Its curved yellow beak pointed at the table, as if it listened keenly to their conversation. The eagle was learning freedom didn't exist for everyone. Only White people. What could he possibly say to assuage Toby and Stella?

"You've paid Toby back here tonight," Stella said to John Dee.

"Oh?"

"You owe Toby your life. As do I."

"Goes both ways," Toby said, with a glance at John Dee.

"What were you two doing in those woods?" Stella asked.

"We'd wandered off from a wagon train."

"Your family was coming west? Where from?"

John Dee sighed. "Our family farm was in North Carolina. See, 'bout a year earlier, Mother got sick and died. Father wanted to leave his memories of her behind. So he moved to Missouri where we had relations. Set up his doctor's office there. After a time, he sent for me. He paid Mr. Tompkins for my place in his wagon. Ol' man Tompkins had sent us out to gather wood, and that's when we came across you."

Toby chuckled. "Mean bastard that Tompkins was. Whipped us good that night when we turned up."

"Did you two meet on the wagon train?"

"Nah, we go back a lot further than that. Father owned Toby, and he let me bring him along for company." The words had come out before John Dee knew what he was saying. What was it about Stella that enabled her to pry out so effortlessly something he never spoke of?

"I see. You two were raised together?"

"Toby's Mammy worked in the house, and she took care of me, mostly, so yeah, we were together a lot." John Dee took a sip. He glanced at Toby, who'd sat back, an eyebrow raised, like he was eager to hear what was coming. Maybe a little concerned. Their bond was deeper than Stella could understand. "Daddy was working all the time between his doctoring and farming. Why, he could go a week without saying a word to me. And Momma, she was sick in her bed 'bout all the time. Truth is, most of the time they didn't want no bother with me. I was with Toby all day, every day."

"That's unusual, isn't?" Stella asked. "A White boy and a Black boy spending so much time together?"

"Maybe so. We liked to do the same things. Explored the woods and the creeks. Shot birds. Went fishing. We built a tree fort." John Dee nodded at Toby. "After a while, you don't even see skin color."

"Least till John Dee went to school," Toby said. "Then I went to work with the women folk. Washing clothes and bedsheets. When I got a little older, I went to the fields. Anything but learning."

Toby's expression was neither happy nor sad. John Dee wished he'd go ahead and lash out because deep inside he must be bitter that Southern society—John Dee's father—had denied him knowledge and advancement. Toby had every right to be furious with the disparity in their educations. John Dee wouldn't have been bothered a bit if he'd called Daddy a mean rotten bastard for the way he always acted on his belief in the superiority of the White race by suppressing Toby's development. Maybe Toby kept quiet about Daddy out of respect. Then again, Toby always said, "Ain't gonna waste time on what can't be changed."

Stella studied Toby as well. Was the corner of her lip turned up in a little smile? Of course, Toby had saved her life so he was her hero and all. She kept looking at him. Maybe she was attracted to him. Lots of women were. Finally, she said, "Well, thank God you were there."

Toby smiled back at her, even though John Dee knew he was the kind of man who wasn't sure if God had a hand in anything.

John Dee finished his whiskey and the three of them rose to leave.

"I don't think I'll sleep a wink," Stella said.

John Dee nearly laughed. He, not she, had put his life in Captain Martin's and the judge's hands. It was the worst gamble he'd ever taken. He didn't know either man. They could have their reasons to lay the blame for Ricky Burton's killing on him. He could be swinging from the end of a rope tomorrow. He wiped at his brow with his kerchief. "Just get some rest. It'll be better tomorrow."

His words surely weren't convincing. He couldn't miss the worry on Stella's face. She could thank her God all she wanted, but the truth was they sure as hell weren't God's warriors sent to protect her. Him, a man in a fancy suit. Toby, a kind Black man on the lower river, which was very much a White man's world. Up against murderous river pirates. She should be worried.

Chapter 6

At nine o'clock the next morning, John Dee glanced at his pocket watch. *An hour!* Standing with Stella and Toby at the top rail, waiting for the captain for more than an hour felt like a prison sentence.

Smoke from the stacks billowing high into the sky meant the boilers were warm and ready. *Let's get out of here!*

Captain Martin finally crossed the street and approached the gangplank. He was followed by two armed, badge-wearing men whose appearance cast a gloom over a seasonable, sun-drenched morning.

John Dee's mouth went dry.

Why the hell is he bringing officers? God, I need a drink! He also needed to clear his head. Should he be relieved or nervous? Would they arrest him? Or Toby? Was the *Lady J* going to shove off? His feet wanted to run. His head told him to stay put.

The captain's climb up the stairs took an eternity. Sam Clemens appeared at John Dee's side and nodded grimly.

Captain Martin appeared at the top of the stairs with the two lawmen.

John Dee fought his urge to run. Only a rash dive into the river could lose the lawmen, and that would likely kill him.

Captain Martin nodded at him and shouted, "Take her out!"

John Dee's taut neck muscles relaxed. He closed his eyes. *I'm free!*

Sam waved to acknowledge Captain Martin's order, then turned toward the Texas Deck and made a "Forward" signal to the pilot with his thumb and forefinger. Roustabouts released the hemp lines and raised the gangplank. Sam hurried away to his duties.

The boilers cranked up with a deafening sound. Massive heights of steam scaped out when the valves were opened. "Last bell" clanged to signal departure like an accompanist to the boiler noise. The big paddle wheels slowly creaked into action, and the boat floated away from the landing.

Six riders approached the shore, led by long-bearded Cliff Burton. Burton pulled back his reins and pointed to the hurricane deck.

"You up there, Franklin? You hear me?" Even shouting at the top of his lungs, Burton could barely be heard over the boilers.

John Dee's heart beat like a drum. Six riders, six guns. All menacing with murderous intent.

Their six mounts snorted and pranced at the water line.

Captain Martin looked down on the Burtons with his hands on his hips.

"You're a d-dead man, Franklin! You and your wh-whore squaw. You're dead!" Burton's screams were faint but unmistakably hostile. He pumped his right fist at the top deck with the intensity of an attacking beast. His disturbed mount jerked its head and bucked in a circle.

Stella's face was frozen. Any doubts about the threat posed by the Burtons were surely gone.

Time stood still as Cliff Burton's scorching threats hung in the air. John Dee's cheek twitched. *Why is this goddamned boat moving so slowly?* All around, passengers took notice of the shouts and came to the rail. Some stared at John Dee. The previous evening's death on the top deck wasn't a secret any longer. Captain Martin huddled up with his two lawmen. John Dee couldn't hear them.

By the time the *Lady J* entered the main channel, Cliff Burton was far out of earshot. The Burtons and their men rode north, parallel to the boat.

"My God! They're chasing us." Fear shone in Stella's eyes like the brightest lantern. Burton's threat made clear she'd have to run for it with him and Toby. At least he wouldn't be fighting with her as well as the Burtons anymore.

"We knew they would." John Dee tried to keep his voice steady even though dealing with the Burtons was the toughest spot he'd ever been in. "I'm gonna keep you safe. I'll make a plan."

Toby, studying the riders, leaned toward Stella. "He always does."

Her eyes were wide open. John Dee sighed. There was no reassuring her. What was he getting into, dragging her along?

"They don't know about you," John Dee said to Toby. "You can stay on the boat."

Toby raised an eyebrow and smiled grimly. "I'll be coming with you."

"Had to give you a choice."

"Reckon so," Toby said. "We've got six to deal with. That's a shit-ton of firepower, pardner."

The *Lady J* passed a point covered in a thick stand of cattails. The riders had disappeared. Dense woodlands on the Mississippi riverbank made a comforting curtain between the boat and the Burtons. But they'd catch up sooner or later. John Dee's twitch returned. What then?

Captain Martin approached. "I take it you handled the Ricky Burton business with the judge," John Dee said.

"I did." The captain took off his hat and mopped his brow. "First time I've seen him shook, Franklin. He read our statements and asked some questions. Then he lit a cigar and stood by the window. His hand shook a little when he smoked. Took his sweet time to think things over. Then he sent his clerk to get his nephew, the sheriff."

John Dee's guard was up.

"He didn't speak again till his nephew turned up. Wasn't like him a'tall. Tell the truth, Franklin, I was wondering if he was a-gonna tear up my statement and cook your goose."

John Dee straightened his back as if bracing himself. Had he been cleared or not? Why the hell all this equivocation? Stella touched his hand to calm him like he was a child in distress. *How's she so calm? Is she listening?*

"But he told his nephew that he was ruling self-defense."

Stella squeezed his fingers as if to say, "You're okay now."

"He said ol' Cliff would be coming, and he posted two armed men at the courthouse door until further notice."

The judge being a familiar local didn't matter. The Burtons threatened him every bit as much as John Dee and Stella.

"But they ain't after the judge," Captain Martin said. "They're coming fer us. You saw 'em. The Burtons and three more men on horseback. Following us north."

"Yeah," John Dee said.

"The judge sent these two deputies with me for firepower when we get to Helena. The ol' boy said Cliff'll be mad as a hornet's nest at me for siding with self-defense." He stretched his collar. "I ain't sure who Cliff'll be gunning for first. You and the squaw singer. Or me."

John Dee stifled a scoff at the captain's fears. He and Stella were the ones Cliff Burton had threatened to kill. They had to get off the boat. But how? *Think, think.*

"My crew can deal with them," the captain said, "but as long as you are on board, good people are at risk. Yer gonna have to get off my boat."

"I understand, Captain," John Dee said.

The entire group fell silent, as if the Burton menace had sucked up all the air around them.

Stella stepped forward. "But, Captain, I can't leave the boat. My troupe—the *Lady J*'s show—is depending on me. Your armed guards can keep me safe."

John Dee sucked in a breath. *Jesus, lady! Couldn't she get it through her head a bunch of ginty murderers were after her? Was she gonna be a giant pain in his and Toby's asses?*

The captain snorted his disapproval. "Didn't you hear Cliff Burton? He's coming for you! I'm not gonna have no shooting war on my boat if I can help it." His expression softened a little. "I'm sorry, ma'am, but you gotta go. Go with these men." He turned to John Dee. "They'll help you, won't you, Franklin?"

"Yeah." John Dee shot Stella a stern look. "From this moment, Toby and I are on the run from the Burtons. No more talk about staying on the boat. And you gotta keep up."

Stella looked from the Captain to Toby as if she were lunging for a life preserver. Both men's expressions were as stony as John Dee's. Finally, her shoulders slumped and she said, "Thank you. I'll keep up."

The Captain straightened his hat. "Come with me to the Pilot House, Franklin. There's a few more details. We've got some things to talk about."

~ ~ ~

Two hours later, constant vibrations from the cranking boilers had lessened to a gentle hum. John Dee dashed up the stairs to the hurricane deck. The riverbank wasn't fading behind the boat anymore. The *Lady J* was slowing. *Dammit!* The Burton gang was chasing the boat. What the hell was the pilot doing?

Sam approached. "Why the hell is the boat slowing down?" John Dee asked.

"Thought you might get a little agitated." He pointed upriver. "We gotta damn-near stop so we don't hit those settlers a-drifting in the main channel. You see 'em?"

Five arks tied together floated in the center of the main channel like a listless wooden island. They were a ways in the distance, and John Dee could barely make out cloth flapping in the wind. Sails? If so, they were in tatters. "Yeah. We'll miss 'em. No need to slow down."

Sam fingered his red mustache like he didn't have a care in the world as he studied the arks. John Dee felt his temples heating up. Didn't Sam realize they were losing time in their race against the Burtons? He or the captain or the pilot had to do something!

"Problem is," Sam said, "the settlers can't steer those contraptions worth a hoot. So, we gotta slow down and get as close to the bank as we can. It's a dod-derned floating village. Seventy-five foot or more across. Wouldn't take much of a squall to swing it around and punch a hole in our stern."

Sam handed John Dee a looking glass.

John Dee studied the arks. Skinny, bearded, shirtless men perched up front. Horses with their ribs showing tied to posts. Chickens scattered all over the decks. A woman holding a baby wrapped in rags. Skinny dogs. A gray-haired lady tending clothes drying in the breeze. A wooden table and a loom. Assorted chairs, crates, and barrels. A plow. A village all right. A sad sack of a village.

"Wait till it gets close," Sam said. "Stinks to high heaven, I'll wager." He looked around. "Where're your friends?"

"Toby and Stella went to get some shuteye. None of us slept much last night."

"Yeah. What about you?" Sam asked.

"Can't sleep."

Stella appeared at the top rail. John Dee waved her over. "Couldn't sleep?"

"Not much. The engines sound different. Have we slowed down?"

"Yep." Sam pointed out the arks, which were much closer now, and their menagerie of ragged travelers, animals, and cargo. "Had to slow down to miss 'em."

"Where are those people from?" Stella asked.

"Those poor souls?" Sam said. "The undiscovered country from whose bourn no traveler returns, as the Bard would say."

Stella's perplexed expression made John Dee roll his eyes.

"That's Shakespeare." John Dee sighed. Sam's free-thinking spirit would never stop with his clever quips, even with evil-doer Burtons on the loose. "For Christ's sakes! We're running for our lives, and you're making fancy jokes."

Sam flashed a sheepish grin and said to Stella, "Oh, I expect they're a bunch of Kaintucks. Coming downriver to make a new life." He took the looking glass back and peered through it, upriver. "We ain't gonna pick up speed for a good while. Once we get past the Kaintucks, there's a deadwood island out there. The captain'll launch the yawl and pole its edges to make sure there ain't no planter snags we can't see."

"We're slowing down for a pile of sticks? There're murderers chasing us, goddammit! We gotta speed up!"

John Dee put his hands on his head and paced in a circle. "Shit!"

Sam put his arm on John Dee's shoulder. "Calm yourself. I'd be a little impatient, too. But these delays might just mean Lady Luck is on our side."

"How can that be?" John Dee asked.

Sam pointed to the riverbank. Thick stands of locusts and willows obscured anything behind them. "The Burton boys are riding a trail half a mile east of the river. Driving their poor mounts like the devil to beat us upriver. The thing is, they're in the woods and won't see the water for hours. They'll pop outta the trees, and we ain't gonna be there. So they'll figure we beat 'em to Helena. Maybe they'll give up?"

"I sure as hell doubt that," John Dee said.

"Are we going to experience these hold-ups all the way to Helena?" Stella asked Sam.

"Truth is, I don't know. But what I do know is a riverboat pilot best have a sixth sense for planter snags, towheads, sawyers, and a bushel-full of other surprises. If he don't, he's better off to plant corn." Sam tipped his cap to Stella. "I gotta get back to the pilot house." He shook John Dee's hand. "And friend, you should get some sleep."

John Dee shook his head. "I'm gonna get a drink."

~ ~ ~

The engine noise paused, startling John Dee. *For Christ's sakes, what is it now?* He drained his whiskey and left the bar. He bounded up the stairs two at a time. Sam and Toby were at the rail, looking down on a small quay on the eastern riverbank. Trees had been cleared back forty yards. Only a tiny shack and long stacks of cord-wood were visible.

John Dee felt like his head would explode. Why the hell had the *Lady J* done Cliff Burton a favor and pulled into a remote, wilderness clearing? A perfect goddamned place for an ambush. "We're stopping! What the hell, Sam? The Burtons are gonna be waiting down there."

"I thought you men might be a tad nervous," Sam said. "We're stopping for a wooding."

"Why the hell now?"

"The *Lady J* burns thirty cords a day, and our bins are damn near empty. Ol' Jacob'll fill them at two dollars and thirty cents a cord. Best price on the river."

"But the Burtons!"

"Easy, John Dee," Toby said. "This may not be so bad."

Had Toby gone crazy? "What?"

"My berth's on the main deck. The captain's got six men with guns at the gangplank. There's two more on the boiler deck. And two lawmen are by the captain's side. Might just be enough firepower to kill the bastards. All this'll be over."

"Ho!" Sam said. "Captain Martin's gonna defend his boat, all right, but the last thing he wants is a gun fight! Innocents could get killed!" He looked at the quay. "I don't see any Burtons, and let's hope they're not here. It don't matter anyhow, boys. Boat burns a shit-ton of wood steaming upriver. We don't have enough fuel to reach Helena."

Stella joined them, and John Dee explained the stop as nonchalantly as he could, but his insides were churning. She wasn't taking it any better than him, darting to the rail and looking for the Burtons.

"Stella," Toby said, "you need to stay away from the rail. They get a sight on you; they'll take a shot."

Stella gasped and stepped back.

Sam raised his palm. "Whoa. No need to rile up the lady. Ain't no sign of the Burtons. They'd-a turned up by now if they were here."

John Dee and Toby stood shoulder to shoulder on the rail and looked down on roustabouts straining to pull their wood-filled cart across the gangplank. Sam was right; no one else was there.

"I'm gonna ask the men if the Burtons have come through," Toby said.

Toby was taking a hell of a risk; what if he came face to face with the Burtons, alone? John Dee had to concede that Toby had the best chance of extracting information since ol' Jacob and his roustabouts were all Black men. "You best have eyes in the back of your head," John Dee said.

"I will."

The *Lady J* took on cart after cart of cord wood. John Dee spotted Toby on the quay, talking with a gray-headed old man.

"Must be ol' Jacob," he said to Sam.

"Sure is."

"Either the Burtons gave up and turned around, which I doubt, or they've passed through," John Dee said.

"They're up ahead a ways, I imagine," Sam said. "I don't have to tell you the boat's been slow as molasses this morning."

John Dee tapped his fingers on the rail, waiting for Toby's return.

Toby emerged from the stairs. "Ol' Jacob said six riders stopped to water their horses near an hour ago."

"Why didn't they ambush us at the quay?" Stella asked.

"They think we're farther upriver," Toby said.

Sam grinned. "Right. They can't see us from the riding trail. Hell, they couldn't have known that the *Lady J* was going to stop."

Steam scaped from the big stacks and the *Lady J* moved away from the clearing. They'd dodged a deadly encounter with the Burtons. But John Dee's cheek twitched again. They'd only delayed an inevitable reckoning with Cliff Burton. He felt it in his bones.

"You hear anything else?" Sam asked.

"Yeah. The riders talked about seeing the whores at the River Belle. Remember the River Belle, eh?" Toby said to John Dee, with a chuckle.

John Dee shot him a look that screamed "keep it to yourself"—women tended to recoil at the mention of a brothel. "The bastards are going to Helena. They'll be there when the *Lady J* lands." John Dee tried to rub the twitch out of his cheek.

Stella's expression reprimanded him and Toby like misbehaving children. Clearly, she'd picked up on his and Toby's familiarity with Helena's well-known bawdy house. He regretted planting a sordid association in her mind between him, Toby, and the world's oldest profession, but it couldn't be helped. Travel the river and some mud stuck to you. Besides, piecing together the Burtons' plans trumped decorum.

"Yep," Toby said. "The Burtons'll be waiting at the landing. Ain't no way we're getting past them."

"And a whole lot of people could get shot up at the gangplank," Sam said. "You can't be on the boat when it lands at Helena."

Stella grabbed his hand. "But Sam!"

"I'm very sorry it's come to this, ma'am, but a shooting war is not on the *Lady J's* itinerary. The captain and I must protect our passengers. We need a new plan." Sam fingered his bushy red moustache as the roustabouts and their carts disappeared from view.

"Let us off, and we'll catch a boat at Ol' Jacob's," John Dee said.

"Nah. Won't work. The Burtons have friends aboard. One of them will spot you getting off and tell the Burtons in Helena. They'll jump on a fast packet going downriver and be back here within a few hours. Hell, Ol' Jacob's is just a clearing. It ain't a real landing. I doubt you'd catch a ride before they're back." Sam struck a contemplative pose. "There's a better way."

"And what's that?" John Dee asked.

"Up ahead, around that next bend," Sam said, "is a sandbar. It's an island, really, just under the river's surface. Gets real shallow, so we'll have to slow down and watch our draft. I'll get you to shore without being noticed. That will be your best bet. Then you'll catch a scow across the river and land somewhere south of Helena. Just sneak into town and catch a cotton boat south." He paused. "I'll make sure we land the *Lady J* on the north end of Helena's landing. If you catch a boat on its south end, you might just stay outta the Burtons' sight."

Stella's eyes widened. "Why in heaven's name would we go to Helena if the Burtons will be looking for us there?"

Sam frowned like an impatient schoolteacher. "Ain't nowhere to catch a cotton boat other than Helena 'til you get to Memphis, ma'am. That's a good sixty, seventy miles. You could walk the trail north, I suppose." He pointed to the trees on the eastern riverbank. "But I wouldn't give a copper penny for your chances of making it past the river gintys in those woods, let alone the Burtons."

Stella opened her mouth to reply, but didn't, apparently resigned to Sam's advice.

"Besides," John Dee said. "Toby and I are friendly with a sheriff's deputy in Helena. Big Jake might help us out if we get in a pickle."

A rumbling sound out of Toby made clear he didn't fancy the door John Dee was opening.

"Dare I ask how you two are friendly with a lawman?" Stella asked.

John Dee remembered the night Big Jake's wife came looking for him at River Belle. John Dee had chatted her up while Toby whisked Jake out the back stairs. "Let's just say he needed a hand, and we were happy to oblige."

He ignored Stella's bemused expression. "How long before we get off the boat, Sam?"

"Just a half an hour or so. I'm going to slip you off at the stern during the mid-day meal. Go pack a bag."

"A bag?" Stella said. "I was hoping to take my gowns."

John Dee chuckled. "One small bag, Stella. No more. We're on the run."

"But—"

"One small bag. We'll buy you new things when we can."

Sam outlined his plan. Within an hour, the luxuries of the *Lady J* would be long gone. Stella stood tall as she listened to the particulars. Wading ashore. Traipsing through the brush for who knows how long. Sleeping in the woods. Hell, they might end up foraging in the trees like squirrels. She didn't want to leave the boat. None of them did. But John Dee knew she'd taken indignity upon shock, without complaining too much, and would do her part. Even so, watching her leave for her room, he couldn't help wondering whether she would see their plan through.

Chapter 7

BE VISIBLE. STICK TO YOUR *routine. Make a little conversation with the ladies.*

Entering the ladies' cabin, Stella's heart raced as she ticked off how to put Sam's plan into motion.

A trio of women sat at the table by the window, same as every other day. Old biddies whose hushed talk about passengers wearing unsuitable attire, gamblers, down-on-their-luck families, and excessive drinkers was just loud enough to be heard by contiguous tables. Quite intentionally, Stella suspected.

The "Silk Sisters." Stella suppressed a smirk recalling her contemptuous nickname for them. They wore silk brocades—one white with blue point, another corn silk with black lace, and the third green-grass silk with white lace—that were too formal for the luncheon. One Silk Sister sniffed at Stella, as if to say, "You are not welcome here, Squaw."

Stella's pink, cotton frock was fashionable enough for the dining hall, but far less expensive than their gowns. The well-fed Silk Sisters could never match its alluring fit on her young and shapely body.

Was the old biddy's enmity rooted in racial prejudice or in the scene at Friars Point? Or both? Word that she and John Dee had been threatened by dangerous rivermen had surely blown through the boat like a wildfire. Stella held her head high and nodded, nonetheless. Just as Sam instructed.

She burned to say what she really felt. *I'm the* Lady J's *singer, and I'm the victim! I have every right to be here!*

Women filled the ladies' cabin, most wearing day dresses and frocks of higher quality than Stella's. A menagerie of yellows, greens, and blues.

Someone tugged on her sleeve. She nearly jumped out of her skin.

A middle-aged woman in a green brocade dress with green linen around the neckline flashed her toothy smile. "Oh, dear, you were magnificent last night!"

"Thank you, ma'am," Stella said.

"You *will* be performing in Helena, I hope?" It came off as more of an order than a question.

"Yes, ma'am."

"Good!" The green lady nodded and walked off.

Could she pull off Sam's clandestine plan with her insides roiling like cream in a butter churn?

The steward announced the mid-day meal.

Conversations halted. Stitching and books were put away. Women rose from their chairs in the sitting area and made a slow procession to the dining tables. Good gracious, so many of them looked alike. Hair parted in the center and drawn back, with ringlets and soft curls dangling down their cheeks. Pale complexions that could have come from the same tube of Crème Celeste. A brooch at the top of the neckline and capped sleeves trimmed with ribbons or braids. Did one of them bark out the order for attire of the day to all others?

Dining tables filled and voices rose in a cruel din.

Instead of being seated, excuse yourself discretely.

That shouldn't be hard. To women like the green lady, admiring Stella's performance was one thing, but lunching together was another. As the *Lady J*'s singer, she had privileges to the ladies' cabin and dining room, but White ladies didn't want a squaw at their dining table. Mr. Jenkins had told her: "Ignore the disdainful looks. Just smile and win them over for the betterment of the show."

Stella meandered between the tables, just as Sam had asked her to do, so any interested party would have ample time to notice her. Dining placements had been set, bowls of English walnuts and pecans put out, and water pitchers filled. *God, how could Sam expect me to stay calm when the Burtons want to put a bullet in me and feed me to the fish?*

Only her castmates sat with her, so Stella scanned the room, looking for one of them. She would follow a castmate toward a table, then peel off, feigning gastronomical distress, which wasn't completely duplicitous.

After slipping away, she was to quickly get to the lower level, at the stern, and sneak off the boat with John Dee and Toby without being seen. An act worthy of the playbill. Her heartbeat hadn't slowed, even a tick.

Stella passed a young Black girl in a white apron, standing at attention and holding a bread basket as the ladies took seats. Stella detected her hint of a smile. Maybe the young girl admired a well-dressed Indian woman moving confidently in the midst of a room of fancy White ladies. If the Burtons weren't on her tail, she'd have stopped and encouraged the girl's own ambitions. No time now.

A familiar-looking elderly woman held a cocktail in one hand and a cane in the other. A steward helped her into her seat. Her light blue hat and parasol set triggered Stella's recollection—of Mr. Jenkins introducing her to the *Lady J*'s highest-paying passengers at the *bon voyage* cocktail reception in New Orleans.

"Call attention to your presence at the meal." Okay, Sam, here is a perfect opportunity.

"Oh, Missus Arbuckle," Stella said, "I hope you enjoyed last night's show."

"What—oh," Missus Arbuckle's expression seemed slightly numbed, presumably from the alcohol, but Stella wasn't much surprised. Many on board had alcoholic drinks in their hands from breakfast on. Missus Arbuckle's recognition kicked in. "Yes, dear. You were magnificent. Do have a wonderful show again tonight in Helena."

Missus Arbuckle made a warm smile, just like she had at the cocktail reception, showing at least a hint of humanity when dealing with a person of darker skin color. Unlike the Silk Sisters.

"Thank you, Missus Arbuckle. I'm sure we will."

Two more women waved. Stella's arm shook a little when she raised it in greeting. Would this masquerade work as Sam intended, or was she just calling attention to her fear of the Burtons?

Sylvia, one of the dancers, approached. Finally! Enough was enough.

"Let's take our seats, Stella," Sylvia said. "I'm starved."

"Oh, dear," Stella said. "My stomach is a bit off. I'm going to pass on the meal and retire to my cabin to get plenty of rest for tonight's show."

"I'm sorry," Sylvia said. "Can I bring you something later?"

"No, please. I believe a good long rest is what I need."

"Okay, dear."

Stella discreetly slipped into the vestibule and onto the deck. She took the stairs to the lower deck and hurried to the stern.

Toby was waiting, sitting on a bench. "Fancy dress you're wearing," he said.

"It's my day frock. Oh, should I have changed? We might have to walk a ways."

"No time. Any trouble?" Toby asked her.

"Everything went perfectly. I slipped out before I was seated, just as Sam planned. The ladies have started their mid-day meal. Men will be next, so John Dee should be along soon." Sam had instructed John Dee to stay for the Spanish olives and gherkins, and then have a few bites of the mutton before he made his excuses and left the table. Then he was to collect his bag and join her and Toby.

Two valises were on the bench next to Toby. Only one was hers. She breathed deeply. How in heaven's name would she ever be invited to join another troupe without costumes and cosmetics? "You only brought one of my valises? I packed two."

"Stella," Toby's expression was pleading, "we're on the run. We can't handle any more baggage."

She paused, wary of irritating Toby, since her escape from the Burtons depended on him and John Dee. But she desperately needed her things, so she said as calmly as she could, "I've got to have some gowns and some cosmetics to start over in a new show. I can't just show up looking like a street girl!"

"You heard John Dee," Toby said.

Heat rose in her temples. "He's not my master!" She put her hands on her hips. "Is he still yours?"

"No!" Toby stood face to face with her, clearly annoyed by her remark. "But he's trying to get your difficult behind to safety. So am I."

Stella took a breath. "That I appreciate. But I'm going to get my other valise." She turned for the stairs.

Toby caught her by the elbow. "Stay here. I'll get it."

Stella stood at the rail waiting for Toby's return. Flags rustled overhead. Rushes of wind on her face felt like they were blowing her career away.

She'd given everything to become the *Lady J*'s headliner. And stardom was damn hard even without the Burton trouble. Delight the paying customers every night, and the troupe made a living. Fears of catching a cold or losing her voice to exhaustion or getting a bad newspaper review kept her awake sometimes. If the ticket window closed, everyone would suffer.

As a woman of color, she'd take the blame. The *Lady J*'s owners would call Mr. Jenkins a fool for hiring a Cherokee squaw for a White woman's work. They'd sack her and put her ashore at some river town that wouldn't want her.

Water oaks swayed in the wind on the riverbank. No wading birds were in the shallows and, unusually, there were no flying birds. It was as if they had all taken shelter.

Tension swelled in her temples. Being forced to leave the show was so unfair—she'd done her part! Sold-out audiences enthusiastically applauded her pitch-perfect voice and acting. Mr. Jenkins had big plans for her. She had even begun to believe that her talents would transcend the *Lady J.* Maybe she could have her own tour, like the Swedish Nightingale.

She'd been assaulted and was the victim, not Ricky Burton. That evil bastard got what he deserved. But now she was running for her life, and to make matters worse, about to be cast ashore on the lower river where many White folks treated her kind as a small step above dogs. Without a role in a show, she wasn't the singing soubrette any longer. She was just another squaw.

Blown away. That's what the Burtons were doing to her career—just when she was at her best—without any fault of her own. A nauseous rumbling bothered her stomach. *The bastards!*

Toby returned with her second valise. She opened it, pulled a shawl, and wrapped it around her shoulders. "It's colder. The weather is changing."

Toby nodded in agreement.

A steamboat chugged downriver, safely to the *Lady J*'s portside. Beyond it, the northern sky had turned a shade of purple. *Those bastard Burton brothers are somewhere on that shore, and I have to get off this boat in a storm?*

Angry white roils rocked the boat. Stella grabbed the rail and widened her stance. The riverbank looked hundreds of yards away. "Good god in heaven! How is Sam going to get us off this boat?"

"We'll manage."

Toby's expression was unchanged. At this moment, no one was more important to her. A day ago, he and John Dee were strangers, despite the long-ago encounter on the Trail of Tears. They were likeable enough, but what did she really know about them?

"We'll get through this."

She didn't reply. What could she make of this stone-faced man? He had an empathy about him that wasn't common in men. He'd come to her defense, twice now, thank God. He had physical strength as well as some disgusting peccadillos, like visiting brothels. Could she count on him?

For God's sakes, did she really have to get off the boat in the middle of a storm? She didn't kill anyone. Why not return to her room and stay there until going on stage tonight? Stay in the cocoon of the troupe and hope the Burtons left her alone. Wouldn't they leave her be and chase John Dee—whom they thought was Ricky Burton's killer? She smiled to herself. It might work if Mr. Jenkins spoke to the captain and convinced him to let her stay. Finally, she said to Toby, "I won't go."

"I know you don't want to." Toby sighed. "You heard Cliff Burton. He'll kill you if you stay on this ship. Besides, the captain said you can't stay. He was real clear about that. Come on now; you gotta think straight, woman."

Toby was right. Burton's screams had been terrifying; his threats had made her want to melt into the deck planks. If she wanted to live, she had to run from him. *God! Why is this happening to me?*

Rain blew in, forcing Stella back from the rail. Making her situation seem all the more hopeless.

"I wish I were a White woman."

Toby's glare made an unspoken demand to explain herself.

"They would have treated a White woman like a princess." If any one of the hoity-toity Silk Sisters had been in her place, her word would have been gospel and the captain quickly would have concluded that Ricky had sexually assaulted her. The judge would have taken her word over that of a river pirate. The crew would have escorted her back to her stateroom for bedrest and vials of White lady medicine until she was good and ready to face the world. "Cliff Burton wouldn't dare kill a White woman."

Toby sat quietly, taking it in.

"Don't you wish you were White, sometimes?"

He sighed. "Don't do a damn bit of good to think about what can't be. Get all that outta your head. You ain't a White woman. You are a Cherokee. A beautiful Cherokee lady who sings like a songbird. Be strong, Stella. And be proud of who you are. John Dee and I'll get you away from the Burtons—to somewhere you can sing again."

She shook her head in disgust. "How in heaven's name are a squaw and a Black man going to survive in little river towns in Mississippi, or Tennessee, or Arkansas, or wherever we are? White folks don't see you or me as real people. They see a slave when they look at you. Me? They see a squaw. Both of us are beneath them."

"I've been in these parts plenty," Toby said. "I can get around." He straightened his hat. "We'll stick close to John Dee. We'll be all right."

"John Dee! He's a White man in fancy clothes. I've met plenty like him, and they only want one thing from me…." Her hands balled into fists. "Why should I trust him? He can walk away anytime and leave you and me to the river heathens. The slavers would sell you down the river. Who knows what they'd do with me?"

"He'd never do that."

"Whyever not? Why do you trust him?" Her voice rose to its uppermost register. "Is it because you two are brothers? Do you have the same daddy?"

Toby grimaced. She instantly regretted her remark, which in the slave-owning South implied Toby's mother had birthed him by John Dee's father, a White man. That meant either Toby's mother had a consensual, illicit affair, or more likely, she had been forced into sexual relations with her master. Neither implication was pardonable given their brief association.

Toby looked away from her. His handsome profile against the darkening afternoon sky was like a sturdy column of granite. Almost frozen, with an imperviousness to her presence. Had she destroyed the goodwill that had been building between them? Finally, he faced her. "John Dee's in this as much as we are," he said, ignoring her paternity question. "He took the blame for killing Ricky Burton. Don't forget that."

Though she hadn't been forgiven, Toby's reply seemed to stitch things up for now. It didn't, however, lessen Stella's suspicions about his and John Dee's common paternity. It wasn't just their similar statures. Their bond cinched tighter every time she spoke to either of them.

The hum from the boilers had lessened, and the boat rocked from side to side. Stella grabbed the bench to steady herself.

Rain came down faster, blowing sideways and forcing Stella farther back from the rail to a dry spot under the ceiling. The shore was a fuzzy green outline. Toby pointed out two bright red shapes approaching from off the stern. Two men wearing red work shirts were poling a keel boat with a wide hull toward the *Lady J*.

John Dee emerged from the deck stairs, bag in hand, followed by Sam.

"What's with the glum faces? Our adventure awaits!" John Dee said.

Neither Stella nor Toby answered.

"Anyone take notice of you?" Sam asked.

"No," Stella said. Toby shook his head.

"The pilot signaled the lighter?" Toby nodded at the approaching keel boat.

"Sure did," Sam said.

Stella hadn't the foggiest what a lighter was or how a boat powered by men pushing it along with poles was going to be useful. Nearly as wide from side to side as it was long, it had a square shape. And no seats.

"A lighter boat?" Stella asked. "I've never seen one before."

Sam grinned, spreading his bushy red mustache from ear to ear. Was he amused at her ignorance or proud of his arcane boat-centered scheme?

"Have their uses," Sam said. "When a packet runs aground in shallow water, this boat unloads cargo to lighten her up. The packet floats free when she's buoyant, and takes back her cargo in deeper water."

"I see. We're not much cargo, are we?"

"Maybe not, but these boys will get paid for a full load." John Dee patted his stomach and smiled at Toby.

Toby nodded. What was the private joke between the two of them?

"So, what's gonna happen here," Sam said, "is that the lighter will pole you right over the sandbar to the riverbank. The hard part's gonna be boarding."

Sam unlatched the gangplank gate. Toby stood at the opening with Stella behind him. The keel's gunwale was five feet lower than the deck she was standing on. The lighter rose on a swell and banged against the *Lady J*'s hull. Stella gasped. Sam expected her to jump down into the severely rocking lighter boat?

"Now, listen," Sam said. "Once you three are on board, lie on the floor until the *Lady J*'s out of sight. The mid-day meal is about over, and if someone looks out, let 'em see nothing but the red shirts poling the lighter."

"Will do," Toby said. He threw three valises into the keel boat. A fourth remained on the bench. Was it one of hers?

Stella opened her mouth to call attention to it, but Sam shouted at Toby. "Time the swells! Wait till the centerboard is at its highest point. Jump on the thwart."

"Got it." Toby crouched at the gate and waited. The keel rose and he deftly hopped onto its thwart beam and down to the floor, executing an athletic maneuver that Stella wouldn't try in her wildest dreams.

Stella's hands shook as Sam took hold of them. Her throat tightened like a vise. His ever-present smile was wiped away by her horrified expression.

"You won't have to do that." Sam gave her hand a supportive squeeze. "John Dee will pass you down." Sam steadied her as she stood at the gate opening, toes over the side.

Rain fell in buckets. Stella's soaked-through frock clung to her body like a second skin. Why hadn't she changed clothes? Sam could have snatched some boy's shirt and trousers that would have been more suitable.

She motioned to John Dee. "My other valise. Hand it to me."

"Don't worry," John Dee said. "I'll get it."

Sam leaned into her for a last word. "Stay close to John Dee and Toby, Stella. They'll keep you safe. Now, good luck to you."

She made a tight smile. "Thank you for all your help. I'll never forget you."

The lighter boat banged loudly against the *Lady J*'s hull. *Oh God!* Sam gave her hand to John Dee and moved away from the gate.

Stella pushed her long black hair away from her eyes. The keel boat seemed impossibly far below. Her heart pounded.

"I've got you," John Dee said. "Just relax. I'm going to hand you down to Toby."

Stella took a deep breath and her feet left the deck. She felt them kick against the *Lady J*'s hull, and then she was falling. "Help!" She put her shoe on the gunwale. The lighter boat rocked violently. She slipped on the wet wood and dropped between the lighter and the massive white hull.

Stella's hysterical scream cut through the howling wind and slapping waves.

"Stella!" John Dee lost his grip on her left hand. He fell to his stomach at the gate opening, clinging to her right hand.

She dangled between the boats. She grabbed for John Dee's right arm with her free hand. The lighter boat lurched upward and rolled to strike the *Lady J*'s hull. Somehow, John Dee lifted her and Toby grabbed her legs. He swung them above the gunwale just as the lighter's centerboard crashed into the hull. Toby cradled her around the waist and laid her on the planks.

"You made it," he said.

Raindrops stung her face and hit the boat's floor with little tings. She had cheated being crushed in half by a split second. Toby held her tightly as rain flowed down his face in little torrents, like a million tears.

"You all right?" he asked. His expression had a stony confidence. Only strength was in his brown eyes.

"Yes."

John Dee had boarded and leaned over Toby's shoulder to take Stella's hand. The keel boat was already fifty yards from the *Lady J* and slowly moving toward shore.

Stella spit out rainwater. "Christ's sakes!" From the fancy dining room to a puddle in the bottom of a workboat in mere minutes. And swaddled by two large men like they were her papa bears.

"Are you hurt?" John Dee asked.

"I don't think so. But I don't know how I'm alive."

He laughed. "If that's the worst that happens on our adventure, we're going to have a grand time."

"Never mind that I'm soaked and chilled to the bone, and my clothes are ruined!"

"You've still got your humor. Good," John Dee said.

The bags Toby had thrown onto the boat were in a puddle of rainwater. "I don't see my second bag."

"Oh, with the excitement of boarding you—I'm sorry," John Dee said.

"Can I trust a word either of you say?" Stella looked from John Dee to Toby.

"Now, now," John Dee said. "First stop in civilization will be the dressmaker's; don't you worry."

The lighter had poled hundreds of yards away from the *Lady J.* Rainwater an inch deep covered Stella in a cold, shallow bath. A splinter from a broken floorboard poked her buttock. "I'm anything but in good humor."

Winds whipped the river surface into angry squalls that slapped the lighter. Rain came at them sideways, stinging her cheeks and every inch of exposed skin. Darkened skies made it impossible to see the *Lady J.* The riverbank was a faint, dark outline. The red-shirted men poled tirelessly toward shore, grimacing as if they wanted off the river every bit as much as their passengers.

"Where are you taking us?" John Dee asked.

"Trapper's cabin."

"How far is it?"

"Behind them trees."

"Where can we catch a scow to take us cross the river?"

The man bristled at the uninvited interruption to his labors and spit a stream of brown tobacco juice into the river without slowing his pace. "Wild Haw Landing. A li'l north of the cabin. 'Spect ol' Dickey'll take you. If you pay 'im."

"What's wild at this landing?"

The man laughed. "Ain't off the boat much, fancy man. Wild Haw's the berry off a Hawthorn. Spit the seeds when you eat 'em."

The red-shirted poler hadn't missed a stroke, and was grinning to himself, apparently savoring John Dee's ignorance of riverbank dendrology. The poler seemed competent at his task, but his grin was lopsided and his teeth were black. Wet long black hair matted to his patchy facial hair gave him a demonic look. The hair on the back of Stella's neck stood up. Would they have encountered this type of man on an overland escape route? Sam had been right.

A wooden cabin situated on a point came into view. Strong winds thumped loose boards against its walls. Stella wiped at her eyes for a good look. Its threshold had no door, and the far corner of its roof was missing. Her throat tightened. Shelter was a rickety shack, deep in uninhabitable wilderness, and that seemed somehow fitting for this nightmare. The flimsy structure surely was no match for the wicked storm.

How in heaven's name was Sam's route going to deliver her back to showboat life? Her ruined dress and glum expression must give her the look of a jilted bride. She didn't know whether to laugh or cry.

John Dee seemed to sense her discouragement and took her hand. "Not exactly the *Lady J*'s stateroom, is it?"

She pulled her hand away, too wet and cold to find any humor in their fix.

~ ~ ~

The trapper's cabin didn't have a hearth or a pump and wasn't much of a dwelling. Kinda like run-down farm sheds in Missouri full of hoes, plows, and dusty old tack. River poles were stacked against outside wallboards. Wind whistled through the structure, shaking it like a drunk's hand. Toby entered its threshold. A cutting table, wooden shelves stocked with rope, fishing twine, a rusty axe, and two spindly chairs were the whole of its interior décor. Rain streamed through several places in the roof.

Toby put down his and Stella's bags. Stella's eyes were as wide as dinner plates. Even John Dee was speechless.

A tree limb slammed against the wall. Toby reared back. *This shack ain't gonna make it!*

"Christ!" John Dee said. "Gale force winds, and we're on an unprotected point."

"We gotta get outta here!" Toby grabbed the bags and led them outside.

He started up a spit of land that connected the shack to the riverbank. Wind blasted him, making every step feel like a slog through knee-deep mud. What the hell had Sam gotten them into? He checked for John Dee and Stella. Still behind him. He pushed through calico bushes. A branch slapped him in the face. Then on into the willows.

"Ow!" Stella screamed.

Toby helped her extract a thorn that had stabbed through her skirt, into her thigh.

"What is it?" she asked him.

"Honey locust, I 'spect. We'll look at your leg once we stop."

A few minutes later, a loud crash stopped them in their tracks. It was somewhere behind them, by the river, but driving rain and heavy foliage blocked the view.

"The cabin?" Toby asked John Dee.

"That'd be my guess."

Toby stopped under a canopy of bur oaks where only a few raindrops got through. He felt the top of a downed tree trunk. Mostly dry. He motioned for Stella to sit. "Let's have a look."

"Okay." She sat and straightened her leg.

Toby hiked her skirt high enough to reveal a puncture wound, lightly bleeding. He applied gentle pressure with his handkerchief. "Not too bad. I'll stop the bleeding and bandage your leg."

"Thank you, Toby," Stella said.

"It's getting dark," John Dee said. "I'll gather some dry wood and start a fire. Someone open a bottle of Claret and set the table."

Toby laughed.

"Quit with the jokes!" Stella said. "We can't stay here! We have to get to Helena."

John Dee chuckled. "My dear Stella, there's not a single lighthouse on the lower river. No scow'll cross in the dark."

"We're just fine," Toby said to her. "Once we get to Helena sometime too-marr-ah, the *Lady J* will be long gone. I'd like to have seen the look on those Burtons' faces when they realized we're not on that boat! Betcha they went straight to the bawdy houses and had their fun. Who knows where they'll be when we get to Helena."

John Dee nodded. "My bet's Sam told Cliff Burton some tall tale about our escape. Five to one, he's sent the lot of 'em to look for us in Memphis or St. Louis."

"I hope so," Stella said. "But we can't dismiss the possibility that the Burtons will be looking for us in Helena."

"That's true," Toby said. "We'll worry on it tomorrow."

The winds had died down, and the rain had stopped. A frog croaked somewhere toward the river. Toby and John Dee cleared an area for a fire. Toby blew like a bellows into kindling and pine combs as John Dee struck a matchstick.

"Shit," John Dee said. "Wet." He struck another. Then another.

John Dee struck his fourth matchstick and puffs of smoke rose. The kindling caught, and Toby fed bigger sticks into the flames. Soon the fire crackled, and John Dee's face flickered in red and yellow hues. "Come sit over here and dry yourself off," Toby said to Stella.

"Shouldn't we go back to the cabin?" Stella asked.

"You heard that pop? I reckon the winds blew it down," Toby said.

"Are you joking? We were standing in it just minutes ago."

"The winds were strong as a damn hurricane. You heard the boom." Toby pointed toward the river. "Either they knocked the cabin down or uprooted a real big tree."

"Is this nightmare ever going to end?" Stella asked.

"Even if that 'ol cabin's standing," Toby said, "rain's gonna pour through its roof. We got better cover here in the oaks."

John Dee had walked off and returned with an armful of leafy branches. "Your comforter, ma'am."

"What?"

John Dee flashed a grin. "I've rung the porter. He'll bring veal chops and glasses of Madeira, soon. After you eat, put on your spectacles, climb under your duvet, and read the latest Dickens by firelight."

Stella leaned back against an oak. "I see. Well, then, do tell him to bring bread pudding and a cup of tea after my dinner."

"Fancy pants, aren't you?" Toby winked. "If you two plan to send me below for my horsemeat and grits supper, I'll have something to say 'bout it."

"Now, Toby," John Dee said, "everybody's welcome at these quarters."

PART II

WICKED RIVER

"The face of the water, in time, became a wonderful book—a book that was a dead language to the uneducated passenger, but which told its mind to me without reserve, delivering its most cherished secrets as clearly as if it uttered them with a voice. And it was not a book to be read once and thrown aside, for it had a new story to tell every day."

— **Mark Twain,** *Life on the Mississippi*

Chapter 8

Toby surveyed the bank from the stern of ol' Dickey's broadhorn. No one in sight. *Good.* Tupelo gums and water oaks lined the bank, and even a few pretty red hibiscus flowers had somehow survived the storm. Calm and scenic as the lower river got, it was all the more sensational after a violent storm. The black water flowed south like a flat road, with only a side-wheeler visible, several miles upriver and no threat to ol' Dickey's boat.

Stella and John Dee sat beside Toby. He reached over to wipe a spot of blood from a cut on her chin. "You did good."

Stella's eyes twinkled. "Thanks, but if I ever see another sticker bush it'll be too soon."

Toby chuckled. God, she'd been a trooper this morning. Waking on a bed of branches. No breakfast. Two hours tramping through brush, bushes, and tree stands until they had reached the landing. Branches had whipped them, and they had stumbled over downed logs and been swarmed by pesky insects. Through it all, she hadn't caterwauled or lagged behind.

When they'd reached the landing, ol' Dickey gladly took their money for a crossing. Now in the main channel, silhouetted against the afternoon sky, he stood on his broadhorn's shack, studying the river swells and working the tiller. The forty-foot flatboat cut against the current with nary a ripple owing to the lightness of the breeze and ol' Dickey's touch. The rudder pole bobbed overhead with ol' Dickey's adjustments to course.

Toby wiped his brow. There was no refuge from the hot, overhead sun.

Stella pointed to the Mississippi side. "Is that where the cabin was? Just past the little island?"

"Probably so. Not a board of it left," John Dee said.

Stella's mouth was open, baring a perfect row of upper teeth. "We would have died if we'd stayed there!"

"Yep," Toby said.

She shook her head and looked away.

It was as close a call as Toby had ever had on the river. Oh, he'd heard of the Big Muddy's power—fierce storms sometimes straightened a river bend in an instant. The explosion they'd heard was the swollen, angry river blasting the shack to pieces and washing away the point on which it sat. Widening the main channel. A few minutes more in the cabin and rushing water would have swallowed up all three of them. Three bodies would have turned up somewhere downriver.

"Last night, the river decided the cabin didn't belong there." John Dee hesitated as a flock of pesty grackle cawed directly overhead. "Next time we pass by, we'll call it 'Stella's Cut.'"

"Very funny." Her stiff smile was humorless.

John Dee rose and called to ol' Dickey, "How long till we land?"

"Well," ol' Dickey said, rubbing his bushy gray goatee as he surveyed the river, "let's see. No wind. Pretty calm water. No boat traffic. Oh, I'd say mebbe forty-five minutes."

"Good. How far south of Helena will we be?"

"Oh, hell. We'll land 'cross just a bit north ah Moon Lake. That'll be five mile or so south of Helena."

"Thank you." John Dee plunked down next to Stella and Toby. "We'll hire a wagon. Should be to Helena late afternoon."

"Once we get there," Toby said, "I'll talk with the roustabouts at the landing. They'll know something about the Burtons."

"I predict you'll find the Burton gang has boarded packets and moved on," John Dee said. "Our first stop will be a dressmaker's, for Stella. Then we'll have a fine dinner. We'll take rooms and catch a cotton boat south in the morning."

"You make it sound so easy," Stella said.

"Positive thinking, dear girl. Positive thinking."

The three of them settled into a comfortable lull. Ol' Dickey toiled in silence, occasionally adjusting the rudder as he navigated across the mighty Mississippi. Toby shaded his eyes with his fingers and marked their course against a massive pine tree, satisfying himself that the boat was making steady progress to the western bank. He leaned back and let his gaze follow a flock of birds overhead. A cooling breeze felt great. An open air seat on the top deck all the way to New Orleans wouldn't be so bad, even in the sunshine.

"I dare say we are profiting from a spectacular boat ride," John Dee said. "A fair day and good company. All we lack is song." He smiled at Stella. "Do you happen to know a nice aria for a sunny day?"

Stella shook her head. "Good lord, John Dee. My frock is in tatters. My face is cut up, and my arms and legs are dotted with insect bites. I haven't had anything to eat. I don't feel much like singing. Though I agree the day is lovely—thank heaven after yesterday's storm."

"Shame," John Dee said. "If you sang a song," he looked up at ol' Dickey, "you'd gain another fan."

Stella rolled her eyes.

"I've been meaning to ask you," John Dee said, "did you have any formal training?"

Toby tensed. How would she take John Dee's probe? Two days' acquaintance surely didn't make the three of them familiars.

Stella hesitated, but then smiled. "Our choir director taught me to measure my breaths and extend my notes. I learned the scales and about octave ranges from her. So, I'd say she helped me greatly with my pitch and the essential sound of my voice."

"Choir? At the Cherokee reservation?"

"Yes. By my teens, my people had built schools. Missionaries, mostly black-robed old men, ran my school." She gazed at the water, as if she were conjuring up memories. "Gosh, they sure pounded Christianity into us. So, we sat in chapel every day and sang lots of hymns."

"You're Christian?"

"I don't know. We read our Scripture. If there's a God, he helped me some. Other times he didn't lift a finger."

Was Stella referring to Ricky Burton's attack and the end of her singing on the *Lady J*, or some other misfortune?

John Dee raised an eyebrow. "The playbill said you started in theater in St. Louis. Did the missionaries send you to St. Louis? To church school?"

Stella stared at the water. She didn't respond. John Dee's questions seemed innocent enough to Toby, but they'd hit something vulnerable in her. Silence hung over the three of them.

"Sorry. It's none of my business," John Dee said.

Waves slapped at the side of the boat. Stella was somewhere far away. After a time, she gazed at John Dee, then at him. Still, she didn't speak. Something needed to come out; Toby felt it deep down inside.

"What is it, Stella?" he asked.

Her eyes, sad as a baby bird with a broken wing, locked with his. "A long time ago, I sang lead parts in our choir. After one recital, the choir director told me that a White man named Mister Bickler had been in the audience and that he liked my voice. He wanted to take me to St. Louis to sing at his theater."

"That was quite an offer."

"Yes, but I didn't want to go. I was young—still in my teens. My choir was my family. I didn't want to leave them. But the director told me to go sing in St. Louis and be a fine example of the talents of the Cherokee Nation." Stella paused. "And she threatened to take me out of the choir and put me in the Cherokee Female Seminary if I didn't go."

"My cynical nature suspects your choir director was paid a finder's fee," John Dee said.

"That crossed my mind. I was an orphan. I didn't have any parents to take my side."

Part of Toby felt the choir director had given Stella a lucky break, whether she profited from sending her student to St. Louis or not, because in the end Stella became the star singer on the *Lady J.* Kind of reminded him of himself. He'd gone along with John Dee from North Carolina to Missouri and then on to become a freed Black businessman. That had turned out pretty well. But Stella hadn't been given a choice, and neither had he.

"A few days later, I was put on the mail wagon up to St. Louis."

"Well," John Dee said, "St. Louis is not a bad town."

"I hated it. Smoke hung over everything like a blanket. I wanted to be home, in fresh air. But mostly, I hated it because of Mister Bickler."

~ ~ ~

St. Louis

Fall 1850

Mr. Bickler's carriage stopped on a narrow lane hidden from the boulevard behind mature dogwoods. He put his arm around Stella's waist and drew her close. She stiffened. Since picking her up, he'd done that twice, once even putting his hand on her thigh for a short time. She had tried to convince herself that Mr. Bickler didn't think of her that way. He was at least twenty years older, judging by the bit of gray in his long, bushy sideburns, and after she'd sniffed uncomfortably at his pungent cigar breath, he'd let her scootch away. Not this time. He tightened his grip, nuzzled his nose into her neck, and sighed contentedly.

"Welcome to your new home," Mr. Bickler said. "Take the path through the hedge to the door. Georgia's in there. She'll get you settled."

"When do I go to the theater?" Stella asked.

"Oh—soon. I'll send a carriage when we need you." He kissed her on the cheek.

She grimaced.

He rubbed her arm. "But tonight, I am going to visit you. I'll be back 'bout seven-thirty. Please have a fire going. We'll have some brandy. Have you ever had French brandy?"

"No."

"It'll be divine." He put his lips to her ear and whispered, "And wear the *lingerie* that's in your bureau. It's from Paris."

He reeked of tobacco. She nearly gagged.

He climbed down from the bench and then helped her out of the carriage. He put her bag at her feet and took her hand. He kissed the back of it before climbing up and taking the reins. The horses trotted off. Stella stood with her bag in front of a small brick house, trying to make sense of what was happening to her.

"Come in from the cold, girl," a middle-aged Black woman called out from the front of the house.

"Are you Georgia?"

"Nobody else. You an Injun?"

"I'm Cherokee. My name is Stella."

"Hmmph." Georgia took Stella's bag, led her inside, and set the bag on a small wooden table. "Damn chilly out there." She closed the door.

The most prominent feature of the small front room was its stone hearth. Left of the hearth, a large crock stood next to a wood bin. To the right were several pots, a basin, and two lime green chairs. A single wooden rocking chair sat in front of the hearth. Two rickety chairs were tucked under the wooden table her bag sat on.

Stella peeked through a threshold into a bedroom furnished to an entirely different standard. A plush, burgundy floor rug. A bed with four carved wooden posts made with a white comforter and fluffy pillows. So warm and inviting, if she could only crawl in there and disappear! Over the headboard in an elegant gold frame was a painting of an idyllic pond scene. A handsome set of drawers was against the wall. A shiny red rocking chair with a velvet back and seat cushion sat in the corner.

Georgia stood stiffly with her hands on her hips as Stella looked around. "Mister Bickler said I should wear a long-ray when he visits me tonight. Is that here somewhere?"

"Long-ray?" Georgia frowned. Then Stella's meaning dawned on her and she chuckled. "Top drawer."

Stella opened the drawer and retrieved a sheer, see-through, cream-colored bustier. "Oh my!" Then she pulled out a matching garter, stockings, and a satin robe. "These? Isn't this what a bawdy girl wears? Whose are they?"

Georgia sniffed. "That's most certainly *lingerie*. Mr. Bickler bought it for his last girl, but she's gone now. I s'pose they're yours."

Mr. Bickler's expectations became very clear. Stella's chest caved in. She sat on the edge of the bed and put her head in her hands.

"What'd you think he wanted with you, girl?" Georgia asked, in a softer tone of voice.

"I'm a singer. He hired me for his theater. Not for—"

"I reckon you'll get to sing. If you give him comfort now and then."

"Mister Bickler's married?"

"Course he is."

"I did not come to St. Louis for this." Stella gathered her strength. "I won't!"

Georgia raised an eyebrow.

Stella picked up her bag and headed for the door.

"Girl!" Georgia's voice resonated like the headmaster's at school. Stella stopped in her tracks.

"Where you think you're going?"

"I don't know."

"Do you have any money?"

"No." She'd left the reservation with less than a dollar in coins. Georgia was right; that wouldn't get her far.

"Do you have people in St. Louis?"

"No."

"How you gonna eat?"

She hesitated. Georgia's questions burned like hot pokers, but there had to be a way to escape from Mr. Bickler. "I'll find work."

"What you think you're going to do. Cook? Clean? Mend clothes?"

That's it! She'd done plenty of chores on the reservation. "I can do those things."

"Child, it don't matter. White folk own us women who do all dat. Ain't no job for a li'l Injun girl here." Georgia took her hand and said, tenderly, "Listen to me. If you walk through that door out into the city, you'll most likely end up dead. Or in a bawdy house. Taking three or four men into your bed every night. Mebbe more. No girl from a bawdy house ever gonna sing in a theater." She patted the back of Stella's hand. "Here, it's just Mister Bickler, and he don't come round but every few days. And he don't stay long."

Time stood still as Georgia's advice washed over Stella. Was there any way out? Walking home to Oklahoma would take weeks or months. She didn't even know the way! How would she eat? Would anyone help a Cherokee girl? If she stayed, Mr. Bickler would use her body. She knew what intercourse was, but she had never imagined she would do it with a man who wasn't her husband. Would Mr. Bickler be gentle, or would he harm her? Would he force her to perform unnatural acts? She felt trapped like a defenseless animal. About to be devoured. A tear ran down her cheek. "I've never—"

Georgia draped her arm around Stella's shoulders. "You'll be all right, child. First time, it might hurt a little. You might even bleed a little. Just close your eyes and try to think of your singing." She hugged Stella. "You can get through it. Now, take a rest, girl. After he leaves, put some water in a pot and heat it in the fire. I'll leave some soap for you. Use it real good. Make damn sure you wash all his seed outta you."

~ ~ ~

"I was a young girl. Mister Bickler was a bad man. When I got to St. Louis, I found out he wasn't just interested in my singing abilities. He had me trapped: no money, far from home, and alone in the world."

Toby glanced at John Dee. Tight-lipped. Disgusted. Like him. Toby was reminded of Ricky Burton looking Stella over like a hungry wolf. This lecherous Mr. Bickler deserved Ricky's fate—he'd tear the hide off the old bastard if given the chance. Talking 'bout those days had to be painful, and he was surprised when Stella continued.

"It took months of his—visits—before he let me sing on stage. Finally, he took me down to his theater, and I got a small part. I did fine and got on well with my castmates. My role grew, and the audience started to notice me.

"All the while, I looked for a way out. About a year after I came to St. Louis, my prayers were answered. Showboats were becoming popular. A friend introduced me to the *Aleck Scott*'s musical director. He was looking for talent and offered to hire me on as a singer. I ran away from Mister Bickler to take the job. Thank God the boat was down the river before he was any the wiser. Later, I sang on the *Banjo* and then on the *New Sensation*. Just last year, Mr. Jenkins hired me on to the *Lady J*."

She made a weak smile. "Now you've heard more about St. Louis than I've ever said to anybody."

Toby didn't know what to say. He knew suffering, but Stella's had been different. She'd been violated. Same as Black women on the plantations who'd been violated by their masters. He'd heard stories. They were powerless to stop it, and so was Stella. Lecherous White men made wounds that left the worst scars—on the soul.

Finally, John Dee said, "I'm so sorry. No woman should have to go through that."

"So am I," Toby said. "That man oughta be whipped."

"Thank you. I don't know what happened to him. I hope I never see him again."

"You're a survivor," John Dee said. "You've got what it takes to get outta this tough spot. We'll get you back to singing and we'll get back to business."

"Here, boy." Ol' Dickey threw Toby a hemp line. The flatboat was angling into a small landing. "Wrap it round that post."

Toby jumped in and splashed to shore. He secured the line and nodded to two Black men tending a small corral of mules. Next to the corral was a rickety dray large enough for the three of them. It would have to do for the next leg of their journey. On to Helena.

Chapter 9

TOBY SURVEYED THE STREET. ALL quiet in the direction of Helena's riverfront, a quarter mile east. He and Stella sat outside a small eatery that had no other customers in the quiet hours before dinnertime. She sipped her tea, but Toby left his glass of strawberry wine untouched. An old woman trudged by, carrying her burlap sack.

"You're worried about the Burtons," she said.

Of course the Burtons concerned him. Six murderous river gintys armed to the teeth. He couldn't get Cliff and Brick Burton out of his mind. Cliff Burton's black lion's mane beard. His beastly screams. An untamable menace who would never give up the chase. Brick was his tool of violence. Riding at his brother's side like a big gun in a holster. Every bit of the evil in these two was channeled toward killing Stella and John Dee. And him if they had the slightest inkling of his role in brother Ricky's death. But these truths didn't need to be spoken.

"Nah," Toby said. "You heard what the roustabouts told me—none of them had seen a Burton since they raised a ruckus when the *Lady J* landed. That was yesterday."

"But that doesn't mean they're gone."

"No it don't, but ain't no Burton man coming here, where the Black folks live. It's a good place to pass the time."

"While we wait for foolhardy John Dee! I can't for the life of me understand why he'd visit a card room. That's exactly the kind of place the Burtons would go!"

"He figures the Burtons moved on," Toby said. "Besides, our boat don't pull out till the morning."

"But what about the chance the Burtons are still in Helena? His gambling puts us all at risk! He should be sitting here with us."

Toby took a drink. "I know how he thinks, Stella. We paid the lighter. Paid ol' Dickey. Paid for the wagon. 'Spect he gave money to Sam and mebbe the captain for helping us get off the *Lady J*. Gotta pay the fare back to New Orleans and then back up to St. Louis. He went to the card room 'cause he thinks he's gonna win that money back."

Toby grinned. *John Dee's gonna win. He almost always does. Then he shares his take, so tonight our money belts will be thicker.*

"The man's impossible!"

Toby could almost see steam rising from her ears. Time to get her off John Dee and his card playing. "Them dresses look real nice on you."

A large box filled with two dresses sat next to her. Just as John Dee had promised, the dress shop had been their first stop in Helena. She'd picked out a taffeta trousseau gown made of silk-like material that gave it a satiny feel and a blue and silver brocade dress. She was wearing a third, a high-necked day dress that had replaced the soiled and torn frock she'd worn when they had boarded the lighter. He stifled a groan, recalling the wad of bills he'd taken from his money belt to share the hefty tab with John Dee.

"Thank you, but my dress shopping contributed to the problem."

"Oh no," Toby said. Damn right, her new dresses drained their money pond some, but he didn't see a reason to guilt her about it. "We would have got you those dresses if we'd a had to steal them!"

"I hope not!"

Toby took another look down the street. Nothing.

"Does it bother you that you aren't allowed to join John Dee in the card room?"

"I ain't a card player."

"You know what I mean."

"I told you before: Some things just are what they are on the lower river." His nostrils flared out. "Don't spend no time worrying about what can't be."

"But doesn't it make you mad?"

"Ah, Stella. What makes me mad is when White men look at me like they're my betters. I'm more honest, smarter, and stronger than a helluva lot of 'em. But it don't matter—cause of my dark skin. I gotta keep my mouth shut and behave or there's hell to pay." He put a hard edge on his words. He sure as hell didn't have to like the way it was.

"Why are you on the lower river?"

"River business is good."

"Wouldn't river business be good up north, too? Wouldn't a free state be a better place for a freed man to work?"

Toby took his time before replying. "Our business is St. Louis to New Orleans. We do real well."

"Good for you. But surely there's good business up north in free states where a freed man is safer."

"Can't do that unless we both agree. Our river business is tontine."

She shook her head. "What does that mean?"

"The survivor gets everything."

"That's just legalities." She raised her hand as if to emphasize the point she was about to make. "It's John Dee's gambling that keeps you on the lower river, isn't it? Everybody knows riverboats are more tolerant of card-playing on the lower river than they are up north."

Toby pursed his lips. What the hell did she know about his business? "He likes his card-playing, that's true. And he's damned good at it. But there's more to it than that, Stella. We've lined up sellers and buyers, boat captains and stevedores at New Orleans, St. Louis, and all the landings in between. We can't just go up north and start doing business."

"All I'm saying," Stella said, "is what's good for John Dee may not be good for you."

"I ain't gonna leave him."

"You sound more like family than business partners."

Toby leaned toward her. "You asking me again if we're real brothers? If we come from the same momma?" He spoke firmly, but not angrily.

She took a deep breath. "I suppose I am."

"I don't know if we have the same blood. Mebbe, mebbe not. Momma never told me one way or the other. Far as I know, John Dee's daddy never told him anything.

But, yeah, we're brothers. Only a brother does what he's done for me. And what I do for him."

"How so?"

Toby had a drink of wine. He took a long, searching look at her. "'Bout ten years ago, John Dee's daddy sent him to St. Louis to bring a fancy carriage back to the farm. And sent me along to tend the horses."

~ ~ ~

St. Louis

Summer 1849

Toby flicked the reins, and the horses pulled the carriage into motion. He and John Dee leaned back against the leather cushion. The thickly padded and velvet plush seat wasn't meant for Toby's dirty workingman's trousers. Seemed to him they'd come a long ways to drive a useless buggy back to the farm.

"Just two seats and no bed—it can't haul nuthin'. What's your daddy gonna do with this fancy buggy?"

"I reckon he'll drive his pretty little bride to town and show her off at church." John Dee pulled two cigars from his jacket and handed one to Toby. "Don't know why the hell he married that girl. She's no older than us! Hell, she's gonna wear him out and break his heart." He lit their cigars.

John Dee didn't know how right he was. The day before they'd left, John Dee's "stepmother," pretty young Katherine, had been on the porch when Toby came up from the barn. She had looked him over, letting her gaze linger below his belt buckle. Then she had flashed a sweet smile, licked her lips, winked, and disappeared into the house.

"Katherine's already made her attentions known," John Dee said. "To both of us, eh?"

Toby chuckled. Damn hard to keep secrets between them.

"Yeah, go ahead and laugh," John Dee said. "Won't be long before she grabs your ass. She already grabbed mine."

A young woman darted into the street. Toby jerked back on the reins.

"Just mind the horses, would you? Helluva lot more people and dogs and wagons and such than we ever see back home!"

Dust kicked up as the horses trotted into the heart of the city. Toby puffed on his cigar. They passed liveries, riders, and buggies. People alongside the road, mostly men in smart business jackets, all seemed in a hurry. Buildings were a nonstop blending of merchant shops, banks, government buildings, and other commercial structures in a landscape as foreign to Toby as the ocean, which he'd never seen either. He glanced over and wasn't surprised to find John Dee wide-eyed.

On Locust Street, a tall, boxy building with windows too small for its walls caught his attention. White men led four young Black boys to a raised platform. The boys looked down, defeatedly, as they trudged up the stairs, linked to one another by chains. Several White men dressed in vests and jackets were waiting for them. Others had gathered below the platform. The Black boys were turned to face the crowd. One of the White men on the platform pulled back a boy's cheek and examined his teeth.

"They're fixing to sell them boys?" Toby asked.

"Looks like it," John Dee said. "Must be Lynch's. I'm told he runs the slave market in St. Louis. Got three slave pens inside that building."

One of the boys looked over the crowd, like he was searching for someone. Maybe he was looking for his momma. Maybe he was dreaming of freedom. Somewhere far, far away from Lynch's slave market.

A White man called out to John Dee: "You there. Stop a minute."

"Me?" John Dee asked.

The man nodded. John Dee motioned to Toby to stop the buggy.

"Would you sell me your big buck?"

"What?"

"That niggah driving your buggy."

"He's not for sale."

"You're wasting him! Letting him drive you round like he's some ol' coon. Christsakes man!" He spit tobacco juice in the street. "Hell, I'd give you twenty-one hunerd for him."

John Dee didn't respond but took a real deep breath. The slaver's big number must have surprised him.

"That's right. You gotta big, strong buck there. Look at his back and shoulders. I could sell 'im to a planter lickety-split. He'd put 'im on his main gang and that boy'd pick 'im three hundred pounds of cotton or cut a couple wagonloads of cane every dod-derned day."

Toby stared at the man, wishing his eyes could burn a hole through his head.

"Don't you worry, boy," the slaver said. "You'll get yer fun. Your massa'll want you humping the mammies to make more stock juz like you." He laughed hysterical-ly.

"There's no call for that!" John Dee said. "Keep your jokes to yourself, mister. Toby here ain't for sale to you at no price."

"You're a damn fool!" the slaver shouted at John Dee.

"Let's go," John Dee said to Toby.

The carriage turned the corner, leaving Lynch's and the slaver behind. City buildings faded away as they rode in silence. They made good time on the road along the Meramec. Neither had said a word as they approached the caverns.

Toby hadn't given much thought to the possibility of being sold. He lived on a farm, outside a small town that was many hours from a slave market. He worked hard, but he had enough to eat, and he and John Dee had plen-ty of time to hunt and fish and play cards and even sneak a drink together in the evenings. Life wasn't so bad. But twenty-one hundred dollars! That would make his mas-ter a rich man.

Finally, he turned to John Dee. "One of these days, your daddy'll sell me down the river."

"No. He'd never do that."

"You heard how much I'm worth. Twenty-one hun-dred dollars. That's a fortune."

"I'd never let him," John Dee said.

"I know you'd never sell me, but it ain't up to you."

"Why would Daddy sell you?"

"Could be lots a reasons. What if the farm has hard times? What if that pretty li'l wife of his wants him to buy her a diamond? What if he catches her winking at me? Or grabbing my ass like she grabbed yours. She'll say it's my fault, and he'll want me gone."

"Ain't no way that's gonna happen. I won't let it," John Dee said.

~ ~ ~

Stella took Toby's story in without saying a word. They sat in silence, neither averting their eyes from the other. His posture was straight-backed, and he had a strong, manly jawline. It didn't matter that his clothes were soiled and out of shape from their night on the river; it dawned on her that he was as handsome as any man she knew. White, Black, or Red.

"So," Stella said, "you and John Dee are together to this day. You never did get sold?"

"No." Toby sat back and relaxed his shoulders. "When we got back to the farm, John Dee asked his daddy to give him owner title to me for his birthday. Well, when John Dee's birthday came, his daddy did it, and the next day, John Dee took me to the courthouse. He had 'em write up my freedom papers, and he signed me a free man."

Stella put her hand on her breastbone. "Oh my." She soaked John Dee's good deed in, trying to make sense of his motives. Could a smoking, drinking, gambling man have a pure heart?

"John Dee's daddy was mad as a hornet. The way he saw things, John Dee gave up valuable property for nothing. Said it was robbery of the family. He weren't gonna pay me a wage as a free man. Or feed me. He told me to get off the farm. I lit out for St. Louis."

"Why St. Louis?"

"Only place I'd seen a free Black man. Anyhows, John Dee caught up with me. So we went together, and we've been working our river business ever since." Toby paused. "Far as I know, John Dee never did see his daddy again."

"It's a rare Southern White man who would do what John Dee did," Stella said.

"Just don't ask me again if he's gonna turn his back on us," Toby said. He finished his wine. "Well, we best get into town. When John Dee's gone this long, that usually means he's fixing to find trouble. Come on."

As they walked back to the riverfront, Stella was struck by Helena's pretty setting. Green hills to the north and the river basin a giant, picturesque vista to the south. Her mood lightened and the Burtons were out of her mind for a short time, until the sights got grittier. In the industrial heart of Helena, cotton and grain warehouses stood next to a foundry, machine shops, and a wagon factory.

At the landing, Helena was downright ugly. A peddler of cheap jewelry and knick-knacks accosted them until Toby shoed him away. A waterside slum took shape with shanty boats and a floating medicine show. Farther down was a floating saloon. Worst of all, Stella spotted numerous men who looked as dangerous as the Burtons or any ruffian she'd seen on the river. She held Toby's elbow in a vise grip.

He steered her clear of a scruffy man holding a whiskey bottle to his chest.

"We call them wharf rats," Toby said.

"Quite fitting."

They stopped at the Magnolia Hotel.

"I need you to go to your room, Stella. Lock your door and stay there. Don't open it for anyone. I'll see to John Dee, and we'll bring you up dinner later."

"What are you going to do?"

"I'm gonna keep an eye on the card room. Make sure John Dee doesn't find trouble."

"Maybe I could help you," Stella said.

"It's not your end of things. Look around—the only women at the waterfront are bawdy girls."

"But, I can help—"

"If I need you, I'll come get you."

"How long will you be?"

"I don't know. Get some rest. I 'spect you'll be needing it."

~ ~ ~

The old man across the table raised the bet steadily, in amounts just low enough to keep John Dee and two other players from folding. The dealer flicked a last card to each player, and the pot was close to five hundred dollars. He nodded at the old man to make a bet.

"Five hun-erd dollars." Either the old man had a helluva hand, or he was bluffing to muscle everyone out. Two men folded, and it was down to John Dee and the old man.

John Dee's hand was just a pair of ladies kissing the felt tabletop. Respectable, but vulnerable. Did the old man's cards match his raises? He slowed his breathing as he considered his play, letting the old man stew. John Dee watched for a clue from the corner of his eye. Then the old man's salt-and-pepper mustache twitched. Fear.

"I'll see your five hundred and raise one thousand."

One of the men who had folded gasped. The old man across the table turned to stone. He looked at the stack of bills John Dee had thrown into the center of the pot and looked at his cards. His expression was incredulous as he folded, throwing his cards face down on the table.

As John Dee scooped up his winnings, the old man said, "You've cooked my goose, Mister—. What did you say your name was?"

"I didn't."

The old man growled from deep in his chest. "Round here, a man gives his name to his playing partners."

John Dee smiled. "You can call me 'friend.'"

"Why, you sumabitch! You don't talk like yer from round here. Goddamned Yankee come down here to cheat me!"

John Dee gathered his winnings and rose from the table. "There sure as hell wasn't any cheating. And I'm no Yankee, but I am thirsty. I'll take a seat at the bar while passions cool." He nodded to the other players around the table and went to the bar.

John Dee ordered a whisky and water and contemplated how long he should calmly sip his drink. He couldn't look too eager to leave with the old man's money, or the codger just might chase him with a pistol.

A man took the barstool beside John Dee. "I'm surprised to see you here, Franklin." John Dee turned. The man was wearing a red vest and bowler hat. Stevie Burton! John Dee glanced around the room but didn't see the other Burtons or their hired guns.

"Who?"

"John Dee Franklin. Sure as hell."

"I'm afraid you are mistaken."

"Don't bullshit me. You're Franklin all right. We couldn't get a good look at you from the bank, but I've seen you on the river. In card games." He nodded at the far wall. "Stood over yonder watching the game to make sure I was looking at the great John Dee Franklin. I sure as hell am. Still gut a sucker as good as anybody, don't ya, Franklin?"

John Dee scanned the room again. Cliff and Brick Burton must be here somewhere. And what about their three hired guns? God! If he only had a pistol! Why hadn't he listened to Stella? *"Just hide out with Toby and me until we catch our boat."*

"Mister, I believe you are mistaken." John Dee hoped Stevie Burton wasn't as certain as his declaration.

"Stop yer nonsense. I know who you are. But I will say you have steel testicles coming in here. If Brick and Cliff had seen you, they'd have skinned you alive by now, cut your pecker off, and stuffed it in your mouth."

John Dee gulped, not so much at the threat but with relief at learning Brick and Cliff Burton were elsewhere. "That's a pleasant thought."

"What you deserve."

"Listen," John Dee said. "Your brother Ricky was about to rape that poor girl. He pulled his pistol and shot at me. Then he pulled out his knife. It was him or me."

"Maybe so. The boy had a wild side."

"Does that mean I don't have to worry about a skinning from you?"

Stevie Burton snorted. "Blood is thicker than water, Franklin. I leave that kind of thing to Brick and Cliff.

'Spect you know that. They'll find you." He smirked. "Even though that skinny, red-headed, bastard cub pilot tried to talk Cliff into chasing you up the river." He paused. "You in cahoots with that boy—Sam Clemens?"

"Who?" John Dee replied.

Stevie Burton ignored him and stood. "What I'll never understand, Franklin, is why you thought a goddamned squaw was worth killing my brother. You sweet on her?"

John Dee felt his neck flush. Stevie Burton had hit a nerve. He felt something for Stella. Romantic attraction? He wasn't sure. A connection of some kind, one that made him damn glad Toby had saved her life. "I don't know the girl. A man has to do the right thing, doesn't he?"

"Fucking preacher, ain't ya? I've seen enough of you." Stevie Burton left the card room.

John Dee finished his drink and got up to leave. All eyes were on him, but he didn't look back. Stevie Burton hadn't said one way or the other if Brick and Cliff were still in Helena, but the hair stood up on the back of John Dee's neck. They were close by. He felt it. Burton was gonna tell his brothers he'd seen John Dee and they'd be coming. He had to find Toby and Stella and get them the hell out of Helena, pronto. He needed a new plan.

He scanned the wooden sidewalk. No one there. Dusk was settling on Helena, making the street ahead look dark gray. It was eerily quiet.

He took a cautious step. Then another. Clomp. Clomp. Only his bootheels made a sound.

John Dee stopped and looked in all directions. Nothing.

A door slammed. *Where the hell was that?* Then quiet. Where was everyone? His forearms twitched.

His boots thumped a steady beat. He passed three buildings. His heart pounded. *Someone's there!*

Stevie Burton leapt at him from between two shops, swinging a knife. John Dee evaded his thrust. Toby appeared out of nowhere and tackled Burton from behind. Then he slammed Burton's head on the planks. John Dee helped Toby drag Burton's limp body into the blackness between the buildings.

"Good to see you, partner," John Dee said.

"This is Stevie Burton, ain't he? Those two nasty Burtons here somewhere?"

"I don't think so. I've only seen this one."

"What do we do with him?" Toby asked.

"You asking if we oughta slit his throat?"

"S'pose I am."

John Dee hesitated. "Nah, that ain't our style. Besides, Stevie, here, has just done us a helluva favor."

"How's that?"

"Once he saw me, he coulda run off to tell his brothers I was in the card room. Instead, he tried to kill me himself. The beauty of it is his brothers don't know we're in Helena. So you hold him down. I'll go get our old friend Big Jake at the sheriff's office. I'll have him lock Stevie up least till our boat leaves tomorrow."

"Think Jake'll do that?"

"Jake'll do anything for a ten-dollar bill—and to keep our mouths shut about the River Belle."

"Probably so," Toby said. "Will Jake charge him with trying to kill you? That's a hanging offense, ain't it?"

John Dee laughed. "Don't get your hopes up. For one thing, we ain't sticking around to testify."

"That's true," Toby said.

"Cliff and Brick Burton are gonna get word Stevie's in jail and walk in there with real nasty attitudes, pistols on their hips, and their hired guns behind them. 'Bout then, Big Jake's sense of justice is gonna melt, and Stevie will walk out with his brothers. I'm hoping Jake'll hold Stevie till our boat's down the main channel a piece." A strange feeling hit John Dee. There had been three of them. "Where's Stella?"

"In her hotel room."

"Good. Think we should tell her about this?"

"Nah," Toby said. "We're gonna board the *Cedar Point* in the morning, just like we planned. Let's not frighten her any more than she already is."

Chapter 10

THE BLACK MEN TOBY HAD spoken with on Helena's waterfront the day before went up and down the gangplank, tirelessly, loading the last of the trunks, band boxes, and carpet bags onto the *Cedar Point*. For a few pennies. Same as every other day. White deckhands screamed at the men like they owned them. Stella's declaration that things were better up North for a free Black man rang in Toby's ears. She was probably right.

He, Stella, and John Dee sipped coffee at a table a hundred yards away. Passengers boarded steadily. Neither Brick nor Cliff Burton were among them. Toby didn't expect either to turn up—they'd be looking for Stevie, who was hopefully still licking his wounds in Big Jake's jail cell.

The *Cedar Point* was smaller than the *Lady J*, known as a fast packet for passengers and the mail. It would make New Orleans in three days. That was the good part. But it didn't have the *Lady J*'s gilded derricks or a calliope. No garnished pilot house. Chipped paint marred its deck walls. Its deckhands didn't wear proper uniforms.

Standing at the gangplank, the captain's smart wool jacket and bow tie over his white-collared shirt contradicted the disrepair of his boat. A deckhand discretely gave the captain a paper bag about the size of a liquor bottle. He tucked it inside his jacket. Oh shit, his captaining skills probably matched the condition of the *Cedar Point*.

"Shouldn't we board?" Stella asked.

"Soon. We'll get on last," John Dee said. "The passengers will be mostly settled. A lot of them will be below-decks or in their rooms. Less chance someone will spot us and get the word to Cliff Burton before the *Cedar Point* floats clear."

Toby smiled at John Dee's caution that he hadn't shown yesterday.

A man approached the gangplank carrying a gleaming leather bag, his gold watch dangling from a suit pocket. A Black man called to him, "Bye, Massa! I'll take good care of the plantation."

"Goodbye, Joseph," the White man replied.

"That must be a cotton planter getting on the boat," Stella said.

"No," John Dee said. "He's a cheat. He wants anyone watching to think he's a juicy sucker—a wealthy planter with a bag full of money to lose."

"How do you know?"

"I've seen him before. He's the best capper on the river. Works with a gambler named George Devol to relieve the real suckers of their money."

"The Black man who saw him off ain't no slave," Toby said. "He's a dock worker. I spoke with him yesterday. The White man musta paid him for the sendoff act." He frowned. "And the captain just put a bottle of hooch in his jacket. We's in for a helluva boat ride."

"Listen," John Dee said to Stella. "The man at the gangplank with the bushy goatee and fancy uniform is Captain Devers. It's his boat, and he isn't known to have many rules. This packet'll be full of card sharks, cheats, drunks, and who knows who else. We're all gonna have to be real careful."

"Then let's wait for the next boat!" Stella said.

Toby shook his head. The real reason they had to chance passage on the *Cedar Point* was that Cliff and Brick Burton could spring their brother from jail at any time. And turn up at the waterfront. Toby was certain he and John Dee were of like mind not to spare a second waiting for the next boat. But Stella didn't know the Burtons were in Helena, and neither man wanted to alarm her.

"Can't do that. I spoke to Joseph—he's the leader of the roustabouts." Toby pointed to a big riverboat to the north. "That's the *May Wing*. It's next out, but Joseph said its captain's waiting on some high-paying passengers who won't be ready to leave till tomorrow morning." He didn't know exactly when the *May Wing* was leaving, but it was certainly after *Cedar Point*. Maybe a necessary lie wasn't really a lie. Or was at least an acceptable white lie. "We oughtn't wait around."

"Besides, it's only three days," John Dee said. "Stick close to me and Toby and you'll be fine."

"All right." Stella picked up her bag. "You two are the rivermen here. We'll do it your way."

The three of them boarded the *Cedar Point*, and the gangplank was raised.

~ ~ ~

John Dee left Toby and Stella on the top deck and made his way to the bar. It wasn't as fancy as many riverboat saloons, with just two four-legged wooden tables surrounded by wooden chairs and a plank-top stand-up bar fronting an array of brown whiskey bottles. It was a quite popular room, nonetheless. The *Cedar Point* hadn't yet made the main channel, but a dozen men had whiskeys in hand.

A poker game was underway at one table. At the other, the fake cotton planter was sitting across the table from George Devol, who shuffled a deck of cards and dealt out three. Devol wore spectacles that made him appear slightly less threatening than his thick head and chest otherwise suggested. A smartly dressed man with slicked back blond hair was also sitting at the table, nursing his whiskey.

"What you doing there, boy?" the fake planter asked, regarding Devol as a stranger.

John Dee leaned back against the bar to watch him and his partner fish for a sucker.

"Oh, I saw a man play this three-card game on my last boat trip," Devol said. "What they'd do, you see, was turn one card up." He turned up a six of diamonds. "Then they'd mix the cards up like this…." He used his hands to slide the cards around and then set them three in a row again. "If you turn up the six of diamonds, you win."

"Looks easy enough," the fake planter said. "I'll bet you twenty dollars I can turn it up."

"Okay. You can try your luck," Devol said. "If we're gonna bet, ol' Stan'll keep it fair."

Both men handed their bet money to Stan the bartender.

"How 'bout you?" Devol asked the blond man.

"I'll sit this one out."

"Okay."

The fake planter turned up the six. "Ha! Must be beginner's luck."

"Wanna try again?" Devol asked.

The fake planter took a drink of whiskey. "Well, I reckon so."

"What do you wanna bet?"

"I've got two hun-erd dollars. Is that too much for you?"

"No," Devol said.

Four hundred was handed to Stan. Devol turned up the middle card, which was a ten of spades, and mixed the cards.

"Tell me, brother," the man next to John Dee said quietly, "do you live on the river?"

"I reckon you could say that," John Dee said, acknowledging his tendency to gamble to another gambler.

"Canada Bill Jones. Pleased to meet you."

"Likewise. I'm John Dee Franklin."

"Watch here," Canada Bill said, out of the Devol table's earshot. "He and I think alike. It's immoral to let a sucker keep his money."

The fake planter turned up the ten. "Ho hey!" After he won for a third time, he slapped the shoulder of the blond man, who was intently watching the game. "How 'bout that, neighbor?"

Devol wiped his brow, feigning distress. "Give me a chance to win it back, would ya? How about five hun-erd this time?"

"Okay."

Each man handed five-hundred dollars to Stan the bartender. Devol turned up a deuce of clubs.

"Dealer," the fake planter said, "fill my whiskey, will ya?" Devol turned for the whiskey on the bar behind him, and the fake planter subtly nicked the corner of the deuce in full view of the blond-headed man sitting at the table.

The blond-headed man's eyes grew as big as the rising sun. John Dee knew the type. He hung around card games to get away from the missus, but he wasn't about to risk his money unless he had a sure thing. And that would be his undoing.

"I'd go five hun-erd myself," the blond man said to Devol.

"You're on," Devol said. He and the blond man each gave their wagers to the bartender. Devol mixed the cards, laid them out, and John Dee waited for the inevitable. The fake planter turned up the card that had a slight nick in the corner. It was the ten, not the deuce. The blond man's eyes were wide with disbelief.

"Damn! Lost that time," the fake planter said.

The bartender handed Devol his winnings.

"You're goddamned cheaters!" The blond man pulled a Colt pistol from his jacket and aimed it at Devol's face. "Give me my money back!"

"Hold on now, fella," Devol said, with the calm of a man who had looked down the barrel of a gun before.

"That's a real bad example for other fellas who have bad luck now and then. Tell you what, hand that pistol over to Stan. I'll put your five hun-erd I just won up against it."

The blond man hesitated, then gave his pistol to Stan the bartender. Devol gave Stan five hundred dollars.

Devol turned up the six of diamonds and mixed the cards. The blond man studied the movement of the cards like a monk studied the good book, making John Dee crack a tiny smile. He hadn't spotted Devol's trick, but he was sure the six was already up his sleeve. The blond man picked the deuce, and the bartender handed Devol his money and the Colt. Devol sprang from his chair and pressed the end of the pistol barrel against the blond man's forehead, between his eyes.

"You're a goddamn bad egg, mister." Devol pulled back the hammer and the room went silent. "Get yer ass to yer cabin and don't come out. If I see you again, I'm gonna shoot you with this goddamn pistol and feed ya to the catfish."

The blond man slowly backed away and left the bar-room.

"Helluva kicker, that one," Canada Bill said.

"Wouldn't expect one in this fine establishment," Devol said, with a smirk.

The men went back to their card games like nothing had happened. John Dee bit the inside of his lip. He and Toby should have known the *Cedar Point* would be too damn risky. It was a rare riverboat that permitted men to carry firearms. Stan the bartender hadn't said a thing to Devol about giving up the Colt pistol. Gambling, whiskey, and guns were the perfect ingredients for hellfire. They should have waited for the next boat.

John Dee shivered a little. Trouble was coming. He had to find Toby and Stella.

~ ~ ~

A pleasing breeze tickled Toby's face. Water oaks on the bank somewhere approaching the Arkansas-Louisiana border faded together into a green horizon. He and Stella sat on the top deck, near the stacks, quite a ways from the large open area at the ship's bow where White people tended to congregate. Not many others were up top enjoying the seasonable afternoon, making Toby wonder where the White people were.

"Here we are again," Stella said, "sitting together while John Dee goes off to gamble. It's a concerning pattern."

"Now, Stella, he was gonna take a look around. I don't think he'll gamble much. He's fixing to learn 'bout the White men on this boat." He paused. "Couldn't very well send me or you to do that, now could we?"

Stella sighed. "I just hope he stays out of trouble."

A loud roar rose from the boat's center.

"What the hell is that?" Toby rose and followed the sound to the center stairwell. Stella trailed him. Men were jammed together from the top to the bottom of the stairs, looking down on the spectacle below. Deckhands positioned at the bottom of the stairwell kept them back.

A shirtless Black man was lying on his back, motionless. His head gushed blood. An old Black man tended the wound.

A thickly-built, shirtless White man pumped his fist at the spectators on the stairwell. They cheered him with a bloodlust. One loud voice screamed, "More!" The man pushed out his hairy, barrel-chest and posed his bicep muscles.

Toby got a good look at his face. Brick Burton! *Goddammit! I watched the passengers board. How did I miss him?*

"Oh God!" Stella grabbed Toby's wrist with a death grip.

"Keep calm," Toby said.

"Does he see us?"

"I don't think so," Toby said. "If he does, he might not know who we are. The riverbank was a long ways from up top on the *Lady J*. I doubt he got a good look." Even so, his heart pounded at the sight of the bald-headed brute.

"How in heaven's name can he be on this boat?" she asked.

"I don't know. We watched people board. How the hell did we miss him?" It dawned on Toby that Brick Burton must not know his brother Stevie was in the Helena jail. "The good news is I don't see Cliff Burton or their hired men." Had the gang split up and gone their separate ways?

Stella tugged at his arm. "We won't be able to avoid him on this small boat! We've got to find John Dee and let him know Brick Burton's onboard!"

Toby breathed deeply to slow his racing heart. He had to stay calm so Stella would.

The old Black man threw water on the injured man's face, stirring him. Two other men dragged him away.

Brick Burton jeered at the injured man with a growling snarl that Toby wanted to knock off him.

"Burton damn-near killed him," Toby said.

"What were they doing?" Stella asked.

"A head-butt contest," Toby said. "All those men on the stairs bet on who'd win."

"How barbaric."

Toby lifted an eyebrow. "Ain't head-butt been on any of the boats you worked?"

"Never."

No sense explaining further. Stella only knew the lower river's showy veneer. He and John Dee roamed its underbelly.

The crowd calmed when a man wearing a flashy gold cravat under a black suit jacket began handing out money. His bushy black beard worked up and down like a dark mop as he called out winners.

Brick Burton paced back and forth along a string tied between the stairwell and a support beam, about waist-high from the floor. He stopped in front of three Black men who were sitting on the floor, just beyond the beam. Two scooched behind the biggest of the three.

"Get up, boy!" Brick shouted at the Black man.

From the soot on their shirts, they were boiler room men, forced by the captain into head-butt combat for the amusement of his passengers. One man shook. Another covered his eyes with his hands. Fear. Fear of what Brick Burton might do to them—they had just watched him severely injure a man. And Toby suspected they feared winning. Defeating a White man might spell trouble on the lower river. Especially if the White man got hurt. The spectators were bloodthirsty White men, and who knew what a Black man who injured a White man might be accused of? They might want blood for blood. The sad reality was there was nothing in this head-butt contest for the Black men.

Brick Burton snorted like a rabid dog. Spittle and snot sprayed his reluctant opponent. This evil leviathan of the Mississippi River would destroy the poor unfortunate. Toby squeezed into the throng of men on the stairwell for a better look at the combatants. Burton's opponent shook with fear, about to be crushed, plain as day. Maybe even killed.

For a second, Toby heard the crack of a whip. He was his young self, back in North Carolina. The White overseer struck a Black man's naked back again and again. Toby flinched every time the whip cracked. He couldn't move a muscle. He'd been powerless to stop it.

Brick Burton licked his lips, as if he were anticipating the exquisite taste of inflicting bone-crushing pain. The Black man was gonna die. Pure terror on the man's face made Toby's decision. His arm muscles tensed like iron. He grabbed a man's shoulder, pulling him out of the way, and took a step down the stairs.

He hesitated. *Don't put Stella and John Dee at risk!* But Stella was right—there was no avoiding Brick Burton on a small stern-wheeler.

Time to settle things here and now.

Toby took off his jacket and threw it to Stella. He pushed through the crowd to the bottom of the stairs. He unbuttoned his shirt. The deckhands let him pass.

"Ah, a taker," the bearded man said to the mob of gambling men. "A nice big buck. Can this boy best mighty Brick Burton? Get your bets in!"

Burton eyed Toby with malice; he was out for blood.

Toby couldn't tell if Burton recognized him. It didn't matter. Two men were entering the ring of battle and only one would survive.

"Toby!" John Dee shouted from the stairwell.

Toby turned. The deckhands were restraining John Dee. "Don't do this!"

"Just bet big," Toby said.

Toby turned his attention to Brick Burton, who was snorting again. Then Burton snapped his head downward, showing Toby his knobby skull like it was a bull elk's rack of antlers.

The bearded man stepped between Toby and Burton and yelled, "Get yer bets in! Brick or the black buck! No state bank specie circulars. No wildcat money. Gold and silver from the US Mint only. I'll take Canal Bank notes." From men on the staircase, he took in fistfuls of twenty-dollar coins and some bank notes, also a gold watch and even a fancy pistol in a glass case. His assistant wrote down the wagers. Finally, the throng quieted, its collective lust for carnage hanging heavy in the air.

The bearded man motioned Toby and Brick Burton to opposite ends of the string. Then he pointed to a ribbon tied in the middle. "Start from yer end, and butt heads at the ribbon. On my signal, boys."

Toby took his place. Burton's face contorted, and his body tensed like a stalking beast.

A ray of sunshine peeking in from the stairwell hit Toby's eyes, blinding him. A yellow explosion of light. He blinked. He blinked again. Burton was a blur at the other end of the string.

"Now!"

Toby rammed toward the ribbon, straining to find an aiming point. His head hit Burton's a glancing blow, knocking Toby off-balance and causing him to somersault and crash into the stairwell.

Burton chortled from somewhere deep in his gut. "Get up, coward!" He threw his arms out at the men on the stairs. "This one's pissing hisself! Hope you got your bets in on me!"

Men on the stairs laughed and jeered. "Put your apron on, girlie."

"We ain't gonna let you run, darky."

Toby took a knee at the opposite end of the string. He lined up for a second pass where Brick Burton had started. Burton glared, but the bearded man pointed toward the end Toby had been at. Burton shrugged and lined up. Toby saw him squint. The sunshine would force Burton to hesitate, just an instant.

Toby dropped into a powerful squat. *It's him or me!* He rolled forward ever so slightly.

"Now!"

Toby sprung off the line like a big cat and aimed for the center of Brick Burton's head. He thrust his hairline up and through Burton's skull like he was driving himself into the back wall. He felt bone give, and when he landed on Burton's legs, everything went black.

~ ~ ~

John Dee dabbed at Toby's face with a wet rag. Finally, Toby's eyes opened. "You alive?"

"I think so," Toby said.

"Stand up and you win."

"Did you bet me?"

"Two thousand dollars. They gave me two to one odds."

"Sweet Jesus." Toby used his elbows to brace himself and sat up. Men on the stairwell mostly groaned at the sight. Toby stood and raised his arms.

Brick Burton was flat on his back, convulsing.

"I think you killed him," John Dee whispered in Toby's ear. "Cracked his head something awful. If he lives, his brain'll be summer squash. I'm gonna collect our winnings." He helped Toby put on his shirt. "Six-thousand dollars of mostly coin ain't gonna fit in our money belts. Can you get a valise?"

"Yeah."

"Okay. Hurry along. Then we gotta find Stella and get off this goddamn boat."

~ ~ ~

John Dee climbed through a trap door down into a dark locker located just forward of the main hatch. Toby and Stella were already there, so he squeezed beside Stella and made a place to sit. He heard the pilot slide an empty barrel back over the trap door. He breathed easier. Sore losers were everywhere on the *Cedar Point*. Maybe if he and Toby hid for a while they could escape with their winnings. And their skins.

He adjusted himself to try and get comfortable. It was too dark to make out Toby or Stella.

"All right," Stella said, softly, "I hurried along and haven't asked any questions. It's time to tell me why we're sitting in a dark hole."

"Speak real quiet," John Dee whispered. "We'd be some dumb hicks to get in a black hole and be found out 'cause we were yakking too loud."

"Okay," she whispered back.

"Well, Stella, we're gonna hide in here till we get off the boat."

"I suppose I shouldn't be surprised," she whispered. "What happened after Toby head-butted with Brick Burton?"

"Nothing yet. The boys that bet on Brick are grousing. They want their money back—bunch of damn kickers. They complained to ol' Turley that Toby cheated."

"Was Turley the man with the black bushy beard?"

"Yes. He ran the bets. Turley was having none of it, but sooner or later, they'll bribe him or Captain Devers to back them up and come for our money."

"You don't know they'd take a bribe," Stella said.

"This is a gambling boat. There's a helluva lot of money on the line. I've seen it before."

"Oh."

Footsteps above. John Dee grabbed Stella's arm to signal quiet. When the thumps faded, he continued.

"It might get worse than that. Some of the losers went to find George Devol. He's on the boat—I've seen him. He's got the hardest head on the Mississippi—never lost a head-butt. They want to put him up against Toby to win their money back. Devol would crack Toby's head clean open."

"Don't be so sure," Toby whispered.

"You getting cocky? I'm trying to save your noggin here."

"I can pass on Devol," Toby added.

John Dee snickered, quietly. "And if neither of those things happen, we'll get robbed. *Cedar Point*'s full of rascals who know I won big. Some of them have their pistols. I saw a man with a Colt in the bar. They'll be coming for me."

"Oh my," Stella said. "So, how do we get off the boat?"

"I paid the pilot fifty dollars for a hiding place and a touch-and-go landing."

"Clearly, we're in the hiding place. What, pray tell, is a touch-and-go landing?" Stella paused. "Getting off the *Lady J* nearly killed me."

"This landing will be easier than boarding the lighter," John Dee said. "See, the pilot's gonna square the rudder across the stern and we'll glide close to the bank."

"And he'll lower the gangplank for us?" she asked.

"Well, no, but—"

"Oh, you want me to jump in?"

"Now, Stella," John Dee said, "we'll be real close, so we're just gonna splash through the easy water next to shore and walk up the bank."

"God is testing me."

"You're doing fine," John Dee said.

"Can we trust the pilot?" Toby asked.

"Gonna have to. He's a friend of Sam's, so I'm hoping he'll be square."

"Where is the landing?" Toby asked.

"That I don't know. It'll be a small clearing made by plantations for loading up cotton bales and getting their mail and goods and such. The beauty of the plan is it's quite normal for a packet to glide close to a landing to see if there's anything to pick up. We'll be off the *Cedar Point,* and it'll be a fur piece down the river before anyone's the wiser.

"The pilot said it would be thirty minutes or so before he powers down. Now, relax and stay quiet."

They settled into a comfortable silence. Stella's arm wedged into John Dee's side, and her dress box poked him in the ribs. The closeness of their bodies comforted him. The truth was that she had been more and more in his thoughts every hour they were together. What a re-markable woman! The purity and beauty of her voice. Too perfect for the river. And the uniqueness of her deli-cate, feminine features, and the grace she carried herself with. Now she was showing uncommon strength dealing with the Burtons' threats.

Did Toby feel the same way?

Toby's whisper broke the silence. "You hear the boil-er?"

"Yeah," John Dee said. "We've slowed down. Now it's wheezing. Means the cylinders are worn and this rickety tub's gonna blow sky-high, so it's damn well time we got off anyhow." He chuckled.

"I'm glad you find all this humorous," Stella said.

"Okay," John Dee said. "Let's give it another minute. Then we're gonna run to the stern."

John Dee pushed up on the trap door. The empty barrel wobbled, then toppled over with a bang. *Shit! The whole boat heard that!* He opened the trap door and jumped up and out of the locker. He took Stella's hand and pulled her up. Toby followed, and the three of them ran to the stern with their valises and Stella's dress box.

Toby lifted her over the rail at the starboard corner of the stern. Then he climbed over. "The pilot said to jump when we're closest to the bank."

"I can't believe I'm going to do this!"

"Shh, keep it down, Stella," John Dee said. "Can't you swim?"

"Yes, but not well."

"You won't have to go far. I'll follow you. You'll be fine."

John Dee judged the pace of the *Cedar Point*'s glide. "Thirty seconds and we'll jump." He leaned to speak into Stella's ear. "When you hit the water, paddle with your arms and kick with all you've got."

"How, pray tell, can I do that without tangling my legs in this long skirt?"

"I'll be right behind you if you have any trouble."

"You got the money valise?" John Dee asked Toby.

"Yep."

"It's pretty damned heavy."

"Don't you worry. I'll keep it out of the water."

"All right. I've got the dod-derned dress box."

"I heard that," Stella said.

"Now!"

Three feet-first leaps into the black water, and they splashed away from the *Cedar Point* to the riverbank on the Louisiana side, somewhere north of Vicksburg.

Chapter 11

A SWEET, WILLOWY, WINTERGREEN SCENT HUNG on a gentle breeze as Toby approached the steep riverbank. A cleared dirt patch served as a landing. No bigger than the open area of the *Cedar Point*'s top deck. At the edge of the clearing, an empty three-sided wooden storage shed stood next to the trailhead cut into the bushes. In the shade of a willow, a Black man sat on the bench of a buckboard wagon, holding the reins to two mules.

Toby scrambled up the bank, but with a heavy carpetbag in one hand and nothing to grab ahold of with the other, he lost his footing on the slick black sediment and slid back into the river.

"Christ almighty," he muttered under his breath. Had John Dee seen his awkward failing? Must have missed it, because his jabs would be flying.

"Toby!" Stella stood waist-deep in the dark water, her long, wavy hair matted against her face like a black curtain. She reached out.

He took her hand and pulled her closer to shore. "Let me get up the bank." This time he swung around to his backside and kicked his boot heels into the muck for leverage. He scrambled up the bank on the seat of his trousers. "Do what I did."

"You must be joking!"

"Come on, now," Toby said.

She plopped on her butt at the edge of the water and gained a few inches up the bank with each thrust. She reached up to him but lost her balance and slid down the bank. She came up spitting river water. "Arrgh!"

"Come on, girl," Toby said. "Ain't you never played in the mud before?"

John Dee laughed loudly. He put out his palms. "Brace your feet against my hands and scooch up the bank."

"It's not funny John Dee!" She squatted and plopped down in the muck and pushed against him. Progress. Stella grabbed for the bank but her hand slipped off, filled with a big glob of mud. "Dammit!"

Toby shook his head. Was she ever gonna get outta the river?

John Dee braced her again. "Once more, Stella. Come on, now."

She straightened her legs against John Dee's palms and thrust her back up the bank. Toby grabbed her hand and pulled her onto dry ground.

She shook mud off her hands. "My day dress is ruined! I'm half-drowned, soaked to the skin, and covered in mud!" She knocked a hunk of black gunk off her hip. "Maybe I should have just let the Burtons' shoot me!"

Toby suppressed a chuckle. Makeup streaked below her eyes, and her dress clung to her lithe body like a skin except where the frilly bottom flared into a tail. The singing soubrette, always captivatingly perfect in her stage dress as an elegant songstress, a sultry dancer, or a folksy skit player. But standing in the mud, she looked like a great blue heron.

"You're cute when you're mad," Toby said.

"Stop!"

"Don't worry; we'll get you another dress."

"Dresses cost money. You've spent too much on me already."

John Dee emerged from the bank and set down Stella's dress box. "Don't worry about that. We'll put a few of the four-thousand dollars we just won into your new wardrobe."

"Four thousand? From the head-butt contest?" Her eyes opened wide as pies. "My lord. That's more than I've made singing on boats all these years!"

"That's right," John Dee said. "Thank Toby's hard head while we travel in style to New Orleans."

Toby held up the bag. "It's right here. I even kept it dry."

Toby approached the man by the shed, still on his wagon bench. He was grinning from ear to ear. *Enjoy the show, friend? You sure as hell didn't lend a hand.* Toby wiped mud off his cheek. "Hello."

"Who the hell are you, mud boy?" the man asked Toby. "And who's your massa?" he asked, pointing at John Dee.

Before Toby could respond, the man shouted at John Dee, "Ain't never been a visitor up tuh Willow Bend or Tranquil Pines swimming in from the river. Y'all some troublemakers?"

Toby replied, "First off, he ain't my master. I'm a freed man."

"All right," the man said.

"Name's Toby. This White man's called John Dee Franklin. He's my partner. The woman's name is Stella. We're traveling to New Orleans." He paused. "What's your name?"

"Jess." He rubbed his chin. "Why'd you jump off the boat?"

"Some bad men were trying to rob us."

Jess took long looks at each of them. Bird songs filled the air, emphasizing to Toby the remoteness of the landing and the fact that Jess was their only source of knowledge of their surroundings.

"Willow Bend and Tranquil Pines are cotton plantations round here?" Toby asked.

"Yep. Just up that trail." Jess pointed to the clearing. "Why you asking? You ain't got nothing for them."

Toby wanted to throw his hands in the air. Would this gatekeeper to the cotton fields tell him anything useful? "You a free man?"

Jess sat up straight, as if he perceived a threat. "Yep."

"Work for the plantations?"

Jess's nostrils flared. "You ask a lot of questions, boy."

"Just trying to find out who we're talking to, same as you," Toby said.

Jess adjusted himself on the wagon bench before he replied. "They pay me to deliver things from the boats. And to load up cotton bales in the fall."

"Why don't the field hands do that?"

Jess laughed. "The massas ain't gonna let those boys anywhere near a boat. Hell, a slave gets a chance, he's gonna jump on and float off."

Toby scanned the rolling black water of the Mississippi. It was hard to imagine that jumping an unfamiliar boat on the big river to parts unknown was much of a chance for freedom. But the younger version of Toby had yearned to be free; he knew better than anyone it was a chance an enslaved man would take.

Not a boat in sight. Jess oughta know the frequency of landings at this desolate place. "When's another boat coming?"

Jess chuckled. "Now how would I know that?" He pointed to a flagpole. "When I wanna call a boat in, why I run up the flag—ain't no flag up there now is there, mud boy?"

"Can you raise the flag?" Toby asked.

Jess raised an eyebrow. "Too late today, big'un. Ain't gonna land in the dark."

"Uh huh," Toby said. At least Jess had dropped "mud boy." But he wasn't getting anywhere. Jess's wariness was understandable—castaways with the flimsiest of explanations. But maybe he could be enticed. "These plantations. They pay well?"

Jess's expression screamed, "Don't mess with me, boy!" Finally, he answered, "It's steady work. 'Bout every other day, I'll hear boilers winding down, and I come to see what they bringing. Might be grain, flour, dress boxes, tools—could be anything. I take it up to the house."

"What do you make in a day?" Toby asked.

Jess shot a steely glare. "Why you asking?"

"I might have some business for you."

Jess scratched his chin. "I got a few men who work for me. Pay 'em fifty cents or mebbe a dollar a day, depending on the load. When we're moving cotton bales and bags of seed, why I can make eight dollars after paying all of 'em."

"How would you like to make twenty dollars?"

Jess straightened up. "What you say?"

Toby suppressed a chuckle at Jess's wide eyes. Finally. Hook, line, and sinker. "We need a place to dry out, something to eat, and a place to sleep. We need to board a boat going south tomorrow. Can you help us? We'll pay you twenty dollars."

"Reckon I can," Jess said.

"And as far as you know, we were never here."

Jess exhaled heavily, as if he were sizing up the risks. "I understand. Load up."

~ ~ ~

Stella climbed onto the bench beside Jess. Toby and John Dee sat in the wagon bed with the bags. She sat on an old blanket as Jess drove the wagon north, parallel to the river, past twisted buttonwood trunks and thickets of blooming calico. Buntings darted in and out of the branches of bald cypress trees. Woodpeckers knocked somewhere in the green canopy that was pierced by occasional sunbeams.

The mules' hooves thumped, occasionally splashing mud. They rode through heavy woods, with the wagon pushing through branches hanging over the narrow trail. Being cloaked in foliage gave Stella a sense of security she hadn't felt on the *Cedar Point*. A natural, nearly uninhabited world where the Burtons would never find her. She sat back, admiring the pretty red hibiscus flowers that dotted bushes along the trail.

A deer leapt across the trail, startling Stella. "Oh my!"

"Gonna come back and shoot that one," Jess said. "He'll feed my family for a month."

"There must be lots of animals here," she said.

"Oh, some bobcats and coyote, but the dogs keep 'em away. Course there's coons and rabbits and snakes and such. And there's turtles and frogs by the river—them's good eats."

Stella cringed at the thought of a turtle supper.

"We catch all the fish we can cook up. Cats. Perch. Bass."

"I see. There's no town around here, is there? How do you get other things you need?"

"Like what?" Jess asked.

"Dry goods. Clothing. Furniture," Stella said. "Things for a household."

"Boats stop here every day or two. Now and then there's a trading post."

"On a boat?"

"Yes, ma'am. Big ol' flatboats. The ones from the North most likely have timber, salt pork, osnaburg or wool, flour and mebbe cheese. From the South, lotta times its sugar or molasses or tobaccy, or mebbe some fine linens."

"And you just go shopping?"

"Trading boats stop to sell goods to Willow Bend and Tranquil Pines. Someone'll come down from the house and pick out things for the massa. After they're done, I'll buy what I want."

"That's handy."

"But, most off, we on our own." He grabbed his collar. "This shirt and these trousers—why, my Lettie girl done stitched 'em from osnaburg. We have a vegetable garden behind the cabin. Grow us maize and turn it into hominy. Also some greens, onion, and ta-may-tuh. Don't need much else."

Jess's gaze was on the trail. His shirt clung to his powerful shoulders. His skin was darker than Toby's, but they shared the same confident expression. Men with a mindset not be trifled with.

"You ever leave here?" Toby asked Jess.

"Not much." He glanced at Toby. "You know why, don't ya, big'un. We got's our freedom papers and all, but in town you gotta watch for those damned bounty hunters. They'd sure as hell sell us for slaves and pocket the money."

"Bounty hunters don't come round here?" Toby asked.

Jess laughed. "Ain't nobody come round these bottomlands—'cept the boats." He nodded toward a clearing. "We're getting close. There's five cabins up here. Five of us freed men and our families. Bounty hunter come up here, he ain't going home."

"Oh!" Stella said.

"What I mean, ma'am, is we keep an eye out for one another."

"That's good," Toby said.

"Why are the cabins a ways from the landing?" John Dee asked.

"We built 'em on the highest ground we could find. See, the bottomlands flood out every few springs." Jess straightened his felt hat. "But yer right, White man. We out here in the sticks. And the lady here's right, too. Once and a while, we'll need some things. Then, a couple of us catch a boat ride to Greenville. We visit the mercantile and get what we need real quick. Come right back. Ain't had no trouble yet."

The more Stella learned about Jess, the more curious she became. He lived with his family in the deep bush, like rabbits hiding from critters. Sheltered from events in the world. He rarely encountered people. Could his be a happy life?

The wagon emerged from a copse of trees, and Jess's cabin came into view. They passed a small peach orchard and a garden. Three barking hounds bounded alongside Jess.

"All right, all right," Jess said to the dogs, smiling.

Stella surveyed the structure, a simple log cabin with a pitched roof pierced by a stove pipe. A plank door centered the front wall, flanked by windows with opened hinged shutters. On its south side, a small extra room sprouted off the main structure, four feet above ground and supported by corner posts.

A few hundred yards beyond Jess's cabin stood another one. A Black man was in the garden, hands resting on top of his hoe. Jess waved at him, and he waved back and returned to work.

"That's ol' Jimmy," Jess said. "Making sure you all ain't no kinda trouble."

Stella nodded.

Two small children whacked at a ball with sticks. A bare-chested boy was in the lead, chased by a little girl in a calico wrapper.

"We played a game like that where I grew up," Stella said.

"Where's that, ma'am?" Jess asked.

"On the reservation. In Oklahoma."

"Uh huh," Jess said. "Kids'll chase balls in all parts now, won't they?"

Jess halted the mules in front of his cabin. A trim Black woman stood at the front door. She wore a striped cotton dress and a headscarf folded cornerwise and tied at her forehead. Her hands were on her hips. There was a strength about her much like Stella saw in Jess. "What's all this, Jessie-beau?"

"We got some business, Lettie girl," he said. "Come meet these folk."

Lettie approached the wagon and helped Stella down from the bench.

"Hello, ma'am. I'm Stella Parrot, and I'm pleased to meet you."

"Don't call me ma'am. I'm Lettie."

"Okay, Lettie." Stella made a polite smile.

Toby and John Dee hopped down from the wagon bed. They introduced themselves to Lettie.

Jess called his children over. He put his hand on his son's head. "This here's Ollie. And this one's Sadie."

"What a beauty you are," John Dee said, extending his hand to Sadie.

Sadie recoiled and hid behind her father's leg.

Jess laughed. "These children ain't never seen a White man or a squaw on this property." He glanced at Stella. "Yer a squaw, ain't you?" He didn't wait for her reply. "But they'll warm up to you." He sent Ollie and Sadie off to play.

Lettie slowly looked over her, and then John Dee and Toby. Suddenly conscious of wet clothes clinging to her body, Stella suspected alarm bells were going off in Lettie's mind.

"A White man. A squaw. A Black man. Been in the river, haven't ya? Hmmph. Just what in heaven's creation are you unlikely collection of folk doing out here in the bottomlands?" Lettie asked.

"Passing through," Toby said.

"You ain't bringing trouble, are you? We don't need none of that!"

"No, ma'am," Toby said. "We just need a place to stay before we catch our boat tomorrow. For a fair wage, of course."

"They paying well," Jess said to Lettie.

Lettie took a deep breath. "I s'pose I'll need to cook supper for these folk?"

"Yes, dear. I'll tend the mules while you do that." Jess led the mules across a clearing toward a grassy knoll. A small barn sat on the knoll, surrounded by a wooden fence. He stopped and motioned to Toby and John Dee to follow him. "Come on, then. You boys help me with my chores. I'll show you where you'll bed down."

Lettie's expression softened, and she took Stella's hand. "Come with me, girl. You can wash up, and I'll put you in one of my dresses. I'll start a fire, and we'll dry your clothes. And we'll get supper ready."

The warmth in Lettie's grip gave Stella confidence that they had stumbled into a fortunate stop. A night of respite in the company of good people. Far from the Burtons.

~ ~ ~

John Dee attacked Lettie's pork and biscuits like a starving man. He took a second scoop of hominy mixed with onions and turnips. Across the table, little Ollie's face hung over his plate, his spoon shoveling in food. Conversation halted as everyone dug in.

Something nudged him. One of the hounds nosed into the space between his deer-skin-wrapped chair and Toby's. The food's aroma was as heavenly as an angel's breath, so John Dee couldn't blame a dog for trying to get at it. Jess snapped his fingers, and the hound slunk back to lay with the other two in a subdued row.

"Lettie, ma'am," John Dee said, "Toby and I haven't eaten like this since we were back in Missouri. I sure do miss good farm cooking."

"I been hoping its passable," Lettie said. "Little early for maize and greens."

"More than passable, ma'am," Toby said.

John Dee marveled at Lettie's ability to put a two-dollar quality meal before them from her small stone hearth pierced by a rod for two hanging pots. A utilitarian kitchen indeed. Two more stand-up iron pots. A water bucket drawn from the outdoor pump. A coffee kettle. Lard and butter crocks. Rough-hewn slats of wood fashioned into a cupboard that stored cookware, plates, and cups.

They'd finished with hardly a scrap left for the dogs' supper. Jess excused Ollie and Sadie from the table.

When Lettie began to clear away, Stella got up and helped. Lettie hummed as she worked. Jess hummed along as he poured water into the wash basin. John Dee recognized the hymn, but he couldn't remember its name, which was no surprise since he hadn't been to Sunday service in many years.

Lettie held the last note of the first verse, and when she started to sing the chorus, Stella sang along:

"Nearer, my God, to Thee, nearer to Thee!"

Lettie paused, and Stella's voice resonated through the room—crystal clear. Lettie's eyes widened as she listened. Jess seemed as startled as his wife, and little Sadie jumped up and down with joyful appreciation. The second verse started, and Lettie resumed singing in her smoky alto while Stella harmonized in her natural soprano range.

"Though like the wanderer, the sun gone down,

Darkness be over me, my rest a stone;

Yet in my dreams I'd be nearer, my God, to thee...."

Stella's and Lettie's voices blended magnificently. They held hands at the head of the table, smiling as they sang. John Dee imagined them on stage on the *Lady J*, mesmerizing an adoring packed theater. When the chorus came round, Jess joined with his deep baritone, strumming along on a banjo. Once they'd completed five verses, they held the last note as John Dee, Toby, Ollie, and Sadie all clapped enthusiastically.

"My, my! That's my favorite hymn. Your voice is as pretty as any I've heard sing it," Lettie said.

"Thank you."

Stella didn't add that she was a professional singer, to John Dee's relief. No need to drop clues that could help the Burtons learn they had passed through.

"You a praying girl?" Lettie asked Stella.

"Used to be. I learned it in chapel."

"Well," Lettie said, "mebbe you'll find your savior again one day."

"I hope so," Stella said.

Ollie and Sadie joined their mother, and little Sadie pulled on Lettie's dress. "My turn!" they said in unison.

"All right, you two," Lettie said, "Let's sing 'Wade in the Water' for our guests. You, too, Jessie-beau." She cued them with a long "oh," and then she and Jess and the children sang:

"Wade in the Water,

Wade in the Water..."

Lettie sang the verses while Jess and the children hummed along. All four of their voices joined for the choruses. The tune's spare, almost haunting emotion flowed through John Dee like a soothing elixir. Stella's eyes were closed. Toby's head bobbed in time, his expression rapt.

The performance ended. John Dee felt a collective satisfaction that warmed the room. Lettie hugged her children. Then Jess encircled the three of them in his strong arms. Their tight, radiant bond was one John Dee had never known in his own family. Simple, uneducated people living in a hovel at the edge of the world. Material pleasures at a minimum. But love and happiness abounded among the four of them.

Stella beamed, even wearing Lettie's simple cotton dress without a dab of her stage makeup. She was just as radiant as Lettie and her family. One day, would she be the queen of a contented and loving family, just like Lettie? If she were, she wouldn't be a riverboat singer anymore. Instead, her family would be the audience, just as Jess's had been tonight.

"Thank you," Toby said. "That was special. I ain't heard it in a long while."

"Where'd you hear it? Back in Missour-a?" Jess asked.

"Yeah." Toby looked at John Dee. "In the slave quarters."

"Come on, children," Lettie said. "It's time for bed." Ollie and Sadie kissed their father and said their goodnights. Then Lettie shuffled them off to wash and change into bed clothes.

Jess spoke. "White man, you know why we sing those words?"

"Wade in the water?"

Jess nodded.

John Dee knew the message, but it somehow felt wrong for him to say it when Jess and Toby had lived it. He, Jess, Toby, and Stella sat in uncomfortable silence.

Finally, Jess took a deep breath. "When a slave runs from his massa, he oughta stay in the water as long as he can. The crick, the river. Don't leave no scent for the dogs or footprints for the slavers."

"You were a slave?" John Dee asked.

"Sure was," Jess said. "Lettie too, and Ollie. Sadie was born free."

"How'd you become a free man?" John Dee asked.

Jess rubbed his chin, as if he were pondering how much to tell a White man he'd just met. "Lettie and I were on a small plantation, an hour ride west of here. Only had ten or so slaves. It was jus' the massa and his wife—they didn't have no children. Massa dropped dead as a stone one day. His widow woman was awful sad. She stayed in her bedroom day after day. Finally, she sold the place and moved back east. 'Fore she left, she set every one of us free."

"God bless her," Toby said.

"She did God's work then," Jess said, "but her man weren't no saint. He cracked his whip too damn much. Hell, I could show ya the scars on my back to prove it." He paused. "Lettie got one, too. She dropped that man's wine glass one night, and he gave her a lash. That wife a his never stopped him once."

Jess's eyes narrowed. John Dee felt the burn of the man's frustration. That slave owner probably died before Jess got his vengeance. A score with a cold-hearted bastard left unsettled.

"You ever think of taking your family up north?" Toby asked Jess.

"We gots what we need here. Food and shelter. Why would I leave ol' Jimmy and the rest of our people?"

"In the North," Toby said, "you walk the street without seeing a slave hunter on every corner. Black children get schooling and learn to read." He paused. "Way upriver is a place called Minnesota. The U.S. of A. just took it in as a free state. Be a good place for a Black man to raise his family, I'd reckon."

John Dee caught Toby glancing at Stella as if she were his confidant. Had she stirred his passion for a life up north?

"Let me tell you something, big'un," Jess said. "When we was freed, we didn't get fed no more. The new massa worked our plantation with his own field hands. He wasn't gonna pay no free Black man a wage. He didn't let us eat with his people. Lettie and Ollie and me had nowhere to go, and we was starving." A tear rolled down his cheek. "Lettie lost our baby then."

Stella took Jess's hand. "I'm sorry."

Jess sniffed and seemed to compose himself. "I got real lucky to be at the riverbank one day when the massa of Willow Bend needed help. Since that day, going on eight years, I've had steady work." He waved his arm across the room. "I built this house for my family. I have food, crops, livestock. Truth is, running carts for the plantations been our deliverance. I sure as hell ain't gonna give it up to take Lettie and our children somewhere I ain't got no job!"

~ ~ ~

Toby sat back, soaking in Jess's words, and his world. A happy, loving place rooted in a spare, hardworking existence. One that was born out of the ashes of slavery. One that lived on the knife edge of White man's wages.

Would he ever come across a Black man's story on the lower river that was secure and promising?

"What's with the long faces?" Lettie asked, having returned from putting down the children.

"Oh," Jess said, "just been a long day is all."

"Stella, I'm gonna get some blankets," Lettie said. "You'll sleep in the river room."

"River room?"

Lettie pointed to stairs on the far wall that led to a small room. "That's where we sleep when the floods come. Jess keeps some barrels and such up there most ah the time. Jess! Clear a space for her now, would ya?"

"Yes, dear."

Toby followed Jess to take a look into the river room. Cramped, but a hell of a lot more comfortable than a bed of straw spread over mule muck on a barn floor.

"Not you!" Lettie said to him. "My Jess showed ya yer place in the barn, didn't he?"

"Well, Stella," John Dee said, "you sung yourself into a comfortable boudoir, didn't you?"

Everyone laughed.

Lettie got Stella settled in the river room. Everyone said their goodnights. Toby and John Dee headed for the barn with their blankets and clothes that had dried at the hearth.

Toby hung Jess's lantern over a barn beam. They made straw pallets and laid out their blankets. Hay bundles stacked against the wall put off a sweet and dusty smell. *Well, this might not be too bad.* Toby stretched out on his blanket and got a whiff of mule muck. "Christ!"

"Not so bad, is it, Toby? That is, if the mules don't snore too loud."

"We've slept in worst places," Toby said.

"That's for damn sure. It's been a good day. Got rid o' one o' the Burtons and made good money doing it. By the way—your head all right?"

"I'm fine," Toby said.

"Then we got outta sight of that nasty Cliff Burton for a while. Had a fine supper and met a real nice family. Good people. Put us up on their land."

"They's good people all right," Toby said, "but I doubt it's their land. Squatters, I 'spect."

"Maybe," John Dee said, "but at least they're free."

"They ain't free!"

"What do you mean? Jess said the widow freed them."

"Open your eyes, John Dee. They live in the woods. Hiding from the slavers. Jess still works for plantations. The massas decide to hire a different cart and his family ain't gonna eat. Besides, their children don't get no schooling. They don't have a church to go to. Truth is, they're out here living scared of the White man just like a slave."

"They're happy," John Dee said.

"Mebbe for now. They should go north. Cause on the lower river they're at the mercy of the White man. And so am I."

Toby felt John Dee's hand on his shoulder.

"But we ain't had no problems we can't handle," John Dee said.

So, he'd hit a nerve. Good a time as any to get some things straight. "We! That's right. I don't have any problems when I'm with you—cause you are a White man."

"You take care of me, too," John Dee said. "Like you did when Stevie jumped me."

"That's not what I'm talking about. Down here on the lower river, if you ain't around, how long would it be before a bounty hunter tried to chain me and sell me?"

"I'd bet on you if some fool tried that. Come on, Toby; I'll always be around."

"What if one of those suckers you best in a card room shoots you dead? What if you take up with some pretty woman?"

"Toby…"

Neither man spoke for minutes.

"We've always been together," John Dee said. "We're best together. Like brothers. Brothers stick together. There—I said it."

The words rang true with Toby as well. They'd never spoken of it, but their bond was as strong as that of any pair of brothers. Blood or not. Even so, tonight Jess's family had helped him see the lower river for what it was. The weight on his chest was racial prejudices on the lower river that shackled a free Black man. If he wanted that weight to lift, his path was becoming clear.

"I'm going up north, John Dee," Toby said. "And I'm hoping you'll come with me."

John Dee sighed. "I've gotta think on this."

Chapter 12

Toby left the shade of a giant water oak and stood on the riverbank. The hot sun was high in the sky. At least a gentle breeze tickled his cheek. He was sick and tired of waiting for Jess's flag to draw a boat. Damn paddle-wheeler traffic had been upriver, except for settler flatboats, barges, and one southbound mail packet that hadn't stopped.

Finally!

A big stern-wheeler veered toward the landing.

Toby nudged Jess with his boot. About an hour before Jess had slipped his hat over his face and napped 'cause he "might juz have to save my energy for a two-ton load."

The *Delta Ray* glided out of the main channel into the easy water, bow angled to the riverbank. Would she be a genteel showboat like the *Lady J* or a gambler-friendly hell craft like *Cedar Point*? He couldn't answer that, yet, but she was damn big. Her massive stacks rose considerably higher into the sky than the *Lady J*'s did. Decorative arches hung under her hurricane deck, and a white wooden railing wrapped the boiler deck.

A dozen or more passengers stood at the top rail as deckhands dropped the *Delta Ray*'s lines.

Christ! John Dee and Stella were in plain sight of everyone aboard! What if Cliff or Stevie were on the boat? Might as well paint a bull's eye on their foreheads. He blew out a deep breath. Cliff ain't there. He woulda put a bullet between John Dee's eyes by now.

A row of cotton bales stacked five high covered the main deck like a dirty wool curtain. So, she wasn't a pretty showboat like the *Lady J*. Must be a working cotton boat. Probably weighed down and low in the water. Gonna be a slow float downriver. Toby wondered idly how many Black men had toiled to load her.

Toby stood with Stella, John Dee, and Jess, waiting for the *Delta Ray*'s gangplank to drop. "Seems sturdy enough," Stella said. "But my word, it's loaded down with a lot of cotton. Is it safe?"

"It'll be fine." Stella's pose distracted Toby. Her hand was at her brow, shielding her eyes from the sun. The silver and blue brocade dress he and John Dee had bought her still looked new, hugging her alluringly lithe figure. Long black hair flowed from a delicate bonnet she'd salvaged. A portrait of beauty. Over her shoulder was the *Delta Ray*'s Texas deck. Up there, the pilot must be staring at her—an unlikely glamorous beacon at a sparse riverbank landing.

"Secure the lines!" was shouted from the boat. Deckhands scurried into action, bringing Toby's thoughts back to Stella's question.

"It's not the weight you gotta worry 'bout. Why, in the fall, after picking, bales'll be stacked on this boat a dozen high, all the way to the top deck. The boat'll float all right, but if the cotton catches fire, it'll go up in flames in no time. Seen it happen once; from two miles that cursed boat burned brighter than a falling star."

"Oh! You've just given me something else to worry about." Stella ran her hands through her black hair.

God, she's cute!

"But it's springtime. Why is there cotton on this boat?" Stella frowned. "Didn't the planters just plant their fields?"

"That's right," Toby said. "Some smart agent musta stashed cotton bales upriver over the winter. 'Bout now, some textile factory in England is running low. They'll pay top dollar for off-season bales."

"Do you and John Dee sell off-season cotton?"

Toby laughed. "It takes a helluva lot of money to pay for a crop and let it sit all winter. No, that's not how we do it."

"We're small operators, Stella," John Dee added. "We'd have to get real cozy with a St. Louis banker to borrow enough money to keep cotton over the winter. The bastard would squeeze us where it hurts if prices went bad or for some reason we couldn't get our load south."

Bow lines were cinched to a massive post and the *Delta Ray*'s long gangplank was dropped. A portly man wearing a blue jacket with a yellow stripe at the shoulder walked out to meet John Dee. To Toby, he didn't look old enough to be the captain, but he sure as hell was well-fed; his jacket barely contained his white shirt's hefty bulge over the belt.

"Sir," he said to John Dee, "I'm Robert Toppins, deck officer of the *Delta Ray*."

"John Dee Franklin."

"Business in New Orleans, sir?"

Of course, Toppins addressed John Dee. A White man at a plantation landing. Took him for a planter waiting on a boat with his wife and two slaves. Toby sucked in the sting of indignity for the greater good of their plan.

Toppins didn't wait for a response. "We've one cabin suite open, Mr. Franklin. It'll be seventy-five dollars for you and the missus from here to New Orleans."

Stella raised an eyebrow at Toppins's marital presumption but wisely refrained from correcting him.

Toppins hardly gave Toby a glance, no doubt taking him for a slave. Toby damn-near bared his teeth at the fat boy who was probably a helluva lot better at eating chicken fry than handling a paddle wheeler. *Get over it! Happens everywhere on the lower river.*

John Dee made a show of pausing and looking over the boat. "That will be fine. Have your man escort my wife and me to our room, please, Mister Toppins."

Toby suppressed a smirk. John Dee read the situation masterfully, as always, and played his part perfectly. The ruse was fine with Toby, though he would have preferred to pose as Stella's husband rather than as John Dee's manservant. But hell would freeze over before an interracial marriage was gonna fly.

"Certainly, sir." Toppins bowed at John Dee and stepped onto the gangplank to return to the boat. As an afterthought, he said, "Your darkies can find a place with the bales and seed bags on the main deck. Five dollars."

"Fine," John Dee said.

Toppins crossed back over the gangplank and disappeared inside the boat.

"I suppose you'll be comfortable Mister and Missus Franklin," Toby said to Stella and John Dee, tongue-in-cheek.

"Don't be bitter," John Dee said. "It's not a bad disguise for Stella and me to pose as a married couple."

"And me as your slave."

"It's just three days, Toby. Come now; in New Orleans, we'll let you the biggest suite we can find in the Quarter. Stocked with champagne and oysters!"

"I'll hold you to that," Toby said.

A deckhand took their bags and Stella's dress box. "I'm going to the room and rest for a while," she said.

"I'll escort you, my dear." John Dee turned to Toby. "I'll meet you on the hurricane deck in fifteen minutes."

Stella shook Jess's hand and whispered out of the deckhand's ear shot, "I'll never forget you and your family."

John Dee thanked Jess and handed him a twenty-dollar gold coin.

Jess's eyes got wide as saucers. Toby smiled at him, knowingly, since he'd already paid Jess his twenty-dollar fee. He'd even given him an additional twenty dollars in appreciation of a terrific evening. Now with John Dee's twenty, Jess had just collected more than his best weeks' worth of pay.

As John Dee and Stella stepped from the gangplank onto the *Delta Ray,* Toby felt a faint change in the dynamics among the three of them. Would the marriage ruse somehow make things different? Would it force closeness between Stella and John Dee that would create some distance between John Dee and himself?

Jess shook Toby's hand and drew him close. "You take care of yourself, now, big'un. That's a wicked river, you know."

"I know it is," Toby said. "I can be a little wicked, too." He patted Jess on the shoulder and let him go, already missing Jess's beautiful family and their simple ways.

~ ~ ~

John Dee and Toby stood at the rail on the hurricane deck, looking across the main channel to Mississippi. John Dee savored the warmth of the sun on his face. The gentle rolling of the big boat was soothing, as was the faint tat-tat-tat of the paddle wheels striking the river far below. Exhaust from the stacks billowed in the sky above them, giving the air a slight sulphury scent and affirming the *Delta Ray*'s progress south.

"Now this is an afternoon to remember," John Dee said. "Perfect weather. Hightailing out of harm's way. Our plan is working."

"Don't get cocky," Toby said.

"In fact," John Dee said, "good fortune calls for a drink. Want one?"

"Sounds real nice."

"Mint julep? Gin sling?"

"Whatever you'll have."

John Dee stopped a steward.

"Yes, sir?" asked a young Black man with mutton-chop sideburns. He wore a clean white shirt under a black jacket.

"Two gin slings, please," John Dee said.

The steward looked nervously at Toby.

"What's the trouble?" John Dee asked.

"Ah, sir, there's a law in Mississippi that prohibits givin' licker to negroes," the steward said.

"We ain't in Mississippi." John Dee pointed to the river. "We're in Arkansas water."

The young man didn't answer.

"Two," John Dee emphasized. "They're both for me."

The steward nodded and descended the stairs.

"Getting me a drink gonna bring trouble?" Toby asked.

His expression hadn't changed, as if the steward's hesitancy to serve a drink didn't bother him. Even so, John Dee loathed the prejudicial slights that his partner endured on the lower river. No doubt, Toby did as well. "They won't let you in the barroom, but no one said you can't stand with me on the hurricane deck. What's it to them if you have a drink? Don't worry; I'll handle it."

"You always do," Toby said.

When the steward returned with the drinks, John Dee paid for them and gave him an extra quarter.

The *Delta Ray* passed several massive logs floating a short ways off the bow. John Dee could see hemp lines dangling off a log. "Looks like all that's left of some poor ol' Kaintucks' river dream."

"Glad we didn't hit those damn things," Toby said.

Toby's remark was callous. If the logs were indeed a busted raft, dead bodies might be bouncing off the hull.

John Dee couldn't remember a trip on the Mississippi without settler rafts floating downriver. Arks, really, crowded with horses, cows, dogs, grandma and babies, and hanging clothes. Adventurers determined to homestead somewhere in the southern frontier or maybe put out at Red River landing and take a wagon to Texas. All of them oblivious to the big river's sandbars and snags, crowded stretches with too many big steamboats without brakes, storms, pirates and gintys, and unforgiving currents and river boils. Any of which could put an end to a family's dreams of a new life.

But Toby had a point: Raft logs could punch a hole in the *Delta Ray* and dump everyone aboard into the river.

They sipped their drinks while watching a small northbound packet pass. A bend to the east came into view a few miles ahead. A few minutes later, high overhead, a dozen or more turkey vultures were circling toward the Arkansas bank.

"Hope it's not your Kaintucks they've spotted," Toby said.

A vision of a family of drowned pilgrims unsettled John Dee. Lifeless, bloated bodies bobbing along the riverbank, now fodder for fish and birds. He took a big drink. "God, I hope not."

"Maybe these Kaintucks didn't make it," Toby said, "but a Kaintuck gots a better chance of a good life than I do in Arkansas or Lou-see-anna or Mississippi, or wherever we are."

"You're serious about going north?"

"Most definitely."

Toby's northern dreams had caught him off guard. They'd traveled the river together from New Orleans to St. Louis and back for years now. The two of them had known plenty of adventures and made some money, and they had certainly sowed their oats. They were still young men due for plenty more adventures on boats, in river taverns, and in the bawdy houses. John Dee had never given a thought to getting off the river. Could meeting Stella have sparked Toby's notion of settling down? Or maybe spending time with Jess and his happy family had opened Toby's eyes to the possibility of a home with a wife and children. Either way, he owed Toby a fair hearing.

John Dee couldn't argue that it would be difficult, if not impossible, for him to settle on the lower river. During their travels, as a Black man, Toby had been restricted; segregation laws prevented him from going into many of the places John Dee could. *Hell, he can't even get a drink on a boat on the lower river.*

Sometimes, it was just easier to let White folk think Toby was John Dee's slave, so that's what they'd done. They'd met some free Black men on their travels, mostly in Natchez and New Orleans. They hadn't been slaves, but like Jess, they treaded lightly around White men. Slave hunters, and the danger of being sold back into slavery, lurked everywhere in the southern states.

John Dee pulled two cigars and gave one to Toby. He looked around the top deck. Only a group of three men and another of two couples were in sight. Must be far fewer passengers on the *Delta Ray* than had been on the *Lady J* or even the *Cedar Point*. Less passengers and more cotton. He lit their smokes.

The more John Dee thought about it, Toby was right about Jess. He was a happy man and a free man—only to a point. Jess lived his life on the down low by avoiding any contact with White men that wasn't absolutely necessary. Toby didn't see that as a way to live, and John Dee understood.

"Minnesota? Is that what you said?"

"Yep."

"What do you know about business up there?"

"Nothing yet."

"Then I suppose we should go to Minnesota and have a look around."

"I suppose we should." Toby's slight smile satisfied John Dee that they'd bridged any gap between them.

"Listen," Toby said. "We're gonna be smart about it. We got good business on the lower river, and we ain't gonna give that up. But mebbe we can add to it."

"Makes sense to me," John Dee said. "There's not much business on the lower river when it's hot in August. Why don't we take a trip north then?"

"Fine."

They clinked their glasses in agreement.

John Dee leaned on the rail, lost in his thoughts. Just three days earlier, on the top rail of the *Lady J*, with Toby and Stella and Sam, Cliff Burton's face had been twisted with evil. As he'd screamed his threats, his determination to even the score for his brother's death had been unforgettable.

John Dee flicked his cigar into the river and finished his sling.

A pleasant afternoon with a cocktail in hand wasn't going to make Cliff and his threats go away.

"Toby."

"Yes?"

"Cliff's gonna learn what you did to Brick. He won't stop till he kills us—or we kill him."

"I know that," Toby said.

"So, we'll have to deal with Cliff and Stevie before we can get back to business."

"I s'pose we will," Toby said.

A lively conversation down the rail caught John Dee's attention. A short, gray-haired gentleman in a fashionable waistcoat gestured expressively to two equally well-dressed couples. Fashionable day dresses, paddle fans with painted designs, and rosy-gold brooches were out of place on a cotton boat. As were the men's tails and top-hats. They sure as hell weren't working the bales.

The older gentleman told the couples. "We'll do more hymns tonight. Why, do you know 'Out of the Wilderness'?" He sang in a dull tone: "'If you want to go to heaven—go in the wilderness—and wait upon the Lord.'"

John Dee set down his empty glass and said to Toby, "Give me a minute." He approached the group.

He hesitated. The three of them were supposed to keep their heads down to minimize any trail for Cliff and Stevie Burton to follow. An opportunity at odds with the plan had presented itself. He knew what Stella would say—keep to yourself! But Brick had gone south out of Helena, alone. Didn't that mean his brothers would have gone a different direction? North? Or east. Or west.

John Dee straightened his collar.

Sooner or later, the Burtons would be dealt with, and in the meantime, he and Toby had a business to run. Well-dressed gentlemen were rarely seen on cotton boats. Were these men wealthy planters? Or bankers? Yes, it was time to find out and do some business.

"Excuse me, kind folks." John Dee extended his hand to the gray-haired man. "I'm John Dee Franklin. I do believe you are the musical director of the *Delta Ray*'s most excellent variety theater?"

The man puffed out his chest and shook his hand. "I am indeed. Theodore Drinkweather. Mister Franklin, I would like to introduce you to Mister and Missus Broussard and Mister and Missus McCombs. Mister McCombs hired my troupe for this passage."

John Dee greeted the two couples. Ms. Broussard made a coy smile at him that he could have sworn screamed "I'm interested." A blond curl dangled below the brim of her hat. Her blue eyes stirred his soul. *Good gracious, not now, ma'am!* He glanced away, hoping that no one noticed.

"That's right, son," Mr. McCombs said. "Ain't got many passengers on my cotton boat, but we gotta be entertained in the evening, now don't we? Drinkwater here's doing all right, but he's gonna have his folks sing some more spirituals, won't ya now, Drinkwalker?"

"Yes, sir, we will. It's Drinkweather, sir."

"Oh, right. You'll come to the show tonight, won't you, Franklin?"

"Absolutely! My wife will be very interested to attend the performance," John Dee said. "As a professional courtesy, of course."

"Oh?" Mr. McCombs said. "And who is your wife?"

"Stella Parrot, most recently performing on the *Lady J.* Currently, she is between engagements."

Drinkweather lit up. "Ms. Parrot? Oh my! The singing soubrette! I read about her in the *Free Trader*." He clapped his hands and said to the Broussards and the McCombs, "She really is quite famous!" Then he said to John Dee, "I do hope she'll enjoy our show! The *Delta Ray*'s a working boat, so of course our show is not as grand as hers was on the *Lady J*, or the shows on the *Banjo* or *Chapman's Palace*."

"I'm sure she'll enjoy the evening all the same."

Drinkweather hesitated, then asked, "Do you think we could persuade her to join us for a number?"

John Dee smiled. "I suspect that can be arranged."

"Well, what a happy coincidence," Mr. Broussard said. Missus Broussard and I would be honored if you and your wife would join us and Mister and Missus Mc-Combs for dinner tonight before the show."

"We would love to." John Dee exchanged parting phrases with the couples and Mr. Drinkweather before returning to Toby and filling him in on the plans he'd made. He suppressed a whoop. These men were from the rich planter class with the deep pockets to fill his and Toby's coffers!

"Christ, John Dee! We all agreed to stay low on this boat. Why'd you have to go and do that?"

"Now, Toby. McCombs must be a wealthy planter. I think we'll get some business outta it."

"Once Stella sings, everyone will know her!" Toby's voice rose. "You shoulda at least asked Stella before you'd said she'd do it."

"She'll be delighted," John Dee said. "She gets to sing. A singer is only happy if she's singing, right? Who knows—maybe this Drinkweather fellow will hire her." His conviction waned as he finished speculating. Toby was right; Stella should have been allowed to decide for herself if she wanted to sing or, for that matter, join two pompously aristocratic Southern White couples for dinner. It dawned on John Dee that he had been seduced by the prospects of dinner conversation with two rich planters leading to business deals for him and Toby. And a little by Missus Broussard's wandering eye. His motives had been selfish, but the arrangements had been made, and he wasn't going to change them.

Toby had turned his attention to the river.

"What are you looking at?" John Dee asked.

"See that small packet? 'Bout half a mile upriver?"

"Yes."

"Something flashed on its top deck," Toby said.

"Like a muzzle flash? Someone shooting at us? I didn't hear a gunshot."

"Nah. More of a sun burst. Probably a looking glass."

"You're worried someone spotted us? Cliff or Stevie Burton?"

"Somebody just got a look at us," Toby said. "Hell, with all the boats on the river, it's a thousand to one it'd be Cliff and Stevie Burton. But I'm gonna be worried 'bout them Burtons till this all ends."

John Dee studied the two-deck stern wheeler Toby had pointed out. It maintained its gap, as if it were stalking the *Delta Ray.* He saw the flash Toby had described. Could Cliff and Stevie Burton have hired out the packet to search the riverboats making their way downriver? If so, they'd now spotted him and Toby. Could they have learned within twenty-four hours of the head-butt contest on the *Cedar Point* that Toby had crushed Brick's skull? *Unlikely, but for goddamned sure anything's possible on the lower river.*

"Me too," he said.

~ ~ ~

Stella held John Dee's elbow and took in the dining room's décor. A barrel-vaulted ceiling with painted beams featured floral carvings and arches. Three levels of gas lamps on a chandelier surely took a crew to light. They passed velvet padded chairs positioned down the sides of a long, rectangular, dark wood table.

Where were these wealthy White Southerners? People John Dee had described as "perhaps a little pompous" when he relayed their dinner invitation and Mr. Drinkweather's invitation to sing. She didn't want any part of either! John Dee had been insistent but, in the end, left it up to her. He could have shamed her into dinner and a song in appreciation of his and Toby's efforts to deliver her to safety. But he hadn't. Nevertheless, she felt a measure of duty and had agreed for that very reason.

She wore her new taffeta gown and a string of pearls John Dee had "borrowed." She hadn't pressed him further about their origin. It wasn't far-fetched to think the pearls had formerly been the property of the wife of one of his cardroom marks.

John Dee pointed to the front corner of the dining table where two empty seats were positioned between two well-dressed couples. Handsome men and pretty ladies much younger than she expected.

Stella's stomach roiled as the White ladies looked her over. Her attire was certainly less expensive than Mrs. Broussard and Mrs. McCombs's festooned silk skirts and bodices. Glaringly obvious precious stones hung from brooches at the tops of their bosoms. Both had blonde hair. They couldn't be much older than Stella. She had to concede they were the most attractive women in the room. Their husbands had distinguished, early middle-aged looks of men of authority. Full glasses of whisky were in front of them.

Following introductions, Mrs. McCombs raised her hand and called for a server. "Well. I say! These are the laziest house niggahs I ever did see. God made 'em to serve us, but evidently he forgot to tell these here." She laughed at her own joke, and after a short pause, her husband and the Broussards laughed, too.

"My dining room at Magnolia Grove runs better than this one," Mrs. McCombs said.

"Oh?" Mrs. Broussard inquired.

"You see, I got an ol' mammie named Tilley, and she runs my house girls tough as the devil. Why, they get outta line and Tilley tans their hides!" She made a satisfied smile. "Any that don't straighten up, why Tilley runs them off to work in the fields. We juz go buy ourselves another."

Stella's blood boiled. John Dee took her hand as if he knew this self-anointed delta queen had lit her fuse.

Mrs. McCombs turned to Stella. "Your skin tone my dear," she said, "is so—unusual. Tell me, are you Melungeon?"

Stella smiled sweetly, trying to keep herself from exploding in indignation at this rich White woman's entitlement to make any offensively inane observation that drifted into her mind. Mistaking a Cherokee for a half-blood Appalachian African? In her entire life had Mrs. McCombs been in the same room with one of either? *How do I get out of here? I can't possibly endure dinner with these extremely racist, privileged Southern aristocratic bastards!*

John Dee squeezed her hand, clearly urging restraint so he could handle the reply. She looked up at him, and his expression seemed to beg forgiveness. Even he, as a White man, recognized that spending time with these bigots was insufferable. How had she come to know him so well so quickly?

"My heavens no!" John Dee raised his eyebrows in indignation. "My exotically beautiful wife is from the House of Bourbon!"

Stella almost chuckled at John Dee's theatrical pose, jawline jutted out and head held high.

"You mean—the King of Spain?" Mr. Broussard asked.

"Daughter of Maria and Ferdinand. Sister to Queen Isabella and sister-in-law to King Francisco himself," John Dee said.

"Ahh see," Mr. McCombs said. "You don't talk like no Spaniard."

"I was raised on a large ranch in Missouri," John Dee said. "I had the good fortune to meet my wife on my trip to Madrid to pick out my Andalusians."

"That a horse?" Mr. McCombs asked.

"Not only a horse—the finest stock the world over."

"Hmm." Mr. McCombs looked at his wife. "I'll have to look into some ah them. Go on, sir."

"I had audience with Queen Isabella and bought several from the royal stable. Stella happened to be there." John Dee leaned slightly toward Mr. Broussard, as if drawing him into his confidence. "She and the Queen are close in age and were always together growing up."

The Broussards and McCombs all stared at Stella. She raised her chin in a regal pose, while wondering if they could be so gullible as to believe John Dee. Mrs.

McComb's mouth was open in a dumb expression, and Stella could almost see her mind calculating how a royal connection could elevate her own social standing.

Stella didn't know anything about Spain's royal court. All she could do was play along with John Dee's charade and hope he didn't make fools of them. Maybe these racist White cotton planters wouldn't be able to distinguish a Cherokee woman's accent or appearance from that of Spanish royalty.

"Mister Drinkweather showed me the piece about the singing soubrette from the *Free Trader*," Mr. Broussard said. "It didn't say a word about royal blood."

John Dee looked in both directions, as if to confirm their conversation had remained private, and spoke softly. "We don't tell just anyone that my wife is from the House of Bourbon. Kidnappers and fortune seekers make it too dangerous to use her real identity. And for that reason, she rarely wears her best jewelry. But you fine people understand the precautions those of us of…a certain social class and wealth…must take in these times."

Mr. Broussard leaned back in his chair, suitably plumed. "Ahh see. Stella Parrot. Her stage name—it's an alias, isn't it?"

"Very astute, Mister Broussard," John Dee said. "Can we count on you fine people to keep my wife's identity in strict confidence?"

The four of them nodded enthusiastically.

"Well then," Mr. McCombs said, "let's raise a glass to cordial relations between the Kingdom of Spain and the great states of Lou-see-anna and Miss-a-sip-ee."

Six glasses clinked.

"Princess, err, Miss Parrot," Mrs. McCombs said, "our plantation is just south of Natchez. Please consider stopping to visit us on one of your tours." Her face lit up in a big smile. "And do bring your cousin, the Queen of Spain, when she comes over! You can tell her the main house is quite grand. We have very comfortable and spacious accommodations for her and her servants, the most beautiful gardens north of New Orleans, and plenty o' housemaids to take care of her every need."

"Thank you for your kind invitation. I'll share it with dear Isabella in my next letter," Stella said in a bad Latin accent, nearly choking on her words. Mrs. McCombs leaned against the back of her chair with a buffoonishly idyllic expression as if she'd already topped the *Free Trader*'s social column.

A steward approached and placed Henry Alcock fine china plates at each setting. A second steward set a tiered silver tray with gherkins, pecans, English walnuts, and olives in the center of the table. Mr. Broussard pointed to his and Mr. McComb's empty glasses and said to the steward, "More whiskey, boy."

"Spanish olives," Mr. Broussard said to Stella. "They musta knew you was coming."

Stella laughed. If John Dee could play along, she could too.

"Will you join another boat's show in New Orleans?" Mrs. Broussard asked.

"Yes. My husband is negotiating with several talent directors to secure my next tour." Her mind raced to her next musical challenge: an ad hoc appearance on the *Delta Ray's* stage based on John Dee's serendipitous encounter with Mr. Drinkweather. She couldn't disagree with John Dee that some good might come from it. The *Delta Ray* was a nice professional credit, at the least, and who knew, perhaps it could turn into a paying engagement? But it wasn't as easy to perform as he supposed! First, one of her numbers had to be in the repertoire of the company's pianist. Fortunately, when she'd met the cast earlier, the piano player's version of "Goodbye, My Lover, Goodbye" was competent. And singing without a proper voice warm-up courted disaster. A few simple two octave pitch glides after dinner would have to do.

"Do you always accompany your wife?" Mrs. Broussard asked.

"As much as I can, ma'am," John Dee said. "Sometimes we must part when business obligations require my presence."

"Oh," Mr. McCombs said. "What business you in, Mistah Franklin?"

"I own a shipping company."

This time, Stella squeezed John Dee's hand in a cautionary signal. His charade was starting to roll downhill like an out-of-control boulder.

Mr. McCombs chuckled. "I done cut you out this trip, Franklin."

"How so?"

"All that cotton piled up on the main deck—why that's mine. Bought a plantation up north ah Rosedale and kept last year's crop till now. Gonna make a fortune selling it off-season in New Orleans. Them Englishmen'll be suckers for it." Mr. McCombs nodded his head up and down as if to acknowledge his own commercial genius. "Negotiated shipping with the captain hisself. Ya see, I hired out his boat! Cut out the middleman."

Mr. Broussard raised his glass to Mr. McCombs. "Here's to a helluva piece of business!"

They toasted.

"Maybe in the fall you can help me ship this year's crop, Franklin," Mr. McCombs said. "I grow too damn much cotton to take care of all the shipping myself."

"We would be honored to assist you," John Dee said.

"You outta New Orleans?" Mr. McCombs asked John Dee.

"Quite a lot of my business is in New Orleans," John Dee said. "We have business up to St. Louis. This summer I'll have a look at the northern port cities."

"Why in tarnation would you do that? Must cost a fortune for a man to do business up there. They're coming in as free states, and ya gotta pay through the nose up north for darky labor! Damned idiots are under the yoke of that crazy fool Horace Greeley. Sum-bitch thinks every damn rube down to the lowest darky is equal with everybody else. No cotton-picking respect for the property owner and man of industry! Least the court had the sense to stop some of the tomfoolery with the Dred Scott case." Spittle clung to Mr. McCombs's lower lip as he finished his rant. He turned to Stella. "Spain's a monarchy. They sure as hell don't think like Horace goddamned Greeley back home, do they, Princess?"

Stella batted her eyes but didn't say anything.

"Well, I haven't been upriver past Burlington," John Dee said. "Think it's time to see for myself."

"Where the hell is that?" Mr. McCombs asked.

"Iowa," John Dee said.

Mr. McCombs clenched his jaw and said with a snarl, "Remember this. We don't need no goddamned Northerners on the lower river. Them crazy northern bastards want to change our Southern way of life. We won't have it! They keep coming down and trying to order us around, and we're gonna be through with the U.S. of A. lickety-split." He stared at John Dee. "Time to pick sides is coming, Franklin. You gonna have to decide if you're with us. Or them."

Chapter 13

BACKSTAGE AGAIN!

Stella dodged a wide-eyed female dancer in a silly pink tutu and a young man wearing overalls who shook with nervous tics. She pulled back the velvet curtain and luxuriated in its fluffy texture. A floppy-hat-wearing clown shimmied across the stage, drawing laughs. Oil-burning stage lamps put off a pleasing rustic smell. Her stomach churned, same as always before she took the stage and hit her first note. God, she missed everything about her role on the *Lady J.*

Her last night on the *Lady J* seemed an eternity ago. What changes had Mr. Jenkins made? Did he put young Mary in her numbers? Yeah, Mary had a stage presence, but her vocal range couldn't handle "The Blue Alsatian Mountains." Did Mr. Jenkins switch songs to fit her? Mr. Jenkins—God, she'd left him high and dry, mid tour, no doubt burning bridges with him forever. Her chest felt a crushing weight at the thought of having to restart her singing career without his help.

Could her showbusiness rebirth possibly happen here, in a small auditorium with plywood prop boards, wooden folding chairs for audience seating, and a fiddler with a silly white hat who looked like a misplaced sea captain?

Put all that aside! So, *Delta Ray*'s stage is smaller and its cadre of performers and musicians sparse compared to the *Lady J*'s. *Who cares? It's time to sing again!*

Stella peeked around the curtain. Less than half the crowd of the *Lady J.* She spotted John Dee in the second row, center stage, next to Mrs. Broussard. So, he was carrying on their charade right through her performance. Mr. Broussard sat on the other side of his wife, and the McCombs in the next seats over.

Toby sat in the last row, with other Black people. Brothers or not, once again skin color separated him and John Dee. She hadn't seen Toby since they had boarded. Playing married to a White man gave her privileges to a lovely cabin and fancy dinner that Toby didn't have.

Mr. Drinkweather tapped her shoulder. "You're on after the next number. I'll introduce you and then just come on stage."

"I will. Thank you," Stella said.

"Remind me, what is your song?"

"'Goodbye, My Lover, Goodbye,'" Stella said.

"Hmm. Isn't there something more up tempo you could do?"

She stiffened. Was this small-show director questioning her musical judgment? "Your pianist Phillip and I reviewed his repertoire this afternoon. I've picked the number he plays with a tone and rhythm that will best back my soprano."

"Very well." Mr. Drinkweather put his palms together under his chin, as if he were praying. "Your decision. You're the singing soubrette, after all."

Stella nodded in a dismissive fashion and peeked around the curtains again. A lively young man moved confidently across the stage, belting out Stephen Foster's popular tune in a strong tenor. "Camptown ladies sing this song, Doo-dah! Doo-dah!" Tattered clothes and cheeks smudged with grime. A perfect vagabond character. "Camptown racetrack five miles long, Oh doo-dah day!" He displayed his smashed hat to the audience. "I come down here with my hat caved in, Doo-dah, doo-dah!" He twirled and turned his empty pockets inside out. "I go back home with a pocketful of tin, Oh doo-dah day!"

The audience clapped along as he sang and danced. Except for Stella's dinner partners. The cotton planters were slumped over, heads bobbing. Hardly a surprise after their prodigious dinner-table whiskey consumption.

Stella caught a glimpse of Mrs. Broussard leaning into John Dee's shoulder. The planter's wife whispered into his ear, and he smiled at her. She took his arm and drew him to her. An amorous display Stella would expect from young lovers, not casual acquaintances who had met only hours earlier. Was John Dee making plans to sneak off with this blonde vixen while her husband slept it off?

Stella's face flushed. She and John Dee weren't really married—or even romantically involved—so she had no right to stop his pursuits of another woman. His consorting with Mrs. Broussard shouldn't aggrieve her, but it was a punch to her stomach. The faux adultery involved betrayed Mr. Broussard, not her. Still, John Dee pursuing a dalliance with Mrs. Broussard, a married woman, was a stain on his character and Stella's, as his make-believe wife.

It hurt.

John Dee hadn't shown romantic interest in her. She squinted at the planter's wife seated next to him. Was Mrs. Broussard more attractive to him? An entitled, racist woman with blond curls and a full bosom! Were John Dee's amorous tastes so shallow? Had she misjudged him?

John Dee laughed at something Mrs. Broussard said. His attention turned back to the vagabond act. Was she reading more into this than either of them intended? John Dee was a handsome young man who undoubtedly had his sexual yearnings. Stella wasn't naïve; he and Toby traveled the wicked river, and they had surely had liaisons. After all, they answered to no one but themselves. A fling now and then was one thing, but taking up with a married woman like Mrs. Broussard was a reckless provocation that could lead to violent conflict with her husband. Especially a self-aggrandizing Southern planter like Mr. Broussard.

Maybe Stella would never understand John Dee. She didn't feel the magnet of sexual attraction to another person like John Dee apparently could. Oh, she dealt with admirers now and then. Some men complimented her on her singing. Others on her beauty. And they asked to spend time with her. She never accepted. She hadn't let a man touch her in that way since Mr. Bickler had killed the part of her that could have romantic feelings.

Someone touched her arm. "Ma'am!" A young woman pointed to the stage.

The curtains opened and Mr. Drinkweather said, "And now our special guest. The singing soubrette!" He extended his arm toward Stella. The audience clapped enthusiastically.

Oh God! My cue! She blinked twice and smiled. Showtime! Forget everything else.

Stella waved to Mr. Drinkweather and took the stage. She flashed a wide smile to all corners of the audience. Then she nodded at Phillip. He hit the keys, and the opening unfolded with the rhythmic feel and slow-burning mood she had envisioned, though a quarter beat too fast. She'd just have to adjust.

At least Phillip's minor key was perfect for her mournful rendition. She gathered her breath as his introduction waned into her opening. "Goodbye, my lover, goodbye; I'm going away to leave you."

As his playing filled the bridge, she glanced up. Mrs. Broussard was leaning into John Dee again. Her right arm was across her body, into his lap—*My God! Was she*—

Phillip's awkward repetition of the final bridge chords snapped her back to the song. She nodded slightly as if to apologize for her lapse and to confirm she was ready to sing again.

"I'm sorry for to tell; Love I can't stay here by myself." The words fit her feelings perfectly. John Dee crossed a line she couldn't quite define; she just knew that his conduct hurt her. She savored the rest of the verses, telling him off through the sorrowful, relationship-ending message of the song, and held onto the final note with a sense of satisfaction.

Everyone stood and applause filled the room. Her audience had absorbed her passion, a measure of acceptance that she coveted. Mrs. Broussard and Mrs. Mc-Combs even roused their drunken husbands for the ovation. John Dee and Mrs. Broussard were suitably spaced, now, but Stella was on to their carnal conspiracy.

She took her bows, acknowledged Phillip, and retreated behind the curtain.

Mr. Drinkweather and the vagabond player greeted her.

"You were sensational," Mr. Drinkweather said. "The audience wants an encore. Can you give them one?"

"Oh, no. I haven't prepared a second number," Stella said.

"Well, I understand. I'll wrap it up," Mr. Drinkweather said. "Would you consider performing a few songs as part of our show on our last two nights before the *Delta Ray* lands in New Orleans?"

Stella hesitated. "I...."

"I can offer payment terms," Mr. Drinkweather said.

The notion of contributing, even slightly, to the funding of her travels with John Dee and Toby appealed to her. Sooner or later, she must find her own way, and that required financial resources.

"Miss Parrot," the young man said, "I'm Ned Halston. It was truly captivating watching you perform. I'm certain I speak for all the cast—we would be delighted if you would join us for these last shows!" A stagehand and a young woman singer, standing behind Ned, nodded in agreement.

Acceptance by her musical peers struck an arrow of joy into Stella's heart. She shook Ned's hand, as well as the hands of the two behind him. "I'd like nothing more."

~ ~ ~

Where was Stella? John Dee took a last look on the main deck and ascended the stairs. He ticked through the places he'd searched. Backstage. Their cabin. He'd inquired at the ladies' lounge. No Stella. He didn't want to wait another second to hear how Mr. Drinkweather and the cast had received her singing.

A gentle breeze tickled his cheek. Stars dotted the sky. He strolled the hurricane deck and found the *Delta Ray* was tied up for the night at a dark, desolate place that reminded him of the landing where he, Toby, and Stella had met Jess. Moonlight illuminated cypress tree branches dangling over the riverbank. He swatted a bug away and lit a cigar. He puffed a smoke ring into the peacefulness of late evening air.

He noticed a solitary figure on the opposite rail.

"Stella! I never expected to see you alone in the dark again after that night on the *Lady J.*"

"Oh. I didn't even think about it. I need to be alone."

He found her reply strange, but he set it aside. "I've been looking everywhere for you."

"Have you now?"

Nothing was making sense. "Perk up, Stella! The audience loved your singing! Well done! What did Mister Drinkweather say?"

"He and the cast were very kind," she said, tersely.

"Will you sing with the troupe again?"

"Mister Drinkweather invited me to join the show for a couple of numbers the next two nights before we arrive in New Orleans."

"Fabulous!"

"Where's Toby?"

"He told me he was turning in for a good night of sleep," John Dee said.

Stella gazed toward the far shore, almost mournfully. Where was the excitement after her night's triumph?

"Why the long face?" John Dee asked.

"I didn't expect to see you tonight," Stella said, ignoring his concern.

"Whyever not?"

"From where I stood on the stage, you and Missus Broussard made your intentions quite clear."

"What does that mean?"

"The woman groped you during my song! Her dead drunk husband had passed out. You two were cuddling with every intention of stealing away together, weren't you?"

"Stella! First off, whatever she was groping wasn't me. You're right. Her husband was drunk. McCombs was, too. After the show, I helped the ladies get the men to their cabins."

"Our marriage on this boat is a charade, but if I noticed you and that woman saying sweet things to each other, someone else did, too. You made a fool out of me."

He puffed his cigar. "I don't deny Mrs. Broussard is attractive. And yes, she showed me some flattering attention. I was polite—maybe we flirted the littlest bit—but I did not return her attentions."

"The littlest bit! You practically let that woman crawl into your lap!"

John Dee laughed. "Touché. Okay, her charms worked their magic on me. But I gathered my resolve! Listen—married women are strictly off limits!"

"Is that so? It didn't seem as if Missus Broussard was at all off limits to you."

"Married women violate my Bitty Brownlee rule," John Dee said.

"What in heaven's name are you talking about?"

John Dee puffed on his cigar. "When Toby and I started in business, a card player named Bitty Brownlee traveled the lower river. Bitty was a small man. Slicked-back black hair and a twinkle in his eyes that women found desirable."

Stella crossed her arms. "Go on."

"One trip south, a dentist spent long evenings in the card room, joining games and drinking whiskey. Bitty disappeared each evening for an hour or so. Now, that was unusual for Bitty; he rarely left the card room. One night, I'd had tough luck and went to my cabin for more funds when I saw Bitty leaving another cabin. He was whispering sweet things to a little lady with a head full of black curls. She saw me and shut the door. I said to Bitty, 'I didn't mean to disturb you and the missus.' Bitty just laughed. 'Missus? She's a missus all right, but not mine.' He leaned toward me and whispered: 'That one's as fine a model of female flesh as God put on this earth.'"

"Good heavens. I see where this is going," Stella said.

"Now, I didn't play in Bitty's card games," John Dee said. "He was the best cheat I ever saw; I never could figure out his tricks. Anyway, on the fourth night on the river, Bitty cleaned out the dentist. Got all his money and his pocket watch, too."

John Dee puffed again.

"An hour later, the dentist came into the card room, following that pretty little lady with the black curls. 'You!'

she screamed at Bitty. 'You've taken all our money.' She grabbed Bitty's collar and pulled him to her, face to face. 'How dare you do this to me?' The dentist wasn't stupid; he picked up on the implication that his wife and Bitty were familiar. He stepped up and looked at his wife, then at Bitty, and back at his wife. The lady looked at the dentist in a way that must have confirmed his suspicions without saying a word. The dentist pulled a Derringer from his vest and shot Bitty right through his heart."

"How awful!" Stella said.

"Taught me never to dally with a married woman," John Dee said.

"What happened to the dentist?"

"Don't know for sure. They gave him to the law in some little river town. Might have been Greenville. I imagine they hanged him."

They settled into a comfortable silence. Waves lapped at the *Delta Ray*'s waterline. Had Stella got over Ms. Broussard? Had she forgiven him?

"If I am mistaken in my suspicions, I apologize," Stella said.

"None needed."

"It seemed strange to me. The way you showed romantic interest in Missus Broussard. Or 'flirted' as you say."

"Why?"

"Well, it seemed out of character for you. For instance, you haven't shown any interest in me."

"Oh, Stella." Was she jealous of his few flirtatious moments with Mrs. Broussard? John Dee hadn't an inkling she was attracted to him, even before their faux marriage.

But he'd intended to keep things on a platonic level. They were in a damn serious predicament, running from the Burton brothers for their lives. It would be best for him and Toby to keep reassuring Stella she was safe and keep her focused on their plan to get to New Orleans. He and Toby were surely of the same mind on this.

Now, had circumstances been different, would Stella be a target of his affections? Of course. Her dark features and almond eyes were night and day different than those of the buxom blonde Mrs. Broussard. But Stella was every bit as beautiful as the planter's wife.

Was she insecure about her looks? She was a performer, the star of the show, and a star had to believe she was beautiful to be at her best, didn't she? Easy enough to placate.

"I had to hold myself back," John Dee said.

"Oh?"

"We're in a damn tough spot here. Didn't want to overcomplicate things."

"Okay."

"And once you told Toby and me what happened to you in St. Louis—"

"I appreciate your consideration," Stella said.

John Dee took her hand. "But if my wife needs me to tell her how beautiful she is—"

Stella laughed. "Don't get frisky, husband."

They leaned over the rail. A gorgeous crescent moon cast a white shimmer across the water surface.

John Dee gently clasped her shoulders and turned her toward him. He pushed a dangling ringlet of black hair behind her ear. With the backs of his fingers, he gently caressed her cheek. He whispered, "You're the most beautiful woman on this boat. And the last boat. And the boat before that."

He looked into her eyes. Passion hung in the air; he felt it. His heart told him to kiss her. He leaned slightly to her. She didn't back away, but she didn't move to meet him. He waited; time stood still with their lips inches apart. He reluctantly told himself it had to be her decision. His heart pounded as he waited for her lips to touch his. But they didn't. Finally, the moment melted away, and he took her hand. He kissed the back of it and said, "Let's get some sleep, my dear."

John Dee led Stella, hand in hand, down the stairs to their cabin.

~ ~ ~

"I'll wait in the hall while you change into your nightclothes and tuck yourself in," John Dee said. "Then I'll take a place on the floor."

Stella scarcely heard him. His gentle touch had awakened something wonderful in her—something she had never felt before. Her heart beat as fast as a hummingbird's wings. She nearly couldn't breathe.

"Oh, oh, yes." When she opened the cabin door, he let her hand go, giving her a sense of loss. "I'll be just a minute."

Her dress was a little tricky to unclasp without assistance, but she managed. She took off her undergarments, folded everything, and put on her nightclothes. The last time she'd put on nightclothes in anticipation of a man visiting her bedchamber was St. Louis. For Mr. Bickler. The thought chilled her. *Quit thinking of that old bastard. John Dee, not Mr. Bickler, is at the door, and he's a good man.*

She took the comforter and one of the pillows and put them on the floor for him. She pulled the covers back. Then she climbed into the bed.

John Dee knocked on the door.

"Come in," Stella said.

"Turn away," John Dee said.

Stella rolled onto her side and stared at the far wall. She heard John Dee take off his boots and the jangle of his belt buckle. She couldn't restrain herself and peeked as he took off his shirt. The bare skin of his muscular back and shoulders faced her. His torso was twice the size of Mr. Bickler's pear-shaped old body. His waistline was surprisingly trim.

She caught a glimpse of his money belt. It was six inches wide and plump. No wonder his waist looked thinner when he was shirtless.

She turned back to the wall, feeling the excitement of his touch all over again. Did other women feel what she was feeling? It was as if a door had opened to something wonderful on the other side. To be held in his powerful arms would be heavenly. Why hadn't he kissed her when they stood at the top rail? If he had, she felt certain they would be coupling right now. Undoubtably, with a passion that she had never felt in St. Louis.

John Dee lay down on the floor. The floorboards creaked as he adjusted himself. She heard him sigh; she felt her own heartbeat. More creaking. He rolled over frequently, likely no closer to falling asleep than she was.

Stella still sensed a warmth on her cheek where his fingers had been. No man's touch had affected her like his. John Dee had shown her so much more could be felt between lovers than she had ever dreamed. Something that was nothing like the intercourse she had endured. Maybe something beautiful.

He groaned. The wooden floor couldn't be comfortable for a large man.

"John Dee," she said.

"Yes?"

"Come up here."

He seemed to hesitate; then the floorboards moaned as he rose. She scooched to the other side of the bed and raised the blanket. He lay next to her, and their faces were inches apart, as they had been a short time ago at the rail.

"Kiss me," Stella said.

He brought his lips to hers and they kissed, slowly and tenderly. His hand was on her shoulders, and then he lovingly caressed her arm. He intertwined his fingers with hers. Passion soared in her, and she put her hand on the back of his head and pulled him to her, kissing him hungrily.

His night shirt was pressed to hers, her breasts to his chest. She raised his shirt, and he raised hers.

A violent pounding on the door froze them.

"Fire!"

Chapter 14

Toby put his shoulder into the door and smashed it open to find John Dee and Stella tangled into a single form under the blanket. A mound of human flesh joined for only one possible purpose.

"Toby!" Stella shouted, pulling the blanket to her neck.

A hazy cloud of shock stopped Toby in the threshold, his body tense like iron, his mind a spinning wheel of emotions. Anger? Jealousy? Betrayal? No time to sort it out.

"Boat's on fire! We gotta go. Now!"

"Your timing's impeccable, partner," John Dee said.

For the first time in a long time, Toby wanted to slap the silly humor out of his friend.

"Give us a minute to get dressed," John Dee said.

"No! Now! Them cotton bales are burning at the stern. Back of the boat's already a funeral pyre!"

"What the hell happened?" John Dee asked as he sat up.

"Don't know. Somebody cut us loose and fired that cotton. Boat's drifting to the main channel."

"Was it Burton?"

Smoke wafted into the cabin. Toby's body tremored like never before. Was there still an escape route? "Move! Flames are gonna ignite the wood stack, and then the boat'll break apart. We gotta get to the bow and jump. Or we're gonna die!"

John Dee and Stella put on their nightshirts. John Dee got out of bed and went for his clothes. "For Christ's sake, what time is it?"

"I dunno," Toby said. He pulled John Dee's arm off his clothes. "Forget yer god-damned clothes! Ain't no time!"

John Dee's eyes lit up like he'd been attacked.

"Just grab yer money belt. I got the bag full a cash."

John Dee nodded. He took Stella's hand and helped her out of bed. "Let's go."

"I can't possibly like this! Let me change clothes."

"No time. Here!" Toby threw a dress and undergarments at her. "We gotta move. Now!" He pulled Stella, still in her nightclothes, into the hallway with her clutching the items he'd thrown her. John Dee followed, in his nightshirt, and the three of them started down the hallway toward the bow.

"Boy!" A White man in a silk robe with disheveled hair stood at his cabin's door. "Niggah-boy! Get me the captain!"

Toby ignored him.

"McCombs!" John Dee said. "Get your wife and get to the bow. Boat's burning fast. Stay here and you'll die."

"That's my goddamned cotton!" Mr. McCombs said. "Every last bale. I'll be ruined! Captain's gotta put this goddamned fire out!"

McCombs went toward the stern where the fire was. "I'll get his ass working…."

"Let's go!" Toby pushed toward the bow, dragging Stella along. John Dee kept up.

Panicked passengers and boat workers scurried everywhere. They clogged the deck at the main stairwell. White men, Black men, women, and children jostled each other to climb the stairs. Smoke wafted over them.

Toby's path was blocked. *Shit! Gotta get to the bow!* He wedged through two men in night clothes, pulling Stella with him.

"We should follow them!" Stella shouted.

"Hell no," Toby said. "They're trying to get away from the flames. Cotton bales on the main deck's burning fast! The boat's going down, and they're gonna have to jump. It's too big a drop from up top. The fall might kill 'em."

A horrifyingly loud crack silenced everyone.

Toby froze as if his boots were nailed to the deck. Stella's eyes were wide as saucers.

Screams filled the air.

"*Delta Ray*'s gonna break up!" Toby shouted. "Come on!"

He, Stella, and John Dee dashed through the ladies' lounge and the dining room. Evening service had been cleared away, and the long table and chairs covered with clean linens. Absurdly neat and orderly, given all of it would soon be sunk in mud at the bottom of the river.

A server in her white apron and a cook stood at the door, both frozen in place.

"Save yerself!" Toby shouted.

"What should we do?" the woman asked.

"Jump in the water," John Dee said to her. "This boat's gonna sink."

"But I can't swim!"

"Find something that'll float and hang on," Toby said. "Come on!" He picked up the pace, almost dragging Stella along to the front of the boat.

They reached the forward stairwell and descended to water level. Five-foot-high cotton bales weighing five hundred pounds each were tightly wedged between support posts in a ring all the way around the bow of the boat.

Smoke was thicker now. Toby coughed. His eyes burned. Screams were constant, coming from somewhere in the smoky haze behind them.

Toby pushed a bale, but it didn't move. "Come on, John Dee. We gotta push three of these into the river. We'll ride 'em till a boat comes."

"You sure they float?" Stella asked.

"Yep. *Violet's* boilers blew on the Arkansas," Toby said. "Knew a deckhand who jumped on a bale and got rescued."

"It's our best shot," John Dee said.

Toby and John Dee rocked one back and forth, nudging it inch by inch toward the river. Finally, the bale's weight shifted and it made a giant splash.

Toby pulled Stella to the rail. "Jump. Get on that bale 'fore it gets too far away."

She looked at him with a hopelessness he'd never forget.

"We'll find you." He kissed her on the cheek. "I promise."

She jumped into the river.

Toby and John Dee worked two more bales free and pushed them into the river.

"Go!" Toby shouted at John Dee.

John Dee shook Toby's hand and grinned. "See you on the rescue boat—or in hell!" He jumped in.

Toby couldn't see Stella. John Dee swam on the firelit river surface toward one of the bales. Other passengers were in the river, struggling to stay above its surface. A woman clung to a big piece of wood, holding a child with her other arm, screaming for help. But there was no help. Then mother and child were gone.

Toby located the third bale, took a deep breath, and jumped toward it.

~ ~ ~

John Dee screamed as loud as he could. "Toby!"
Nothing.

"Stella!" No response.

Distant, pitiable screams of doomed passengers filled the air. John Dee's throat tightened listening to the cacophony of tortured sounds from souls fighting to stay above water. The devil was at work in the big river.

He didn't make out Stella's voice. Or Toby's.

His shoulders sagged. Was this it? His life with Toby ended in the black water? All the effort to outrun the Burtons ended here? *Don't think like that!* The cotton bale's holding. A boat will come along.

John Dee lay on his belly, spread his legs, and hooked a foot on each side of the bale so he didn't slide off. At first, he'd sat up, and the bale had rolled and he'd gone into the water. Had a helluva time climbing back up on it.

Once he'd figured out how to lay flat, he knew he'd make it a long while. But it sure as hell wasn't comfortable. Little stem pieces pricked him every time he moved.

How much time had passed since he'd jumped off the *Delta Ray*? Fifteen minutes? Half an hour? An hour? He wasn't sure. He hadn't spotted Stella or Toby since they'd jumped. He'd spotted a few others in the river, struggling to stay afloat. Now, the fire was nearly out and screams for help were less frequent. The dark river was a watery graveyard.

Something grabbed John Dee's foot. "Mister!" a man's voice shouted. "Pull me up!"

John Dee grabbed the man's hand. His torso rose out of the water.

"Th...th...thank you, mister!"

"Hold on!" the cotton bale tilted. John Dee slid toward the man.

The bale was sinking!

John Dee pushed the man back in the water.

"No! No!" The man gurgled river water.

John Dee grabbed his hand again. "It can't hold us both. Look; grab onto that!" A section of the *Delta Ray*'s wooden railing floated by the bale.

The man grabbed the rail.

"Is it gonna hold?" John Dee asked.

"Maybe." The poor bastard's voice wasn't much more than a whisper.

"Good luck, brother." John Dee lost sight of him in the gloam and didn't see another passenger for several minutes. His cotton bale was lower in the water. *Dammit, it's not gonna hold me much longer.*

When was help going to come? He remembered the *Delta Ray* had been tied up for the night at a remote landing. No settlement or riverboat nearby. No help was coming till sometime after first light.

God help me. God help us all.

~ ~ ~

Toby's cotton bale drifted along in the current of the main channel. He lay flat, trying to spread his weight. He stuck his finger in the bale at its water line. Soggy clearthrough. *Damn thing's gonna sink like a boulder real soon, and I can't swim for shit.* How long could he keep his head above water once the bale sank?

Firelit wreckage of the *Delta Ray* was long gone. He couldn't see any passengers. He had no idea where John Dee and Stella were. Hell, they might be a mile away.

John Dee and Stella under the blankets was the biggest damned shock he'd had in a while. Oh, he'd seen John Dee rolled-up with a bawdy girl like that a morning or two in St. Louis, or in Natchez, Helena, or New Orleans, when he'd had to wake him to get moving. Not only that, sometimes they'd entertained women in side-by-side bawdy-house rooms with real thin walls. So, Toby was well aware John Dee had his carnal appetites. Just like he did.

But with Stella it felt different. Was it because he wanted her for himself? Yeah, he wanted her. He desired her. Her womanly curves stirred him; her dark eyes cut to his soul when she smiled. But he felt something more for her than just the satisfaction of his urges. He could spend time with Stella; deep in his heart, he was sure. Maybe even make a life with her. Did John Dee feel the same way? Did Stella?

He sighed. Neither of them had said Stella was off limits. He had no call for a grievance with John Dee.

Now their tryst was the least of his worries. Were they alive?

"Help me! Help me" A woman splashed just out of his reach.

"Swim to me," Toby said.

Flailing like a crazy lady, she reached for his hand. "Let me up!"

"This bale's sinking," Toby said.

She pulled his arms in a desperate attempt to climb onto the bale, forcing Toby to slide into the water. She grabbed his shoulders, pushing him under. He struggled to control her.

"Easy, woman!"

Something grazed his back. A ceiling beam from the *Delta Ray. Thank God in heaven!* "Grab that!"

She put her arm around the beam as he steadied her. "I can't hang on!"

"Calm yerself now. I got it." He pulled the beam underwater, testing its buoyancy. It popped back up. Good. Toby put his bag on the beam and grabbed the beam with one arm and the woman with the other.

"Okay. We can float a while like this." His arms and shoulders tensed like steel, trying to support himself and the woman. But holding onto another person in the dark, cold river was better than facing his grim reaper alone.

"Help me!" the woman said. "I'm so tired. And I'm cold."

"You're all right now. I got ya. We just gotta hold on till morning. A boat'll pick us up."

"Just don't let go a-me," she said.

"I won't, ma'am."

Her face was just a foot or so from his across the beam. The moon cast faint light on her blond hair and high cheekbones. Must be a real looker in the daylight. The only White women he'd been this close to had been bawdy girls. Cost him a dollar or more, but none of them had been as pretty as this White lady.

"What's in the bag?" she asked.

"Most important thing in the world. My freedom papers."

"You're a free nig-gah?"

"Don't call me niggah unless you want to swim by yourself. We's equal on this here beam!"

"I'm sorry! Don't let me go!" she shouted.

Toby squeezed her hand to make her understand she wasn't going anywhere.

"I don't mean nuthin' by it," she said. "It's jez what we call Black folk."

"Just call me Toby."

"Okay."

She stared at the bag.

"I'll drown before I lose those papers," Toby said.

"Can I ask you sumthin' without you gettin' mad at me?"

"Go ahead."

"Why'd your master set you free? You're big and strong. You must be worth two thousand dollars or more."

Toby laughed. "I've heard that before. Maybe you can ask him yourself tomorrow. He's in the river here somewhere, just like us."

The woman flinched. "Who's that?"

"John Dee Franklin."

"Franklin? Are you kidding me?"

"No, ma'am. He's my partner."

"I'll be damned! My husband and I had dinner with him last night! Him and his wife—the princess of something or other. She sang on stage."

Toby belly laughed. "Stella, a princess? She kind of looks like a princess, I guess."

"She ain't a real princess?" the woman asked.

"Hell no."

The woman frowned. "I knew their cock-and-bull story was a lie. But they snowed my husband. He don't know shit from apple butter when he's into whiskey."

"You got separated from your husband?"

"He's dead. I know he is."

"Maybe he's floating like us." Toby's arm ached. "Can you wrap your arm around the beam? I need a little break here."

"I'll try." The woman kicked and rose slightly out of the water, circling the beam with her arm. "This better?"

He loosened his grip on her slightly. "Yeah."

"Far as my husband, ain't no doubt he's dead. The stewards came to our cabin and told us to get out 'cause the fire. Now, he'd passed out drunk, so I had a helluva a time rousing him. Finally, he said he weren't going anywhere till he shaved and dressed. A steward grabbed my arm and pulled me outta our cabin. Didn't give me a chance to argue. About then the ceiling crashed. I ran for my life. Down the hall and out the door. I jumped and my robe caught on the rail! I hung there screaming for help till somebody cut me loose and I dropped into the river. Heard the big smokestacks fall and the boat broke up. Ain't no way Reginald got out alive."

"I'm sorry," Toby said.

"Thank you. I'm not sure I am."

Toby let that go. He adjusted his torso to lessen the strain on his arms.

"You all right?" she asked.

"I'll be fine," Toby said. "Just hold on tight. What's your name, ma'am?"

"Adelaide Broussard. What'd you say your name was?"

"Toby."

"Just Toby?"

"You can call me Toby Freeman."

"That fits, I guess. There aren't no freemen where I'm from."

"Where's that?"

"Loo-see-anna. We have a sugar plantation," Adelaide said. "It's called Grace Vale."

"You have slaves?"

"Oh yes. Mebbe a hundred and fifty."

"You're big planters, then. You got a son whose gonna help you run the place if yer husband's passed?"

Adelaide hesitated. She sniffed like she was misty eyed. "No. Don't have no children. But I got pregnant twice. First one died 'fore it was born. Then we had a son. He got sick and died at age one. That was ten years ago."

"I'm sorry, Adelaide."

She stiffened. "I ain't never had a nig-gah call me that before—oh! Sorry—Toby. But you saved my life, so I guess you can be first." She squeezed his forearm. "Well, anyhow, we never had another baby. Didn't try to make a baby much to tell you the truth."

"Uh huh," Toby muttered, mostly disinterested in hearing more about this planter's wife's troubles. But it was just the two of them, and there were hours to pass. "Why's that? The whiskey?"

"Nah. Reggie was more interested in his visits down to the slave quarters at night."

A rage ran through Toby like a fast-burning fuse. Black slave women were powerless to stop the advances of their masters, same as Stella with Mr. Bickler. A White overseer named Jones back in North Carolina came to mind. Bastard always wore his black hat. He'd would take a young girl named Bessie into the barn now and then. Little Bessie weren't no more than fifteen and had a tear in her eye every time. Toby knew an old Black doctor in New Orleans who'd said, "There weren't a fine-featured Black woman on the lower river who hadn't had to deal with a White man."

The men involved were evildoers of a heinous nature. Had this White woman stood by and knowingly let her husband have his way with enslaved Black women? She wasn't a damn bit better than him.

Adelaide was studying him to the point of annoyance. Toby asked, "What are you looking at?"

"It was Franklin you say who set you free?"

"Yes," Toby said.

"You two got the same Daddy?"

"What?"

"Don't get huffy," Adelaide said. "With yer lighter skin, you have the look of a mulatto or maybe a quadroon. You surely know that! I can see a little of Franklin in you."

Toby sighed. "We was raised together. Been together a lot of years. So, we're real close, like brothers. Truth is, I don't know if we have the same Daddy."

"Thought you must be close with him if he set you free."

Toby didn't respond.

"Look," Adelaide said, "I don't mean nuthin' by it. We're just passin' time."

"Yeah," Toby said. "We got a few more hours till dawn. Talk all you want 'cause we can't fall asleep if we wanna live."

Adelaide sniffed again, this time as if she were upset. "I know about mulattos and such 'cause we got quite a few of them at Grace Vale. I can see Reggie in some of the children." She sniffed again. "I never said anything about this to anyone before."

"Not even your husband?" Toby asked.

"Especially not him," she said. "He'd like to have killed me before admittin' such a thing."

"Ever think about them poor girls he stuck his pecker in? You shoulda stopped him."

"I know I shoulda. But you don't know Reggie. The man woulda beat me if I accused him of bein' with the slave women." She paused. "I was too weak to say sumthin'."

So, the White man held power over his own wife as well. But she got a comfortable life in return for keeping her eyes closed and mouth shut. He could understand Adelaide's inaction but would never respect it.

"You know my secrets now, Toby. I figure that's okay since you saved my life and we're probably gonna die anyway. It's kinda nice to get 'em off my chest."

"I'm not gonna lie; I don't like any of it, not one bit. But I'll keep your secrets, Adelaide."

Neither spoke for a few minutes. Then Adelaide said, "I'm so cold."

"Keep your legs moving. You gotta keep yer blood flowing, and you can't fall asleep! We have to stay awake till morning!"

"I don't think I can."

"You can! Just a couple of hours, now. River's over sixty degrees here. Least we ain't upriver where the water's real cold! We keep moving, we'll make it till a boat comes. Tell you what, if something bigger than this beam floats by, I'll get you out of the water."

"But I'm real cold, Toby."

Toby dove under the beam and came up on Adelaide's side. He hugged her tightly and used his palms to massage her arms and back.

"But—" Adelaide said.

"I gotta keep you warm," Toby said. "Only way to do it."

"It's unnatural…."

"Because I'm a Black man?" Toby asked.

"Uh-huh. And because you ain't my husband."

He continued to rub her back.

"But it's helping," Adelaide said.

He rubbed her thighs. "Your legs are cold. Kick 'em till they warm up."

Adelaide started to kick between his legs. Her buttocks wedged against his pelvis. Even in the cold river, fighting for his life, he couldn't help himself from stiffening with her body pressing into his. *God, not now!*

"That's better," she said, apparently not noticing his plight. She held on to him with both of her arms around his neck, face to face. She crossed her legs around his waist. He strained to hold on to the beam and support the weight of both of them.

"Keep me warm, Toby." She hugged him tightly. "Are you okay?"

"I'll manage," he said, trying to even his breathing and conceal his arousal.

The rolling river lifted them apart and brought them back together in a rhythm that only fueled the fire in him. A miraculous entwinement with a Southern planter's beautiful blond-headed wife he could have never dreamed up. Not quite intercourse, but still the most sensuous coupling he'd ever had. For those minutes, everything was gone—the river, the cold, John Dee and Stella, the Burtons, inequalities—except this serendipitous intimacy.

Her breathing was faster. Then she spoke in a whisper. "I've never had a Black lover, like Reggie did. You ever had a White woman?"

"You ask a lot of questions."

"You wanted me to keep talkin'!" She laughed.

"I s'pose I did. I'm gonna say that ain't none of your business."

"If I were guessin'," Adelaide said, "I'd say you've had White women. Now, I'm not sayin' I couldn't take a Black lover, if it was the right man and all. Especially now that Reggie's dead."

Adelaide's foot rubbed his lower leg, below the knee. What a firecracker. Then she kicked him in a way that felt playful and threw her head back. "What I need right now big, strong, Mister Toby Freeman is for you to get me rescued."

"I'm trying my best."

"I know you are."

Adelaide held onto the beam and kicked her legs. "I'm feelin' a little better. A little warmer."

"Just keep moving," Toby said. "We'll kick together for a while. Then we'll take a rest. Then we'll kick again. It'll keep us warm, and 'fore we know it, it'll be morning."

"How long?"

Toby looked into the murky gray sky and listened for birds. Nothing yet.

"Dawn's coming in an hour or two," he said. Might be a while longer than that, but he had to give her hope.

"Okay. Where we kickin' to?"

"New Orleans."

"You're being funny," Adelaide said.

"Yeah. We'll try and kick a ways toward the riverbank. But I doubt we can get outta the current."

"Okay."

They kicked for a while and then relaxed, drifting with the current and letting their breathing even out.

"If we survive, what are you gonna do?" she asked.

"I'm gonna find John Dee, and we're gonna get back to business."

"Where's that?"

"Oh, we ship goods up and down the river. Got a load due into St. Louis. I 'spect we'll go up there and make sure everything's handled."

"John Dee Franklin is really your partner? A White man?"

"Yep."

"He ain't married to that singer, now, is he?" Adelaide didn't wait for Toby's answer. "He fed Reggie a crock-ah-shit."

"And what are you gonna do?"

"Go back home to Grace Vale, of course."

"I hope you treat your people better than your husband did."

"What do you mean?"

"Forcing himself on the women. Why, if he did that, he musta been the kinda man who whipped his slaves."

"I didn't have nuthin' to do with that!"

"You saw 'em whipped, didn't ya?"

"Now and then."

"Did you try and stop your husband?"

"That weren't my place! I told ya—when I got into Reggie's business, he'd beat me! All I know is Reggie said sometimes he had to. 'Cause they were lying or stealing or being lazy or such."

Toby trembled, and it wasn't from the cold. "Didn't want to lose your pretty dresses and your diamonds, now, did you? And your servant girls and your fancy parties at your fancy house. Ain't that right?"

"Yer shamin' me," Adelaide said.

"Hell yes, I am."

"Mebbe I should a said somethin'. But he woulda hurt me, Toby. You don't understand."

"How bad you think it hurts to be whipped?" Toby asked her.

"I don't want to think about that!"

"Feel my back! Between my shoulder blades."

Adelaide slipped her hand under his shirt and ran her fingers over the ropey scars along his spine. She gasped.

"Yeah," Toby said. "When they whip ya, them wounds are open and bleeding. They hurt like hell every time you move. Makes you sick a few days. Tell me, White lady, does any person made by God deserve this?"

"I don't reckon they do," Adelaide said.

Her blind eye to the dark side of Grace Vale made his blood boil. "Hell no, they don't. I'm gonna tell you sumthin'. John Dee and I have been to lots of plantations. Doing business with 'em. Know what we see?"

"What?"

"Planters that treat their slaves right make the most money."

"How's that?" she asked.

"They give their people fair rest. Plenty of good food. Clothes and shoes aren't too worn out. Mebbe even a li'l spending money for tobaccy and sweets. They let families live together. They let their people have a Sabbath and church time. They let 'em sing and have fun after the work's done. And they never whip 'em. See, when they do all that, everyone has a decent life and the Whites and Blacks are all working together for the good of the plantation."

"Reggie always said, 'You give 'em an inch and they take a mile.'"

"He was a damn fool."

Neither spoke as water lapped at the beam.

"You'd be wise to sell the place and all your slaves," Toby said.

"Now why would I do that?"

"How are you gonna run a sugar plantation without a husband?" Toby asked. "You don't know a thing about cutting cane. Besides, one day, mebbe soon, slavery's gonna be through. How you gonna grow cotton if you gotta pay the pickers a dollar a day? Your plantation ain't gonna be worth a nickel."

"How do you know that?"

"I'm friends with a Black doctor in New Orleans. He spends time with White docs who come down there from the northern states. They told him slavery's like a powder keg in the North. Politicians want to end it, and they'll get their way—it's just a matter of time."

"Why do them northern men care what we do?"

"My doctor friend told me that," Toby said. "Why, in the North, there's factories and businesses like we never seen down here. They make steel and clothes and saddles and windas and toys and carriages—everything you can think of. Everything. And the workers are for-'ners. Germans and Irish and such. But the factories pay a wage to the for-'ners cause they's free men. Well, the politicians don't think it's fair their factories pay a wage and you don't on your sugar plantation. They're gonna change things."

Adelaide rested her head on her forearm.

"Don't you fall asleep," Toby said.

"I ain't sleepin'. I'm thinkin'."

"What about?"

"There's a lot of sense in what you say. It'd be nice if Grace Vale were a happier place. I'd like to see my girls who help me around the house with smiles on their faces. Do you really think—Black folks and me—we could all get along and work together?"

"You're the boss lady now," Toby said. "Make it so."

"I can't do it by myself! The men'd think I was crazy if I started giving the orders. I'll tell you something, Toby. I never set foot in Grace Vale's slave quarters since the day Reggie brought me there."

Toby fought an urge to lay into Adelaide for her indifference to the lives of dozens of enslaved people who lived on her property. But now wasn't the time. She was inching along toward the right thing. "You can do it, Addy."

"Addy. I kinda like that. If you help me, mebbe I can."

"What?"

"Once we get off this river, come to Grace Vale with me. Help me change the way Reggie ran things. You can speak with my people. There's a strength in you: they'll listen and do what you say. I'm sure of it."

She took his hand. "And I'm gonna think on what you said about selling Grace Vale."

Was she serious? What did he know about running a cane operation? What did he know about managing one-hundred-and-fifty slaves? What did he know about this White lady who all the sudden wanted to change her ways? He knew what Momma would tell him: "Only a fool believes a tiger'll change its stripes."

"Say you'll come!" Adelaide pleaded.

The powerful connection he'd felt with her made his questions disappear. "Mebbe for a while."

They floated, contentedly, her hand resting on his. The early glow of dawn appeared to the east. A bird cackled in the distance. As strange as the thought seemed after a night in the cold river, Toby wanted time to slow down while he floated with Addy, just the two of them, away from the rest of the world.

"Sun'll be up soon, Addy," Toby said. "A boat'll come along. We're gonna make it."

"You saved my life."

He squeezed her hand.

"Toby?"

"Yeah?"

"When you were warmin' me up."

"Yeah?"

"When I was holdin' onto you, real tight."

"Uh huh."

"Did you feel—did you feel somethin'—somethin' real good?"

"I most surely did."

She leaned over and kissed his arm. "When you come to Grace Vale, you'll be stayin' in the big house."

~ ~ ~

A distant rumble and John Dee looked up. A dark shape. A boat! Must be a small stern wheeler.

"Help!" John Dee shouted. "I'm here! Help me!"

A lantern shone at its rail, silhouetting a man against the lower deck. Another man leaned over the rail.

A woman screamed. She screamed a second time, even louder, more hysterically. Stella! Being pulled out of the water by her hair. A long beard hung from the face of the man pulling her into the boat. Cliff Burton!

"You out there, Franklin?"

God, it's him! John Dee's heart was racing.

"Got your squaw whore. You's hearing me, boy?"

John Dee's mouth went dry. He swallowed hard and screamed back, "Let her go!"

"It is you!" Burton laughed loudly. "Ain't gonna do that, Franklin. She's mine now."

"Don't hurt her!"

"Oh, don't you worry! Won't do nuthin' to her that you haven't, right, Franklin?"

"Give her to me," John Dee said, trying to collect his thoughts. What would Cliff Burton listen to? "I'll pay you."

"Goddamned right you'll pay! With your life, boy." A rifle shot rang out. Bullets pinged the water a distance away as Burton shot in the dark toward his voice. Only a miraculously lucky shot would hit him.

John Dee drifted farther from the stern wheeler.

"Franklin!" Burton shouted. "You want her back? Come get her in New Orleans. She'll be whoring down there! That's right—I'm-a gonna sell yer squaw to a whore house!"

Burton's wicked laugh cackled and faded. The stern wheeler vanished into the black. John Dee's heart dropped. The things Burton said he'd do to Stella! Would he ever see her again?

The sheer evil of Burton's actions made John Dee shudder. Stalking the *Delta Ray* till he found them. Firing the cotton, with complete indifference to the deaths of passengers and crew who had nothing to do with his brother's death. Searching the desperate survivors and disregarding every drowning soul except Stella. For vengeance.

John Dee slapped the water's surface again and again. *The bastard! The evil bastard!*

Cliff Burton had to be stopped.

And killed.

PART III

THE CRESCENT CITY

"I have termed New Orleans the crescent city...from its being built around the segment of a circle formed by a graceful curve of the river at this place."

—Joseph Holt Ingraham,
The South-West, by a Yankee, 1835

"I spent weeks in New Orleans.... I doubt if there is a city in the world, where the resident population has been so divided in its origin, or where there is such a variety in the tastes, habits, manners, and moral codes of the citizens."

—Frederick Law Olmsted, *The Cotton Kingdom: A Traveller's Observations on Cotton and Slavery in The American Slave States, 1853-1861*

Chapter 15

Toby took Addy's hand, balancing her as she stepped off their rescue boat. She tiptoed through rocks and puddles to the riverbank.

"Ouch!"

"Got's soft feet, don't ya?" Toby said.

"I most surely do. I'd give half ah Grace Vale for a pair of shoes."

Toby savored the sensation of solid ground under his feet. He didn't even mind the pungent, sulfur-tinged air coming from brackish river water. Sunshine warmed his face, promising a hot day, even though the cool early morning had Addy holding her arms tightly against her body. Better a little chilled than swimming for her life in the river.

He helped her and several other survivors climb the bank to a remote river landing, with only a woodpile and a wagon with a broken axle next to a path that led into the woods. Two skinny White men with greasy, long hair stood at the pile, smoking. *Who the hell are these gintys?* Toby tightened his grip on his moneybag.

"At least we're alive, Addy girl."

"Yes! Yes, we are! I never thought we'd make it, but we're finally outta the river. Ow!" She raised her foot. "Damn rocks."

Toby helped her settle on a patch of grass.

Five other survivors plopped down beside her. Two White men—Irish from their nearly undecipherable English—and a Black man. All about his age, their expressions as worn and weary as Toby felt. Two young women, one White and one Black, wore night dresses that were nearly in tatters. Five workers from the *Delta Ray*. Eyes closed almost immediately. Surely in exhaustion. Maybe seeking solitude to thank their Savior for deliverance from the big river. Maybe just savoring the grassy clearing's earthy and sweet scent.

"I hope other boats pull a helluva lot more survivors outta the river," Toby said.

"God, I hope so," Addy responded.

He propped himself on his elbows, overlooking the river, and put his valise between them. Two dead bodies from the *Delta Ray* lay on the bow of the flatboat they'd arrived on. An Irishmen called "Chappy" and an old woman in night clothes.

Another flatboat glided in from the main channel. Four red-shirted *voyageurs* worked it, but Toby didn't see any passengers, or *Delta Ray* survivors. How many bodies were on board? Would Stella or John Dee be among the dead? *God, please, no.*

"Where 'bouts are we?" Addy asked.

"Well," Toby scanned the river, "don't see no town here. Flatboat man told me we're not far from the Old River. I don't know exactly where that is. I 'spect we're somewhere south ah Natchez. On the Lou-see-anna side."

Addy rubbed her shoulders. "Hope it warms up soon. Think I can board a boat here that'll take me home to Grace Vale?"

"Mebbe." Toby winced. Was she gonna steam out of his life as fast as she had appeared? "This landing's small. Doubt many boats'll stop here. Might have to wait for days. You'd be best off to go down to Baton Rouge and catch a packet south outta there."

"This nightmare will never end."

"Least you're alive."

"Thanks to you." She hugged him. "My big, strong rescuer."

He gently pushed her away and whispered, "That feels real good, Addy girl. But don't do that when folks can see us. Might bring trouble."

"'Cause I'm White and yer Black?"

"Course."

She lay back on her elbows. "You'll be coming with me, won't you?"

He hesitated. "First off, I gotta find John Dee and Stella. John Dee and I promised we'd get her to New Orleans."

"I gotta wait fer all that 'fore you come to Grace Vale?"

"I reckon so," Toby said.

"Hmmph!" Addy closed her eyes tightly for a moment, then opened them and spoke firmly. "Tell me something: What does this little princess girl mean to you and Franklin?"

"If you gotta know, there was trouble with river gintys on Stella's last boat. We're taking her to New Orleans to get far away from the bastards. She'll find another show to sing in."

"What kinda trouble?"

"Nothing we can't handle," Toby said.

They sat silently watching the red-shirted workers tie up the arriving flatboat.

Finally, Addy said, "Have you known Stella for a long time?"

"No."

"So, she's paying you well?"

"No."

"This all seems fishy. You sweet on her?"

Toby suppressed a belly laugh. It had been John Dee between the sheets with Stella, not him. "We's just helping her out. That's it." He stared into Addy's eyes. "I helped you out, didn't I?"

She smiled. "Yeah, but you're sweet on me, ain't ya? I want you to come with me to Grace Vale, straight off. I need you there."

A powerful urge to take her into his arms almost overcame him. But not here. Might be dangerous. "I'll come. But it's best you go to Grace Vale alone. What if your husband turns up?"

"He won't," Addy said. "He's dead. Drunk-assed Reggie stayed in our cabin and the ceiling fell in on him. I was there. Told you so, didn't I?"

A tear ran down her cheek.

Toby discretely touched her hand. "I'm sorry."

Addy sat still as a statute with her head bowed between her knees for several minutes. Finally, she sighed and looked at Toby. "I've been with Reggie since I was a fifteen-year-old girl. He brought me from South Carolina to Grace Vale after our wedding. It's been me and him and the plantation ever since. We hardly ever left there. I was lonely at first, but he was handsome, and

I loved him. And you're right—I came to settle into my life as his wife and the lady of Grace Vale." She fiddled with a loose thread in her torn nightshirt. "But our boy died, and things changed 'tween us. So, these last many years, I didn't love him no more, and I don't think he loved me. But he was with me, at every meal, in and outta the house all day, sleeping in the next room. Tell you the truth, Toby, I don't know how to feel."

A *voyageur* wearing pantaloons approached. He had long red hair, a red beard, and wore a red shirt to match. "Morning, ma'am."

She nodded.

He stiffened at the sight of her tears. He shot a hard look at Toby. "You all right?"

"Oh, it's just been so hard."

"You were on the *Delta Ray*?"

"Yes. So was Toby, here. He helped me survive in the river last night."

The man nodded at Toby.

"He's a free man," Addy said.

The *voyageur* didn't react one way or the other.

"We picked up ten bodies. Must all be from the *Delta Ray*. Would ya both come look 'em over and see if you know any of 'em?"

"Okay."

The three of them boarded the flatboat. Toby carried his valise. At the rear of the vessel, ten bodies of various shapes and sizes lay in a grisly line. Addy and Toby gasped at the sight of a large White man with dark hair, face down on the deck.

"Reggie!" Addy shouted.

Startled, Toby stared at her for a second. Were they looking at the back side of her husband? Or was the corpse John Dee? Toby rolled the body over and to his relief the clean-shaven man was not John Dee Franklin. "Is this your husband?"

"No. No, he's not," Addy answered, flatly.

Toby pointed to the man on the far right. "He was a deckhand on the *Delta Ray*. I'm sure he was, but I don't know his name."

The *voyageur* nodded.

"What happens to these poor souls?" Addy asked.

"The sheriff's on a boat upriver looking for survivors and fishing out dead bodies," said the *voyageur*. "He told me to take these bodies aboard and lay 'em at the next landing so any interested party can get a look at 'em. Mebbe some'll get identified and the sheriff can let kin know they's drowned. Someone'll be along in a few days to bury 'em."

"These people are gonna get buried before their families take them home? With no funeral? At this godforsaken place?" Addy asked.

"If nobody knows who they are or what to do with 'em, I reckon they will," the man said. "'Cause they's gonna stink to high heaven in a day ur two."

"Will ya help get these bodies laid up a ways in the clearing?" the *voyageur* asked.

"Yes, sir," Toby said. "Why don't ya take the bag and go sit a while," he said to Addy.

"All right." She strained under the weight of Toby's bag. "Good gracious! Thar rocks in here?"

He drew back. "Ah, no rocks. Just some tools."

The *voyageur* raised an eyebrow.

Addy shook her head and lugged Toby's bag to her resting place in the grass.

It took a good twenty minutes for Toby and the *voyageurs* to situate the bodies on shore. The last one, a young girl no more than twelve years old, brought a tear to Toby's eye.

"Goddamned miserable job," the red-bearded man said. "Appreciate yer help. We's gonna start a fire and fry some bacon. Yer welcome to some."

"Toby!"

Addy tugged his valise back and forth with one of the skinny White men he'd spied at the woodpile earlier. The skinny man jerked it free, turned and ran. Toby sprinted after the man and his valise.

The thief disappeared into the trees. Toby followed the snap of twigs. The bastard's brown cotton shirt popped in and out of huckleberry bushes. Toby surged, making up the distance. He leapt onto the thief's back and tackled him. He grabbed a handful of brown shirt and pounded him to the ground. Thud! The thief groaned. Toby snatched his valise.

"Put it down, boy!"

Toby looked into the barrel of a musket. The second skinny man pulled the hammer back. "Now!" Patchy facial hair twitched on his cheeks like willows in the wind.

Toby put down the bag but kept his grip on its handle.

"Take yer hand off that bag, boy!"

"You might as well shoot me," Toby said.

"You got money in there?"

"Nah."

"What, then?"

"My freedom papers."

Skinny man laughed. "I'll be burning those, boy. I'm a-gonna sell you down the river for a pretty penny!"

"Drop yer musket!" a hidden voice shouted. "Drop it now!"

Skinny man dropped his musket. Toby breathed easier as the red-bearded *voyageur* stepped out of the brush, his pistol pointed at the thief. "Goddamned river rats! You two thieving bastards git! Ah see you again I'm shooting on sight!"

The skinny two long-hairs disappeared into the trees.

"Thank you," Toby said.

"Yer welcome. I saw that little river rat snatch the lady's bag. I ain't partial to thieves."

"It ain't her bag. It's mine."

"Huh."

Would the *voyageur* have come to his aid if he'd known a Black man was the bag's true owner?

"Well, you helped me move those bodies. That weren't no fun."

"My name's Toby."

"I'm Red."

They shook hands.

"Did I hear you're a free man?"

"Yep."

"Why you all friendly with that White woman?"

Toby studied Red. Was his opinion about Black and White relations the same as other White men on the lower river? A Black man's romantic familiarity with a White woman was a lynching offense. But the look in Red's eyes wasn't hateful. "She was about to drown last night. Helped her hold onto a wooden beam and kept her head above water. At dawn, a little flatboat came along. I got her outta the river."

"Yeah," Red said. "Tough dod-derned night for you people on that boat. Well, figures yer her hero and all now. But don't let her get lovey on ya in front of White men. Now, it don't bother me none, but on the lower river, they'll string a Black fella up for loving on a White lady. You know that, don't you, boy?"

"I reckon so."

"Got yer bag?" Red asked.

"Yep."

"Let's go. Whatever's in there that's worth getting shot fer—I'd keep a closer eye on it."

~ ~ ~

"Stop here, would you?" John Dee asked the captain.

The captain steered his stern-wheeler tug into a small landing. Dead ahead on the riverbank was a long row of corpses.

John Dee gulped in a deep breath. *Stella's in Cliff Burton's clutches, but is Toby gonna be in this line of bodies?* Still in his nightshirt, John Dee hopped over the gunwale into ankle-deep water. His feet hit the shallow river bottom and a wave of relief flowed through him just as it had when he'd scrambled over the rail onto the deck.

The captain looked down on him, just as he had two hours before, when he'd grabbed his hands and hauled him onto the tug. "Don't be long."

John Dee nodded. He owed the captain his life.

He climbed the riverbank and solemnly filed by the dead. Old. Young. Black. White. Female. Male. Stiff limbs and gray pallor. At least someone had closed their eye lids. *Christ! I must look nearly as dead as these folk after my night in the river.* He finished his grisly tour and breathed easier: Toby wasn't among them.

John Dee spotted more bodies a few yards farther, under cypress trees—just as motionless but very much alive. Lucky *Delta Ray* survivors, stretched out in the grass, getting much needed rest after a night in the river. One of them was Toby.

John Dee nudged Toby's leg until he stirred. "Fancy meeting you here."

Toby squinted in the sunlight, then nodded. "Good to see you, partner."

John Dee chuckled at the sight of Toby holding his valise tightly to his chest. "Always could trust you with the goods."

"Oh this." Toby sat up and put the valise next to him. "It's been in high demand round here. You still got your end of things?"

John Dee patted his money-belt-padded mid-section. "Sure do. Gonna have to let this cold cash dry sooner or later."

A blanket next to Toby stirred. A feminine voice moaned, and a woman rose, her blanket bunching around her waist. Adelaide Broussard! The neck of her nightshirt stretched below her shoulder, revealing the cleavage of her ample bosom. She didn't seem to notice. Or care. She sat up and yawned. She leaned her head against Toby's shoulder.

"Missus Broussard! Thank God you're alive!"

She tilted her head toward him. After a moment, she said, "Franklin! I'll be damned."

Her loud belly laugh stirred other lounging survivors. What was so dod-derned funny? He glanced down his nightshirt to his toes. Barefoot in a torn cloth rag that barely clung to his shoulders and hung to his knees. A damn circus clown!

"You ain't meeting the King of Spain today, are you, shit-talker?"

"Addy." Toby straightened her nightshirt over her shoulder. "There's no call for that."

"Addy?" John Dee looked from one to the other and flashed a knowing smile. "Ah, what happens on the river stays on the river." He chuckled. "Musta been quite a night."

"Listen, Franklin," she said, "Last night, I was going under. Toby helped me and got me through till a boat came. He saved my life."

"He has a peculiar habit of saving lives," John Dee said.

"I don't know what the hell that means, but we got to talking."

"Did you now?"

"Course we did! Thought we was gonna die. Said a whole lotta things back and forth. Well, I know you set him free and you're his partner and that singing squaw ain't your wife and all that Spanish royalty talk last night was a crock full-a horseshit."

"I see," John Dee said. "Bared your soul as you contemplated meeting your maker, Toby? At least you finally found someone who understands me."

"Oh, don't ruffle yer feathers. You can call me Addy, too, if you want. Toby's been calling me that, and I kinda like it."

"Okay, Addy. What about your husband?"

"He's dead."

"Oh," John Dee said. "You're sure?"

"He was sleeping off a real good drunk when they came to our cabin. He weren't gonna move. They pulled me out 'cause of the fire. He didn't come. I got down the hall and the roof fell in. He's dead all right."

"I'm sorry."

"Thank you."

Addy was anything but a grieving spouse. Her terse response and her advances at the theater the previous evening suggested a hollowness to her marriage to Mister Broussard. Toby looked to have drawn close enough to Addy to learn all about it, so he'd ask to be filled in later.

Addy seemed to read his thoughts. "I ain't gonna shed a lot of tears for Reggie for a whole lot of reasons."

"Understood," John Dee said.

"But what about the queen or the princess or whatever you called that singing girl you brought to dinner?" Addy asked.

"Stella," Toby said. "Where's Stella?"

John Dee sighed. "It's bad, Toby. Cliff Burton got her."

"Damn!" Toby balled his fist. "It was Cliff and Stevie Burton on that stern-wheeler watching us."

"I imagine so," John Dee said.

"What happened?" Toby asked.

"I had been in the river a good while when I saw a tugboat. Damn near ran me over! Cliff Burton was shining a lantern on people who'd jumped off the *Delta Ray*. But the bastards didn't pick up a single poor soul who was in the river. Then Burton spotted Stella on her cotton bale. He pulled her outta the river by the hair. Dragged her over the rail onto his boat. Musta hurt her real bad 'cause she was screaming. I was yelling for her, and he shot at me but never came close—'cause it was dark— and the tug pulled away. He taunted me he was gonna have his way with her."

"Christ!" Toby said.

"Last thing he yelled, 'Come find her in New Orleans.' Said he was gonna sell her to a whorehouse when he was done with her."

"That poor girl!" Addy's eyes narrowed. "Who's Cliff Burton? What the hell is going on?"

Toby walked away without answering. He stared into the river. Was Toby feeling empathy for Stella's plight, John Dee wondered, or was it deeper than that? Had he emotionally connected with her in their short time together, maybe even sowed the seeds of love? *Oh God!* Toby had found him under the sheets with Stella. Their coupling seemed like an eternity ago, but it had happened just a few hours before and must have shocked Toby like a hammer to the forehead. Was Toby furious? He hadn't had a helluva lot of time to think it over. John Dee sighed. No matter what, he wouldn't let a woman drive a wedge between them.

And what about Addy, the woman Toby had bonded with in the river, with an obvious intensity, as they had stared death in the face? John Dee glanced over at Addy's quizzical expression. Was she wondering about the Burtons or what the hell the triangle was between him, Stella, and Toby?

Toby returned. "So, that sonofabitch set the *Delta Ray* on fire just to get the three of us. He didn't give a damn about other passengers who had nuthin' to do with his brother."

"That's the size of it," John Dee said.

"I'm gonna kill the bastard. Him and his brother both."

"Not if I get 'em first."

"His brother?" Addy asked. "What did his brother have to do with the fire? And who's Stevie?"

Toby sat beside her. "This is bad business, Addy. Cliff Burton and his brothers are a gang of river pirates up Miss-sip-ee way. Cliff's brother Ricky boarded the *Lady J* and tried to rape Stella after her show. We came upon him in the act and killed the bastard."

Addy gasped.

"Now Cliff Burton wants his revenge. We took Stella south to escape the Burtons. But the bastards found us."

"We're going after Stella," Toby said.

"Hell yes, we are." John Dee looked to the riverfront. "My friendly captain already pulled out. We gotta find another boat."

Red and his *voyageur* mates were untying their flatboat. Toby approached him. "Heading toward Baton Rouge, Red?"

"I surely am."

"Would you take the three of us with you?"

"My scow ain't got much room, and it sure as hell ain't too damn comfortable."

"That's no matter," Toby said.

Red looked them over. "You got two bucks each in your bag?"

"Yeah."

"U.S. currency. I ain't taking no note offa some half-arsed bank I never heard of."

"Yeah."

"Then I reckon I will."

After paying Red, Toby, Addy, and John Dee boarded the flatboat. She sat on a pile of cut pinewood and they on barrels.

"How long you figure to Baton Rouge?" John Dee asked Red.

"Oh, depends on the current. 'Spect a few days."

The *voyageurs* poled the flatboat out of the easy water into the main channel. Bright sunshine and a light breeze made for a pleasant float downriver. A side-wheeler steamed by. Another steamer made its way upriver. John Dee estimated it'd pass by in ten minutes.

"How we gonna go about finding Stella?" Toby asked.

"First thing," John Dee said, "we'll find a tog shop in Baton Rouge. We can't very well show up in New Orleans in these rags."

"And we'll buy you things you can wear home to Grace Vale, Addy," Toby said.

"Grace Vale?" John Dee asked.

"My home," Addy said. "Downriver outta Baton Rouge. But I ain't going there."

"You're not?" Toby asked.

"Nope. I'm coming with y'all. I'm going to help you find Stella."

"Now," Toby said, "how you gonna do that?"

"If she's in a bawdy house, you'll need a bawdy girl to look for her."

John Dee laughed.

Addy glared at him. "Don't think I can be a bawdy girl?"

"Being a little forward is a far cry from a bawdy girl!"

"Just you wait, Franklin! Toby's gonna buy me some fancy French *lingerie*. I know for damn sure that bag he's been hugging like a lover has more than a few legal papers in it."

John Dee laughed. "Think so, do you?"

"I know so! Toby ran fast as a bobcat after a river rat fella who grabbed it from me."

John Dee turned to Toby. "Full of surprises this morning, now aren't you, partner?"

Toby grinned. "He didn't get too far. Red here helped me out."

Red nodded.

"You'll see, Franklin," Addy said. "I can walk right into a bawdy house, bat my eyelashes, shake my beehind, and find her. I know what she looks like—from dinner when you spun yer tales."

"It might get rough, Addy. I don't think you're cut out for this type of thing."

"I can do it, Franklin! Toby wants me to come, don't you?"

John Dee knew Toby better than anyone — desire sure-ly raged in him to be with Addy. He didn't blame him; Addy was a helluva woman. But it was damn dangerous for a Black man to take up with a White woman on the lower river. Might be up to him to keep his friend think-ing with his brain instead of his pecker head.

"Course he does," John Dee said.

"What the hell do you three know about bawdy hous-es in New Orleans?" Red asked.

John Dee, Addy, and Toby stared at him.

"Y'all think I'm deaf? I'm standing right here listening to every word of this nonsense."

"You might be surprised," John Dee said, "about all Toby and I know about bawdy houses."

"Is that right?" Addy said.

Toby's shit-eating grin was her answer.

Addy turned to Red. "All right, mister whorehouse expert, tell us."

Red chuckled. "Well, there's all kinds of bawdy hous-es in New Orleans." He said to John Dee, "Mister, you look like a Kaintuck in that rag yer wearing. Now Kain-tucks and dockworkers and immigrants and free Black men like yer pal here go to Gallatin Street. Plenty ah shitholes to choose from. Dutch Pete runs the California House; then there's Archy Murphy's and the Amsterdam House. And a crazy bitch named 'One- legged Duffy' runs the Green Tree Tavern. That's just a few of the shitholes down there. Now, if yer girl's on Gallatin Street, I'm gon-na say you'll be lucky to find her alive. Been told a lot o' whores in that vermin-infested, godforsaken district are dead in a month."

Addy gasped. "For God's sake!"

Red took off his hat and smoothed his red hair from his forehead. "Yep. While back I had a traveler on board from England. A seafaring man, this one. Been on frigates his whole life. That fella told me Gallatin Street was the most dangerous two-block waterfront stretch he'd ever been to. Anywhere in the whole derned world."

"We know about Gallatin Street," Toby said.

"You do?" Addy said.

"Had to go to Gallatin Street and find our hired men a time or two. But we sure as hell didn't go in there after dark." He dropped his eyes a little. "There's better bawdy houses down toward Canal."

"That's right, boy," Red said. "There, and toward the park. Hell, there's plenty of bawdy houses in New Orleans for a man in decent clothes with some money in his pocket." He looked at Toby. "Even a freed Black man like you."

"The Yellow Rose," John Dee said.

"Hell yes," Red said. "And Marguerite's."

"And Pink Gardens," Toby said.

"What is this?" Addy said. "Trading yer debaucheries in front of a woman!"

Toby laughed. "You said you wanted to be a bawdy girl." He paused. "We ain't married men, Addy. We got our needs."

"Well, Red." Addy ignored Toby's last remark. "If we're searching for a pretty woman who has been sold to a bawdy house, where should we look?"

"This pretty one…is she a bawdy girl?" Red asked.

"Hell no," John Dee said. "If she's in a bawdy house, she'll have been placed there against her will."

"All right," Red said. "That means they'll break her to get her to take on customers. Beat her. Or drug her. Or both. And if they're gonna do that, I imagine they'll be doing it somewhere there ain't no rules and no law. That's Gallatin Street."

Chapter 16

"GET OVER HERE, SQUAW!" SALIVA sprayed from Cliff Burton's beard-obscured lips.

Stella froze, unwilling to comply. She inched backward until her back hit the wall of her prison room. She crossed her arms over her breasts, which were barely concealed by her still damp nightshirt.

The bearded demon grabbed her collar and with a stern jerk brought her to him. Rancid breath gagged her. Cold, gray eyes cut into her soul. She blinked, again and again, wanting to be anywhere on earth but close to him.

He flung her chest-down on a large wooden crate. He put his hand between her shoulder blades and pressed her torso into the wood.

"Ow!" Slats dug into her stomach and breasts.

He hiked up her nightshirt. He was going to—

No! God help me!

His belt jangled. His trousers rustled and dropped. She gulped for air. His thighs jammed into the back of her bare legs.

This can't be happening! She tensed for his thrust. It didn't come.

Burton grunted. Then he pushed his legs into her buttocks, bucking her forward on the crate. Why didn't she feel his hardness? The back of his hand was on her thigh, pumping up and down. Was he exciting himself? He bellowed like a ravenous beast. He thrust and his manhood rubbed against her buttocks. Soft. A limp, rolled-up rag, unable to perform the act.

He grabbed her hips and shook her until the room spun. He howled like a raging demon. She cried for help, but no sound came out. Violent lurches smashed his thighs against hers and hurt like hell. Venomous grunts and wheezes pierced the musty air of the storeroom.

She cried out in agony. "God, no, please don't."

He growled. Her pain must excite him. She bit into her cheek to deny him his pleasure.

He stopped, grabbed the back of her nightshirt, and lifted her body off the crate. Then he slammed her down.

Stella fought for breath. She groaned.

A primeval scream rattled her prison room. Was the cold bastard bellowing his triumph to his men?

She knew the truth. The scream expressed his frustration.

He grabbed her hair and raised her head. His beard scratched her ear. "Bitch."

He mashed her face into the crate. An evil growl from somewhere deep inside him chilled her. Was he going to kill her?

But he released her.

God, it hurts! My face must be a battered mess. She grimaced against the wood. Inside, she took solace. *He's less than a man, and I'm still here.*

His belt buckle jangled. Boots clomped across the planks. He left without a word.

She slid off the crate, onto the floor. Everything went black.

~ ~ ~

A splinter from the plank floor poked her upper arm. Stella sat up. How long had she lain in the fetal position? Minutes? Hours?

Just a few slivers of light peeked through the door frame. If only she could shrink into a tiny speck and escape through the cracks. The darkness of her prison mocked her. Black and bleak. Only several barrels, the wooden crate, and a few scattered boxes, all sealed tight. There was no escape. She backed into the corner farthest from the door, pulled her knees into her chest, and curled her toes into the bottom of her nightshirt.

God, she hated that crate. Its wood-burned "McIntyre & Sons" brand on its broad side was etched in her mind forever. Her body ached from Cliff Burton's rough treatment. At least he'd stopped short of breaking her bones. And she thanked God for the tender mercy that he couldn't harden. If he had, terrible would have become unimaginable. Like with Mr. Bickler. Even worse.

But the bearded demon's impotence was a small mercy. Her life was over. The familiarity and comfort she had built with John Dee and Toby were gone. Her romantic interlude with John Dee was a cruel, fleeting dream. Neither man could help her. No one could. There was no way out.

The latch rattled and the rickety door swung open. Light blinded her.

"Get in there, Jasper." A fat, gray-bearded man pushed someone into the room. Her eyes adjusted. It was a much younger man with a patchy, thin beard and dusty blond hair. The kid almost seemed startled.

"You heard Cliff, boy," the old man said in a high-pitched cackle. "Time to make you a man. Give it to her good! Make her scream, boy."

Stella's blood chilled.

"Don't mind if I watch, do ya, boy?"

"What? Christ, Pete!"

"Shy 'bout yer little pecker, are ya, boy? Then get to it!" Old man Pete slammed the door shut.

Jasper advanced on Stella. "Get up."

She slowly rose and faced him. Darkness obscured his expression. His breathing was even, nothing like Cliff Burton's beastly panting or even Mr. Bickler's lusty shallow breaths.

Stella held hers, waiting for him to grab her like Burton had. Nothing. His breathing stayed steady. He didn't move.

Why? Was he scared? Was it his first time? Did he have a sense of right and wrong that the bearded demon didn't?

"You don't have to do this," Stella whispered, quietly, trying not to be heard by the old man's prying ears.

"Yes, I do." Jaspar's voice was quiet also. A good sign. But then he took a step toward her and grabbed her sleeve. "When Cliff gives an order, you do it."

Her body tensed, fearing rough treatment. "Cliff Burton hurt me." She backed away. Tears came quickly and fell down her cheeks. "Please don't hurt me."

Jaspar let her go. Their faces were inches apart. Was he having second thoughts?

Finally, he pulled out a handkerchief and dabbed at the corner of her mouth. "That blood?"

"Yes. I thought Burton was going to kill me."

Jasper gazed at her, almost cherubically. Time stood still. She felt some goodness in him.

Finally, he said, "I have to."

She put her hand on his arm. "No, you don't."

Jaspar looked at the door and back at Stella. Was he searching—for the right thing to do? Time stood still while she studied him. Would he help her? Could she trust him?

"Old Pete's listening. Just outside the door."

"It's okay," she whispered. Then she screamed. "Ahhh! Don't! Ow!" She picked up a wooden box and threw it. It crashed against the wall.

Jaspar was wide-eyed.

"Moan real loud," Stella whispered.

He moaned.

"Now grunt."

He made a noise like a pig's oink.

"No!" She ripped the bottom of her nightshirt. Then she pulled the crate over and it hit the floor with a bang. "Please stop!"

She whispered into his ear, "Scream 'Yes' as loud as you can."

Jaspar screamed.

"Now, 'Like that bitch!'"

He looked at her funny, but did it.

She whispered again, "You are a good man. You need to get away from these bad men."

His jaw tensed. "You don't know nut-thin," he whispered back. "I ain't gonna violate you 'cause it ain't Christian. Just leave it at that."

"Thank you. But Cliff Burton and the others will keep hurting me. They're gonna kill me."

"I can't do nut-thin 'bout that."

"Help me, Jaspar! Don't let them hurt me! Don't let them kill me! Jesus wants you to help me; you know he does!"

Jaspar looked away and didn't say anything. When he turned back to Stella, his expression was pained, almost haunted.

"Please, please, help me."

He leaned toward her and steadied himself, as if he were gathering strength. "I…I…wish I could."

She squeezed his hand. "Please, Jaspar, please. Come tonight and unlatch the door. If you don't help me, I'll die."

~ ~ ~

Time passed painfully slowly in her black cell. She was cold and sore and on edge like a thousand needles poked into her skin. Every creak and thump put her heart in her throat. Was it the tromping boots of her next attacker?

Would Jaspar help her? It took backbone to stand up to the Burtons, and Jaspar might not be up to it. It was a helluva lot easier to feign sympathy for a battered woman on the way out of the cell than to unlock the door. Did he have the guts to cross Cliff Burton—most certainly risking death if Burton found him out? If Jaspar didn't help her, this would end only one way. She'd die. The bearded demon wouldn't lock her up, violate her, and let her live to tell the story.

Wait! Hadn't Burton shouted something to John Dee about selling her to a whorehouse? Would Burton rather take money for her than kill her? But she wasn't a whore. How could a whorehouse make her lie on her back and take on men for money if she didn't want to? Would she be better off dead than a whore?

Think straight. The bearded demon wants revenge. It's in his eyes—one way or another, he wants me as dead as his brother. She'd be gone, wiped off the earth. No legacy, no history. A leaf in the wind. People who cared about her— the *Lady J* troupe, her new friends John Dee and Toby— would have no idea what became of her.

She balled her fist. Sitting in dirt, in the darkness, cowering and whimpering didn't do no good. The next time—*I'll fight the bastards! Slam a wooden box on the rapist's skull. Punch, kick, bite, whatever it takes. Repel him.* It felt good to imagine inflicting pain on Cliff Burton.

But that wouldn't work. Burton and the others were too big and strong. They'd overpower her resistance and beat the hell out of her, probably to death. *Think. Think. Endure whatever they do.* Jaspar gave her hope. *Survive till nightfall. He'll unlatch the door. Then escape! Believe in Jaspar. Believe his faith will give him the balls to unlock the door.*

But where was she? Where would she go? *Think. Think.*

The boat must be south of Natchez. *It's gonna stop for the night, won't it? Yes, it'll stop.* The riverbank would be close. *Pray that Jaspar unlatches the door. Then jump over the side and make it to shore!* Perhaps a town would be nearby. If not, a sugar plantation.

Then what? Wherever she turned up, she would be an Indian squaw, disheveled and dressed in a dirty nightshirt. Would White people believe her story? Would they help her?

Should she seek out the enslaved people? Would they help her or turn her away?

Stella took a deep breath. Those worries come later. Just get off the boat. And find a way to New Orleans.

Hours passed. The door remained shut. Somewhere beyond the walls of her prison, voices shouted, laughed, and cursed. No man came for her. Every passing second without one of them appearing was a blessing. She prayed to God like when she was a schoolgirl. She hadn't prayed in years. Was she even a Christian? Didn't matter—praying was all she could do. But she doubted God would listen. Why should he? What was she to him? God hadn't stopped Mr. Bickler. He hadn't stopped Cliff from pulling her out of the river.

She heard a sound at the door. A snap or a click. But the door didn't open. Had Jaspar unlatched it?

She waited until the voices quieted. Minutes went by. Ten? Twenty? She couldn't be sure. *Do it! Put a hand on the door and push!* It opened slowly. It made a faint creak. She held her breath and dared a quick peek. It was dark, but as far as she could tell, no one was there. She followed the wall to a vestibule where she made out the grayish murk of the night sky. Water swished against the hull. Croaks. Chirps. A faint outline of treetops. Good. The bank was near. She tiptoed across the deck to the rail and swung a leg over the gunwale.

Her spirits soared. Freedom was the river.

Someone grabbed her arm.

"No!" Stella screamed.

A lantern shone over her. A bushy black beard mocked her. Cliff Burton! Her heart was in her throat.

"Out for some air, squaw?"

The gray-bearded old man appeared. A dimly-lit gap in his crusty broken teeth taunted her.

Burton trained the light on the old man and the figure at his side. "Who ya got there, Pete?"

"Got the boy. Found him topside."

"It's me, Jaspar," the boy said, meekly.

"How'd she get loose, boy?"

"I don't know."

"What were ya doing up top?"

"Pissing."

Burton smirked. "Nah. You unlatched that door, didn't ya, boy?"

"No, Cliff, I didn't."

"Now, why would ya do that? You partial to this squaw, boy?"

"No, sir."

Old man Pete laughed. "You weren't partial enough to fug her now, were ya, boy?"

"Uh, yes I did," Jaspar said.

"No, boy. I looked in," old Pete said. "That bitch was whispering sweet things in yer ear. You a-planning to run off with 'er, weren't ya?"

"No!" Jaspar looked at Stella like a condemned man.

Burton jerked her arm and flung her toward the old man. "Hold onto her." He set the lantern on a bench and put his arm around Jaspar's shoulders.

"Boy, I understand being young and stupid. We all been there, ain't we?" Burton winked.

Jaspar's shoulders relaxed. Was the bearded demon going to show the boy mercy?

He gripped Jaspar's chin and turned him so they were nose to nose. "But what I don't cotton to is weakness. And most of all, I don't cotton to disobeying my orders."

He raised Jaspar's chin. With his other hand, he pulled a long-bladed knife and made a swift cut across Jaspar's throat. Blood spurted onto the deck. Stella screamed. The bearded demon heaved Jaspar's body over the side rail into the river.

"Gimme yer bottle."

Old Pete reached into his coat and handed Burton a whisky bottle. After a long drink, he jerked Stella away from the old man.

"You see that, squaw? Takes a strong man to kill another sum bitch with a knife." The bearded demon squeezed her cheeks together, forcing her to look at him. "I don't think Franklin's strong 'nuff to best Ricky in a knife fight. Hell no, I don't." He leaned in close. His whiskey breath nearly overwhelmed her. "Franklin was with a big, strong niggah on that cotton boat. That Franklin's niggah?" He didn't wait for her answer. "Franklin's niggah killed Ricky; ain't that right, squaw?"

Stella's mouth opened. Be careful! If she admitted the truth, she would be signing Toby's death warrant. And telling Burton something that contradicted what she and John Dee had told the judge. "You know Mister Franklin killed your brother to stop him from assaulting me," Stella said.

"Y're a lying bitch. I outta throw you in the river with yer lover boy." Burton took another drink. "Ah hell, y're gonna be worth good money in New Orleans. I'll bet 'ol Dutch Pete or Kitty or Archie or one ah them other whoring bastards'll buy ya. Might's well keep ya and get sumting outta ya."

A lightness she hadn't felt since before the fire floated through her. A whorehouse in New Orleans had to be better than being his prisoner. Or tossed into the river with Jaspar's body. *Just make it to New Orleans and run away! Find a boat and sing again! Just maybe—*

He pulled her in close. His grip squeezed her upper arm like a vise. She bit into her cheek to keep from screaming in pain.

"I'll tell ya a secret, squaw. Once the whorehouse makes its money off ya, I'll be coming back. Yep. Then I'm gonna gut you like a fish and throw you to the hogs."

Stella couldn't stop shaking.

He grinned and growled softly, evidently savoring her discomfort.

"That's right, bitch. Shoulda stayed away from my brother." He grabbed her long black hair and jerked her head back. He yanked her hair downward, forcing her to her knees.

"Ow! No!"

The bearded demon's heinously evil laugh chilled her to the bone. He dragged her by the hair to her prison room.

Chapter 17

Toby stood at the bow staring at black patches in a gray, early-dawn sky. Steamy humidity portended a steamy Louisiana day. He twisted his torso to loosen his back. Hours lying on the packet's plank deck, wedged between a horse stall and a row of hogsheads, had damn near made him a bent-over old man.

He tapped his boot heel, anxious for *Patsy*, the packet he, Addy, and John Dee had caught at Baton Rouge, to pull into the main channel and steam southeast. New Orleans was just a few bends downriver.

Daylight crept over the southern sky. Paddle-wheelers were gonna pop up, one after another, steaming north. In the distance, past thickets of buttonwoods, the faint shape of a big house could be seen on the south riverbank. Oak Alley? Glendale? Maybe even Homeplace? Might be just an hour or two from port.

Would that bearded river ginty Cliff Burton be waiting with his greasy band of pirates? Bound and determined to shoot him and John Dee dead. *Nah, how can he know where we're landing? Or when we're gonna turn up?* But he'd sure as hell be setting a trap in New Orleans. Burton was trouble for damn sure—the kinda trouble that wouldn't be hard to find.

Storks splashed near shore. Everyone was gonna be up before too long.

Here I go again, into the fire with John Dee. Toby shifted on his feet. This time with John Dee chasing after his lover. Could he keep a straight head about Stella when he'd just tumbled with her? *Christ. Cliff Burton sure as hell knows what he wants. Our heads. Is John Dee up to Burton's threat? He's gonna have to be. Fact is John Dee's all I got to back me up. Least he's always been there before.*

Something banged at the stern. Must be the crew getting ready to throw off the lines.

Toby brushed some dirt off his coat. *Goddamned smelly-planked stable deck!* Be a shame to ruin these fine togs he'd just purchased in Baton Rouge. He chuckled to himself, recalling the moment he, Addy, and John Dee had arrived at the haberdashery in their river rags. The clerk's contempt, and his threat to call the authorities to remove them, disappeared into a welcoming smile when John Dee pulled out a handful of twenty-dollar gold coins. Then he and John Dee were into new clothes in a flash. And Addy ran the clerk ragged fetching dresses. She musta tried on a dozen, posing in each one in front of the mirror. And him. Damn, the woman was a goddess in every danged dress! She settled on three, each a different color, but all low-cut at the neck like a bawdy girl wore. Truth was, he'd sat there, enjoying the modeling show, damn near salivating at the prospect of peeling one of those dresses off her.

Addy's a looker all right, and for damn sure there's a fire lit. Christ. Careful man. You ain't stayed alive on the lower river rushing headlong into things.

At least the right city was up ahead. New Orleans was more tolerant toward Black folk than anywhere else Toby'd been. The place sure as hell had its debaucheries. Even so, caution must be the word. He knew about laws on the books against amalgamation—interracial sex— even in New Orleans. If he happened to show Addy affection in front of the wrong White man, it'd be a trip to face the recorder, then on to a whipping.

Gotta be smarter.

Besides, why get wrapped up with Addy when there were the Burtons to deal with? Time had come to face Cliff Burton and his gintys.

~ ~ ~

John Dee stood aside as Toby helped Addy into their carriage. She was a sight in her low-cut dress, with its ribbon-trimmed sleeves and a rosy gold brooch decorating the top of her bosom. When she made a "come hither" smile at Toby, he chuckled to himself.

Course, Toby was a sight, too, in his sharp gray wool waistcoat and black hat.

Their finery stood out on the wharf. Roustabouts in shabby work clothes shouted in an indecipherable international jumble of French, English, Spanish, and German.

Drays splattered mud everywhere. Haphazard weighing stations, cargo stands of casks and barrels, and piles of coal were scattered like debris from a storm.

John Dee climbed up and took the bench opposite Addy and Toby. He sucked in steamy air heavy with the stench of stale wine or maybe horse piss. Time to move on.

The driver turned and asked, "Where to?" in thick Irish brogue. His eyes widened at the sight of Toby sitting close to Addy, her armed wrapped around his at the elbow.

"Problem, friend?" John Dee asked.

"Don't want no trouble."

"On account o' these two?" John Dee pointed his thumb at Toby and Addy.

"Some White men round here don't take kindly to it."

Toby sighed, patted the back of Addy's hand, and scooched several inches away from her.

"Now then," John Dee said, "the Saint Charles Hotel."

"*Oui*, yer 'onor," the driver said.

John Dee leaned toward Toby and Addy. "Be a little careful, would you two?"

Addy sighed and looked off.

They settled into a comfortable silence as the iron-rimmed wheels crunched the mottled surface of the port road: clam shells, fish bones, the remnants of wooden crates, and broken bits of pottery and other goods. A well-traveled road, which gave John Dee confidence that an inevitable clash with the Burtons wouldn't occur here.

Finally, Addy asked, "How long to the hotel?"

"Oh, a good while," John Dee said. "*Patsy* landed downriver from the Quarter. It's a-ways to town. First, we'll come round the human river rats on the waterfront. Whorehouses and taverns."

"We ain't stopping there, are we?"

"Nah. We'll let rooms and make a plan. I suppose it'll be onto the whorehouses on Gallatin Street."

"Okay."

"Closer to town, the carriage way's gonna roll through some residences and down by Jackson Square. Past some gardens and the cathedral."

"That sounds better."

"By a damn sight."

A few minutes later, the carriage emerged from cypress trees and clattered over the rutted road that ran along a canal. Bricked salt warehouses sat behind deep troughs of curbstones half-full of stagnant water. The stench nearly gagged John Dee. Just past the warehouses, a building had broken shutters and an open back door.

The horses stopped while one relieved himself. A short man in a blue sailor suit stood on the back stoop of the dilapidated building. A young woman with red hair and gigantic breasts joined him and waved at John Dee, Addy, and Toby. "You there! Come on over for—a talk. Your woman, too. A real good, pleasurable talk."

"Good God!"

Toby laughed at Addy. "What's the matter? Don't want to be a bawdy girl after all?"

"Not like that one! I'll be a classy lady who just happens to play a bawdy girl."

John Dee snorted out a laugh. "Gallatin Street's short on classy bawdy girls these days."

"Look at all them shit-hole buildings," Addy said. "Far down as you can see."

Back sides of the tenements faced the canal. Broken roof tiles, discarded furniture, and piles of garbage were the norm.

"Can't tell a tavern from a whorehouse round here," Toby said.

"They're all the same," John Dee said.

"You really think Stella's in one of these nasty places?" Addy asked.

"We're gonna find out," Toby said.

The carriage rattled on, leaving the bawdy houses behind, proceeding through narrow streets lined with residences. Several blocks into the neighborhood, giant lanterns swayed over the carriage way from cables connecting high poles. Sea-salt-battered stucco walls fronted houses that featured high-arched windows and doors, balconies and entresols. Some had lacy-patterned iron railings. All were partially shrouded in Spanish moss, giving the area a mystical aura.

"Good gracious, these houses are on top of one another," Addy said. "You'd knock elbows with your neighbor."

"Ain't used to the city, are you, Addy girl?" Toby asked with a grin. "Gotta take the bad with the good. Fine restaurants, merchants and shops, and plenty o' people to keep you entertained come along with the tight spaces."

"'Spose so," she said.

John Dee smiled at Toby and Addy getting to know each other. Small talk, gaining comfort with one another. God, she'd come a long way. Just a couple of days ago, she would have treated Toby no better than dirt under her shoe. Did it make any sense that one night in the river truly forged a deep bond between them and tempered her prejudices? Or was her lust for Toby concealing her true nature, for now.

Soon, they passed stucco buildings of commerce with stately pillars. Features like domes, cupolas, and steeples proclaimed New Orleans' architectural dominance of the Western Frontier.

"Ahh," John Dee said, "charming New Orleans. When I come this way, I feel home."

"That right?" Addy pointed to a garbage heap. "Is it the stink, the hucksters, or the whores? Or all of it?"

"Addy! There's no call." Toby squeezed her hand.

John Dee just smiled.

The carriage approached the courthouse, past the expansive grounds of Jackson Square and its equestrian statue. Drays and hastily constructed merchant stands clogged the square, and clanging pots and pans augured the midday meal. Cooking smells wafted over them. Gumbo, bread, and coffee.

St. Louis Cathedral loomed beyond the square. Hooves clicked along the brick roadway. When the driver slowed his team at a large, public garden, John Dee enjoyed the scent of lemon. Vines with pretty yellow flowers draped the fence. Perfectly-shaped laurel bushes and creeping myrtles with purple flowers lifted his mood.

"This is more like it," Addy said.

They passed an English-style pub, and suddenly, people were everywhere. Whites, Blacks, Mulattos, Indians. At the cathedral, cripples and beggars called out, some in English, others in French. Some White, others Black, all mixed together in a pitiful integrated scene that John Dee couldn't remember seeing anywhere else. An old priest opened the lid of his box as they approached. John Dee tossed coins into it.

"What're you doing?" Addy asked.

"Filling his poor box," John Dee said. "Good for the soul."

The driver halted the horses.

"Why'd you stop?" John Dee asked.

The driver pointed to a large, black carriage with iron bars, coming from their right.

"That's the Black Maria. Bad luck to cross in front of 'er."

Four large horses and the Black Maria trotted by. The driver tended his team from a high bench. A rifleman sat beside him. Female faces stared at John Dee, Toby, and Addy through the iron bars.

"Who are they? Where are the going?" Addy asked.

"Bawdy girls," the driver said. "Recorder sent 'em to the workhouse."

"What?" Addy shook her head. "There's whorehouses everywhere! Do they send all the bawdy girls away?"

"Nah," the driver said. "These are the dumb-arsed bitches that get drunk and swear round church people. Some of 'em might-a stole money from their tryst-man."

John Dee took Addy's hands. "Back on the river, I told you this ain't no game. Sending you into Gallatin Street's gonna be dangerous." A rebellious gleam in her eye alarmed him. Stella was in grave danger; that couldn't be helped. Addy would be in just as much danger if she took her cavalier attitude into the waterfront flesh-peddling cesspool. "I don't think this is for you."

Addy pushed him away. "I'm gonna help find that girl. And I'm gonna be careful about it. Toby'll be there to protect me, won't you?"

"Sure will," Toby said.

"Just worry about yourself, Franklin," Addy said. "You can find trouble here just as easy as I can."

"Yah!" The driver snapped his whip and the horses clip-clopped past brick shop buildings with shutters pulled back. Merchants displayed muslins, silks, and shawls.

Addy's spirits seemed to lift. "I'll be coming back here."

"Reckon so," Toby said.

Several blocks later, the grand, Grecian portico of the St. Charles Hotel took John Dee's breath away. Marble and stone columns shimmered in the sun, and the building was adorned with intricate carvings he'd never seen the likes of. Good ol' Aphrodite, and maybe the Dying Gaul. And there was the Winged Victory. Impressive.

A man smoking a pipe stood near the marble stairs. He wore a top hat and formal black waistcoat, and he was observing John Dee, Toby, and Addy. Two women tugged up their light-colored hoop dresses as they ascended the stairs. Their sleeves were capped short for the warm weather. Servants followed behind, carrying their bags.

"Thank God!" Addy said. "Civilization at last. A bath. A feather bed. I've done come to heaven!"

"Finest hotel in the world, ma'am," said the driver. "Least this side of Killarney."

John Dee gestured to the doorman to wait a moment before approaching their carriage. He leaned into Toby and Addy. "Wait here. I'm going in to let three rooms." He looked at Toby. "You're a Creole plantation owner from down Lafayette way. And Addy's the wife of a planter who's a client of mine." He turned to Addy.

"Be discrete with your affections, would ya? You heard the driver: White men may not take kindly to you two canoodling. Stella's in enough trouble without dealing with more of your creation!"

"Don't you worry," Toby said. "We're gonna get our bags to the rooms, wash up, and go look for Stella, ain't we?"

John Dee noticed a little color in Toby's cheeks. Hotter than a firecracker to be with Addy. "Tell ya what. I've got someone to visit who might just help us out."

"Who's that, Franklin?" Addy asked. "A bawdy girl? Then don't be worried about what Toby and I'll be up to."

John Dee sighed. "Just where do you think I'll find out something about Stella? Church pews?"

Addy laughed. "Figured you were gonna mix business with pleasure."

"Christ! I'll be back in a couple of hours. You two— rest up." He smirked. "We'll meet in the Paris parlor in two hours. Then we'll head out and search for Stella."

~ ~ ~

John Dee's bootheels sank into plush Persian carpet. He approached the bar, which was adorned with a red metallic cover and brass fixtures. Bottles stood in clusters in cubbies of the rich, cherrywood back bar.

He breathed deeply. A lavender scent? Even the air was elegant in this bawdy house, the opposite direction and a world away from Gallatin Street.

He felt a light touch on his shoulder.

"Hello, dear," a sultry voice whispered in his ear.

"Miss Marguerite! Truly a vision you are. Southern Belle extraordinaire." He kissed the back of her gloved hand.

"Been too long, John Dee Franklin." Her eyes twinkled. Did she do that for all her men? Her expression was joyful, with rouge-highlighted cheeks framed by ringlets dangling from her center part.

"Indeed it has. You are as beautiful as ever, my dear."

"Thank you. And you are as handsome as ever." She looked around. "Where is your handsome friend, Mister Toby Freeman? You two are virtually inseparable as I recall."

"Oh, Toby's in town. Just tied up for now."

"Shame. Eloise will be so disappointed. A drink?"

He kissed her lightly on the cheek. "Absolutely. Let's take one upstairs with us, shall we?"

"What's your hurry, dear?" John Dee smiled. "Your charms entice a man to action, my lovely." He turned to the bartender. "Whiskey and water. A brandy for the lady."

A few minutes later, drink in hand, John Dee sank into a leather chair in the corner of Marguerite's room. She closed the door, making a sultry smile and a sweet cooing sound that stirred his loins. Standing between his legs, she removed her gloves, and lightly dragged them across his cheek. Tossing them away, she put her hands on his chest and surely felt his pounding heartbeat. Her hands drifted to his shoulders, inviting his embrace.

She frowned at his lack of response. "What's troubling you, sugar?"

"You know me so well," John Dee said.

She leaned into him and placed her finger on his chin. "Sure do. Your manly dimple. The cute little half-moon scar on your hip. That thing you do—"

Still, he didn't reach for her.

"What is it, darling?"

"A friend of mine's in trouble here in New Orleans," he said.

"What kind of trouble?"

"Some river pirates took her and are gonna sell her to a bawdy house."

"Oh my! Why?"

"To get back at me."

"What did you do to them?"

"Killed one of 'em when he assaulted my friend."

Marguerite drew back. "Hmm. What's the name of this pirate bunch?"

"The Burtons."

"They don't come round here."

"Didn't reckon they do. Too many politicians and judges and such visit you girls."

"This friend of yours—do you love her?"

John Dee sighed. "Her name's Stella. Stella Parrot. I care about her."

"How can I help?" Marguerite sat on the bed and patted the mattress.

John Dee sat next to her. "Stella's no bawdy girl. The Burtons are gonna sell her against her will."

"Oh, honey. It's a pitiful shame." She sighed. "That puts your girl in a very bad situation, but I expect you know that."

"We know that, my darling."

"So this girl is Toby's friend, too?"

John Dee nodded. "S'pose some mean bastard's gonna drug her or beat her or both to make her take on trysts. We're guessing she's being held at a grimy whorehouse on Gallatin Street."

"That's most likely true," Marguerite said. "The heinous way some of these monsters do business—you've heard of 'White lady medicine'?"

"Yeah. Some drug, isn't it?"

"They mix opium with alcohol. Listen, dear; a girl here called Candy has taken up with an Irish policeman who knows plenty about Gallatin Street establishments. Candy's mick cop told her that nasty brothels down on Gallatin Street make the girls drink White lady medicine to keep 'em numb to the depravities. Don't take long before a girl can't live without it. She'll do anything for a swig."

"Turns my stomach to think some bastard is forcing Stella to drink poison." John Dee squeezed Marguerite's hand.

"Might just be a woman who's doing it. A Madam like Dutch Kitty or Sugar Marie. They're just as rotten as the men." She hugged him. "I'll have Candy inquire with her mick about your girl, discretely. Tell me more about her."

John Dee described Stella's appearance and gentle manner. He found himself nearly tongue-tied trying to explain her singing talent, and left it at "Well, she's the finest singer I've heard anywhere, anytime."

Marguerite's kind, understanding smile was comforting, but the cold truth was her elegant house was a world away from the cesspool he and Toby needed to dive into if they were going to find Stella on Gallatin Street. The sooner the better.

"Your soft side comes out when you tell me about Stella," Marguerite said. "It's the romantic in you, John Dee. Makes me squishy inside. I imagine Stella feels it, too." She took his hands. "But Gallatin Street ain't warm and squishy. It's blood and guts and balls and nerve. Getting a girl outta there won't be easy. It'll be dangerous. Real dangerous. I don't know if you and Toby got that in you. Maybe you should find a gunman to search for Stella."

John Dee stood. "I got it in me. Toby does, too." He put a coin in Marguerite's hand and kissed her cheek. "I'll check back with you, soon."

"Promise?"

He winked as he disappeared through the door.

Chapter 18

I MAGES CAUGHT IN A TORNADO hurtled over Stella's head. Shattered brown wood. Gleaming sunlight too bright to look at. Dark liquid sloshing in a drinking glass. Unattached hands darting back and forth over her face. A large, angry woman with breasts the size of pumpkins floating like a ghost.

Stella strained to sit up, but her arms and legs refused to move. *What's happening?*

Rows of enraptured faces drifted overhead. Another face, this one with bushy red eyebrows rising and lowering over a big nose and red mustache.

Sam, what do I do?

John Dee appeared, smiling.

Help me! Hold me, John Dee!

Cliff Burton's nasty face loomed with sneering lips. Black snakes slithered in his beard.

Stella screamed. No sound came out. Or did it? Echoes blasted through her brain. She bucked her torso. She banged her head against the bedframe. Where was she…? Who did this…? What could…?

~ ~ ~

Stella's eyes opened slowly, adjusting to the light. Ropes dug into her wrists and ankles, jamming them into the bedframe. Only her head moved freely. She slowly surveyed her surroundings. A small room, with planked walls, a shabby, splintered wooden ceiling, and an old wooden chair. Was she back in her prison on Cliff Burton's boat? No. The floor wasn't rocking, unlike the boat's. *This room is somewhere else.*

Who was keeping her prisoner?

Good God! The stench! Was something dead in the room?

Stella stretched her neck to the right. There, a rusty bedpan was nearly full of brown and yellow ooze. Her throat constricted. Her stomach clenched.

Who is doing this to me? Is any of this real?

She struggled to free herself. The skin on her wrists and ankles burned.

Why did I leave the Lady J*? For the love of God!*

She'd gone over its side into a stormy river on a hope and a prayer with two men she barely knew. She'd flailed in the river, escaped a burning boat, and been beaten within an inch of her life. This room promised worse. She should have taken her chances on the *Lady J* with her troupe.

Forget that! Like Toby said, "Don't do a damn bit of good to think about what can't be." Okay, so where was she? Was Cliff Burton here? Or had he sold her to who-ever owned this grotesque shack—just like he said he would. Had he sold her to a whorehouse? *My God no!*

She tried to calm herself. *Think straight. Someone will come. Figure out how to escape. Stay strong!*

She stared at the ceiling. Time passed. Was it minutes? Hours? The trail of every chip and splinter in the wood overhead burned into her brain like her road to nowhere.

A hunger ate at her. It wasn't for food.

She rolled her tongue around the insides of her mouth. *Ahh.* A pleasingly faint burning taste. Not quite brandy. What was it?

The door creaked open.

A massive, scowling woman, with flaming red hair pinned up on top of her head stood at the end of Stella's bed. Her low-cut dress barely contained massive breasts and revealed cleavage the size of a gopher hole. Hands on her hips, she stared at Stella.

"Hmmph. 'Spose you'll need to eat sum-ting."

"Un-tie me!" Stella bucked, struggling to free her arms and legs. Bedposts bounced on the plank floor. She made no progress and collapsed, huffing and puffing in futility.

"You done, squaw?" The redheaded woman glared. "Ya ain't get-tin' no food till ya calm yerself." She bent down and squeezed Stella's chin in her hand. "Listen here, girlie. I paid good money for you." Spittle struck Stella's cheeks. The redheaded woman's face hovered inches closer. "You're mine now! Quit wasting my time and money, or I'll feed ya to the hogs!" The woman's chin and jowls quivered hostilely.

Stella shuddered. "Where am I?" she asked in not much more than a whisper.

"Yer in my house. Near the docks. On Gallatin Street. If you fly right, I'll clean you up and you'll be one of my girls."

"What do you mean?"

"Don't act a goddamned, dumb-assed, black-eyed Susie, squaw!" The woman squeezed Stella's jaw again until it hurt like hell.

"Ow!"

"Yer gonna hurt a lot worse if you don't calm yerself and follow my orders!"

The woman's fiery eyes provided a glimpse into the pit of hell.

"What do you want from me?" Stella asked.

The redheaded woman stood up, towering over Stella, with her hands on her hips. "I think you know. So, jus relax, squaw. Once yer ready, the girls'll bathe you and dress you up real nice. Why, with yer dark skin, you may be a looker. Then you'll take care of my men customers just like the rest of the girls do. Hell, maybe even a woman here and again." She chuckled. "Do a good job and I'll let you keep a coin now and then."

The woman let that sink in. Stella could hardly breathe. Was she in hell?

"Ain't all bad, is it?" the redheaded woman asked.

Stella cringed, imagining dirty, smelly dockworkers pinning her down, laughing, taunting her. Poking her. Hurting her. Tossing her about like a rag doll. Grunting and straining. Finishing, and pushing her away like a piece of trash.

"Open yer eyes!" the woman shouted. "Don't you cry like a goddamned baby."

"I'm...I'm not a bawdy girl. I'm a singer!"

The redhead roared with laughter, her ample belly jiggling up and down. "A singer? Are you now? Then sing a love song to your tryst-man, and maybe he'll toss you an extra coin."

Her cackle at her own joke chilled Stella.

"Calm yerself, girlie." She turned toward the table and grabbed a glass of brown liquid. "Here, girlie; take your medicine. It's gonna make you feel a whole lot better."

The sight of the glass warmed Stella's insides. *Yes.* The brown juice had made her feel happy, like she was far away from here. Then she drifted off to sleep. Another drink—that's what she needed. She raised her head to meet the glass.

The redheaded woman brought the glass to Stella's lips and let her sip. Then she drew back.

Stella licked her lips, craving more.

"Good, ain't it?"

Stella puckered her lips for more.

"It ain't free, squaw. You ain't getting no more unless you calm yerself and let my girls clean you up. Understand me?"

"Yes."

The woman returned the glass to Stella's lips, and she greedily drank down the liquid. A burning sensation traveled down her throat and warmed her insides. She closed her eyes.

When she opened them wide, the redheaded woman was gone. Everything was clear. She was imprisoned. In a New Orleans whorehouse. Taking "White lady medicine" until she capitulated. Then she would whore for this evil madam.

The wooden ceiling became puffy brown clouds.

No one would come for her. Georgia's sad face popped into her mind. That was the moment Stella had realized she had no choice other than to satisfy Mr. Bickler. Now, there was no choice other than to satisfy the madam's customers.

A Black man and a White man stood shoulder to shoulder at the foot of the bed. Strong. Honorable. *Toby! John Dee! Come for me! You're my only hope.*

John Dee extended his hand to her. She tried to reach out, but the ropes....

Her eyelids flickered. Her vision clouded over like a dingy sunset, and her two saviors shattered into dozens of puzzle pieces.

She laid her head back and waves of relief surged through her body. Ecstasy. She concentrated solely on the feeling. Seismic waves lifted her high into the sky and lowered her gently, as if she were weightless.

Images floated above her again. A Bible. Toby—reaching out for her. *I'm here, Toby! Here!*

Her eyelids flickered.

A red bustier. A gap-toothed, grinning man with a scraggly beard. A gold coin, flipping end over end.

Her father's stoic face, his long black hair lying over his collar.

Teddy, pounding the ivory piano keys.

The black surface of the river.

Stella gulped for air, flailing in the water once again. She couldn't raise her arms or legs. She couldn't swim. Desperate to stay above water, she struggled.

Help...help....

Chapter 19

ADDY ROLLED ONTO HER SIDE and grabbed a handful of satin bedsheet. Little tingles flickered up her arm to her very core. She lifted her palm to place it on Toby's powerful shoulder. He wasn't there. Her breathing quickened as panic shot through her. She sat up. *Thank God, he's here!* He stood next to the bed, putting his muscled arms into sleeves and pulling his shirt over his manly torso. How heavenly, being embraced by that body—

"What's your hurry?" she asked.

"We're gonna meet John Dee," Toby said. "And hunt for Stella."

"I 'spose so. But I'd rather have you come back into bed with me for a while longer."

Toby kissed the back of her hand. "We've just started, Addy girl. There'll be more loving later. For damn sure."

"Better be. Best I ever had, and I want more."

He grinned.

Her passionate confession had rushed out like a waterfall. It was true, coming from somewhere deep inside of her. A piece of her just for him.

"Toby."

"Yeah."

"I want you with me."

He sighed. "I want you, too, Addy girl."

"I mean always. I think…I think I…."

"Stop, Addy girl. Don't say what you don't mean. You ain't had time to think on that."

She rose from the bed, letting the sheet fall off her shoulders. She pulled him to her naked body and squeezed him tight. She cradled his cheeks and kissed him. "Okay, then. When I say it, you'll know I mean it."

"Damn. You make it tough to leave this room." He kissed her hungrily. "Get yourself dressed, Addy girl."

She made pouty lips but gathered her clothes.

Toby took a chair and pulled on his boots. She flashed a mischievous smile as she slowly fastened her lace stockings with a garter. Then she dressed herself with one unhurried piece of clothing after another. The lust in his gaze hung in the air. Slow, deliberate brush strokes to apply her rouge had him squirming in his chair. She slipped on an elegant blue cape that covered her bustier.

"Gotta hide my bawdy girl clothes in this fancy hotel."

"Yes, you do, but hiding the body of a goddess is a damn shame," Toby said.

She blew him a kiss. "Ready?"

Toby rose. "One more thing." He pulled a knife from his coat and made a long slit in the side of the mattress.

Her mouth fell open. "Toby?"

He flattened his valise and stuffed it inside the mattress. Then he patted it smooth, pulled up the sheets, and placed the pillow at the head of the bed.

"Trusting me with your future, are you?" Addy asked.

"Well, the Burtons know about John Dee and me, but they don't know about you. If they come looking round this hotel, the money oughta be safe in your mattress."

"Gonna be a real temptation, lover." Addy grinned. "All these fancy shops in the Quarter."

Toby pulled her close. "I know where to find you."

"I'm counting on that."

He kissed her with the passion of new lovers before he reluctantly drew away. "We gotta go."

"You go on down, first. We ain't s'pose to be together in front of all them men in the lobby. Besides, I gotta touch up my makeup."

"All right." Toby disappeared through the doorway.

~ ~ ~

Toby pulled his hat low on his forehead. He stood next to a stone column in the vast lobby of the St. Charles Hotel, scanning the room for John Dee while clerks scurried about the hotel counter. Over their heads, massive tapestries depicted idyllic Greek or Roman garden scenes of toga-clad men sipping wine and appreciating young women with bare titties. Reminded him of looking down at Addy half-covered in satin sheets.

His grinning lips stiffened. A mustachioed man wearing a dark suit jacket over zouave trousers was eyeing him. Long black hair hung under a military-style hat that gave the observer an air of authority. Toby lifted his chin, placed his lapel between his thumb and forefinger, and puffed out his chest in his best impression of a vainglorious, upcountry, Creole planter. Someone called to his observer, and Toby used the momentary distraction to move across the lobby, behind a column at the far side of the counter.

Where the hell is John Dee?

"Simply not acceptable! *Monsieur* Chalmette is here, and you must summon him!" A tall, pear-shaped, and gray-headed guest screeched at a wide-eyed clerk. The old man wagged his finger like a weapon at the harried young man.

Toby stifled a laugh.

The clerk stammered, "I'm sorry; did you say your name is Mister…Mister…Bickler—? I've checked our records carefully and there is no—"

Mr. Bickler? Toby's mind raced back to Stella's St. Louis story. Bickler—the bastard who cornered her and had his way. Could he be this man?

"*Monsieur* Chalmette is most certainly a guest at this hotel! We have a very important meeting at this very hour! I board a boat to St. Louis in two hours, so time is of the essence here!"

St. Louis. This must be the same bastard who had scarred Stella's soul.

"But, sir," the clerk said with wilting conviction, "I've searched our book—"

"Then consult whoever you have to! Find him!" Mr. Bickler demanded with fiery rage while rapping the counter like a judge banging his gavel.

The clerk scurried away, down the counter and through a door to the back.

Bickler turned and scanned the lobby, apparently searching for Chalmette. Pursed, thin lips and beady eyes. Toby's gut turned with surety. *Here is the evil bastard, and it's time to deal with him.*

Toby removed and folded his jacket, then placed it and his hat under the cover of fern fronds overflowing a stone floor vase like an opened umbrella. He unbuttoned the collar of his shirt to mimic a look befitting a manservant enduring late spring heat. He approached the counter.

"Excuse me, sir," Toby said. "You be Mister Bickler?"

The old man drew back. Maybe in shock. More likely in fear of a much younger, stronger, Black man. He eyed Toby up and down, apparently calculating whether he might be Chalmette's manservant sent to fetch him.

"Oh, I'm sorry to startle you, sir," Toby said. "It's juz—Master Chalmette told me to come round and bring you to see him at the Four Roses on Tchoupitoulas."

Bickler's expression transformed into a satisfied grin. "Very well." He took a second, searching look around. "But his letter said to meet here, at the St. Charles. We have very important business to discuss."

"Yes, sir, very important. Master said to bring you right down to de-scuss things 'bout your theater." Toby tried his best to pantomime a house slave's dialect and demeanor. *Acknowledge your theater, old geezer, and it's case closed.* "It's juz master's meeting's run over down at Four Roses."

"Very well then. Yes, your master and I have most important things to discuss about my theater."

It was him, all right!

"Would ya please follow me, Mister Bickler? I gotta get you down to the Four Roses lickety-split."

Toby led Bickler down Canal Street toward the river. The old man walked with a slight stoop, reflective of the decade that had passed since Stella arrived in

St. Louis. Toby's blood boiled. A young woman of color shamed and sexually abused by a powerful White man. He'd heard it all too often. Despicable! Her painful telling ate at his soul. Time for one of these bastards to pay!

He led the old man onto a side street opposite Sazerac House. Too narrow for a sidewalk, they kept to the right side of the lane to dodge an oncoming carriage. They stepped over piles of horse muck. The stench of vegetable tannins from saddles displayed in front of a run-down wooden building hung in the air like a curse.

Bickler tugged on Toby's sleeve. "Boy, you sure this is the right way?"

"Oh, yes, sir. Master said bring Mister Bickler to the Four Roses juz lickety-split." He snapped his fingers for emphasis. "This here's the fastest route. We'll be there in no time."

"Okay."

"Mister Bickler, sir?"

"Yes, boy?"

"I've been to your theater in St. Louis."

"My theater?"

"Yessir. One time Master brought me 'long. He was in the seats up front, course, and I was back uh the rail. Most wonderful place I been in all my life!"

Bickler's face lit up. "Well, thank you, boy."

They passed a white fence with half its pickets dangling and several post caps missing. The brick building behind it had broken shutters and shattered window glass.

Bickler sniffed with obvious nervousness.

Toby casually surveyed the street. No one in sight.

"Here, sir." Toby guided Bickler into a narrow lane between an abandoned groggery and a locked warehouse.

"Are we close, boy? I don't like this—"

"Oh, yes, sir. Very close. Juz a minute or two more." He whistled two lines of "Swanee River" like he didn't have a care in the world. "Why, in that beautiful theater of yours, you had the best singer in all a Missour-a. You remember that Indian girl, sir? What her name?"

"Oh, her." Bickler grimaced. "She had a fine voice. But she was a disloyal red-skinned bitch. Left me for the boats without a word." He rubbed his chin. "What was her name? Oh, Stella—Stella Bird? Stella Crow?"

Toby grabbed the sleeve of Bickler's coat and stopped them behind the warehouse.

Bickler stiffened. His eyes widened with fury. "Release me, boy!"

Toby glared back. Bickler's superiority melted.

"Her name is Stella Parrot."

Bickler didn't respond.

"You abused that poor girl."

Bickler's nostrils flared. "I did nothing of the sort. I made that girl a singer!"

Toby moved closer, almost nose to nose with him. "Stuck your pecker in her when she didn't want you to, didn't you?"

"She got what she wanted, and I got what I wanted!" Bickler's neck quivered. "Enough of this! Take me to *Monsieur* Chalmette immediately!"

"Who?" Toby asked.

Bickler turned white as a sheet. He opened his mouth to scream. Toby grabbed the back of his neck and pressed the palm of his other hand against Bickler's lips, silencing him. Bickler grabbed Toby's arms, but he couldn't break Toby's stronger grip.

"Now I'm gonna get what I want." Toby backed Bickler toward a horse trough and drove him under the surface, splashing up brownish water, foamy scum, and bits of straw. He held Bickler's head under for several seconds. When he pulled him up, guttural gasps escaped bluish lips.

Toby's heart pounded like a drum. Everything inside him screamed *Finish the bastard!* He plunged the old man back under. No one ever deserved it more. Toby savored the feeling of Bickler's weakening struggles.

Finally, Toby sighed and pulled Bickler's head out of the water. Water spewed from the old man's mouth and nostrils. Once he caught his breath, Bickler looked up at Toby with eyes pleading like a slave facing his master's whip.

"I ain't gonna finish you 'cause Stella would be merciful." Toby shook Bickler for emphasis. "Listen, old man. Get yer ass on the boat and outta New Orleans. I see you again, I'm gonna kill you. Understand?"

Bickler nodded.

Toby released his grip.

~ ~ ~

John Dee weaved through a sea of White men in wool tailcoats. He took a seat in the Paris Parlor, off the lobby of the St. Charles, and ordered peppermint tea. Where the hell were they? Toby was always prompt. Early most times. His infatuation with this blond planter's wife-vixen was just going to slow them down.

Addy approached. The sight of her busty neckline and cape-covered, perfect, womanly form took away his breath. *I guess I understand, partner.*

"Toby let you outta bed?"

"Watch your mouth, Franklin!" Addy said with a sneer. "Toby left the room a good fifteen minutes ago. He's not here?"

"Haven't seen him." John Dee rose and scanned the lobby. "Hmm."

"You worried?" Addy asked.

"He'll turn up. He always does." John Dee pointed to a paisley-patterned loveseat. "Please, sit down. May I pour you some tea?"

"Thank you." Addy seated herself.

John Dee took a long look at Addy as she sipped her tea. Flowing blond hair, liberally-applied rouge, and a voluptuous bustline would more than appeal to any tryst-man on Gallatin Street or anywhere else in New Orleans. The sassy boudoir apparel he and Toby had purchased for her in Baton Rouge would be sure to attract lecherous customers like bees to nectar. None of this added up—why the hell was a privileged cane planter's wife mixed up in a mission to the debaucherous whorehouses of New Orleans?

"What exactly are you doing here painted like a two-dollar soiled dove?" he asked.

"Wh—what do you mean?"

"Where we're going ain't no place for a lady like you."

"I'm gonna help Toby."

"That so?"

She took a sip of tea. "He said he can't come to Grace Vale with me till y'all find Stella. So, I'm gonna help him."

John Dee's throat tightened. "You think Toby's gonna go with you to your sugar plantation upriver?"

"Why, yes." Her head tilted as if she anticipated John Dee's fears. "Now, don't worry, honey. He ain't gonna cut cane or nothing. He's gonna help me run Grace Vale a lot better than Reggie did. He's gonna help me with the Black folks. We're gonna treat every-one better."

John Dee sat back, soaking that in. How goddamned smitten was Toby by this woman's charms? Thinking with his pecker-head! Grace Vale was as risky a place as there was on earth for Toby. What if this blond Aphro-dite lost interest in him? One wrong move and he'd find himself shackled, sold to the highest bidder.

"A cane plantation ain't no place for Toby."

"Whyever not?"

"He's a freeman, Addy. A businessman. He comes and goes as he pleases and sure as hell can't be tied down on a cane plantation!"

"Toby wants to come with me. We have a connection!"

"Okay. He pulled you out of the river. He's your hero. Get your fill of him the next couple of nights and go home."

"You don't know anything! Yeah, I care for Toby and want him with me. But it's business, too, for him. He's gonna help me sell Grace Vale."

Blood rushed to his temples. "I don't like this one bit."

"Just what exactly is Toby to you, Franklin? Seems to me he's following you around like Sancho Panza. Yer crazy enough to be Don Quixote from those tall Spanish tales you tell."

Calm, calm. Don't lash out at this delusional blonde planter queen, least not till you've talked to Toby.

"Nah," Addy said. "I know what it is. Don't want to separate from your brother, do you?" She smirked.

"What'd you say?"

"I see the same cheekbones and square jaw in you two boys. Got the same daddy, don't you?" She leaned closer. "Or is it appearances? You kinda like walking round boats and river towns with your big buck trailing behind you, don't you? Makes you look like a big man, now don't it?"

An explosion bubbled, and John Dee took several deep breaths. "Just know this—if Toby comes to your plantation, I'll be checking in on him. If anything happens to him, you'll answer to me."

"That a threat, Franklin?"

"Tea time, is it?" Toby said, interrupting them. He chuckled. "Well, John Dee, she works you up, same as me!"

John Dee sat back and relaxed his jaw. "Sugar princess here just told me about her plans for you. We have some things to talk over, you and I, partner."

Toby turned to Addy. "Told him you want me to come to Grace Vale?"

Addy nodded, sheepishly.

"We'll all talk this over once we find Stella," he said.

"Where the hell you been?" John Dee asked.

"I was down here waiting on you two, and I don't imagine you'll ever guess who I came across."

"Oh?"

"Mister Bickler, from St. Louis, was passing through."

John Dee thought for a moment. "That theater man Stella told us about?"

"That's the one."

"You're sure it was him?"

"Yep," Toby said. "Even got him to admit what he did."

John Dee sat back in his chair. "For God's sake, please tell me you didn't gut the bastard and drop another dead bird on the doorstep."

"Nah. Well, almost. Let's just say he got the rough treatment he deserved."

Addy raised her arms. "What the hell is going on here?"

John Dee rubbed his chin. "Toby here just gave Stella some long-overdue justice. A good omen, if you ask me, for our prospects of finding her and getting her back to her singing."

Addy tilted her head like she didn't have the foggiest notion of what he was talking about.

"But enough about that," he said. "Let's get to Gallatin Street."

Chapter 20

Toby waited with Addy and John Dee for a coach-and-four to pass so they could cross Ursuline to Gallatin Street. A woman wearing a wide headdress peered out from the window opening in the U-shaped, red-lacquered carriage, her head positioned directly over a coat of arms. Her gaze fell on Addy, and what a sight to behold! Busty, with her blond curls tied high, leaving a few loose strands to frame her beautiful face. The rich lady squinted like she was stuck in a rancid outhouse. In her world, visitors to Gallatin Street were 'bout as welcome as turds.

"For Christ's sakes!" Addy tiptoed over cobblestones to minimize the splash-up when the walkway disappeared into a brown, muddy blob. "This damned mud's gonna ruin my shoes and spot up my stockings!"

Toby took her hand to help her step up from Ursuline Street to the banquette. A sinking feeling hit him. Muddy shoes were gonna be the least of her problems. He pulled a rag from his jacket and bent down at her feet.

"I can always count on you." She shifted her shoe, and he wiped off the mud.

"Don't let her step on you with that pointy heel," John Dee said.

"Stow it, Franklin!"

Toby shook his head. John Dee and Addy at each other's throats again. Just what the hell had happened during dinner with the planters and their wives and John Dee and Stella? Maybe John Dee's disdain for rich Southern planters, evident on more than one occasion, was driving his ire. But what about John Dee fired Addy's pistons?

The sulfuric stench of garbage piled on the street nearly gagged Toby.

"Christ!" Addy said. "What in the world is that? A dead cat?"

"Nah," John Dee said, "just rotten onions and cabbage thrown out by some mick vegetable trader. See the broken crate slats?"

"This ain't supposed to be a market. You said it's a row of bawdy houses."

John Dee laughed. "We're in the right place."

A redheaded boy darted into the street from an alley between brick buildings, chasing a scrawny black and tan dog.

A third-floor window opened. "Tad-hg!" a female voice shouted. "Get back in 'ere!"

Addy looked at Toby, wide-eyed. "Families live in this shithole?"

"Some of the Irish just off the boat squat on top floors. Might see a few of 'em 'cause it ain't dark yet."

"Stay away from 'em," John Dee said. "Yellow fever spread through here like a wildfire a couple of summers ago. Don't touch a damn thing."

The nearest building was three floors of nondescript, sooted bricks. Rusting metal doors suggested a warehouse. "I don't see nothing like a bawdy house," Addy said.

Toby chuckled. "Have a peek."

He pulled the iron latch and the door creaked open. A stale, overpowering stench of stale beer wafted out like a cloud of fog. He waved away the stink and stepped over the threshold. Addy was beside him.

A fat man wearing a blue sailor's jacket was on his back in the middle of a room lined with barrels. His mouth opened in a dumb grin. "Amphitrite! Sweet Amphitrite! Sail on in. Come aboard with me."

Toby pulled Addy back outside and shut the door. "After dark, the whole floor'll be stacked with sea dogs."

"Haven't the foggiest idea who that drunk thought I was, but he was kinda funny."

"Come on," John Dee said. "We ain't got time for barrel houses, disorderly tippling houses, or low groggeries."

A guttural scream came from somewhere up the street. The three of them stopped in their tracks. Toby looked at John Dee and then at Addy. Had he made a horrific mistake bringing her to Gallatin Street?

She nodded, slowly, like she read his mind and was acknowledging the danger. But she didn't retreat. Must have more backbone than a sugar princess.

"Dance houses are just a little farther," John Dee said.

Half a block on, a man pissed in the street. Three swerving drunks, arm in arm, approached him, bellowing unmelodious chants of "Blow the man down." One wore a sailor's jacket and had long, plaited hair. Another was shirtless, with blood streaking from his shoulder.

The sailor steered their human chain toward the pissing man. The pisser straightened and pulled a dirk from his jacket. He slashed the air in front of the drunks. "Piss away, swabbie! I'll butcher you, I will!"

The sailor backed off and nudged his shirtless mate with enough force to knock their third down. Momentum from linked arms pulled all of them onto the bricks. "Arrgh!"

The knife-wielding pisser returned to the building.

The sailor and one of his companions rose with the awkwardness of newborn foals. The shirtless man stayed down. "Come on, Mick!" The shirtless drunk didn't move. "Ah, leave 'im!"

John Dee pointed to a sign at the entrance that read "Boatmen's House." "This here's a bawdy house." He grabbed Addy's shoulders. "That little flare-up's just the start of what you'll see. I say Toby outta take you back to the St. Charles and let me look around."

Addy didn't flinch. "I came here to ask about Stella, and I'm gonna do it. Shall I start here?"

John Dee sighed. "I'll visit this one. You and Toby go into the next one. Toby'll wait outside while you ask around. When they ask yer name, tell 'em you're Sugar Marie."

Addy snorted. "You're a goddamned joker, Franklin! You really think I'm gonna call myself that?"

"If you say your real name, you're an idiot."

She handed her blue cape to Toby and pushed up her bosom. "Worry 'bout yerself, Franklin!"

"Don't let nobody take you to the back, down the stairs, up the stairs, or anywhere outta sight. And for damn sure, don't drink nothing. They give you something with a knockout drop in it, Toby and I'll never find you."

"I got all that, Franklin. You get yer information, and I'll get mine."

While John Dee entered the Boatmen's House, Toby escorted Addy to the next building. Wood-burned signage of "Mother Bee's" hung from a triangular iron bracket. The door was cracked open, and he peered in. A bearded man danced with a curly-headed lass to the happy chords of the piano player's rollicking rendition of "The Arkansas Traveler." Her red velvet hemline flopped above her knees with each high step.

Addy smiled and entered. As Toby closed the door, shutting her in, he swore the music stopped. *Christ, Addy's called attention to herself right off the get go!* He backed against the outer wall, resigned to sweat out each minute until she reappeared.

John Dee was still inside the Boatmen's House. Toby wasn't worried about him. He knew his way around a brothel.

Toby put his ear to Mother Bee's door. Nothing. He couldn't hear a thing. *If Addy finds trouble, how in the world will I know she needs help?*

He said a little prayer to himself: *Lord, make this worth it. Let one of them learn something that leads us to Stella.*

Stella, oh Stella. What had they done to her? Was she in one of these hellholes, taking on paying men? Did they beat her? Drug her?

He closed his eyes, knowing Stella might be dead by now. Maybe Cliff Burton had slit her throat and tossed her in the river. Toby cringed at the thought that Burton might have beat her, making her endure blow after blow in a slow, painful death.

A man in a black suit approached from the east, holding out a bottle. "Here, boy. You need my elixir. Just fifty cents! It'll cure you from seeing the elephant!"

"Elephant?" Toby said. "Ain't no elephant here."

The man laughed. "Yer here in this seedy cesspit of humanity for a large time of fun and frolic, ain't you, boy? At any cost to your health and your soul! This here elixir will be your salvation from lues, the clap, pox, and all of Cupid's diseases!"

"Don't need none of that, sir."

"Suit yerself." The medicine man walked on, toward Ursuline.

The front door of Boatmen's House opened, and a man flew from the threshold across the sidewalk, landing in a heap in the street. "Stay the fuck out!" The door slammed shut.

The prone unfortunate was about the size of John Dee and wore a black jacket. Toby approached for a closer look. Not John Dee. Toby sighed with relief. The man scrambled to all fours and spewed a vile liquid on the cobblestones.

John Dee emerged from the Boatmen's House and approached the man in the gutter. "Rough treatment they gave you, friend."

The gleam of a steel blade caught Toby's eye.

"John Dee! Back!"

The man sprang up and slashed his blade. John Dee leapt back. Toby caught the man's arm and jerked it unnaturally straight. A loud crack echoed; the man screamed and dropped his knife. Toby slammed him back into the street. He lay face down, moaning.

"You all right?" Toby asked John Dee.

John Dee held out his lapel, showing off a six-inch slice through it. "I'm just quick enough to keep my innards, but poorer a new coat on account of this dodgy bastard."

"Can't leave you boys be for ten minutes," Addy said, appearing with her hands on her hips.

Toby exhaled with relief. They'd survived their first stop on Gallatin Street, even though the fur flew all around them.

"Okay, what'd you two find out?"

"First off, we came at the right time," Addy said.

"How's that?"

"The madam, some bitch called 'Irish Eve,' don't come round till dark. That means the girls could talk to me."

Toby looked in both directions. No one within earshot. Good. "What'd they tell you?"

"Well, when I asked if Mother Bee's needed another girl, they said I don't look like the type. I told 'em I was sick and tired of making just a dollar a day off the doctor I work for."

John Dee chuckled. "You're worth that much?"

"Goddamn you!"

Toby sighed. "Easy, Addy, girl. Just go on." He turned to John Dee. "For Christ's sakes!"

"Okay, okay," John Dee said.

Addy continued. "A little thing—said her name was 'Star Lila'—laid it all out. Eve'll charge me ten bucks a week for my bed. And I'll have to give Eve fifty cents a tryst."

"What do the girls charge these days?" John Dee asked.

"Lila said most of the girls get two bucks a tryst, but I'm pretty enough to get three."

Toby detected a smug smile on Addy's face.

"Lila said I'll make a helluva lot more at Mother Bee's than that cheap doctor pays!"

"Well, Addy," John Dee said, "many apologies if I implied earlier you were a two-dollar whore."

"I outta put my shoe up yer ass, Franklin!"

"Christ," Toby said, "you're a couple of damn children! Anything else?"

"Just that there ain't no Injun whore at Mother Bee's. Star Lila said she ain't seen no squaw round Gallatin Street, neither."

"How 'bout you?" Toby asked John Dee.

"There was no sign of Stella in the Boatmen's House. I asked around. Nothing." John Dee grimaced. "We're looking for a needle in a haystack. There's a couple dozen more whorehouses on Gallatin Street. Then a bunch of lowbrow dance houses on Sanctity Row downriver at Elysian Fields. More at the lakefront at Pontchartrain. Then all the 'respectable' whorehouses."

"Where do we start?" Toby asked.

"One of the girls mentioned the 'River Swan,' about a block farther on. It's known for having more than its share of dark-skinned beauties. Black ancestry, Indian, Creole, some Spanish." John Dee nodded to Toby. "You take your *Nymph de Pavé* and see what you can find out at the Swan. I'll check out the Lion's Den, which is down that way as well."

Addy took Toby's hand. "Let's go, sweetie."

Toby's chest tingled. How the hell would they avoid trouble at the next stop?

~ ~ ~

The River Swan's door opened, and Toby stepped onto a massive black stain on a threadbare rug. Someone's vile spew? Blood? A half-dozen armchairs were lined up against the wall, under a painting that had a blotchy brown stain on the body of a white swan.

He smiled at two girls who stood to greet him. Both wore tight bustiers, but similarities in appearance ended there. A wide-hipped, aging whore had painted her cheeks with white cream, presumably to hide tell-tale crow's feet. Next to her was a lithe young girl, though droopy, baggy eyes put an older woman's face on the kid's body.

The younger girl approached, took his hand, and led him to a chair. Her skin was the color of coffee stirred with milk. She sat on his lap.

"Honey," she said, "'bout time a strong, handsome man like you came through that door."

Addy, who had entered a few minutes earlier, was at the bar, talking with a redheaded woman. When Addy turned her head slightly, fire lit in her eyes.

Ain't no time for jealousies! I gotta play the game with the whores, woman! Toby nodded, discreetly, hoping to calm her, and to turn her attention back to learning anything she could about Stella. Then he resumed his own investigation.

"Well then," he said to the young whore, "pretty little thing, ain't ya? Not sure a young'un like you can handle me."

The girl's expression bristled. "Don't you worry about that, mister! I'll ride you like a bucking horse!"

He laughed. "Maybe you would. But, all the same, you seem too damn young to be in the Swan, girlie."

She put her finger on Toby's chin. "Listen here. I been in the Swan for four months, and I take care of a man better 'n any of these old hags! Shit! I used to scrub the floor of a public house for food scraps. I'll take this merry life any old day!"

Toby chuckled.

The door opened. A massive, bald-headed man entered. He sported a thick, black mustache and was half a head taller than Toby. He called out to the redhead at the bar. "Char-let! Iz pretty new girl! Let *mich* try 'er out. A doll-ur fur a romp!"

Addy's eyes widened like pie saucers, undoubtedly betraying her fear that the redhead would accept the big German's offer.

Shit! Toby's heart raced. Bringing Addy to Gallatin Street was nothing but a peck of trouble.

~ ~ ~

Addy's mouth went dry. This beastly German man on top of her? His heft would squish her! *Oh God, no!* Judging by his height, bulk, and big ol' square bucket-head, his pecker must be the size of a wagon wheel spoke.

Toby's eyes were afire, as if he were ready to toss the little whore off his lap and come to her rescue. *Yes, baby, get me out of this!*

"Uh, uh, Charlotte, I...." She couldn't find the words to make her excuses and leave the River Swan.

Charlotte patted her arm, as if to calm her, and said to the big German, "Now, Otto, can't you see I'm doing business with Sugar here? Maybe later, love. For now, why don't you have a dance with Ruby Jo?"

Charlotte pointed at the cream-faced old whore, who was batting her eyes at Otto. He grunted, and let Ruby Jo lead him through the door at the back of the bar.

Addy slowly exhaled a relieved breath.

Charlotte turned back to her. "Now, Sugar, what were you saying 'bout this squaw?"

"Her name is Stella," Addy said. "We're good friends, see. Worked together at the same dance house in Natchez till she came downriver. Her letter said she's working here. I answered that I'd come join her."

"Stella...Stella," Charlotte said. "We have a couple a Injun girls. Prairie Fire and Pocahontas. Course one of 'em's real name could be Stella. Let's go find yer Stella."

Charlotte nodded at the door to the back. Should she follow? Toby and John Dee had said not to leave the public area, but this was her best chance to find Stella. And Charlotte didn't expect any whoring just yet; she'd sent Otto off with Ruby Jo. *I'll just have a quick look around, only a minute or two.*

Addy glanced at Toby. He still had the little whore on his lap. His expression turned to a frown, which apparently was meant to question where she was going. Rather than worry about her, he better concentrate on keeping his pecker in his pants as he played his part in this charade. *Or I'll skin him alive!* She nodded at him and followed Charlotte.

Charlotte led her into a dingy, dimly lit hallway with numbered doors every ten feet or so, like a rooming house. Grunts and moans carried through the walls. Charlotte smiled. "Some of my girls are already hard at work. Gonna be a good night."

Toward the end of the hall, she knocked and then opened a door. Addy peeked over her shoulder. A dark-skinned woman was brushing her long black hair.

"Charlotte!" a female voice screamed from somewhere down the hall. "Goddammit, Charlotte! These bitches stole my lavender perfume!"

Charlotte sighed. "Some 'ah these girls ain't worth a barrel o' shot. Let me tend to this. I'll be right back."

Charlotte walked off, and everything was quiet again. Addy glanced both directions and found herself alone in this cesspool of a cathouse. Was Charlotte fixing to trap her? Maybe she oughta hightail it back to the front room. That's what Toby would tell her to do.

The woman in the room lowered her brush and stared at Addy. Her eyes were misted over, making it seem she were looking straight through Addy to somewhere far away. Definitely not Stella.

"Are you Prairie Fire?"

"Yes. Who's asking?"

"A friend of Stella Parrot. Know her?"

The woman shook her head.

"Where's Pocahontas?"

"Upstairs. On the right. By the owl sconce."

"What the hell is an owl sconce?"

"You'll know it when you see it." Prairie Fire turned away and resumed brushing her hair.

"Thank you." Addy closed the door. No sign of Charlotte. She took a deep breath, considering her next move. Return to the safety of the front room, knock that little whore off Toby's lap, and get outta the Swan? Or delve deeper, unescorted, into the carnal catacombs of the Swan on a long-shot lead? *Ah, hell, I've gotta have a look at Pocahontas.*

A long shadow flickered like an apparition, causing her to nearly jump out of her skin. Nothing there. Just candlelight.

The deserted stairwell was quiet as a tomb as she climbed to the second floor. When she stepped into the hallway, the moans and grunts returned.

God, what a pathetic sound! No one in sight. *Good.*

Something thumped. Her heart pumped like a piston. Who was there?

She stood still as a statue. No sound followed the thump other than passionate wailing. She tiptoed on.

About halfway down the hall, a candle flickered. Addy went closer. Light danced on an oval-shaped copper sconce. Decorative smaller copper circles on its top and bottom had small etchings that could be an ol' hoot owl's eyes and talons, if her imagination opened wide.

The closest door was partially open. Addy peered in. An Indian woman whose long, black hair was parted into two braids was naked to her waist. She had darker skin and a thicker torso than Stella's, most certainly. Her hands were on a man's belt buckle. His long hair hung over the collar of his unbuttoned dungaree shirt, which revealed a thick mat of chest hair.

The woman looked at Addy. The man took notice.

"You there, blondie," the man said. "Get on in here. Take off them fancy clothes and join us. I got an extra dollar for each of you."

A shudder swept through Addy. She drew back into the hall and turned directly into the naked, hairy chest of Otto, the gigantic German. An impenetrable wall.

"*Fraulein*! We meet a-ken."

Addy froze. She took a step back.

Otto circled his arms around her and lifted her in a bear hug. She gasped for breath.

"Vere is yer room?"

"No! No! Toby!" She screamed as loudly she could muster between her gasps.

Otto squeezed tighter.

Addy couldn't make another sound.

"Ve'll take dis one." Otto thrust his butt into the nearest closed door, popping it open. He pivoted so Addy's back was to the bed. He drove her onto it, landing on top of her with all his weight.

Everything went black.

In seconds, which could as well have been hours, Addy awakened to a crash. She was falling. The footboard was gone. Toby and Otto had blasted through it. Toby's arm was around Otto's neck, and he slugged his other fist into the back of the German's massive bald skull. Otto bucked Toby off, rose, roared like a lion, and charged. Toby braced for the blow, but the momentum of the big man's bulk crashed them through the flimsy plaster wall into the hallway.

Addy sat up, recovering her breath.

Toby's fist pounded Otto's ribs, but the big man didn't budge. He swung wildly, but Toby dodged the blow. Toby charged Otto and encircled his waist. Otto got a grip on Toby, grunted like a bull taking his heifer, and raised Toby five feet above the hallway floor. Toby slammed onto the floorboards. He shook his head, groggily. Otto laughed.

"Otto! What the hell is going on!" Charlotte screamed from down the hall.

Toby was on one knee, moaning.

"Come on!" Addy grabbed his arm and pulled him toward the stairwell. They scrambled down the stairs to the first floor, arm in arm. She led him into the front room, pushed two whores out of their path, and charged out the front door to Gallatin Street. They ran toward Ursuline and safety.

"You all right?" she asked Toby.

"I think so. Shoulder hurts a bit. That big bastard slammed the hell outta me."

"I got some advice for you."

"What's that?"

"They grow 'em bigger than you in Germany. Don't be going there. They'd like to kill you."

~ ~ ~

Happy banter from diners at dozens of wrought-iron tables on the gas-lit café's patio belied John Dee's frustrations. He pushed his little plate of pralines away. "We're whistling in the wind. Four goddamned-awful whorehouses, and each one of us damn-near got killed. How are we gonna survive visiting dozens more?"

"You just gonna give up on your girl?" Addy asked.

"Now, goddamn it. I didn't say that!"

"You two gonna be the death of me," Toby said. "Put your claws away. Both of you. We gotta decide what we're gonna do."

"What's your thought?" John Dee asked.

"First-off, Addy here is done playing whore. It's too damn dangerous."

"Now hold on!" Addy said.

A young boy approached, stopping her from arguing further. "You be Mister Franklin?" the boy asked.

John Dee nodded.

The boy handed him a folded piece of paper. He tossed the boy a piece of Mexican silver. The boy weaved his way through tables and out of the café.

John Dee locked eyes with Toby. How the hell did someone know to deliver a message to this table? Toby undoubtedly sensed what he did—whatever this paper said was gonna change everything.

"Well? What's it say?" Addy asked, her brow furrowed with concern.

John Dee opened the paper. Large and sloppy hand-printed words filled the page: "Lafon's tomb at St. Louis Cemetery at 2AM. Bring yer nigger and two thousand cash. I'll give you yer squaw. If ya don't come I'll deliver her in pieces."

None of the three spoke immediately. Electricity filled the air like an approaching lightning storm. John Dee fingered the decorative *fleur-de-lis* on the iron arm of his chair as he thought.

"It's a trap, sure as hell." Toby grabbed the paper and looked it over. "Ain't signed."

"It's Burton all right," John Dee said. "Gotta be. He knows we're here. Surprised he ain't attacked us."

"Wants to be sure we have money on us, I 'spect," Toby said.

"Why do you have to go?" Addy asked.

Toby bristled at her question. "I'd be going whether the paper mentioned me or not. John Dee and I are in this together."

"I don't like it one bit," she said.

"Hell," John Dee said, "none of us do." He rose and put on his hat.

"Where you going?" Toby asked.

"I'm gonna get us a couple of Colt 1851s. And I'll see you back at the Saint Charles."

Chapter 21

ASOLITARY CAW BROKE THE SILENCE. John Dee's gut tightened with wariness. The tortured soul of a cemetery resident presiding in the form of a black crow? Or a warning?

The moon hung over St. Louis Cemetery like a rich planter's silver platter. John Dee led Toby down a gravel path, the crunch of their boots the only sound. They wove through sections of illuminated crypts with surnames of past generations. Some in French—Archambeau, Barbier, Fournier. Some Creole—Boudreaux, Thibodeaux. The vaults varied in height from quite low to peaked and featured an incongruous mix of stones of all shades and sizes, bricks, and iron—all lifted over the flood line to keep inhabitants sealed within dry.

Not until Toby's boot hit the back of his calf did John Dee notice he'd slowed to a snail's pace.

"Scared of the spirits, are you?" Toby asked with a snicker.

"Christ." John Dee narrowed his eyes, but the tightly packed ghostly residences spawned dark, shadowy places untouched by the light of the moon. The unnatural quiet raised the hair on the back of his neck. "Come on."

He turned right at a bricked, pyramid-shaped crypt surrounded by spike-topped iron fencing.

John Dee held his Colt in his right hand, close to his chest. *Just what the hell are we doing here?* This was a fool's errand. A task of soon-to-be-dead fools. Cliff Burton and his men were, without a doubt, lying in wait. But neither of them could cotton sitting around to wait for Burton to start delivering Stella's appendages. Because the evil bastard sure as hell would make good on his threat.

The God's honest truth was no way in hell John Dee would desert Stella. But why? Sure, she was a looker and fired his loins, but so had plenty of other women. And he'd moved on from every one of them. Gotten his fill and gone back to the river and more business and adventure with Toby.

Something about Stella stirred his soul. It had happened on the *Lady J*'s top deck when they landed at Friars Point. When she opened her mouth to sing. In those magical moments in her bed before the fire.

He couldn't turn his back on what was building between them. If he did, a big piece of his heart would die. Even more than that, Stella was a good soul and sure as hell didn't deserve what Cliff Burton had done to her.

Between the crypts were shadowy patches of gray and blackness. Potential hiding places at every corner. John Dee's neck hair stood on end. Mortal danger was out there. But where?

What did the old man say? *Turn left at the Aubert crypt and it be at the end of the section.* Lafon's tomb was said to be a solid stone monstrosity with several levels of pull-out chambers towering over its ghostly neighbors.

A snap brought John Dee up short.

He and Toby raised their Colts.

"What is it?" Toby whispered.

"Quiet."

No other sound.

"Bastards are hiding among the ghosts," Toby whispered.

"Yeah. Come on. It's just a little way."

John Dee took a tentative step. Then another. Just moonlit stone death homes on either side of the path, and he couldn't see anything between them. Perfect for an ambush. His and Toby's Colts pointed ineffectively into the darkness.

Ahead, Lafon's tomb had four stone doors stacked high over four stone ledges. A stone behemoth two stories taller than anything nearby. The patriarch's progeny could lay their bones on top of the place where his had been set nearly forty years before.

Next to Lafon's tomb, a sarcophagus in the shape of a casket had been disturbed. Its massive stone top crisscrossed its side walls.

Oh shit.

"That's far enough, Franklin."

John Dee couldn't see the speaker. It had to be Cliff Burton.

"Bring yer money?"

John Dee patted a money bag inside his jacket. "I got it. Where's Stella?"

"Put the money on the ground first."

"Show yourself, Burton! Show me Stella!"

"Put yer damn money on the ground!"

John Dee scanned nearby crypts and pointed his Colt into the darkness, aimlessly. Neither Burton nor his brother Stevie nor any of their men were visible. Somewhere behind the structures, in the blackness, pistols had a bead on Toby and him. Toby made a barely audible growl.

His hesitation produced a click. A pistol being cocked. Swallowing, John Dee opened his coat and pulled out a bag. He laid it at his feet.

Silence. Moments passed.

A crunch. Gravel under a boot heel.

His heart pumped like a piston. *Get out before it's too late!*

Another click. And another. And another. Too many pistol hammers to count. A shadowy figure stepped from behind Lafon's tomb. John Dee thought he made out Stevie Burton pointing a rifle at him. Another dark figure to the right. More gravel crunched to the left.

John Dee stood side by side with Toby on the center pathway, in open ground, discernible enough to draw a bead on. Moonlit targets for shadowy figures he and Toby couldn't defend against.

Christ!

"Drop 'em!" Cliff Burton's voice was firm and steady.

"I think I see two to the right," Toby whispered. "I'll take 'em. Get the ones on the left."

"Hold on," John Dee whispered back. "There're too many, and we can't see for shit."

"Put yer pistols down," Burton said, calmly. "Then I'm gonna pick up the money. I'll tell ya the name of the whorehouse where yer squaw is."

Shoot? Run? Play along? John Dee's stomach twisted as he mulled his next move.

"Drop 'em or we'll shoot ya where you stand."

Cliff Burton stepped forward. His crinkled nose and black mane of a beard were twisted into a grimace like a blackthorn in the dark forest. He pointed his pistol at John Dee's face. Boots shuffled. Men emerged from all directions.

A goddamned posse! All with pistols pointed at us.

"Now!"

John Dee put his Colt on the ground. He gently touched Toby's arm, and Toby slowly lowered his gun and placed it next to John Dee's.

Cliff Burton picked up the money bag. Gold pieces clinked. He handed it to Stevie, who lowered his Enfield and fingered through the bills.

"Where's Stella?" John Dee asked.

Cliff Burton laughed. "Why do you give a shit, Franklin?"

"I paid you!"

"Yeah, yuh did. Okay, Franklin, yer whore squaw's at Miss Kitty's. Sucking the cock of some sailor boy right now. How's that make you feel?" He chortled. "Wish it were yers, don't ya!"

"We're done here," John Dee said.

"Not by a damn sight, Franklin." Burton stood face to face with him and put his pistol barrel under John Dee's chin. "I said I'd tell ya where yer whore squaw is. I never said I weren't gonna kill ya."

Toby jerked backward. Two gunmen advanced and put their guns in his face.

"This our niggah?" one asked.

Burton chuckled. "That's right." He turned to John Dee. "Might make ya feel better to know I ain't killing yer blackie here, Franklin? He's worth a lot more than you are. See, these boys are gonna sell him upriver. To a planter or mebbe one of the mines. He'll cut cane or pick cotton or break rocks till his back gives out."

"Toby's a free man!"

"Not no more he ain't."

"You bastard!"

A bearded, burly man stepped forward with a length of chains. The manacles clinked. John Dee's insides felt hollow. *How the hell could I let this happen?*

"Pay my brother first," Burton said.

The man handed over a wad of bills. Stevie Burton fanned through the money and, satisfied, stuffed it in John Dee's money bag.

"Don't do this, Burton!" John Dee's body quaked. "Ricky was my doing, not Toby's! He don't deserve this!"

Cliff Burton growled. "First off, I don't think yer man enough to best Ricky in a knife fight." He moved close enough that John Dee smelled tobacco fumes trapped in his beard. "Don't matter anyhow. It's good business."

One of the gunmen held a pistol barrel to Toby's forehead.

"Hands out, boy," the burly man said. "Now!"

A second gunman added his pistol to Toby's temple.

Toby reluctantly held out his hands.

The burly man locked iron cuffs around his wrists. "Ain't all bad for a big buck like you. Your massa'll want you breeding the mammies. Work by day, romp dem mammies by night. Young ones, old ones. Fat ones, skinny ones."

"Shit," Toby said. "I've heard that before."

The burly man laughed and locked a second set of cuffs around Toby's ankles. "Party's over, boy."

He yanked on the chain. Toby dropped to his knees.

"You gonna walk, boy, or am I gonna drag you?"

Toby stood and looked at John Dee. Fiery eyes and a face of granite. *Toby isn't done yet. It's not gonna end like this. Goddammit! It can't end like this.*

"I'll come for you," John Dee said.

Cliff Burton laughed hysterically. "In hell, Franklin! You two'll see each other in hell!"

Chains rattled a hollow dirge as the four gunmen led Toby away.

"You're an evil bastard, Burton," John Dee said.

"I s'pose I oughta take that as a compliment coming from you."

"You fired the *Delta Ray* and killed dozens of people who didn't have anything to do with your brother Ricky."

"Maybe they didn't, but there's something you don't understand, Franklin. Mess with a Burton and kin's gonna get ya, whatever it takes."

"Enough talk. Your time's up." Stevie Burton poked his rifle barrel at John Dee's chest, forcing him closer to the sarcophagus.

Cliff Burton grunted. "Juz wish Brick was here to see you die."

"That ain't likely," John Dee said.

Cliff Burton squinted and surged forward. He pressed the circular end of his pistol barrel deep into John Dee's cheek. "What're you saying, boy?"

"Your brother picked a fight he couldn't win. On the *Cedar Point*."

Burton's expression hardened to stone. "That the boat Brick went on, Stevie?"

"Yep."

"Juz what the fuck happened, Franklin?"

"He got killed."

"Who did it?" Burton's face was beet red.

John Dee didn't answer. Burton smashed the butt of his pistol into John Dee's face, doubling him over. His jaw seared with pain. He tasted blood.

Burton jerked John Dee's collar upward, forcing him to face him. "You shoot 'im dead?"

"Nope."

"Then who?"

John Dee glared at Cliff Burton and spit out blood. "Somebody bigger and tougher than Brick, I guess."

"You sure Brick was dead?"

"Looked dead to me."

Burton shook John Dee like a rag doll. The bearded man's anguished scream reverberated through the cemetery. "W—what'd they do with him?"

"Don't know. Was a lot of commotion. Got off the boat."

Burton smashed John Dee's face again. Blood streamed from John Dee's lips.

"That's two of my brothers, Franklin. Yer the goddamned cause of all of it! Now yer gonna rot on a pile of bones with maggots coming out yer eyeballs. It's what you deserve!"

Stevie Burton jabbed the Enfield's barrel into John Dee's chest hard enough to knock him backward. He jabbed again. Another step back.

John Dee looked into the sarcophagus and made out a white skull and ribcage. His throat tightened. He could hardly breathe.

Again, Stevie Burton pushed him with the gun barrel. His buttocks hit the wall of the sarcophagus.

Stevie Burton poked lower this time. The barrel hit his money belt, which was cinched across his midsection. Stevie hesitated. He stared at John Dee's stomach and tapped the money belt with the tip of the barrel. "What the hell is this?" Stevie probed the contours of John Dee's money belt.

"What is it?" Cliff Burton asked.

They greedily eyed John Dee's stomach.

Now!

John Dee grabbed the Enfield's barrel and pulled Stevie Burton close. He snatched Stevie's collar and rotated him to face Cliff Burton just as he fired his pistol.

The shot hit Stevie square in his chest. He gasped. Cliff's eyes went wide as saucers.

John Dee flipped the Enfield and pulled the trigger. The blast knocked Cliff backward, into the base of a square-topped crypt.

Stevie's body fell to the ground, motionless. John Dee knocked Cliff's pistol out of his hand with the rifle barrel. Cliff's eyes were trained on him, with devilish hatred that John Dee would never forget.

He emitted a wheeze. "Franklin...."

"Burn in hell, Burton."

Then Cliff Burton was silent. Eyes looking straight ahead and lips parted. Dead as the bones at the bottom of the sarcophagus.

John Dee gripped Stevie Burton's body under the arms and lifted him so his upper torso hung over the wall of the sarcophagus. He grabbed Stevie's boots and flipped the body into the vault. When Stevie landed, bones cracked. He dragged Cliff Burton's body to the sarcophagus, lugged him over the opening, and dropped him on his brother for all eternity.

John Dee put his shoulder against the weighty stone lid. He grunted and pushed with everything he had until it rotated ninety degrees and dropped into place.

He sat, back to the stone sarcophagus, spent and huffing to catch his breath. His jaw ached. The taste of blood repulsed him.

Four dead Burtons, but he couldn't rest and damn sure couldn't celebrate. Even in death, they'd had their revenge. Toby in chains and Stella whoring.

Get up! Toby and Stella need you!

John Dee gathered Stevie Burton's Enfield rifle musket and powder bag and Cliff Burton's pistol. A Colt, good. He pulled back his jacket and tucked it under his gun belt. Plenty of bullets.

He snatched up the money bag and his and Toby's Colts. He sprinted toward the cemetery entrance at St. Louis Street. And kept running toward the river.

Chapter 22

JOHN DEE RACED SOUTH ON Dumaine Street, willing his legs to go faster. Moonglow cast eerie shadows on structures, and nocturnal debaucheries were everywhere. A hooting fool. A squeaky tin trumpet rattling from the windows of a candle-lit dance hall. A wretched, prone figure in the street.

Farther along, he passed empty, dilapidated belvederes. Large, greedy rats darted in and out of stinky garbage piled in front of eateries.

A city part alive, part dead.

Ain't nothing to do but run like the wind. But run where? Where the hell were the slavers taking Toby? Didn't Cliff Burton say they'd sell Toby upriver? So, they must be leading him to their boat. *Keep running. To the river. Like a fox with dogs on its heels.*

For a moment, Toby was running with him. Boys and a dog bobbing through a field of wheat flowing in gentle, golden waves. Into the woods where leafy branches swooshed and twigs snapped as they made their path. Through the creek with clear, chilly water splashing into their faces with every bounding step.

I'm coming for you, Toby!

John Dee's lungs burned. Now, every step was labored. He stopped and bent over, hungrily gulping in air. He puckered and spit a mouthful of blood.

A horse whinnied. At the corner, a wagon driven by a gray-headed Black man was about to cross Royal Street.

"Sir!" John Dee raised his rifle as a sign to stop. "You see slavers pulling along a Black man in manacles?"

The man crinkled his eyebrows. The wagon halted, but he didn't respond.

"The Black man's about my size. And my age."

A set jaw betrayed the man's reticence to get involved.

"Woulda been just a minute or so ago."

Finally, the man said, "Lose yer darky, did you?" He snapped the reins and his horse perked up. "Ain't seen 'im."

John Dee grabbed the lead. "He's my brother."

"What'd you say?" The man's voice rose a pitch.

"Toby's my brother. Slavers got him, and they're gonna sell him upriver. I gotta save him. He's a free man!"

The man studied him. "What the hell happened to you?"

John Dee wiped away blood at the corner of his mouth. "Damn slavers."

"You and Toby got the same daddy?"

"Yeah."

The man scratched his chin. "Dem soul drivers put in the river up a ways from the whorehouses. Come on!" He motioned for John Dee to climb aboard. "Yer gonna have to beat 'em to their boat."

"Thank you." John Dee took a seat on the wagon bench and extended his hand. "John Dee Franklin."

The man shook his hand. "Name's Reuben."

"What are you doing out here in the dark, Reuben?"

"On my way to the bakery. Gonna load up tarts and pralines and such and get 'em delivered at daybreak."

"Well, thank you."

Reuben nodded at the rifle. "Gonna be trouble?"

"I 'spect so," John Dee said. He pulled Cliff's pistol from his belt and put it on the bench. "Can you handle this?"

Reuben nodded again.

"Yah!" He snapped the reins and the horses set off at a quick trot.

"Where you going?"

"We's gonna hightail to the salt shed 'bout quarter mile 'fore the canal. This time a night should be real quiet. Dem boys are gonna come out of the trees, and the moon'll light 'em up real good. We'll be in the shadows and draw a bead on 'em. If we're lucky, they'll drop their weapons and hand yer brother over."

John Dee laughed. He picked a cartridge out of Stevie Burton's pouch and snipped the end off with his teeth.

"What's so funny?" Reuben asked.

"The bastards got the drop on Toby and me in the moonlight and put their guns in our faces when they captured him." John Dee poured powder down the rifle barrel and put a bullet in the muzzle.

"Works both ways," Reuben said.

"Sure does." John Dee withdrew the rammer and tamped the bullet home. He half-cocked the Enfield and replaced the spent cap. He took his and Toby's Colts from his jacket and put them on the bench next to Cliff's.

"There's just the two of us!"

"But there's four slavers," John Dee said. "Gotta be locked and loaded if words don't work." He filled empty pistol chambers with powder and lead balls. "We'll use these pistols first. Six shots each. Oughta be plenty."

"I'd say." Reuben scratched his chin. "This brother of yours—his name's Toby?"

"Yeah."

"Well, ain't a big surprise you got a Black brother. Quite a few White men round here gots his 'other family.'"

John Dee nodded.

"Yeah. Folks call it a left-handed marriage when a White man has children with his *plaçée* woman."

"That what folks in New Orleans call a woman with Black blood in her?"

"Yep, one who makes a union with a White man, anyways. See, a good White man'll support his *plaçée* and her children just like a second family. So, lots of White men got dark half-brothers round here. But I don't know one of dem White men who'd risk his neck for his half-blood kin."

"Listen here," John Dee said, firmly. "I would. And Toby would for me."

"That right?"

"It's just been the two of us since I was eighteen. We're partners."

"What do ya mean?"

"We got a river business together. Tell you the truth, we do everything together."

"Huh," Reuben said. "You both working for your daddy?"

"Hell no. Ain't seen him since I was eighteen. Toby neither."

"Your daddy make Toby a free man?"

"Nah. I did. Daddy didn't like it one bit; I think he'd have cut my balls off if he'd had the chance. So, Toby and I ran off."

"I'll be." Reuben studied the road ahead. "Salt shed's just a little ways. Shouldn't be no one around. I'll leave the wagon out back, and we'll hide in the shadows until the soul drivers and yer brother come up the path."

Reuben parked the wagon and led John Dee to the front of the salt shed. They settled into shadowy crevices within a large stack of wooden barrels. Just twenty-five feet away, the moonlit road's base of white rock and shell fragments shone milky gray. John Dee could even make out wagon wheel ruts. Perfect.

"Pretty sure they're coming this way?" John Dee asked.

Reuben nodded. "Yeah. Soul drivers tie up at the canal just down yonder."

"And Gallatin Street's that way?" John Dee pointed in the opposite direction.

"Yep." Reuben grunted. "You a whoring man?"

John Dee ignored that. "It's my next stop. Toby and I are gonna rescue a friend from Miss Kitty. She's made our friend a whore against her will."

"Christ's sakes!" Reuben glared at John Dee. "You chock full-a crusades to fight! What kind of a hot flash you get me into?"

"Just help me free Toby. That's all I need from you."

"Well, now I's curious. What the hell is going on here? I imagine Toby in chains and a girl kept prisoner at Gallatin Street is all the same story."

"Yeah. But let's hope I don't have time—"

"Quiet!"

Chains clinked before John Dee saw anyone. The bearded, burly man appeared first, leading Toby by a length of chain. One armed man walked beside him, and two others trailed Toby.

John Dee's fingers twitched on the grip of his Colt. He let the group advance to less than a stone's throw from the salt shed.

"Stop!" he said.

The burly man's head jerked up.

"We got guns on you!"

One of the guards reached for his pistol.

John Dee fired into the road. "Don't."

The guard's hand froze in place.

"There's just one of you!" the burly man yelled. "You best get the hell outta here, boy!"

"Nope!" Reuben yelled back. "We's got three repeating Colts aimed at you boys. Ready to blow you to hell!"

"Wadda you want?" the burly man asked.

"Unlock the manacles!" John Dee shouted. "Wrists and ankles."

The burly man didn't move. One guard grumbled.

John Dee pulled from his money bag the wad of bills the burly man had given Stevie Burton in St. Louis Cemetery. He tossed it at the man's boots. "Ain't this the money you paid for Toby here earlier?"

The man's mouth fell open as he looked at the wad of bills. "You gonna show yerself?"

"Nope."

The man rubbed his bushy beard. "Huh. I didn't reckon you'd get outta that cemetery. And here you are with the money bag." His expression changed into something like admiration. "Hmm. Where's Cliff Burton?"

"You give a damn 'bout that bastard?" John Dee asked.

"No, I don't reckon I do."

John Dee threw several more bills at the bearded man. "Two hundred dollars. Fifty dollars a man. Makes it a profitable night. Now take the chains off."

"Goddamn it, John Dee!" Toby shouted. "Don't you give these slaver bastards a nickel. Shoot 'em all!"

A guard reached for his gun. John Dee shot him in the arm.

"Ahh-damn!" The wounded guard dropped to his knees.

"Stay down, boy. Keep away from that gun!" John Dee shouted at the wounded man. "Shut your mouth, Toby! I'm doing business here. Me and this fella are gonna make our deal, and that'll be the end of it. Right, mister?"

The burly man nodded. "Throw me another twenty-dollar piece to tend to the wound and you got yerself a deal."

~ ~ ~

Horse hooves and iron-rimmed wheels crunched stones and shells as Reuben's wagon rolled toward Gallatin Street. The road was eerily empty, though Toby tried to discern spying eyes in the dark places between trees, bushes, and buildings. Just a few more minutes to Stella.

He rubbed pinched skin on his wrists.

Shadowy, tumbledown commercial buildings gave way to neglected, balconied colonial houses. Breathing in a rotten stench assured Toby they were closing in on their destination.

Toby glanced at John Dee. Moonlight illuminated a knot on his face the size of an apple.

"Tough night, pardner?"

"Oh, this?" John Dee lightly fingered his cheek. "You should see the other guys."

Toby chuckled. "Doubt I'll be seeing them anymore."

"No, you won't."

"I need your kerchief." John Dee pulled it from his jacket and handed it over. Toby rubbed at dark streaks from John Dee's mouth.

"Ow!"

"Hold on; it's dried." Toby wet the handkerchief with his saliva and wiped the blood away. "Gotta make you presentable if yer gonna visit the ladies."

John Dee didn't respond. He stared straight ahead. Must be thinking about Stella. Neither one of them had ever said much about their feelings for women, but Toby sure would like to know more about how John Dee saw things with Stella. Damn, so much had happened in a few days. The Burtons, Stella, Addy. Where did that leave things between the two of them? *Well, John Dee came for me. And I woulda come for him. We'll sort out where everything stands later.*

"We sure appreciate your help, Reuben," John Dee said.

"Yeah." Toby continued to rub his wrist. "We sure do. Them damn manacles gouged me like a rusty whittling knife."

Reuben laughed. "Ain't nuthin compared to being chained up in the hold of the soul drivers' boat!"

"S'pose so. Anyhow, drop us up here, please."

Reuben looked straight ahead into Gallatin Street. "Nah. I'll be coming with you. Ain't had this much fun in a while, boys. Besides, I still got an hour 'fore dawn."

"All right." Toby turned to John Dee. "Where we gonna find Stella?"

John Dee hesitated as a drunken man in a knit cap stumbled off the sidewalk and fell face first into Gallatin Street. He didn't move. "This shithole don't sleep! Well, to answer your question, Burton said she's at Miss Kitty's. Just down on the left."

"Tell me; you ain't gonna give a whoring bitch all our money, are ya?" Toby asked.

"Ain't planning on it. You still sore I paid the slavers?"

"Damn right I am."

"Hell, Toby, if we'd all started shooting at least one of us would be dead."

Toby sighed. John Dee had a point.

"Besides, I feel I made out."

"How's that?"

"We woulda paid Burton two thousand dollars to get Stella back. That is, if he hadn't double-crossed us. Got her whereabouts outta him, and I've only spent two hundred and a gold piece."

"Plus, the iron gouges in my wrists and ankles and the wound on your face," Toby said. "And we don't have her back yet. Give me the dod-derned money bag; I'll be a damn sight tighter 'bout giving any to a kidnapping whore madam."

John Dee chuckled. "We both will be."

Reuben halted the horses in front of Miss Kitty's. "What's yer plan?"

"John Dee and I are gonna walk into this cathouse like a couple of liquored-up tryst men," Toby said. "We're gonna piss off Miss Kitty and draw out her hired gun."

"Who's that?"

"Oh, Miss Kitty'll have a big German or Irishman around in case there's trouble. Every one of these shitholes has a hidden gun or two."

"Okay."

"Then you're gonna come in and keep a pistol on Kitty's man while John Dee and I find Stella."

"Might just work," John Dee said.

"Gonna have to."

Toby trailed John Dee up creaking steps into a rundown tenement. A frayed, blood-red floor rug and sleeping poodle met them at the entrance. Toby nearly choked at the smell: Alcohol? Cheap perfume? Or both?

Four public women stood in a line in the front room, displaying their feminine wares, but only the youngest-looking smiled. The chunky, burgundy-headed lady pushed up her sagging bustline, highlighting what were nevertheless her best assets. One of the others had a bruised cheek and another, bags under her eyes like she hadn't slept for days. Late into the night as it was, just how many men had these pitiful wenches already serviced?

The plump redhead took John Dee's arm. She stared at his swollen face. "There, there, honey child. I'm gonna make it feel all better."

"Drink!" John Dee shouted. "Get me a drink!"

The eagerly smiling, skinny, young girl approached Toby.

"I'll take you, a bottle of whiskey, and the new squaw," Toby said.

"Who?"

"There's a new squaw here, and I want her!"

"I don't know no squaw," the girl said.

"Goddammit, there's a squaw!" Toby said, shouting now. "Cliff Burton told me so. I pay good money. Somebody get me the damn squaw!"

The door to the back opened. A busty, middle-aged woman with red curls tied high up on her head stormed through. "What the hell is going on here?"

"These girls won't get me yer new squaw!" Toby said.

"You see a squaw here?"

"Don't bullshit me, Kitty! Cliff Burton told me you bought his squaw." He pulled the skinny girl close. "I want this one. A bottle of whiskey. And the squaw."

"Cliff told you that, huh?" Kitty's frown revealed displeasure with Cliff leaking their dealings.

"Tell ya what, big man. Come back ta-marrah for the squaw." She nodded at the young girl. "Tonight, you can have this one and a bottle." She pointed to the other girls in the front room. "Hell, take one of them, too."

Toby grabbed Kitty's arm. "Get me the squaw goddammit!"

Kitty tried to break Toby's grip. "Jens! Get yer ass out here. Now!"

A vest-wearing, bald-headed, and bearded big man stormed through the door. His predatory glare settled on Toby. Jens lurched toward him.

"Stop!" John Dee pulled his Colt and aimed it at the big man's face.

The big German froze and raised his hands.

"What the hell?" Kitty shouted.

Toby flung her onto a settee and pulled his pistol. He pressed the end of its barrel against her forehead. "Shut yer trap, wench!"

Reuben entered.

"Keep your pistol on this one," John Dee said. "Shoot him in the face if he moves an inch."

Toby jerked Kitty to her feet. He shoved her toward the door to the back. "You're taking us to the Indian girl. Now!"

"You sons of bitches can't come inna my place of business and pull this shit!"

John Dee put his pistol barrel into Kitty's mouth. "My partner told you to shut yer trap! Got it?"

Kitty mumbled something inaudible with the gun barrel bulging out her cheek.

"What the hell's she saying?" Toby asked.

John Dee removed the barrel.

"I'll kill you bastards! You sonsa—"

John Dee reinserted the gun barrel, this time ramming it deep into Kitty's throat. She dropped to her knees. Her eyes watered. She grabbed her throat and made a retching sound. John Dee maintained pressure, and her lips gripped the Colt's chamber like a calf on a teat.

"It's been a real long night, bitch," John Dee said. "We ain't taking no more of your shit." He snatched her arm and jerked her to her feet. He removed the barrel, and this time, Kitty just glared at him. "That's better. Keep your trap shut. And take us to the girl. Maybe we'll let you live."

Kitty grunted. She led them through the door to the back and into a hall lined by girls' rooms. She took them up creaking back stairs, past a broken window on the second-floor landing, to a third-floor room at the back of the building.

Toby gagged at the malodorous odor. Stella was bound, wrists and ankles, on the small bed in the tiny room that had probably once been a closet. Just the bed, a rickety wooden chair, and a bedpan for décor.

Stella turned her head toward them without the faintest hint of recognition.

"Stella!" John Dee dropped to his knees and took her face in his hands.

She seemed to purr, but she didn't speak.

Toby pulled his knife from his jacket and cut her wrist ties, then moved to her ankles.

Kitty picked up the chair and swung it at Toby. He blocked the blow and drove her back into the wall. He put his knife blade to her throat.

"No," Stella said in a voice so soft the sound was more a coo than a word.

Toby tasted a bitter tang. Oh, how easy it'd be to slice this evil woman's throat open. But he couldn't.

John Dee picked up Stella. She put her arms around his neck and buried her face in his chest. He hesitated at the door. "You heard her, partner."

"Yeah."

"See you downstairs." John Dee carried Stella away.

Toby took his knife off Kitty's throat and flung her onto the bed. She screamed out. He stuffed his handkerchief into her mouth. As she flailed at him with her fists, he drove his knee into her chest and came down with all his weight. She gasped for breath, defenseless, while he bound her wrists to the bedposts. Then he bound her ankles.

He stood over her. She mumbled through her gag and twisted and writhed, trying to free herself.

He shook his head. "Evil bitch."

He picked up the bedpan and poured its contents over her. He tossed the pan onto her stomach on his way out.

Toby descended the stairs and joined the others in the front room. John Dee gently stroked Stella's cheek. Her expression was peaceful; her eyes were locked on his. Two of the whores sat on the couch and the other two in chairs. A couple of them had pallid, expressionless faces, and the others stared at Reuben's Colt and shook like tambourines.

"Where's Kitty?" John Dee asked.

"Lying in shit like a dirty sow should."

John Dee chuckled. "Good."

One whore snorted. When Toby glared at her, her gaze dropped to her lap.

"What about this one?" Reuben nodded at Jens. Reuben's pistol was still aimed at the man's chest.

"Oh, him." Toby blasted Jens with a powerful punch to his jaw. Jens collapsed onto the floor and didn't move. "Time to get the hell outta this shithole."

~ ~ ~

Dawn's chalky white sky settled over New Orleans. Reuben's horses clip-clopped over the cobblestones as the wagon approached the St. Charles Hotel.

John Dee cradled Stella in the back of the wagon. He pulled up to her chin a blanket he'd taken from Kitty's. Whatever the madam had given Stella stupefied her something awful. Her gaze was vacant, though now and then it seemed to lock on his face with something like contentment. She'd said his name twice, but she was a far cry from coherent. The path ahead became clear. Get her into bed and find someone who knew how to rid her body of Kitty's drugs.

"How can we ever thank you?" Toby asked Reuben.

"I told you boys; ain't had so much fun in a long time."

Toby climbed down from the bench. John Dee gently handed Stella to him. Her eyes were open, and her head rolled from side to side as if she were trying to make sense of her surroundings.

"Know anyone who can help her?" John Dee asked.

"Matter ah fact, I do," Toby said. "There's an ol' doc I know who has cured juz 'bout every kind of malady. Doc Joe. Lives up 'round Congo Park."

"Know him?" John Dee asked Reuben.

"Everybody knows Doc Joe," Reuben said. "He'll know what to do. See, he's treated White folk all these years—even got a White other side of da family like I was telling you 'bout. Doc Joe travels in all circles…. Hell, when he ain't doctoring, he makes beautiful paintings he sells to White folk. They'll let 'im into yer hotel."

"Can you get word to Doc Joe to come to the St. Charles Hotel, right away?"

"Sure will."

"You are a great man," John Dee said.

Reuben made a half smile.

"You're gonna have some explaining to do at the bakery, aren't ya?"

"Don't you worry 'bout that."

John Dee pulled from the money bag as many bills and coins as he could grab with two hands. He put it all on the bench beside Reuben.

Reuben's eyes widened like saucers.

"When you get to the bakery, if they give ya any horseshit 'bout being late, just buy 'em out."

Chapter 23

Stella sipped her steaming hot coffee, looking at five steamboats moored at the wooden piers that jutted into the river between Jackson Square and Canal Street. John Dee's hand was on the back of her chair, and his warm smile lit up her insides. A gentle breeze and awning shade made their table the perfect waiting spot.

Toby and Addy sat across from them, both idly watching the activity on the wharves. Yellow and red parasols. White and blue bonnets. Dungareed workers shouting in various languages. Braying mules. Wagons clickety-clacking over the wooden planks. Stacks of cargo boxes, fresh-cut lumber and sugar barrels. Bustling scenes bringing to life a kaleidoscope of color and sound.

It dawned on her that her nightmare was over. She'd soon leave the Crescent City behind, at least for now.

She fed John Dee a bite of her praline. "Delicious, isn't it?"

He smiled and kissed the back of her hand.

He'd come for her. He'd come for Toby. A fading, but still angry purple bruise on his cheek displayed the price he'd paid. Over these past weeks, his wound had healed just as she had.

Even with the imperfection, his manly, handsome gaze made her stomach do little flip-flops. Night after night, he sat at her bedside, holding her hand, feeding her bits of cracker and giving her sips of water. Just a pallet of pillows and blankets on the floor for his rest. He ran errands for the doctor and washed her clothes, like he didn't have a thing to do but bring her back to the living.

Addy's profile caught her eye. Perfect, high cheekbones and blonde curls riding the breeze. The look of an angel. One who had been at the doctor's shoulder, helping him and John Dee. Pressing cold towels to her forehead and sitting with her when John Dee was gone. Holding her hand and whispering gentle encouragements when her sweats came and voices demanded she find some of the evil opium elixir.

Had it been three weeks? God, her opinion of Addy had changed like night and day. Three weeks ago, on the *Delta Ray*, Stella had seen an uppity, racist planter's wife with hot pantaloons for John Dee. A despicable creature. One Toby would never stomach. But there was more to Addy than a sugar princess. She had proven it to Toby; Stella was certain of that. Addy's caring aid at her own lowest moments washed away ugly first impressions.

Yes, Toby was smitten with this blonde widow woman. Stella was happy for him, but also fearful. Love with a White woman on the lower river was a dangerous game for him. Even so, she had picked up on the absolute certainty that Addy and Toby had gotten in a whole lot of loving during these weeks in New Orleans.

John Dee, on the other hand, hadn't been intimate with Stella. Oh, he'd been attentive, showering her with caring, loving kisses on her cheek, on her forehead, and on the back of her hands. Nothing more than that while she recovered. These last many days she'd thought back to their intimacy on the *Delta Ray*. Fondly. *God, let me feel the heavenly pleasure of his touch again.* She tapped her fingers on the table. It was up to her to convince John Dee that she wasn't broken anymore. Soon. It would be time to take his hand and enter their season of sunshine.

"Ahh," John Dee said, "our esteemed guest!"

Sam Clemens approached the empty seat at their table; the corner of his bushy red mustache turned up in a sly grin. He leaned over and kissed Stella on the cheek.

"I'm so sorry; John Dee told me what you've been through."

"Thank you, Sam," Stella said. "These folks are my guardian angels in every way. And you deserve the greatest thanks. If you hadn't got John Dee, Toby, and me off the *Lady J*, I don't believe I would be alive."

Sam nodded, respectfully. "John Dee told me a wench madam down on Gallatin Street forced you to take the opium poison. Tell me; I'm curious. How did they go about curing you?"

Stella stared vacantly at the river scene. She tried to recall her treatment plan, but her thoughts took her back to the moment Cliff Burton had pulled her from the river. And her captivity. Her throat tightened. Memories of his violence and Kitty's demonic rants jumbled with her people's horrific walk on the Trail of Tears. Pain that she lived with.

"I can't say I remember much at all about that, Sam." She nodded at John Dee with unspoken authorization to answer Sam's questions.

"The credit for Stella's recovery goes to an old doctor named Doc Joe," John Dee said.

"Doc Joe. Hmm. Doc Joe Sawyer. The artist?" Sam asked.

"This Doc Joe's a doctor—the very best." John Dee rubbed his chin. "I believe Joe did mention he paints landscape scenes when he has the time. Know him?"

"Most certainly. I've seen some of his paintings, and they're magnificent! Why, last summer he was a passenger on my boat far as Baton Rouge. Was heading up there to deliver several to a rich planter up that way." Sam grinned. "Had a grand time with him in the parlor. The man knows a little 'bout everything, and can sure command a room."

"I'll be," John Dee said. "His doctoring is top notch."

"How so?" Sam asked.

"Doc Joe did exactly what I didn't think he'd do. He kept giving Stella little doses of laudanum. God, that stuff was awful. Smelled bad, had a reddish-brown color, and a bitter taste."

"Huh," Sam said. "You like to think he'd a just stopped her from taking more poison, wouldn't you? Maybe given her plenty of water, simple foods, and something to make her sleep."

"Exactly. But Joe said if Stella stopped cold, there was a high risk she would have fits—convulsions he called 'em—that could kill her. So, he gave her little doses, and over a few weeks she was herself again."

Stella hardly remembered any of that. Joe's doctoring was just fractured scenes fogged by her addiction and his remedy. Even so, she would never forget his kind face. And just a day or two ago, when he was with her, she sang again. "Amazing Grace." Doc Joe hummed along in his deep baritone. A harmonizing bass beat worthy of any orchestra she'd sung for.

What was it he had said when they'd finished? *"I know about the Showboat* Soubrette. *It's time for your gift to come alive again."*

Then he'd quoted something that seemed like it should have been familiar. Shakespeare maybe? "Be not afraid of greatness. Some are born great, some achieve greatness, and others have greatness thrust upon them." Doc Joe had taken her hand and made the kindest smile in all the world. "Go forth and sing for the people, Stella. Share your gift. Share your greatness."

"Are you back to normal?" Sam asked Stella.

"I'm much better."

"She'll be coming to my plantation to rest up," Addy said. "Good, clean country air'll set her right."

Sam's gaze darted from Addy to Toby, undoubtedly noticing their shoulders nearly touched. He raised his eyebrows. "You two?"

"Just who is this redheaded, nosy fella?" Addy asked no one in particular.

Toby patted her hand. "John Dee and I have known Sam for a long time. Like Stella said, Sam saved our skins by getting us off the *Lady J*." He turned back to Sam. "Yeah, this little lady and I have spent time together. Hope it's gonna continue."

"It will!" Addy lifted from her chair. "Toby's coming to Grace Vale with me. Stella and Franklin are coming, too."

"And where and what is this Grace Vale?" Sam asked.

"It's my sugar plantation in Louisiana. Little south of Baton Rouge."

Sam's mouth fell open. "Do you mean a sugar plantation where Black folks are slaves? Do you mean your husband's plantation?"

"Toby's a free man! Surely you know that if yer his 'friend.' He ain't gonna be cuttin' no cane at Grace Vale." Addy shook her finger at him. "And I'm a widow woman. I'll bring whoever I choose to Grace Vale. Even you if Toby thinks you're a suitable guest."

"Does that mean Toby's the new man of Grace Vale?" Sam's voice trembled slightly.

"He's my man all right. But we're gonna have to play the game long as we're on the lower river. That ain't gonna be forever."

"Oh?"

"Toby and Franklin here are gonna help me sell Grace Vale. That'll give us enough money to go somewhere that the color o' yer skin doesn't stop a man and a woman from being together."

"You got somewhere in mind?"

"Well, I heard tell that Paris, France, may be a place Toby and I can go."

Sam chuckled. "Paris, France. Well, why not, Toby? One of the two most adventurous men I know is going on his biggest adventure yet."

Toby patted Addy's hand. "I can't bear the thought of being away from this little lady. But me and John Dee got our business dealings, too. It'll all get sorted, on the by and by."

"What about you, Sam?" John Dee asked. "Once you finished up the *Lady J* run, you musta caught a packet from St. Louis down here to New Orleans?"

"That's right." Sam took Stella's hand. "After the *Lady J* left Helena, I told Mister Jenkins and the cast how Ricky Burton attacked you and his brother Cliff threatened you. They all understood that your choice to leave the boat was for their safety as well as *Lady J*'s other passengers. Every one of them, including Mister Jenkins, wants to work with you again once your trouble with the Burtons is over."

"Thank you, Sam. I've been terribly worried about how things were left with the troupe." Stella kissed him on the cheek. "You've set things right. I'm so relieved."

"Where you off to?" Toby asked Sam.

"Upriver. Tell you what, Toby. I just wanna get my pilot's license."

"Well, you've put in your time on the river, so you should."

"Yeah," Sam said. "And I find I've been keeping myself busy with some writings. Now and then, I send correspondent letters out to river-town newspapers. Truth is, I got some stories to tell. Some of 'em are even better than you boys and Stella and the Burtons!"

Toby and John Dee laughed.

"So, John Dee," Sam said, "you back to business?"

"Well, Stella and I'll stop into Grace Vale with Addy and Toby for a short while."

"How short, Franklin?" Addy asked.

"Not sure. Long enough to figure out where I've gotta go to fetch Toby if he don't get back to business with me!"

Toby laughed. Addy crinkled her nose, then laughed along with him.

"Stella and I will take a boat to St. Louis," John Dee said. "I'll get to work, and we'll find a good place for her to sing again." He put his arm around her shoulders and hugged her close.

"We all look forward to hearing your beautiful voice again," Sam said.

"Thank you," Stella said. "It's been going on a month since I sang in a show. I've got work to do to make my voice strong enough to sing again."

"How will you do that?" Addy asked.

"Oh, some scales work and pitch glides. I'll sing in my low register at first, and work my way to high notes." She winked. "And drink lots of tea and honey!"

Everyone chuckled.

"Where will you sing once your voice is ready?" Sam asked.

"Maybe at a theater. Maybe on another showboat."

Sam raised an eyebrow. "Thought it might be a long time before any of you were on the river again."

"Ahh," John Dee said. "There's danger everywhere. Besides, there's bound to be a damn site of new suckers at the card tables when I get on board!"

Sam chuckled. Then he took a deep breath and struck an unusually serious pose. "You all be real careful on your travels on the lower river, now. Things are changing."

"How so?" John Dee asked.

"Northern men and Southern men. Anymore, it's like putting mercury fulminate and potassium chloride together with a fuse."

"I don't know what that means, but it must not be good," John Dee said.

"Boom," said Sam. "My boat stopped in Memphis coming down here. Wandered to town for dinner and noticed quite a commotion. Turns out a traveler admitted to being from Kansas. 'Bleeding Kansas,' the locals said. One of them called him a John Brown man. Another said the poor bastard had been at Pottawatomie. The crowd damn-near beat him to death."

"You think things are gonna boil over? Gonna be a war?" Toby asked.

"I sure hope not. But hardly a day goes by without someone saying, 'It's time to pick sides.'" Sam glanced at the riverfront. "Which one's your boat?"

"The *Liberty Rose*," John Dee said.

"Ahh, the *Rose*," Sam said. "Good. She's got a helluva pilot. Name's Davey Ambrose. Give him my regards, would ya?"

"Sure will."

Stella followed John Dee's gaze to the *Liberty Rose*. Quite a handsome profile, with red bunting hung from her top rail. White pickets partially obscured tables and chairs under shady eaves. She sighed contentedly, anticipating sitting there with John Dee, Toby, and Addy, taking in riverside vistas with a cold drink.

She twitched at a loud bang. The gangplank was rolling out.

"'Bout time. A nice leisurely boat ride up the big river with a fine pilot and no Burtons." John Dee hugged Stella again. "I'm looking forward to this!"

"Yep," Sam said, "you took care of every one of the Burton men...."

"But?" Toby said.

"But they have a sister. Bessie Burton. Bessie married Butch Claymore. I'm sorry to tell you boys this, but you oughta hear it. Butch'll see you the mean of Cliff Burton and raise you a Ricky and a Brick. A bad fella. Real bad."

Stella's heart beat faster. John Dee and Toby made loud sighs at the same time.

"Last I heard," Sam said, "Butch was in Memphis."

The *Liberty Rose*'s whistle screeched its boarding call.

"On that happy note." John Dee rose, helped pull Stella out her chair, and took her hand as she stood. On the other side of the table, Toby did the same with Addy.

John Dee shook hands with Sam. "It's been a helluva journey, my friend. Fare thee well!"

THE END

Notes and
Acknowledgments

THE SEEDS OF SHOWBOAT *SOUBRETTE* might have been sown decades ago, when Dad packed us into the station wagon for a drive to Hannibal, Missouri, and the world of Mark Twain. I remember traipsing around the cave he made famous, marveling at a replica of his white-washed fence, but most of all begging to be able to take home his books from the gift shop. *Tom Sawyer, Huckleberry Finn, A Connecticut Yankee, Pudd'nhead Wilson.* I wanted all of them!

Ultimately, extended family lore led me to this story. We have a charcoal portrait of a beautiful young Cherokee woman. She was referenced in a family letter from long ago that indicates this woman walked the Trail of Tears in 1838. We also have an old letter describes the family's migration from North Carolina to Missouri in the Antebellum South. A little White boy traveled across country by wagon train accompanied by a young Black boy. I don't have other details about the lives of these three. My book is a "whole cloth" imagining of how they might have interacted.

To understand a historical period, I've found the best sources are often the words of those who bore witness. My examination of riverboat life in Antebellum times started with Twain's *Life on the Mississippi*, which captures the majesty and navigational dangers of the mighty Mississippi during his cub pilot days. Frederick Law Olmsted was a renowned Northerner (he later was one of the developers of New York's Central Park and served as a commissioner of that unique urban park) who left an invaluable account of his travels through slave states in the decade preceding the Civil War: *The Cotton Kingdom: A Traveller's Observations on Cotton and Slavery in the American Slave States, 1853-1861*. Olmsted's memoirs record societal racist attitudes and practices teeming with an abject cruelty that is almost beyond belief today. Solomon Northrup's tragic story of being kidnapped and sold into bondage in the Deep South for twelve years is recounted in *Twelve Years a Slave*. George Devol was a long-time riverboat gambler who recounted many violent, lawless, and sometimes humorous incidents in his autobiography: *Forty Years a Gambler on the Mississippi*.

SHOWBOAT *SOUBRETTE* draws on these and many other resources. I've molded a story that is perhaps grittier than my first two historical novels, THE FOUR BELLS and ANGELS *and* BANDITS. I searched for goodness that could surely be found amid the violence and racism that permeated the Antebellum lower Mississippi River.

Thank you so much to my editor, Cindy Vallar, who was incredibly supportive and helpful with this project. Tyler Tichelaar and Larry Alexander at Superior Productions were terrific in polishing and laying out the book. The incredibly talented Sue Millard, who shaped up my first two historical novels, was a great help on early chapters. Thanks so much to my author friend Kris Abel Helwig—we go way back to high school!—for a great critique I really needed. My son Zack took a break from his law school studies to give me some great ideas for SHOWBOAT *SOUBRETTE*. Thank you so much to Marcia Stafford for your invaluable feedback and your friendship.

To my wife Sue and sons Zack and Dane, I love you all, and thank you for always being there for me during my writing journey!

About the Author

B RODIE CURTIS IS THE AWARD-WINNING author of *The Four Bells*, a novel of The Great War, and *Angels and Bandits*, which focuses on The Battle of Britain. Curtis loves American history and the history of the World Wars and has reviewed novels for *Historical Novels Reviews* for over six years. More than 150 of his published reviews and additional short takes on historical novels can be found on his website: BrodieCurtis.com.

Be Sure to Read All of Brodie Curtis' Books

Angels *and* Bandits

THE BATTLE OF BRITAIN RAGES and two young RAF pilots from very different stations in life must somehow find common ground—and stay alive.

On the eve of World War II, working-class Eddy Beane is a flight instructor in London. He successfully completes dangerous espionage missions for Air Commodore Keith Park and takes on society-girl June Stephenson as a student. Her ex-fiancé, Dudley Thane, is also a flyer, but upper-class and Cambridge-educated. When the German Luftwaffe attacks England in 1940, Eddy and Dudley end up serving in the same Spitfire squadron. Aerial combat is intense, and both men show their skills and courage, but can they set aside jealousy and class differences to become fighting brothers for the defense of Britain?

The Four Bells

Aㅤ Christmas toast to the past...

Damaged World War 1 veteran Al Weldy revisits his home town on Christmas Eve 1931, intending to raise a toast to his dead comrade-in-arms, Eddie Beane. Behind the bar of The Four Bells he finds Eddie's sister Maddy, his one-time flame.

Maddy, now a widow, confides how the Great War damaged her husband and draws  from a reluctant Al the details of his army service with her brother Eddie. Al's stories reveal how he and Eddie went to war with youthful enthusiasm, but came of age in the tumult and tragedy of battle. He reflects on the Christmas Truce of 1914, when British and German soldiers laid down their weapons for an uplifting encounter on a battlefield gone quiet.

Maddy is delighted when she learns that Eddie found romance in Flanders with Therese, a beautiful Belgian refugee. But, in the end, she must endure the news of Eddie's brave, rebellious death in the trenches.

...and the future?

As Al and Maddy reopen the old wounds the war caused, they find that their youthful romance has transformed into a more mature emotional connection, and possibly a new life together.

Brodie Curtis's books are available at
www.BrodieCurtis.com, Amazon, Barnes & Noble,
and other booksellers.